JUST
ONE LAST NIGHT…

BY
AMY ANDREWS

MILLS & BOON

First published in Great Britain 2011
by Mills & Boon, an imprint of Harlequin (UK) Limited,
Eton House, 18-24 Paradise Road, Richmond, Surrey TW9 1SR

© Amy Andrews 2011

ISBN: 978 0 263 88597 2

Printed and bound in Spain
by Blackprint CPI, Barcelona

For Olwyn Deane and Lillias Jensen—
two wonderful women who have enriched
the fabric of my life since the day I was born

CHAPTER ONE

DR GRACE PERRY hated feeling unprepared. She'd happily lived her entire adult life totally prepared for all situations. She liked being prepared. Loved it, actually. It gave her power and a sense of control.

She loved control.

And order. And predictability.

Otherwise there was just chaos. And Grace hated chaos.

Unfortunately there'd been precious little order and too much chaos in the last eighteen months.

So today she planned to take back control.

All she had to do was get the job.

An interview she was feeling totally *unprepared* for after her early-morning flight from Brisbane and Tash's door slamming condemnation from last night still ringing in her ears.

Grace sighed as she pushed the lift button. How could a sullen fifteen-year-old girl have defeated her—broken her—so utterly? Taken her nice, neat, ordered, *controlled* world and turned it totally on its ear.

Grace hated defeat.

The lift arrived and Grace put the rare moment of self-pity aside as she strode into it and pushed the button for the eighth floor.

Such negative thoughts did not bode well going into the interview of her life. And however hard it had been on her to become guardian to her niece and nephew, it had been a thousand times worse for Tash and Benji.

The doors opened at her destination and Grace took a moment

to straighten the dark grey skirt that flared around her knees, balancing out the flare of very feminine hips. She did up the large buttons on her matching jacket.

You can do this, she lectured herself as her strappy pumps sank into plush carpet. You are a fantastic emergency physician with fifteen years' experience and a respected manager.

You are outstandingly qualified.

Opposite the lifts was a large reception desk and she made her way to it.

'Dr Grace Perry to see Dr John Wilkie,' she said, injecting a note of calm assurance as if the interview was no more trifling than a sutured finger or a strep throat.

The starched-looking receptionist peered at her over half-moon glasses and frowned. She consulted her watch and then some paperwork. 'You're early.'

Grace blinked, feeling as if she'd committed some horrible transgression. 'Yes. It's a terrible habit of mine.'

Or it used to be anyway before chaos had taken over.

'Sorry,' she added, feeling the need to apologise to the un-amused woman in front of her. Then she smiled to reassure the receptionist it wouldn't happen again and to vanquish the horrible feeling of being caught on the back foot.

The receptionist sniffed then stood. 'Please follow me.'

Grace did as she was instructed—she didn't dare not to—following the woman's brisk march through a series of corridors until they reached a door and entered a lounge area.

'Take a seat. Dr Wilkie's conducting another interview.' She sniffed again. 'He may be a while.'

'That's fine,' Grace murmured, sinking into the nearest lounge chair. 'I have some work to do,' she said, patting her bag.

The receptionist departed and Grace was left to her own devices. Self-directed as ever and rather than think about who was on the other side of the closed door opposite, making a play for *her* job, she hauled out her laptop, placing it on the low table in front of her. She adjusted her glasses and waited for it to power up.

Twenty minutes later she was fully engrossed in a report when her mobile rang. Distracted, Grace searched through her bag for it. Normally she'd have it attached to her waistband but she had this bloody impractical skirt on today instead of her regulation trousers with their convenient loops so she'd thrown it in her bag.

It trilled insistently as Grace pulled out the entire contents of her bag onto the table in an effort to locate it.

Where could one little phone hide, for crying out loud?

She finally located it and pushed the answer button. 'Dr Perry,' she said.

'Hello, Dr Perry, this is Juanita from Brisbane City High.'

Grace gripped the phone harder as a surge of dread rose like a monster from the deep inside her. 'What's she done now?' She sighed.

'Natasha hasn't shown up today. Again. That's the third time this week.'

Grace shut her eyes. 'I see.' She knew her niece had been dropped at school. There'd been a text from Jo, the nanny, when she'd disembarked in Melbourne that morning, telling her so.

'Right, thanks. I'll deal with it.'

Grace's hand shook as she tried Tash's mobile. It went to the message bank and Grace left a terse message. She rang Jo next and informed her, then texted her niece.

Get your butt to school. Now!

Grace wasn't overly worried about Tash. If her niece ran true to form, she'd be at the local shopping centre.

Hopefully not shoplifting this time.

Grace was pretty sure Tash had learned her lesson from her brief foray into petty crime. But that boy would probably be there too. What was his name? Hayden? Jayden? Braydon? Something like that… And that was cause for concern.

Caught up in the drama as she was and the sick feeling that

had been fermenting in her gut for eighteen months, Grace startled when the door opened abruptly and two male voices intruded on her disquiet.

'Thanks John, I look forward to hearing from you.'

'No worries, Brent. The successful applicant will be informed by the end of next week.'

The hairs on the back of Grace's neck prickled and it had nothing to do with the way the two men shook hands, slapped backs and generally interacted like the outcome was a foregone conclusion.

And everything to do with Dr Brent Cartwright.

Her first love.

She rose abruptly to her feet as if she'd been zapped by some sort of divine cattle prod. Shock waves buffeted her body as twenty years fell away in an instant and the memories flooded back.

His deep, rich voice. The rumble in his laugh. The way he'd looked at her like she was the only woman on the planet. How he'd enjoyed teasing her. The way he'd told stories. His generosity. His intellect. His attention to detail.

The heat of his mouth.

The smell of his neck.

The way he'd filled her more perfectly than any man ever had.

The way he'd shaken his head, his angry words when she'd broken their brief engagement. Broken his heart.

Broken both their hearts.

'Ah, Dr Perry,' John Wilkie greeted her from the door. 'Edwina said you were here already. Give us a few minutes, would you?' he requested as he backed through the door and shut it again.

Grace nodded dumbly, her pulse tap-dancing a frantic beat at her temples, but had eyes only for an equally stunned-looking Brent.

Brent stared. He couldn't help it.

Grace Perry.

The one that got away.

He was momentarily speechless. Twenty years and yet the memories rushed out at him. Walking hand and hand through the uni campus as the leaves had changed and they'd fallen in love. Skipping classes. Staying in bed for days in a row. Talking endlessly into the night. Eating cold leftover pizza for breakfast too many mornings to count.

Drinking cheap cafeteria coffee as they swatted up for anatomy exams, desperately trying to catch up on the things they'd missed.

She'd been his first love.

He took a step towards her, reached out a hand. He felt as gauche as a schoolboy. As unsure as the eighteen-year-old man who had considered her way out of his league but had wanted her anyway.

He finally found his voice. 'Gracie…'

She stiffened as his endearment yanked her back to the present. 'It's Grace,' she said, taking a step back. 'Just Grace.'

Brent stilled as her don't-touch-me vibe sparked other memories. The cold stab of her *it's-over* speech. The hard bite of the solitaire engagement ring she'd curled into his palm. The straightness of her spine as she'd turned away from him.

He stuffed his hands into his pockets, embarrassed by the impulse and surprised how, even after all these years, it was automatic for him to reach for her.

But if she could be cool and collected, so could he. 'How are you?' he asked politely. 'You're interviewing for the head of emergency?'

Grace nodded. 'You too?'

'Yes. I've been acting in it for the last four months.'

His voice flowed over her like warm butterscotch sauce oozing into long-forgotten places and Grace's heart banged like a bongo in her chest. It had no right to betray her. It should be sinking in her chest, not thumping merrily along like it wasn't aware of the implications of Brent's words.

What hope in hell did she have of getting the job if there was already someone acting in it?

She groped around for another subject. 'Have you stayed in Melbourne all these years?'

Brent nodded, keeping his face neutral. 'Some of us don't consider that a hardship, Grace.'

It had been twenty years but the slight clench of his jaw still gave him away. *She'd pissed him off.* She raised her chin and forced herself to shrug.

'It wasn't meant to be a criticism.'

Brent, oh, so familiar with that little chin lift, regarded her for a moment. She'd changed. And yet she hadn't. Her hair was shorter. Her hips were even curvier. She wore trendy glasses instead of contacts. And fashionable clothes. Her make-up had been artfully applied.

But her grey eyes still looked at him the same steady way they always had. The same old frankness was there. And her full lips still parted softly the way they always had, as if silently begging to be kissed.

Her lip gloss was the same too, he noticed absently. It still glistened like dew on cobwebs and its heady vanilla essence curled delicious fingers around his gut. He didn't have to try it to know it would still taste like honey.

But he wanted to.

He wondered how many years apart it would take to erase that tantalising aroma from his memory cells. The one that occasionally drifted elusively through his dreams.

Brent stared at her mouth for what seemed an age and Grace felt heat build everywhere as she ruthlessly suppressed the nervous—or was that wanton?—urge to trace the outline of her lips with her tongue.

But even more dangerous to her equilibrium was the storm surge of emotions welling inside her. Feelings she'd long since buried spluttered to the surface. The sense of rightness and belonging he'd always stirred inside her. The feeling of completeness when he'd held her.

All of which she'd rejected twenty years ago.

Maybe emotions like that were just too strong to ever truly forget?

She shook her head, fighting to wrest back control.

This was crazy.

Certifiable!

It had to stop…

And then the door behind Brent opened abruptly and John Wilkie was smiling and calling her in, before disappearing back into the room.

'Coming,' she said, dragging her gaze from the searing heat of Brent's.

She turned back to her bag, the contents still strewn over the table, stuffing it all back in, shutting her laptop lid and shoving it in too. Aware of Brent's heavy stare the entire time—feeling it in her breasts and her belly and her thighs.

But mostly in her heart.

Items slipped through her useless fingers, dropped to the floor, rolled out of reach. Grace wanted to weep she felt so clumsy and…

Out of control.

Chaos reigned again.

Damn it!

She forced the last item in and stood, taking a couple of deep, calm breaths. This interview was important. And she was the best one for the job. She needed to be composed. Prepared. In control.

She drew in three more cleansing breaths before turning to face Brent again. 'It was…nice…seeing you again,' she said politely, before gathering all her bravado and walking past him, her head high.

And her knickers twisted into the mother of all knots!

Nice? Nice! Brent stared after her until the softly shut door completely obscured her.

Nice?

It had been surprising. Shocking. Startling.

Cataclysmic.

He sat down on the nearby lounge and shook his head.

Nice? Damn, it was *anything* but *nice.*

Even now his body was stuck back in first-year uni, skipping class to stay in bed with her all day. It was a wonder the two of them hadn't contracted a vitamin D deficiency. Or turned into vampires.

They'd certainly had insatiable appetites!

Brent absently rubbed his jaw as the memories played like an old film reel in his head. He'd never quite managed to erase the images of her. Not through twenty years of distance or even two impulsive marriages and their subsequent fallouts.

And here she was. At Melbourne Central Hospital.

Déjà vu.

Confounding him again. Making him feel things again. Challenging all his assumptions about her being firmly in his past.

He dropped his head in his hands and shut his eyes. For some reason he'd been so sure they'd never cross paths ever again. Her goodbye had been so final—he'd never doubted she meant it even when he'd wasted two years harbouring secret fantasies about a reconciliation.

Meeting her today had been a huge jolt.

And very far from nice.

Dear God. What if she got the job? *His job.* What if he had to see her every day? Hear that laugh he'd loved so much. Watch that sway to her hips.

Smell that damn lip gloss?

Brent opened his eyes on a silent groan, his gaze falling on an object near his foot. He reached for it, realising it was a photograph. Grace must have dropped it from her bag when she was stuffing everything back in.

He stared at the image for a long time, trying to comprehend what he saw. Two children, a boy and a girl. The girl looked about twelve. The boy four, maybe five. Brother and sister?

They were laughing at the camera, their arms slung around each other's necks. Trees and a clothesline could just be seen in the background. They looked happy and loved.

And remarkably like Grace.

The girl more so. They both had her grey eyes but the girl had long blonde hair that fell in a white-blonde curtain to her waist, just as Grace's had back when he'd first known her. The boy looked more like Grace around the mouth. He laughed like her.

Grace had children.

His brain tried to reject the notion but he knew it somewhere deep in his gut. Just like he'd known all those years ago that she'd meant it when she'd said she was never coming back.

Grace had children.

Was she married also? Had she been wearing a ring?

A storm of emotions built inside him and he gripped the corners of the photograph hard. What the hell had happened to remaining childless? To *never, ever*?

That's what she'd said the day she'd given him back his ring. The day she'd received her second-year anatomy results and discovered she'd failed the subject. The day she'd totally flipped out, blaming them—blaming him—for derailing her career.

'I'm the eldest of ten children, Brent. I've lived in chaos and clutter and noise all my life. I've fed and changed and bathed and rocked and carted and carried and kissed skinned knees and babysat my entire life. And they're my family and I love them but I don't want that for me and I never want to do it ever again.

Never, ever.

I'm done with it all. I want to go far away. Live and work and experience somewhere else. Somewhere different. I want to be totally selfish for the rest of my life. To not have anyone but me to worry about. I'm going to make a great aunty—the best—but no babies for me.'

Brent stared at the picture—she'd lied.

* * *

Grace felt confident as she shook John Wilkie's hand half an hour later. Facing a panel interview was always nerve-racking and with the fates conspiring to knock her totally off balance before she'd even begun, she could have easily messed it up.

But she'd clicked into doctor mode, treating the interview like a multi-trauma case, drawing on the focus for which she was known. And she'd nailed it.

The get-the-job plan was looking up.

The last thing she expected when she exited the room was to find Brent waiting for her.

He gave her a rather grim look and stood. Grace's breath caught in her throat as he unfolded himself. She'd forgotten how he redefined the whole tall, dark and handsome thing. How broad his shoulders were. How his hazel eyes looked tawny in some lights. How his cleanly shaven jaw was impossibly smooth.

'How did it go?'

Grace blinked at the terseness of his tone. He seemed annoyed with her and she felt her hackles rise. Just because he was already in the damn job it didn't mean it was his. She really didn't have enough time or room in her life for his male ego.

'I nailed it,' she said bluntly.

Brent snorted. Of course she had. Grace had always done everything well. Failure was not acceptable to her—he'd learned that the hard way.

He passed the photo that had been eating a hole in his gut back to her. 'You dropped this.'

Grace frowned and took it. Her expression softened as she realised what it was. Tash and Benji. Back before their world had been turned upside down. Before Benji had cried himself to sleep every other night. Before Tash had dyed her hair black and pierced her nose.

They'd been so innocent.

She looked back at Brent, who was looking at her expectantly. Like she owed him some kind of explanation. And suddenly his terseness made sense.

It wasn't about the job at all.

She lifted her chin. 'Thank you.'

Brent scrunched his fingers into fists by his sides to prevent himself from reaching out and shaking her. 'You have kids.'

It wasn't a question and Grace hesitated for less than a second. She did. She did have kids. She may not have given birth to them, she may not have a clue how to deal with them, but they were blood and they'd been living under her roof for eighteen months.

And she loved them.

So, yes, she had kids. 'Yes.'

Brent nodded, shoving his fists into his pockets. Part of him had been hoping she'd deny it. 'You're married.'

Again, not a question. 'No.'

Brent rejected the slither of hope her denial engendered. 'Divorced?'

'No.'

'Widowed?'

'No.'

'In any kind of a relationship with their father?'

'No.'

Brent regarded her for a moment. She looked so aloof behind her glasses and her salon-styled hair. It was all layered and shaggy at the back with multi hues of blonde and brown. Her bangs swept across her forehead and the sides neatly tucked behind the ears. She looked like a poster girl in an optometrist's window.

Gorgeous but untouchable.

'In any kind of relationship at all?'

Grace raised her chin. None of this was his business and she was damned if she was going to unload the whole sorry story on him just because once upon a time he'd been a really good listener. Even if she did feel absurdly like doing just that.

The details of her personal life were on a need-to-know basis only. And he *did not* need to know.

'I hardly see that as being relevant, do you?'

So that was a no…'I thought you *never, ever* wanted kids.'

Grace did not appreciate his accusatory tone. 'I was twenty years old, Brent.' *God, had she ever been that young?*

He nodded. 'I do believe I made that point at the time but you were pretty adamant.'

Grace was weary. She spent most of her days arguing with a recalcitrant teenager. She didn't have the emotional energy to play one-upmanship with an ex-lover.

Even if he'd been her first.

And the best.

She shrugged. 'It was two decades ago, Brent. So sue me.'

Right now suing her was the last thing on his mind. Shaking her, on the other hand, was looking more and more viable. Putting her over his knee and spanking her even more so.

But there was a tiredness to her words, to the set of her shoulders that gave him pause.

She was right.

It had been twenty years. An age ago. They'd been kids. Young and in love and foolish.

And it belonged in the past.

He sighed. 'Would you like a tour of the department?'

Grace eyed him warily. The doctor in her was exceedingly interested in a tour of Melbourne Central's state-of-the-art Department of Emergency Medicine. She was, after all, hopefully about to become its director.

But the woman inside was urging her to run away. Fast. Do not pass go. Do not collect two hundred dollars.

Do not do anything that prolonged their time together.

Do not be foolish.

She'd been foolish with him before and where had it got her?

Flunking medical school.

She thought back to that day, that horrible day when she'd got her anatomy results. The fail had viciously yanked the blinkers from her eyes. Burst the happy little love-is-enough bubble she'd been floating around in.

She'd been on a scholarship, for crying out loud. With twelve mouths to feed her parents hadn't been able to afford to send her to uni and she'd worked her butt off to earn that full scholarship.

One that had demanded academic success. Not failure.

She'd known right then it was medicine or Brent. Both of them were all-consuming. Both of them demanded a singular focus.

She'd had to choose.

She'd wanted to be a doctor since she'd been eight years old and had had her appendix out.

She'd loved Brent for two years.

And in those two short years he'd made her forget all her career aspirations and long-term goals. He'd made her fail anatomy. He'd put her scholarship on the line.

Ending it, transferring to another uni, had been the logical thing to do.

But it had hurt. Oh, how it had hurt.

Twenty years on the stakes were even higher. Her life was careening out of control and this was her chance to get it back on track. It wasn't just about her any more. There were two kids involved.

But how foolish would it be to pass up this opportunity? She needed to be informed and who better to do so than the current—if temporary—director? The doctor inside, the pragmatist, knew it made sense. And she'd got through the last twenty years, made a success of her life by listening to the doctor and not the woman.

It would be foolish to start doing so now.

CHAPTER TWO

BRENT put everything, including the fact that Grace was a rival for his job, aside and gave her the full tour. When he'd been seconded to Melbourne Central he'd been far from enthusiastic about the change. After fifteen years at the Royal Melbourne he had been utterly dedicated to his old hospital.

He'd planned on taking the helm, keeping the ship running until they found the right candidate and then head back to the Royal.

But since moving into the brand spanking new Melbourne Central he'd changed his mind. He'd realised he'd grown stagnant staying in one place. Roots were all well and good but the challenge of heading a new department, if only temporarily, had been exhilarating. And working with top-notch equipment in state-of-the-art facilities had been a luxury he'd quickly grown used to.

He'd put his stamp on this place and he was proud to share it with Grace. To show her that the boy with dreams she'd once known had more than fulfilled his goals.

He showed her around the twenty cubicles and seven resus beds, introduced her to the staff and demonstrated the central monitoring and fully integrated computer system that was run from the central work station.

Afterwards he took her around the other side of the station and opened a door. 'And this is my office.'

Grace looked inside. It wasn't palatial. But it was big enough, with a decent-sized desk and a very comfortable-looking leather chair. She looked at him. 'You mean my office?'

Brent gave a grudging half-laugh. 'Okay, the director's office.'

His laughter slipped over her skin like a satin nightgown—light and silky—and Grace smiled. For a moment. Before reality intruded. 'What will you do if I get the job?'

Brent regarded her for a few moments, wondering whether to tell the truth. He decided to give her no quarter. The old Grace hadn't liked to be mollycoddled.

'I hate to be the bearer of bad news but I really don't see that happening, Grace. I've been here since the beginning. They're only advertising the role because they have to. It's just a formality.'

Grace held his gaze. It was surprisingly gentle, considering the impact of his words, and had come over all tawny again. She appreciated his frankness. Hell, she'd suspected as much when he'd told her he was acting in the position.

Still, it irked. She needed it. Jobs like this at her senior level, with regular hours, didn't grow on trees. She wasn't just going to cede it to him.

'Well, we'll see about that, won't we?'

Brent saw the chin tilt again. 'You want it that badly?'

'I need it,' she corrected.

Brent knew the concession wouldn't have come easily to Grace and he saw in her gaze she was already regretting it. 'Need it?'

She hesitated for a moment, already cross with herself for giving away more than she should have and hyper-aware that they were standing very close in the small doorway. She could smell his aftershave wafting towards her and memories of how good it had felt to bury her face against his neck assailed her.

She took a step back, out of the doorway. 'More regular hours for the kids would be a blessing.'

Brent noted her withdrawal, pleased for the breathing space. It seemed twenty years hadn't dulled her effect on him. 'What are their names?'

'Tash…' Grace cleared her throat. 'Natasha and Benji.'

He nodded liking the way her voice softened as she said their names. She sounded like a mother and it called to something primitive inside him. After all, he'd once hoped she'd be the mother of his children.

Children she hadn't wanted.

'You could still come and work here you know, if this position doesn't come off. We're always looking for staff. You could have a job with flexible hours.'

Brent surprised himself with the invitation. But good hospitals needed good doctors. And he knew she wouldn't be being interviewed unless she was damn good. He wanted the best for the Central, for his department. Their history was immaterial.

He shrugged. 'The offer's there, anyway.'

Grace glanced at him, startled. That was a big call. And very generous. But it also had danger written all over it. Her life was complicated enough, without repeating past mistakes.

'Thanks,' she said, filing it in a mental bin. 'So…' she looked around '…is there a minor ops room somewhere?'

Brent stared at her for a moment longer then took the hint. 'This way.'

They walked to a corridor that ran along the back of the department with several more rooms evenly spaced along its length.

'That's X-Ray through there,' Brent said, pointing to the door at the far end of the corridor. 'This here…' he indicated, opening a door '…is for minor ops.'

Grace perused the layout and equipment before they moved on to several other rooms, including a storeroom, medication room and an examination room for eye patients housing an expensive specialised microscope.

'Dokator Brent!'

'Oh, hell,' Brent groaned at the raised female voice from nearby floated towards them. He looked behind him at the trail of black scuff marks his shoes had left on the polished linoleum floor.

'Dokator Brent!'

The heavily accented voice was closer this time, more insistent, and Grace looked at Brent, perplexed. 'Who is that?'

'That's Sophia,' he said, frantically scrubbing at the nearest mark with his shod foot. 'She's the department's cleaner. She's a dear old thing, has to be about ninety years old. Russian or Slavic or something like that. Salt of the earth but takes fanatical pride in her floors. Does not like having them besmirched, and these damn shoes always leave horrible marks.'

As Grace watched he moved on to the next black smudge. She stared at his shoes. They looked expensive—a far cry from the tatty sneakers he'd worn when they'd been young and in love.

'I don't usually wear them, except of course I had the interview today. She'll give me a terrible tongue lashing,' he groaned, the sole of his shoe erasing the marks.

Grace smiled. She couldn't help herself. Brent Cartwright terrified of a little old lady. She laughed then, unable to stop herself. Twenty years fell away and she was back at uni with him, goofing around.

He looked up at her laughing face and it took his breath away. She was looking at him like she had back then, like the intervening years had never happened. Like they were still lovers.

'Oh, you think it's funny?' He grinned at her, letting the years disappear. 'Just you wait. Trust me, no one wants to be on Sophia's bad side.'

She laughed again as he smiled and his foot scrubbed at the floor. Another 'I vill find you, Dokator Brent' came from very close by.

Brent stopped what he was doing, grabbed Grace by the hand. 'Quick,' he whispered, and pushed her through a nearby door, pulling it closed after them.

Grace didn't register the small confines of the room or the

fact that it stank of the cleaning products that weighed down its three rows of shelves. It seemed to be a supply room. Not much bigger than a cupboard really. She was laughing too hard to even notice how close they were standing.

'Shh,' Brent whispered.

Just then the door opened abruptly, pushing them even closer together as they huddled behind it to stay obscured. He put his hand over Grace's mouth to help stifle her laughter. He felt the texture of her lip gloss as a waft of vanilla and honey drifted his way.

What was it called again? Honey something…

Sophia called out, 'I know you here somewhere, Dokator Brent.'

The door shut again but not before Grace heard Sophia muttering under her breath in some strange tongue.

Grace pulled his hand aside and burst out laughing again. 'Oh, God, I'm so sorry, Brent.' She grabbed his shirt as she leant forward a little, trying to catch her breath and laugh at the same time.

'You should see your face. I can't believe that the big important *Dokator* is afraid of a sweet little old lady.'

'She isn't so sweet when she's pointing a mop at you.'

He grinned down her. She was so…familiar, so…*Gracie* it was impossible not to.

Impossible also not to be aware that her hand was warm on his chest and her breasts kept grazing the front of his shirt as laughter spasmed through her rib cage. Or the vanilla aroma of her lips, which somehow overpowered the smell of bleach and hospital-grade disinfectant. Or that his hand was firmly planted on one of her hips and all he needed to do was exert minimum pressure and she'd be pushed against him completely.

Grace slowly became aware of his fading smile and his growing silence and the fact that she was scrunching his shirt in her hand. She felt tense beneath her grip and he was staring at her mouth. He was big and warm and so very near.

So very Brent.

She eased her hold on his shirt and absently smoothed it with her palm. 'Sorry,' she muttered, as she became aware of the heavy thud of his heart beneath her fingers.

'I needed that,' she said, to ease the growing silence.

Today had been stressful, and this unexpected laughter had been the perfect release. Still, the fact remained that she was in a cupboard with Brent, giggling like a teenager.

It was insane.

She straightened slightly and put her hand on his chest, levering some distance between them.

'Pleased me and my shoes could be of assistance,' he said, moving back, as much as he was able in the confined area, placing temptation further out of reach.

Grace smiled at his joke. 'I think it's safe to go out now.' She checked her watch. 'And my plane leaves in a couple of hours.'

'That's a flying visit. Are you not even dropping in on your parents?'

Grace shook her head. She hadn't told her family. She didn't want to get anyone's hopes up. 'I saw them a couple of weeks ago,' she lied. 'I have to get home to the kids.'

There was Tash to deal with. And Benji hadn't coped well with changed plans since his parents' accident.

The kids. Brent still couldn't wrap his head around that one. 'Who's looking after them now?'

'The nanny.'

'Very suburban mum,' he murmured, as an incredible surge of something potent—jealousy, longing—clawed at his gut.

Grace felt the husky edge to his voice all the way to her toes. And all the places in between.

She straightened her clothes, finger-combed her hair, adjusted her glasses. 'I have to go.'

Brent nodded as he watched her reach for the doorknob. 'It was…nice…seeing you again, Grace,' he murmured.

His chest bubbled with absurd laughter at the irony of his understatement.

Grace's hand stilled in mid-twist. 'Yes. You too.'

Then she opened the door and walked out without looking back.

'I hate you,' Natasha said as the plane touched down at Melbourne's Tullamarine airport six weeks later.

Grace sighed. 'Yes. I got that.'

They'd been over and over her decision to move them all back to Melbourne. She wasn't about to have the same conversation in front of a couple of hundred strangers.

'I love Jayden. He loves me. How could you rip us apart like this?'

Grace looked into Tash's tear-stained face. Her heavily kohled eyes, the same colour as her hair, looked raccoonlike as her mascara ran. The twinkle of a shiny stone chip in her niece's previously perfect nose winked cheerfully amidst all the teenage angst.

Somehow, it managed to look even more ridiculous.

Grace was sorely tempted to roll her eyes and tell her niece to stop being so melodramatic. That being in love at the grand old age of fifteen was absurd and, contrary to popular romantic myths, the world would not end.

Even though she'd been a scant few years older and had, in actual fact, felt exactly like the world was going to end when she'd walked away from the only man she'd ever loved.

But she just looked at Tash and said, 'If he truly loves you, he'll want the best for you. As do I. And this is the best thing for all of us right now.'

She wanted to say, Do you think I want this? Do you think I want to uproot myself and my career and sell my lovely house I slaved countless hours to pay off and leave my friends and a job that I love? Do you think it was my plan to upend my entire life to accommodate two orphans? So I could live with a pissed-off teenager and an emotionally fragile little boy?

Do you think I wanted my sister to die?

But she didn't.

'Look,' said Benji, sitting on his haunches in the window seat, his nose pressed to the glass, 'we're here, Tash. We're here.'

Natasha, mouth open and about to let loose what Grace felt was no doubt another embittered teenage diatribe, turned to her brother, scrubbing at her face and forcing a smile on her face. 'Yep, Benji.' She squeezed his hand. 'Grandma will be waiting for us and all the cousins.'

And in that instant Grace's heart melted. Behind all that horrible teenage surliness and you-don't-understand-me façade was a really great kid. Whose whole carefree existence had come to an end in a crash of twisted metal.

She sucked in a breath and reminded herself to be patient.

Grace felt unaccountably emotional as they walked up the sky bridge into the terminal to be greeted by her entire extended family. The Perry clan—her parents and eight siblings and assorted progeny—surged forward and Grace felt as if she'd come home.

After fleeing Melbourne twenty years ago she hadn't expected to feel such a strong sense of homecoming. She'd happily made her life away from it all. And it had been a very good life. One that she'd been more than a little reluctant to leave behind.

But the events of the last eighteen months had been climactic and Grace felt like she'd been slowly sinking in quicksand.

And it was now up to her neck.

It felt good to know her family were throwing her a lifeline.

'Welcome home, darling,' her mother said, wrapping her in a tea-rose hug. The scent of her childhood.

'Mum,' she said, hugging back, holding on tight.

Her mother had aged so much since Julie's death. For a woman with ten kids she'd always been remarkably spry. Full of energy and lust for life. Grace had constantly marvelled at how she did it—goodness, she herself was exhausted just trying to keep track of two!

But Trish Perry was greyer now, more pensive, less energetic. The sparkle in her eyes had been replaced by shadow. The spring in her step had disappeared completely.

And the same for her father. They were just…less.

Grace stood back to let her parents hug their grandchildren. A lump rose in her throat as a tear slid from behind her mother's closed lids. A spike of guilt lanced her. Had it been wrong for her to take the two most tangible connections to her sister so far away?

But Natasha had desperately wanted to get away from Melbourne. Sure, she'd made a song and dance about always having wanted to live in the Sunshine State but no one had bought that. They'd known that she had wanted to get far away from the memories.

And, in the end, they'd all agreed that it might be for the best.

How were any of them to know it had been an unmitigated disaster?

'Come on,' Trish said over the general din, wiping at the tear before disentangling herself, all mother-of-ten business-like again. 'Let's get you all home. I've made roast lamb, your favourite, Benj, and for you, young lady…' Trish ruffled Tash's hair '…I made chocolate crackles.'

Grace tensed and waited for Tash to primp her hair back into place or scoff at her grandmother's offering. The way she had when Grace had made a batch the week the kids had come to live with her—after a particularly harrowing night shift—because she'd known that they were her niece's favourite.

Tash's vehement *'You're not her'* had been cutting and Grace had been walking on eggshells ever since.

'Cool. My favourite,' Tash said.

Grace expelled a breath. *Teenagers!*

The next couple of weeks were crazy busy. Grace re-en-rolled the kids in the school they'd been in prior to moving to Queensland—the school she herself had attended a million moons ago—and spent a small fortune on books and uniforms and all the assorted paraphernalia.

The school was local to the Perry family home, and was also attended by the current generation of Perry children. None of Grace's siblings had flown too far from the nest, all setting up house within a ten-kilometre radius of the family home and sending their kids to the same school they'd attended.

She had been the only black sheep.

With the kids settled, Grace went house-hunting. Her parents wanted her to continue to stay with them and she was happy to until she found somewhere else. But Grace had been inde-pendent for too long to move back home at the grand age of thirty-nine.

Her brothers and sisters may have been happy to stay close but Grace had always wanted more. And while she was grateful to have the amazing support of her family after doing the whole *mother* thing alone, she needed her space too.

Her parents' home was just too chaotic—even more so than it had been growing up—with thirty grandchildren from babies through to teenagers coming and going at all hours of the day and night.

Grace had missed the love and laughter but not the sheer noise of it all. She'd forgotten how loud and busy it always was. And how everyone was in everyone else's business.

That was something Grace hadn't missed.

In short, she needed privacy. A place that was quiet. Still. A place that was hers.

It had been tempting to look at real estate on the other side of the city, close to her new workplace. Had she moved back to Melbourne in different circumstances it would have been exactly what she would have done. Found a dinky little terraced cottage in the inner city close to cafés and shopping.

But the point of coming home was to be close to family. Was to have them as an extended support system. Multiple places the kids could go and stay when she invariably got stuck at work. Always someone to pick up the kids if she couldn't. Cousins to have sleepovers, share homework or catch a movie with. Aunts and uncles to spoil them and take them places and keep an eye on them. Grandparents to babysit.

No more nanny.

So Grace very sensibly looked only at houses for sale in the immediate vicinity of the school. The market was much more inflated in Melbourne and Grace was shocked at the prices. Luckily she'd made a good return on her investment with her place back in Brisbane and she calculated she could afford a three-bedroom house without going into a hideous amount of debt.

Julie and Doug had provided for the children's expenses in their wills but they'd been heavily in debt at the time of the accident so there hadn't been much money left. And what there was Grace hadn't wanted to touch. It belonged to Tash and Benji and she knew her sister would have wanted the money to be put towards the kids' university educations.

By the end of the second week she finally found what she was looking for. It was about a kilometre from the school in one direction and even less from her parents' in the other. It was a post-war, low-set brick with a small backyard. It needed a little TLC—the décor definitely needed modernising—but it was of sturdy construction and she could afford it.

Tash had stared aghast at the lurid shagpile carpet in the hall-way and the childish wallpaper in her room the day Grace had taken them to visit their new home. She'd also been completely unimpressed that she was going to have to share a bathroom with everyone else.

Benji had been kinder, his interest lying only in the fact that due to the backyard a puppy might be in the offing. Grace had fobbed him off, promising to think about it for Christmas.

But maybe, Grace thought as she signed the contract, she and the kids could work at modernising it together? She could let them make over their rooms—involve them. Working part time would be very conducive to a DIY project.

She had to try and engage Tash somehow. She'd hoped her niece would get over her resentment at being forced to move from Brisbane but it was just one more thing for Tash to hold against her. She was stubbornly recalcitrant where Grace was concerned. She was pleasant enough with everyone else but cut Grace no slack.

It broke Grace's heart. She'd always been Tash's favourite aunty. Cool Aunty Grace. Whenever Grace had come back for holidays Tash had been Grace's shadow. They'd chatted on the phone every few days since Tash had been old enough to speak.

But those days had long gone.

'Be patient,' her mother had said.

Except patience had never been a virtue she'd mastered.

She was losing Tash. And she couldn't bear it. But she just didn't know what to do. How to reach her. She was a fifteen-year-old girl who had lost her parents and shut herself off from the one person she'd once been closest to.

The one person who could help her the most.

And with all this weighing on her mind, Grace would have expected there to be no room for thoughts of Brent Cartwright.

But she'd been wrong.

It had been eight weeks since she'd seen him, since that awkward moment in the supply room, and tomorrow she had to face him again.

And every day after that.

A heavy feeling had been sitting like a lead lump in her

stomach ever since she'd accepted the job. Nervousness. A sense of dread.

And that she could cope with.

It was the rather contrary bubble in her cells and the fizz in her blood that made her uneasy.

Very, very uneasy.

CHAPTER THREE

'ANXIOUS about today, darling?'

Anxious? Grace was so nervous she could barely pick up her cup of tea without it rattling against the saucer.

Why her mother was the only person on the planet not to have switched to mugs was a complete mystery.

She looked around at the expectant faces at the table. It had been nice to slip back into the family breakfast ritual but this morning she could have done with a little less companionship.

The kids were inhaling cereal like they'd never eaten before. Her father was reading the paper. Her brother Marshall had called in on his way to work to drop off his two kids and was currently eating his second breakfast of the day.

'No.' Grace shook her head and forced down the toast that her mother had insisted on making her.

The food was in imminent danger of regurgitation but at least it gave her something to think about other than Brent.

Chew. Chew. Chew. Swallow.

Chew. Chew. Chew. Swallow.

'You'll be fine once you get stuck in,' Marshall added.

'I have a five-day hospital orientation first. Boring stuff like fire lectures and workplace health and safety stuff, so I won't be getting stuck in until next week. But at least its nine to five.'

'I hate starting a new job.' Marshall shuddered.

Trish nodded. 'It's always hard starting over somewhere new.' She squeezed her daughter's hand. 'I know you're my oldest and you haven't been little for a very long time, but I'll still worry as if it was your first day at kindy. It's not easy walking into a place where you don't know a soul.'

Irritated by being babied and by their incessant need to talk about what was making her feel incredibly nervous, she blurted out, 'Brent works there.'

There was a moment of double-take around the table that would have been quite comical to an outsider. Her mother sucked in a very audible breath. Her father looked up from his paper. Marshall stopped chewing in mid-mouthful.

'Brent Cartwright?' her father said.

'You didn't mention that before,' her mother said.

'Wow. That's a blast from the past,' Marshall said.

Tash looked from one adult to the other. 'Who's Brent Cartwright?'

'Grace's old boyfriend,' Marshall said, reaching for his fourth slice of toast.

Grace glared at him and turned to Tash. 'He was someone I knew a long time ago. We went to med school together.'

'I didn't think you were still in touch with him?' Trish said.

'I'm not.' She shrugged with as much nonchalance as she could gather. 'I…bumped into him when I came down for the interview. He works at the Central.' Grace kept it deliberately vague.

'Well, how is he? What's he been doing with his life? Goodness…it's been, what…twenty years? Is he married? Does he have kids?'

Grace realised she couldn't answer any of the personal questions about him. She hadn't asked about his life and he hadn't volunteered.

Had he been wearing a ring?

The lump of lead sank a little deeper into the lining of her stomach at the prospect. Which was utterly ridiculous. Of course he'd be married by now. With a swag of kids to boot. It was all he'd ever wanted.

A family to call his own.

She shook her head. 'I don't know, we barely talked,' she said.

'Well, how'd he look?' Trish sighed and fluttered her hand against her chest. 'He was always such a handsome boy.'

Marshall gave a hoot and Grace shot him her very best I-used-to-change-your-nappies look as she stood. 'I guess he still looks okay,' she muttered, figuring she was probably about to be struck down dead and that would, at least, cure her horrible bout of nerves.

He'd looked incredible. Just like the old Brent but with a maturity that had taken his sexiness to a whole new level. 'Anyway, gotta go.'

She bustled around to the other side of the table and dropped a kiss each on Tash and Benji's heads. Benji gave her one of his sweet smiles but Tash fluffed her hair as if to erase it.

Grace ignored the pointed action. 'See you both about five-thirty,' she said, picking up her case and turning to go.

'You should invite him to dinner one night. It'd be lovely to see him again.'

Grace stopped in mid-stride. She looked at her mother, ever the hostess. 'Mmm…' she said noncommittally, ignoring Marshall's wink in her peripheral vision, and headed towards the front door.

That was *so* not going to happen.

As it played out it wasn't until lunch of her third day that she finally met up again with Brent. She was standing in line at the cafeteria when a familiar sense of him surrounded her. She didn't have to look to know he was near.

It had always been like that between the two of them.

'Grace.'

She gripped her tray as his quiet greeting brushed her neck and nestled into her bones as familiar to her, even after all these years, as her own marrow.

She didn't bother to turn and face him. 'Brent.'

'What are you having? They do a good Chicken Parmigiana.'

'The quiche.'

Brent frowned at the continued view of the back of her head. 'Let me guess. With chips drenched in vinegar?'

Grace smiled. 'Yes.'

The waitress interrupted them and Brent let her order.

'That's twelve dollars fifty, Doc.'

'Here,' Brent said, smiling at the middle-aged woman behind the counter, 'add up mine too and take them both out of this.'

Grace, who was handing over her card, froze and finally faced him. 'I pay my own way, Brent.'

A man would have to be deaf, blind and stupid not to pay heed to the ice in her tone and the chill in her gaze.

But somehow it just made him more determined.

He shrugged. 'For old times' sake.'

A surge of molten rage erupted in her chest so fast it took her breath. Hadn't he learned anything from the *old times*? He'd wanted to take care of her and all she'd wanted had been for him to realise she could take care of herself.

She hadn't needed a carer. She'd wanted a partner. An equal. Someone who didn't need the trappings of the traditional to be validated. But Brent, a product of a broken home and an even more broken foster-system, had craved the conventional.

He'd wanted roots. A wife, some kids, the whole white-picket-fence catastrophe. And she'd just wanted a career.

'No.'

She didn't mean it to come out as a growl but she suspected from the rounded eyes of the nurse standing behind Brent that it had. 'Put it away.'

Brent nodded and withdrew his money, cursing his stupidity under his breath. It had been the wrong thing to do and the wrong thing to say.

Why did he suddenly feel like a gangly eighteen-year-old

around her? Trying to prove he was a suave urbane gentleman and not some gutter urchin who had been dragged through a system that had been underfunded and overstretched?

She hadn't treated him as if he'd been unworthy back then—why would she now?

Grace paid for her meal. 'We need to talk,' she said, before she stormed off to an unoccupied table as far away from the nearest lunchtime customers as possible.

Grace continued to fume as she watched Brent charm the woman at the register and then his unhurried stride towards her. He'd been in a suit that day of the interview, which had only hinted at the perfection she knew lay beneath. But today he was in trousers and a business shirt that left nothing to the imagination.

Was it possible that he was even broader twenty years on?

'I'm sorry,' he said as he placed his tray on the table and sank into a chair. 'It won't happen again. In fact, I think you should pay for me next time. I reckon I could set up a tab here and have them bill you at the end of each month. You could also pay for my parking if you like.'

Grace, who'd opened her mouth to launch into her how-dare-you diatribe, shut it again. He was grinning at her and it seemed like nothing had ever gone wrong between them. How many times had they sat in a cafeteria, eating some awful uni food and laughing at his silly jokes?

It seemed like yesterday.

She raised an eyebrow. 'Surely the director of emergency medicine gets his own car space?'

Brent grinned again. 'Yeah, you got me there. So, just my cafeteria bill, okay?'

Grace felt all the angst melt at his infectious smile. *Seemed like she was still a sucker for that mouth.*

The urge to reach out and stroke the rich-looking fabric of his shirt, as she once would have done, prowled inside her like a living, breathing beast. She forced herself to pick up her cutlery instead.

As they ate they chatted about her orientation and Grace also told him about the house she'd bought. Twenty minutes passed easily. He loved listening to her talk. Her voice was just the way he remembered—soothing and melodic.

In fact, so many things about her were the same. Familiar. Her great big smile. Her mannerisms.

But the way her eyes crinkled at the corners when she laughed was new. She'd obviously done it a lot and he was torn between being happy for her and annoyed that she'd obviously had a rich and full life without him.

Of course her hair was completely different. And then there were the glasses. He knew she was severely long-sighted and was essentially as blind as a bat without some kind of corrective device, but what had made her switch from contacts?

'So, why the glasses?' he asked as conversation dwindled.

Grace shrugged and adjusted them with sudden nervousness. This was moving into personal territory.

'I've had so many problems with contacts over the years. Glasses are simpler. And they're excellent splash protection. I can't tell you how many times I've copped an unexpected spray of blood in my face and they've saved my eyes every time.'

Brent nodded. Having had a couple of splash injuries over the years, he could relate to that.

He liked the glasses very much—they, along with the short, layered hairdo, took her to a whole new level of sexy. There was a maturity to her sex appeal now that pulled even more treacher-ously at his libido than it had when he'd been a teenager.

She seemed all schoolmarm, all touch-me-not.

Perversely, it had the opposite effect.

He swallowed his last mouthful and pushed his plate away, sinking back into his chair. 'Have you been avoiding me?'

Grace looked at him, startled for a moment, before forcing herself to calmly pick up her cup and take a sip of her tea.

They'd definitely moved beyond hospital safe-lift policy and dreadful wallpaper.

'The boss of the emergency department has an ego, I see,' she said dryly.

Brent chuckled. 'Is that a yes?'

Grace fought the urge to shut her eyes as his laughter bathed her in testosterone. *No one chuckled quite like Brent.* 'It's been a busy few days—that's all.'

'If you say so.'

Grace ignored the jibe and watched as he picked up his coffee cup the way he always had. His long, strong fingers disregarded the convenience of the curved handle, preferring to encompass the whole cup.

No ring. 'You're not married.'

The statement slipped out unchecked. Not surprising since his marital status had weighed on her mind since her mother had put it there.

But not something she'd wanted him to know she'd been thinking about.

Brent looked at her for a moment before looking down at his bare left hand. 'No. Not now.'

Now? Oh. 'Divorced?'

Brent nodded. 'Twice.'

Grace blinked. 'Twice?'

He nodded. Marrying twice and failing at both wasn't a record he was proud of. 'In my early twenties.'

After Grace had walked away Brent had been determined never to date another career-woman. And while party girls had been fun and up for anything, the reality of married life with a poor medical student or an overworked, underpaid resident had soon lost its sparkle.

'They were both brief. My first one didn't see out a year. The second one didn't see two. Both of my exes have since happily remarried. One now lives in Hong Kong. The other in Darwin. They were both amicable.'

'Okay,' she said. Because frankly she didn't know what else to say. She certainly hadn't expected that.

Deep down she'd secretly thought he'd never find anyone to replace her. That what they'd had was a once-in-a-lifetime thing. She'd certainly never found another man who'd come close to measuring up to Brent.

Brent could see she was grappling with the news. 'I was looking for… I wanted…'

He stopped. He hadn't known what he'd wanted.

Grace. But not Grace.

She nodded. 'Yeah…I know.' He'd wanted connection. Family. Roots. The perfect white-picket life he'd never had. 'Any kids?'

Brent shook his head. Forty years old and the kids he'd always imagined he'd have hadn't panned out.

He'd never been short of partners. In fact, he'd earned quite the playboy rep. But the problem with dating party girls was that they were as reluctant to settle and have babies quickly as career-women were.

And after two divorces, the idea of the perfect family had taken a battering. He'd resigned himself to the fact that he just wasn't meant to be a father.

'I guess I never found the right person. It just hasn't happened.'

Maybe perfect only came along once? Maybe he'd been holding out for another Grace? Sitting opposite her, he suspected that it could possibly be true. The thought alarmed him and he opened his mouth to distract himself from it.

'I coach a football team, though. Made up of kids in the system. It's run by a Melbourne-based charity.' He smiled, thinking about his beloved Little Warriors. 'They range in age from five to twelve. They're a bit of a ragtag bunch, but they're keen and they love their Aussie rules.'

Grace watched as Brent's face softened, his sexy mouth moving into an easy smile. His admission didn't surprise her.

His time in foster-care had given him deep insight into a fraught system. That he would be doing his bit to improve it all these years later was typical of the Brent she'd known.

And after remembering him with her siblings, it was easy to visualise him running around on a field, chasing after a bunch of kids, a whistle in his mouth, laughing.

'Every few weeks I hire a corporate box at the MCG and we all go and watch a game together.'

Grace whistled. That wouldn't be cheap. 'They're lucky to have you.'

Brent shook his head. 'I'm lucky. They're great kids.' He gave a half-smile. 'They keep me young.'

Grace wished she could say the same about her kids. Tash was single-handedly turning her grey. 'Sounds great,' she said, trying not to sound resentful. Coaching a bunch of kids who hero-worshipped you for a couple of hours was very different to parenting day in, day out. *Especially when you weren't wired that way.*

'Enough about me,' he said, looking directly at her. 'You never married?'

She shook her head. 'Nope.'

'Why?'

There was a certain amount of amazement in his voice and she laughed. 'Women do chose to stay single, Brent. It's not a crime. Especially in a field like medicine where the climb to the top is a long, hard slog. I made a choice to put my career first.'

And it hadn't even been difficult. Sure, there'd been relationships over the years but none of them had stimulated her like medicine. Or Brent. She'd always figured she'd had her shot at grand love and blown it.

And if sometimes, deep in the night, she'd craved a man's arms around her, dreamt about Brent, it was the price she'd paid. And she didn't have any regrets.

At least she hadn't until Brent had swept back into her life, reminding her of things that could have been.

'And yet you had children?'

Grace frowned. It took a second for her to understand what he was saying. He still thought Tash and Benji were hers…

'Ah. Actually…I have a confession to make.'

Brent raised an eyebrow. 'Oh?'

She took a deep breath, already dreading the way she knew this conversation was going to go. Rehashing all the grief and opening all the wounds again. 'They're not mine. Tash and Benji. They're Julie's.'

'Julie? Your sister?' She nodded and he continued, a smile lighting his face. 'Do you remember that time she called us at three in the morning from that nightclub? She was underage and had drunk too many West Coast coolers and she was scared she was dying from alcohol poisoning?'

He laughed at the memory. 'What the hell she thought two green medical students could do I have no idea.'

Grace smiled the familiar ache in her chest roaring to life. She remembered it as if it was yesterday. Julie hadn't touched a drop of alcohol since that night.

They'd been so close. With only eleven months between them they'd been more like twins—inseparable. And when Grace had made the heart-wrenching break to Brisbane to finish her medical degree she'd missed her sister almost as much as she had Brent.

'She threw up for a day,' Grace murmured. 'I had to come up with that elaborate lie for Mum and Dad.'

Brent chuckled. So the kids were her sister's. It certainly made a lot more sense. The notion of Grace having kids had been completely foreign to him and he'd spent a lot of time in the last weeks trying to wrap his head around it.

But that didn't explain why she hadn't set him straight from the beginning. Had she wanted him to think they were hers as some kind of proof that she'd been fine without him?

'So…you let me believe they were your kids because…?'

Grace cleared her throat of the huge lump that had suddenly taken up residence. 'Because they are. Mine. That is. Julie and Doug were killed in a car accident eighteen months ago. I'm…' She drew in a shaky breath. 'I'm their legal guardian.'

Brent felt his gut twist at the huskily imparted news. He sat very still for a moment, watching Grace fight to stay contained, observing the thick mist of grief clouding her grey gaze.

'Oh, no, Gracie…' He reached for her across the table, his hand squeezing her forearm. He knew how close they'd been. 'I'm so sorry.'

His touch and the way he said her name, like he could see deep inside her bruised heart with just one glance, nearly brought her undone and she snatched her arm back. She would not break down in front of Brent.

In a public cafeteria.

For God's sake, she hadn't seen him in two decades!

It was ridiculous.

And if she started to cry now, she didn't know if she could stop. And then he would haul her into his arms and the way she was feeling right now, she'd go willingly.

Absurdly, he'd been the one she'd secretly craved most after Julie's death. Having him so near now was dangerous. Her life was complicated. Chaotic.

There wasn't room for any more.

'Thank you,' she said stiffly, refusing to acknowledge the flash of emotion she saw in his hazel eyes at her rejection of his touch.

'What happened?'

Grace filled him in briefly on the accident. 'Doug died instantly,' she concluded. 'Julie was cut free but died shortly after arriving at the Royal.'

Brent frowned. 'I must have been on holidays when it happened.' He thought back. Yes, he had been. He'd gone skiing in France with friends. 'I wish I'd been there when she came in.'

Grace sucked in a husky breath. She wished he had too. It would have made it somehow easier to bear to know that Julie had had a familiar face with her that night. To know that maybe she might not have been so frightened.

It should have been her.

If she'd been there, maybe she could have saved her sister. Maybe Brent could have.

'Me too.'

Brent nodded. She was hugging herself now, so removed, so shut down. It was clear she was hurting and it killed him. He'd do anything to take her pain from her. But she was as closed off, as forbidding as that day she'd told him she was leaving and excised him from her life.

And it hit him—any thoughts he'd been harbouring deep down that they might have a chance at rekindling their relationship were utter fancy.

She was no closer to committing now than she had been back then.

And he was no sadist. In the aftermath of their devastating break-up and two failed marriages he'd hardened his heart to relationships and happily settled into a life of playing the field.

After a childhood of being pushed from pillar to post, Brent knew all about loving the one you were with.

He wasn't about to lose his head to her a second time. She'd walked away last time. And he was damned if he was going to allow nostalgia open the door to her again.

'I wish I'd known,' he said, falling back on polite socially acceptable conversation. 'I know it's probably too late but is there anything I can do...'

Grace shook her head. 'You already have. I'm very thankful that you offered me this job when I didn't get yours. Not many places offer part-time work at my level and I really appreciate it.'

Grace had been devastated when she'd been informed she hadn't been successful. And had rejected Brent's job offer that had come soon after. But then Tash had gone AWOL after school a few days later, scaring the absolute daylights out of her, and as much as she knew it would be challenging for them to work together again, she'd known she needed to come home.

So she'd swallowed her pride and emailed him.

He shrugged. 'I want the Central's emergency department to be the best. It makes sense to hire the best.'

Grace paused, trying to decide whether to mention the elephant in the room or not. But she'd always believed in tackling things head on. 'I appreciate that it's not easy, given our history. I know it'll be awkward to start with.'

Brent nodded. Then he held out his hand. If they set the boundaries at the beginning, they'd both be on the same page. 'So let's make a pact. The past is the past. Today is a new page. Friends?'

Grace's heart thunked in her chest as her hand slid into his and his warmth flowed up her arm and through her body. 'Friends.'

Brent felt it too and quickly withdrew his hand. 'We kinda skipped that part, didn't we?'

Grace gave a half-smile. They certainly had.

She suddenly felt on steadier emotional ground. She looked at her watch. 'Gosh. I have to go.' She stood. 'Thank you. For… being so understanding.'

He shrugged. 'What are friends for?'

Grace smiled, picked up her tray and departed. Brent watched her walk away. The sway of her hips drew his gaze to their hourglass curve and her cute bottom and he had to remind himself of the pact he'd made just a few seconds before.

Friends.

CHAPTER FOUR

GRACE was pleased to get her first day in the actual department started. She loved emergency medicine and even a few weeks away from it had left her yearning for the hustle and bustle.

It was the sort of work that was completely absorbing, leaving no time to worry about anything in the outside world. And now she and Brent had agreed to be friends, there was no reason for apprehension.

It was actually a respite for Grace to come to work.

She'd been too free to over-think her situation over the last few weeks, and the problems with Tash and the uncertainty of what would happen next had been unsettling.

She never felt unsettled at work. At work there was certainty.

And control.

As she entered Melbourne Central's emergency department via the sliding doors fifteen minutes before her official start time of eight a.m., Grace pulled in a deep lungful of hospital air. The smell of antiseptic and floor polish was as familiar to her as her own minty toothpaste breath and she almost sighed out loud.

She wanted to stop in the middle of the all-but-deserted waiting area with its rows of hard plastic chairs and announce, 'Honey, I'm home.'

She smiled to herself as she kept walking, nodding to the nurse at the triage desk as she made her way to the empty staffroom. Stowing her bag in the locker she'd been allocated, she fixed herself a quick cup of coffee at the kitchenette and wandered out to the handover room where she knew the night medical staff would be passing on information to the day doctors.

The handover room, used by both medical and nursing staff, was an office off the main medical station that formed the central hub of the department. It wasn't very large and consisted of an overflowing desk, crammed bookshelves weighed down with medical texts and several chairs.

There were two large glass windows so comings and goings could be watched, and on one wall was a large fixed whiteboard with various patients' names and conditions corresponding with the cubicle number they currently occupied.

Grace introduced herself to the assembled residents and registrars. A large glass jar that sat on the desk containing assorted lollies was passed around and the handover began. Two minutes later Brent strode into the room.

'Sorry, I'm late,' he apologised. 'Bloody traffic is getting worse. Terrible impression to give the new kid on the block. Sorry, Grace, I know how you hate tardiness.'

Grace bristled as she felt the force of several speculative gazes. Yes, she did abhor tardiness. Growing up in a family of twelve, they'd rarely been on time anywhere, and punctuality was one of the things since flying the nest that she'd always prided herself on.

But the familiarity of his greeting, not to mention the way his damp hair curled around his collar and the distinct soap and aftershave aroma he'd brought into the room with him, rankled.

He'd filled the room with such effortless masculinity and, in the process, transported her back twenty years.

When what she really needed was to be in the here and now.

'I'll make sure HR docks it from your pay, Dr Cartwright,' she murmured.

It scored her a couple of laughs but also, she hoped, delivered her message loud and clear. Friendship had its limits.

Brent heard it loud and clear. Obviously being friends didn't entail anything too familiar.

Fine by him.

But still, as the report progressed he realised how hard it was going to be in reality to ignore their history. He was super-conscious of her. Of knowing that beneath her tailored trousers and cotton shirt lay very familiar territory.

He remembered what she looked like naked.

How she liked to be touched.

And what she sounded like when she came.

It may have been twenty years but those memories were still just as potent today. He'd forgotten nothing.

'So what time is the ultrasound booked for the suspected gall bladder?' Grace asked the night reg.

Brent, who hadn't realised he'd tuned out, dragged his mind out of Grace's underwear and tuned back in to the hand-over. Hopefully, seeing Grace regularly like this—at work, as colleagues, in a non-sexual way—would blunt those old memories.

Hopefully, they'd eventually dissipate altogether.

Hopefully.

It took all of Grace's willpower to block out Brent's presence in her peripheral vision but once she had, she found herself enjoying the relaxed atmosphere of the handover. Her new colleagues stopped every now and then to have a joke or throw in an anecdote.

The department was in its early morning lull so there was no need to rush. Not every morning was like this so it was great to be able to take their time when they could.

Brent joined in with his own witty observations and Grace could see how respected he was. The junior doctors deferred to him and he was generous with his support and knowledge. But he also challenged them to think laterally and to look outside the box when answers were elusive.

And he was liberal with praise, murmuring, 'Good catch,' when an apparent case of heartburn at two in the morning had been correctly diagnosed as an impending myocardial infarction.

She also wasn't blind to the level of interest other than professional. Two of the female residents were looking at him like he'd been dipped in chocolate, all but smacking their lips, watching him from under half-closed eyelids. Had they been the ones clocking off she might have put it down to exhaustion but as they were only just starting their shift, Grace wasn't fooled.

He'd always been a chick magnet. Even when they'd been a hot and heavy item. Secure in his love for her, she'd found it amusing, often teasing him about it.

She wondered how many women had shared his bed since.

'All right, then, thanks, folks, go home,' he addressed the night staff. 'Get some sleep.' He stood and looked at the day shift. 'Let's get this day started.'

Grace blinked, surprised they were finished. The others also stood and started to file out of the room and she followed suit automatically, trying to erase images of Brent and bevies of faceless women.

'Grace, can I have a word, please?'

Grace paused and held back, waiting for the room to empty. She felt off balance, confused, and grappled to claw back control.

Brent reached for the jar of lollies and helped himself to one. He contemplated apologising for the over-familiarity earlier but decided to put it down to teething problems with this new relationship they were trying to forge.

'Just want to check you're all set for your first day. Were you happy with your department orientation last Friday? Sorry I wasn't here for it. Do you need me to go over anything else with you?'

Grace wasn't sorry at all if the last twenty minutes in his distracting company was any indication. 'I'm good,' she said. 'Raring to go, actually. I think I'm okay with everything, thanks. But I'll ask if I'm unsure.'

Brent nodded. Of course she was on top of things. Grace was always on top of things. 'I'm going to be in a meeting for most of the morning. Do you think you'll be okay? Sorry, I did want to be around for your first shift.'

Grace was relieved that he wasn't going to be around. She'd be too self-conscious anyway. And not just for personal reasons either. Professionally she had a lot to prove.

Even though they were at the same level, technically he was her boss and his opinion of her medical skills mattered to her. She tried to tell herself it was professional pride and it was, to a degree. But it went deeper than that.

They'd been med students together, weaving dreams of medical greatness. On a personal level, his approval also meant a lot.

Maybe even more.

'I'll be fine,' she confirmed. She'd rather get a feel for the place first before she had Brent scrutinising her every move. 'Don't worry about me. I promise not to kill anyone.'

Brent smiled. 'Good to know.'

'Right, well,' she said, glancing at the door and then back at him. 'I'll…see you around, then?'

Grace didn't wait for his acknowledgement. She turned on her heel and left the room.

The morning turned out to be fairly standard fare for an emergency department. An assortment of minor incidents and accidents—a broken arm, an asthma attack, a case of angina. And then the usual mishmash of things that should be seen in a GP clinic—sore throats, a case of the flu, an ingrown toenail.

It was perfect to allow Grace to ease into the routine. To get to know where things were, who was who and how to work things like the computer system and the different forms. Of course, she would have coped with being thrown in at the deep end too but slow and steady was preferable for her first shift.

The nurse manager for the department, Ellen, was lovely and obviously highly experienced, and even formally introduced her to the intimidating Sophia. The older woman gave her the once-over, paying particular attention to Grace's shoes.

'You wear good shoes,' she said. 'Leave no marks. Is good. We will get along.'

'Er…excellent,' Grace said, relieved to have passed the Sophia test.

'Don't mind her,' Ellen said as Sophia hobbled away. 'Her bark is worse than her bite. She'll do anything for you. Underneath all that bluster she's a real sweetheart.'

'Dr Perry? Ellen?'

They turned to find Barb, the triage nurse, approaching. 'The bat-phone just rang.' The nickname they gave to the phone that provided a direct link to the ambulance coms centre rolled easily off Barb's tongue.

'Stabbing at St Barney's high school. Seventeen-year-old male with knife wound to his central chest. Conscious, orientated, no visible signs of bleeding, obs stable, saturating at ninety-eight per cent. Eight minutes out.'

Ellen looked at Grace. 'Game on.'

Grace felt the familiar kick of adrenaline buzz through her system as they hustled to the resus area. She welcomed it. She knew it would sharpen her instincts, hone her responses, help her make the split-second decisions needed in situations such as these.

'A stabbing at school?' she said to Ellen as she rang the lab to activate the massive transfusion protocol.

'We get a lot of stabbings, not usually school kids, though. Melbourne's got a bit of a seedy underbelly and the inner city has quite a high crime rate. Gunshot victims, stabbings and other violent assaults are quite common.'

Grace nodded. She'd grown up here. Gangland killings had been part and parcel of Melbourne's street life throughout her formative years. But in Brisbane shootings and stabbings were the exception rather than the rule. Grace realised she was going to have to adjust her expectations.

'What's happening?' Brent asked, joining them in Resus. 'You paged me?'

'No.' Grace looked around. 'I didn't.'

'Sorry, I did,' Ellen said. 'This could get messy and I thought it would be better to have as many hands as possible.'

Grace read between the lines. Ellen didn't know her. Fair enough. The nurse couldn't know that Grace had spent a year in Chicago's busiest ER and could crack a chest open with her eyes closed.

A lot of doctors of her experience would have been annoyed and she could see Ellen bracing herself for consequences. But Grace knew the nurse manager was only being cautious and admired her for her initiative. Hopefully, after today all the nursing staff would have faith in her abilities.

'Sure, the more the merrier,' Grace confirmed.

Brent smiled at her, relieved Grace hadn't gone all prima donna on Ellen. A lot of his colleagues would have had their noses totally put out of joint by Ellen's presumption but Grace had taken it in her stride.

It was a good sign. He hadn't known until now what kind of a doctor she was. Sure, she had an impressive CV, but he'd never experienced her in the role, worked side by side with her as a doctor. Often what applicants looked like on paper bore no resemblance to what they were like in action.

In his experience a good doctor wasn't just clinically brilliant but was a team player. And one who didn't recognise that nursing staff were their partners in this crazy thing they did day after day was very shortsighted indeed.

And he was jazzed to be finally working with her. After all, this was what they'd dreamed about twenty years before. Living, loving, laughing, working together. And although the first three might not apply now, he was excited to be finally fulfilling the last.

Watching Dr Grace Perry in action was going to be a real treat.

They bustled around, donning yellow paper gowns and gloves, preparing drugs and instruments, alerting Theatre, readying chest tube and thoracotomy trays.

'You want airway or wound?' Brent asked as the distant wail of a siren punctuated the activity.

'Wound.' She didn't hesitate. She needed to prove herself today and that was the quickest way.

The siren got louder and they rushed outside to greet the ambulance. Brent reached for the back doors and opened them to reveal a paramedic doing chest compressions with bloodied gloves.

'He crashed about thirty seconds ago.'

The paramedic stayed on the trolley, giving a rapid-fire handover as he continued to administer CPR and they rushed the gurney into Resus. He jumped off as the team quickly transferred the critical teenager onto their trolley.

'Get the O-neg started, stat,' Grace said as she placed a stethoscope against the chest wall, working around Ellen who'd taken over compressions and another nurse who was hooking the patient up to the monitor.

'Size eight ETT,' Brent said to the nurse who was assisting him.

'Stop compressions,' someone said. Ellen stopped and they all looked at the monitor. V-fib.

Ellen recommenced as Brent announced, 'I'm in. Let's bag him.'

'I need to crack his chest,' Grace said, pulling the stethoscope out of her ears. The knife had obviously severed a major vessel in his chest or maybe even his heart, and they didn't have time to mess around.

'He's full of subcutaneous emphysema,' she said to the registrar opposite, 'Place a chest tube.'

'Let's give some adrenaline and atropine,' Brent ordered.

A nurse pushed an open pack towards her and held out a pair of sterile gloves. Grace thrust one hand and then the other into them as if she'd been a surgeon for the last fifteen years.

'Thanks,' she said. 'Could you prep?'

Ellen stopped compressions as some iodine was squeezed over the chest.

'Still VF,' Brent said.

'One litre from the chest drain and rising,' the registrar announced, as blood flowed into the collection chamber.

'Come on, kid, do not die,' Grace said as she made a swift incision.

Her hand was rock steady and her focus laser sharp but somewhere at the back of her mind she realised she didn't even know his name. She was about to stick her hands in his chest and she didn't even know the most basic thing about him.

'What's his name?' she asked no on in particular.

'Dean.' The answer came from the back somewhere.

Dean. *Such an innocent-sounding name.* 'Retractor.'

A gloved Brent slapped it into her hand and she positioned it, cranking it slowly apart, watching as more and more of the chest cavity came into view. Blood welled up and poured from the wound. 'Suction!'

'Can you see it?' Brent asked, peering over her shoulder.

'Too much blood,' she muttered, running her gloved fingers over the surface of the fibrillating heart, going by feel alone. Her fingers slid into a groove. 'Yep, got it—must have pierced the right atrium.'

'Sutures?'

Grace nodded and he handed her a loaded needle. The operative field was clearer now the collected blood had been sucked away and she could visualise the rapidly oozing wound on the surface of the heart.

'Tell Theatre we'll be ready in ten,' she said to Ellen as she deftly placed some very rough sutures to close the defect. It wouldn't win her any needlecraft awards but it didn't need to be perfect—just effective. The surgeons could do the rest.

'Still in VF,' Brent murmured, and every set of eyes switched to the monitor.

'Internal defib,' Grace said. She squeezed Dean's heart between her two hands as Brent readied the paddles.

'Here,' he said, passing them to her. They looked remarkably like a pair of salad tongs or long-necked spoons. 'Charged to fifteen joules.'

Grace applied them to either side of Dean's heart muscle. 'Go.'

The small electric current charged through the heart. Grace did not remove the paddles as her eyes sought the monitor.

'Still V-fib.'

'Again,' Grace ordered. Come on, Dean! *What the hell are you kids doing, taking knives to school?*

The paddles were charged again. 'Go.' Everyone held their breath.

This time the frenetic green squiggle changed to a different rhythm. It was slow but essentially normal and Brent announced triumphantly, 'Sinus brady.'

Grace swore she heard the exhalation of a dozen collective breaths. They'd done their jobs, now it was up to the surgeons.

And to Dean.

He was by no means out of the woods.

Brent squeezed her shoulder. 'More adrenaline. More atropine. Hang more blood,' he said to the nurses working with the drugs and fluids. 'Let's get him to Theatre to finish the job.'

Ten minutes later Dean had been whisked off to the operating theatre by the surgical team, who had swarmed in like an efficient army of ants and taken over his care.

'Well done, team,' Brent said as they watched the rapid departure of Dean's trolley. 'Fantastic effort. Amazing result.'

The resus bed area looked as if a bomb had hit it. Grace's gown, along with several others, was covered in blood. They were all looking a little in shock. But it was insignificant at that moment.

Brent's words had given voice to their own thoughts. It *had* been amazing, Grace acknowledged as she rode an adrenaline high, allowing herself to recognise it for the first time.

By God, they'd done it! Pulled a seventeen-year-old boy back from the brink of death.

'Well done to Grace especially,' Ellen said, stripping off her gloves and gown. 'It's going to be a pleasure working with you, Dr Perry.'

Grace, also stripping off her bloodied garments, grinned at her co-workers as they all nodded in agreement.

She'd passed the test.

Grace was on a high for the rest of the shift. They'd heard from the surgeons that Dean had made it through his op and was in the ICU. He'd started to wake and they were feeling optimistic about his long-term prognosis.

Today was an excellent day.

It was so good she didn't want to go home and spoil the buzz. Why was it that she could stick her hands inside the chest of a human being and sew up a hole in a heart but she couldn't figure out how to deal with a fifteen-year-old girl?

Grace shook her head to dispel the insidious thought. For now she *was* at work and she'd ride the high while she could. There was time enough for downers later.

As the afternoon progressed Grace spent a lot of it dealing with Dean's case. As it was an attempted murder investigation there were protocols to follow and the paperwork was endless. She'd also been interviewed by three sets of different police.

Nothing like that for a buzz-kill.

An hour before her shift ended she was reviewing X-rays with Adam Mather, a resident, on a suspected bowel obstruction case, when she heard Brent's voice. She looked up and could just see him through a crack in a pulled curtain around a nearby cubicle. He was talking to a very anxious-looking man as he listened to the man's chest with a stethoscope.

Brent said something she couldn't make out and the man laughed. The furrows in his forehead disappeared and his face cracked into a smile. Brent laughed also, taking the stethoscope out of his ears but leaving his hand on the man's shoulder.

So this was Brent the doctor.

A strange flutter vibrated through her rib cage. It was a revelation for her—this Brent. She'd never actually seen him in action as a fully qualified doctor. Not even this morning. She'd been too intent on what she'd had to do, on her own actions, to pay any heed to his.

Twenty years ago they'd spent a lot of time wondering what they'd be like as qualified doctors. Talked about it. Shared their hopes and aspirations. But she'd walked away from him after two years in medical school and had never seen the result.

She hadn't ever doubted he'd be good. Not just brilliant, compassionate too. Brent's earlier life had been full of harsh realities but instead of making him hard and bitter it had made him determined.

Determined to not treat people as numbers. To protect dignity and preserve self-respect.

Her heart swelled to see that he hadn't grown too big, too important to take a little time with an anxious patient. To crack a joke. To squeeze a shoulder.

A woman could love a man like that.

'Dr Perry?'

Grace blinked as Adam's voice intruded on her wandering thoughts.

Crazy thoughts!

Where the hell they'd come from she had no idea but they were *not* welcome. Last time she'd loved Brent it had smothered the life out of her.

And this time round there was no time for love at all.

CHAPTER FIVE

THE next two days in the department were comparatively un-eventful—thank goodness. Grace had had a real baptism of fire and while she didn't mind a challenging case, where it was *go*, *go*, *go* with no time to think or breathe, she didn't want one every day either.

Okay, this was Melbourne, twice the population of Brisbane—she knew there'd be more. And she knew that she'd lose some. But Dean was doing well in ICU and she'd live on the glow of that success for as long as possible.

On this, her third day, she finally felt as if she was getting a handle on things like the layout and the forms and the different procedures. Her next run of shifts would help to cement that further but that wasn't until next week so she was concentrating hard today on consolidating what she'd already learned.

She couldn't quite wrap her head around working just three days a week. Brent had been very generous with her rostering. She would have to work an occasional weekend and do rare on-call cover, as did he, but essentially she was no longer a shift worker.

After fifteen years!

It was a big adjustment for her. But as hard as it was to be at home more, fighting her uphill battle with Tash, the extra days off did give her an opportunity to connect better with the kids. Grace just hoped that one day Tash would appreciate it. That one day she'd accept the hand that Grace kept holding out. And that Tash kept biting.

Grace was reviewing a CT scan on one of the desktops at the central station when she heard a familiar voice.

'If she's busy, don't bother her. I'll just tell her I was here when she gets home this afternoon.'

Mum? Grace stood. Yep. There was her mother standing at the triage desk, talking to Gabi. What on earth was she doing there?

Tash?

Grace almost groaned out loud. She checked her watch. There hadn't been a wagging incident since Tash had started at the new school. Trepidation squirmed through her belly as she shut down the screen and went to greet her mother.

'Mum? What are you doing here?'

Trish smiled at her daughter. 'Hello, darling.' She hugged Grace. 'Sorry, I hope you're not busy?'

Grace shook her head. 'Is everything okay? Is Tash okay?'

'Of course, everything's fine. I was just passing so I thought I'd drop in to see if Brent would like to come to the family barbecue on the weekend.'

Grace blinked. *Was she mad?*

'Er, Mum?' she said, pulling her by the arm out of earshot of Gabi, the lovely but gossipy triage nurse whose interest in all things Brent was borderline obsessive. She'd already filled Grace in on Brent's very active dating life.

'He's a very busy man, Mum, and besides...I really don't think Brent is interested in attending some family thing of ours.'

'Oh, but, darling, he used to love to hang out at home.'

Yes, he had. Brent had never been more at home than amidst the chaos of her noisy, crazy family.

She sighed. 'Mum that was twenty years ago. Brent—'

'Hello? Yes? Did I hear my name?'

Grace recognised Brent's powerful frame in her peripheral vision before she squeezed her eyes shut. *This could not be happening.*

'Brent!' Trish laughed as Brent swept her into a big hug.

'Mrs Perry. What a lovely surprise. How nice to see you again after all these years.'

'Oh, please.' She batted his chest. 'Call me Trish!'

Grace rolled her eyes. Was her mother *flirting*?

'What have you been up to? Grace tells me you're the director of emergency medicine here.'

Grace stood in agony for five minutes while Brent and her mother chatted away.

'Trish, I was so sorry to hear about Julie. Grace told me. It's just so tragic.'

For the first time since Trish had hugged Brent Grace saw her mother's smile slip. She gave him a pained smile, so sad it broke Grace's heart all over again. 'Yes, it is. We miss her a lot.'

Brent reached for Trish's hands, engulfed them in his own and squeezed. He'd been shocked to see how Grace's mother had aged. He laid the blame squarely on the grief blazing in the older woman's gaze.

'*C'est la vie,*' Trish murmured with a shrug, and cleared her throat of the emotion threatening to overwhelm her. 'Anyway, I was just saying to Grace, we're having a family barbecue his weekend and would love it if you could come along too. For old times' sake, you know? It'd be lovely to catch up with you.'

Brent was momentarily taken back. This he hadn't expected.

'I told Mum you were probably too busy.'

Brent flicked a glance at Grace. She looked like she'd rather have Ebola come to the barbecue. But then he glanced back at Trish and the misery in her eyes was his undoing. He couldn't bear to see anyone this sad.

'I would be delighted to attend.'

Trish grinned. 'Really?'

'Really.' He smiled back.

Trish clapped her hands and gave him a quick hug. 'Oh,

that's great. Wait till I tell Lucas, he'll be so pleased. We often wonder about you. Won't it be great, darling?' she asked, turning to Grace.

Grace nodded. 'Peachy.'

Brent suppressed a smile at Grace's underwhelmed response. Luckily Trish seemed oblivious as she rattled off the details and then departed.

They stood in the waiting room and watched her go.

'I'm sorry. I realise that you'd rather I wasn't there. I just…' He looked down at her. 'She seems so sad. I didn't have the heart to say no. But I won't go if you don't want me to.'

Grace nodded, seeing the compassion and concern in his face reflected in the tawny shimmer of his hazel eyes. 'You can't back out now, Brent.'

'But you wish I hadn't said yes, right?'

He seemed suddenly intense and the heat smoking in his gaze travelled all the way down her spine and curled fingers deep inside. 'I don't think it's a good idea for us to see each other socially,' she prevaricated.

Brent's gaze dropped to her mouth. Her vanilla honey mouth. What was she afraid of? 'We said friends, right? Isn't that what friends do?'

Well, he had her there…except the way he was looking at her mouth didn't feel friendly. Neither did the rat-a-tat-tat of her heart.

Grace drew in a deep breath and took a conscious step back—how had they got so close? 'Of course,' she said with as much primness in her voice as she could muster. 'And the family would love to see you again.'

Brent became aware they were standing in the waiting area not far from the triage desk, with one very interested-looking Gabi and several waiting patients checking them out.

She was still capable of making him lose his head.

'Good, it's settled, then. Midday Sunday.'

'Midday Sunday,' she repeated.

High noon...

The doorbell chimed at precisely midday while Grace was half-way through chopping up a kilo of onions. She'd drawn the short straw, apparently because wearing glasses somehow protected the chopper from the fumes.

She dabbed at her inflamed eyes with a clean tea towel—*obviously not.*

She washed her hands under the tap, feeling her pulse rate kick up a notch. It had to be him—everyone else had arrived an hour ago. 'I'll get it,' she called out.

Brent was about to push the bell again when the door opened abruptly and a small 'Who are you?' drifted up to him.

Brent looked down over the top of the bunch of bright red gerberas he held in his hands.

'I'm Brent. And I think you must be Benji, right?'

Benji squinted at the man on the doorstep. 'How do you know that?'

'I've seen your picture in your Aunty Grace's bag.'

Grace slowed her footsteps as she drew closer to the exchange at the door. She leant against the wall on the other side of the foyer, absently drying her hands and actively eavesdropping.

'You know Aunty Grace?'

'We're old friends. We went to medical school together.'

Benji considered that for a moment. 'Are you the man who broke her heart? Mummy always said Aunty Grace never got married cos a man in medical school broke her heart.'

Brent blinked, momentarily speechless. 'Er...' What was he supposed to say to that—*Well, actually, young Benji, it was the other way round*?

If she'd been heartbroken, she certainly hadn't shown it. Echoes of her unemotional severing of their relationship rampaged through his head. Her gutting announcement that she was leaving to complete her studies in Brisbane, far away from the distraction of him, clanging like a great gong in his brain.

Grace straightened and dashed from her hiding place to rescue Brent. 'Benji,' she said, sidling up quickly, slipping her hands onto his little shoulders and avoiding looking at Brent altogether, 'here you are. I think Uncle Marshall's looking for you.'

Benji smiled at his aunt. 'I told him I was the best at lighting fires. He said he might need my help.'

'Okay. But be careful,' she called after him, a familiar clutch of worry grabbing at her gut. What was it about boys and fire? Marshall was as fascinated by it now, at thirty-five, as he had been at Benji's age!

She turned back to Brent, who was still standing in the doorway. Filling the doorway actually, the warm day outside blocked from her view. He was wearing jeans and a casual navy T-shirt that hung out over his waistband. It moulded his biceps and stretched nicely across his shoulders, pecs and abs.

He looked all warm and relaxed and utterly sexy with his cleanly shaven jaw and some amazing scent that made her want to track down its origin.

With her tongue.

'Sorry about the Spanish Inquisition. I'm learning that seven-year-olds don't have much of a filter.'

Brent held her gaze. 'Is it true?'

She contemplated playing dumb but she'd never been very good at artifice. She shrugged. 'I never got married because I was busy building a career. You know I never wanted the whole white-picket-fence thing and I've never regretted my choices. Julie is a romantic who thinks everyone should be married.'

Brent held his breath at her slip and watched as it dawned on her face. Watched the flash of grief streak through her eyes like a lightning bolt. He noticed the red rimming her eyes. Had she been crying? Family events like this had to be difficult.

'Was,' Grace corrected herself.

Brent didn't say anything for a moment. 'You've been crying.'

Grace frowned, his words dragging her back from an emotional abyss. 'No,' she shook her head. 'Onions. I've been chopping onions.'

'Oh,' he said, and laughed. 'Sorry.'

She smiled back at him. 'No, I'm sorry. I'm being a very bad hostess.' She held her arms out for the flowers. 'Thanks for these, they're lovely.'

'Oh,' Brent said again, looking from her to the flowers and back again. 'Sorry, I actually brought them for your mother.'

It was Grace's turn to laugh this time. 'Whoops. That was embarrassing. Sorry.' And then she laughed again.

Brent grinned, relieved to see the shadows gone from her eyes. 'So are we going to stand in the doorway and trade apologies all day or can I come in?'

Grace slapped her hand to her forehead. 'Of course, come in.'

She stepped aside and admitted him, a magical mix of aromas wafting past her—flowers, sunshine and something quintessentially male. She drew it deep into her lungs and felt a corresponding tingle in her blood. Her mouth started to salivate as if she'd just walked past a bakery and spied a very tempting pastry.

'This way,' she said, keeping a safe distance between them as she led him through the house.

It felt strange having him here again. It gave her a weird sense of déjà vu—almost like the first time she'd brought him home. Her new boyfriend. Her first proper boyfriend.

She'd been nervous then too. But for different reasons. She'd wanted him to like the sprawling home she'd grown up in. Her father, a carpenter by trade, had added to it over the years in several different renovations to create more room for his ever-growing family. It wasn't very conventional.

And she'd desperately wanted him to like her family.

She'd been acutely aware that his childhood had been very different from hers. And she'd been scared that he would run a mile after witnessing the chaos of it all. Her youngest sibling, Barry, had only been four years old. Five of her siblings had still been in primary school. It had been a lot to ask anyone to digest.

But Brent had embraced it all—family, crazy mishmash house and all the associated noise. She'd fallen in love with him that day.

Brent followed her through a house he hadn't set foot in for over two decades. One that was still surprisingly familiar. Happy memories of family dinners and many noisy nights of babysitting. Finally getting the last child to bed and then making out on the couch in front of the television.

He smiled to himself as his gaze drifted to the swing of Grace's backside. Her hips had always been generously curved but were even more so now, with maturity on her side. Her jeans skimmed and hugged in all the right places.

It made him want to get her out of them.

Really, really badly.

Except, of course, they were friends.

She stopped just inside the back door and turned abruptly. He started guiltily, dragging his gaze up to her face. But it snagged momentarily on the way her red V-necked T-shirt stretched across her breasts. Those babies had always balanced out her hips perfectly.

Grace sucked in a breath as his eyes moved upwards, lingering on her cleavage. It was such a physical force it was as if his breath had fanned over her instead of his gaze. She willed her nipples not to react but it was futile.

Then his gaze met hers and there was a moment when everything else fell away and mutual sexual attraction roared into the silence between them.

Grace swallowed. *Pull yourself together!*

She cleared her throat and placed her hand on the doorknob.

The noise outside was muffled but more than evident and she was grateful for it to help focus her scattered thoughts.

'I suppose you've forgotten how crazy it was around here all those years ago?'

Brent concentrated on the racket beyond the door and not his pounding chest or the uncomfortable tightness of his jeans. He smiled. 'No, I haven't. I loved the craziness.'

She nodded. He had. He really had. 'Good, cos it's multiplied considerably.'

He shrugged. 'Bring it on.'

Grace rolled her eyes. 'Don't say I didn't warn you.'

And then she turned and opened the door and stepped into the tornado that was a Perry family get-together.

There was a moment when the entire activity in the back yard ceased and all eyes flew to the open doorway. Like some bizarre sixth sense, the family had all smelled new blood.

Then cries of 'Brent!' rang out and he was sucked into the vortex.

'For you,' he said to Grace's mother, presenting the flowers.

'Oh, Brent, they're lovely,' Trish said, plonking a kiss on his cheek.

'You always were a crawler,' Marshall said, slapping Brent on the back and shaking his hand.

'Wendy, you're closest—could you pop these in some water, please?'

'Here, I will,' Grace volunteered, relieving her sister of the job gratefully as Brent was drawn into a bear hug by her father.

Grace faded back into the house to fill a vase at the sink. The large picture window in front of her gave her a full Technicolor view of the backyard, which made it impossible to ignore the activity.

Brent was being greeted like a long-lost son. Even Barry, who'd been six years old when she'd left for Brisbane and surely wouldn't remember Brent at all, was shaking Brent's hand with vigour.

Grace's heart gave a painful squeeze. Were they all just filling the gap today?

The Julie gap?

It was plain wrong to have everyone here except her.

They'd spent the last hour pretending there wasn't a great big gaping hole in their family unit. Because that's what they did now. Laughing and joking. Talking and telling jokes and being positive.

And being loud. As loud as possible.

Pretending.

For each other. For Tash and Benji.

Trying to be *normal*.

And Grace was sure, from the outside at least, they would have appeared quite normal. Just a regular, albeit rather large, suburban family having a regular weekend celebration in the back yard.

But the hole never really went away.

Maybe having Brent back helped. Maybe it took them all back to happier times? When the family had been complete and nothing could touch them.

The good old days.

As for Brent, he was lapping it up. Grace smiled despite the heaviness in her heart and her misgivings about him being there.

Misgivings totally justified after their moment at the door.

It was as if he'd never left, slipping into his *Grace's boyfriend* shoes and making himself comfy.

Except he wasn't.

And he wasn't Julie either.

Grace pulled herself out of her funk and rejoined the Perry clan. 'Here she is,' Trish proclaimed. 'We were about to send out a search party.'

'I see you've met everyone, then,' Grace said.

He smiled at her as he passed her a boutique beer. She took it, the frosty glass a stark contrast to the warmth pulsing through her everywhere at the sheer sexiness of his smiling face.

'There are a few more of you than the last time I was here.' He grinned.

'We're going to test you in an hour,' Trish teased.

Brent let out a hoot of laughter. 'Oh, I see. I have to earn my supper.'

'Around here you do.' Grace's father grinned.

'I see the old tree house is still going strong, Lucas,' Brent said to Grace's father.

He took in the sight of the enormous sycamore tree that dominated one corner of the large back yard, branching over the fences on either side and providing shade for several sets of neighbours also. It was truly magnificent.

The tree house was just as grand. The Swiss Family Robinson couldn't have built a better one. Brent raised the beer bottle to his mouth to hide the smile that came to his lips as he remembered the night he and Grace had made love in the tree house.

'Yep. Grandkids use it now.'

Tash approached, her permanent scowl firmly in place, and Grace tensed. 'Everything okay, Tash? We should be eating soon.'

Before she could acknowledge—or ignore—Grace, Brent jumped in. 'Ah, so this is Tash,' he said, holding out his hand. He would never have recognised this girl as the smiling girl with long blonde hair from the photo. 'Nice to meet you.'

Tash blinked and Grace watched as her niece's lips parted slightly and the scowl slipped. A sort of stunned look took its place and she even managed a small smile.

Grace couldn't believe the transformation. Although she could understand the impetus. Brent Cartwright seemed to have that effect on all women. From toddlers to grannies.

Tash darted a nervous look in Grace's direction. 'You…
seen a photo of me?'

Grace knew exactly what she was thinking—*Oh my God,
what was I wearing? How old was I? It wasn't that naked-in-
the-backyard-pool one, was it?*

'Your Aunty Grace showed me. I thought how much you
looked like her but now I've seen you in the flesh you're the
spitting image of Julie.'

Grace heard her mother's indrawn breath as her own muscles
tightened to an unbearable tension.

'You…knew Mum?'

Brent flicked a glance towards Grace and Trish, who had
visibly paled. 'I did. She was fantastic.' He paused, unsure of
what to say. 'The world is a poorer place without her.'

Tash stared for a moment or two then Trish jumped in. 'Okay,
then, come on, love.' She ruffled Tash's hair. 'Let's go and see
how those snags are doing.'

Tash let herself be bundled along and Brent watched them
go. 'I'm sorry.' He grimaced, looking down at Grace. 'Did I
say the wrong thing?'

Grace shook her head. 'Not at all. We're all walking on eggshells around her. She usually hates to even hear Julie's name
mentioned. We never quite know how she'll react.'

'Has she had counselling?'

Grace nodded. 'A couple of times. But then she refused to
go.'

Brent heard the sadness weighing down Grace's voice. It was
unbearable. 'She needs to be able to talk about her mum.'

Grace felt a prickle of resentment. 'I know that.' She was a
doctor, for crying out loud. Didn't he think she knew that? 'I'm
just trying to take one day at a time,' she said defensively.

What clue would he have? A footloose, fancy-free bachelor?
She was doing the best she could, damn it. She'd been living
a single woman's life all her adult years and had never been
blessed with maternal instincts. This was all new to her.

Brent nodded. 'I'm sorry, I didn't mean to criticise. You'll get through this. I know you will.'

And because she looked like she needed it, he put his arm around her shoulder and pulled her into him. He was surprised when she plonked her head against his shoulder, accepting his comfort with no resistance.

It was just like the old days.

She must be worn down.

Grace shut her eyes, briefly letting his warmth and his solidness and his deep reassurance ease the worry lashing her insides.

'Who's for cricket?' Marshall yelled above the din, hitting a tennis ball high into the air with a bat.

A deafening affirmative response followed and Brent gave her arm a squeeze. 'Gotta go whip some Perry butt.'

Grace laughed. 'Good luck with that.'

They grinned at each other for a moment and Grace's heart rate spiked. Then he was away and she absently rubbed at her suddenly cold arms.

It was seven o'clock before Grace knew it and the crowd was starting to thin. Tired Perry children were being bundled up by their parents in preparation for home and everyone was in clean-up mode. The night air made her shiver despite the warmth of the afternoon and she had to remind herself she wasn't living in the Sunshine State any more.

'You don't have to clean up, Brent,' she said, as he pulled up beside her and started to gather plates.

'Nonsense,' he said. 'I helped make the mess. I can help clean it up.'

Grace laughed. 'Oh I'm sure we noticed your mess amongst the thirty-odd kids' plates and debris scattered everywhere.'

'Aunty Grace?'

Grace turned to find Tash standing behind her. She was fidgeting with her mobile phone in her hands and not quite making eye contact. Grace quelled the impulse to tense and smiled at her niece. 'Yes?'

'I'm off to the movies. I'll be back by eleven.'

Grace blinked. Her pulse beat loudly in her ears as Tash threw the fait accompli at her like a great big rock.

Grace took a breath. *She's a teenager. She's testing the boundaries. It's normal.*

Grace folded her arms. 'Er...no. No, you're not.'

Tash stood her ground. 'Yes, I am.'

The tips of Grace's fingers dug into the flesh of her arms. 'It's Sunday night. Tomorrow is a school day.'

Tash glared at her aunt. 'I'm not a little kid.'

'No, you're not. But you still have to follow the rules.'

'The rules suck,' Tash said belligerently.

Grace nodded. 'Yep. Mostly they do.'

'Please, Aunty Grace. Just this once,' she wheedled.

Grace blinked at her niece's rapid-fire change of tack. 'No.'

'I'll never ask again.'

Grace suppressed a snort. Would that that was true. Still, at least she was asking this time. That scary afternoon she'd run off and Grace hadn't been able to find her for hours had aged her a decade. 'And how do you propose to get there? And who exactly are you going with, Tash?'

Tash was back to belligerent as she gave a careless shrug. 'Some kids from school.'

'Do they have names?'

Tash's lips tightened. 'Just kids. Friends.'

Grace drew in a breath, reaching for patience. 'Trinny and Simone and Justine?'

Tash shook her head. 'New friends.'

Grace felt her unease grow. Since she'd been back Tash had shunned her old friends. It was concerning—old friends were part of the reason for moving the kids back to Melbourne.

'If you want to go to the movies next weekend, I'm sure we

could arrange it. But I'll need to meet your friends first and know transport details. I'd also like phone numbers for their parents.'

An incredulous look came over Tash's face as if Grace had asked her to provide police background checks and urine samples for drug screening. 'That's bloody ridiculous,' Tash yelled. Tears welled in her eyes. 'Mum would have let me go.'

Grace sucked in a breath as Tash's accusation slammed into her. She felt a warm hand on her shoulder. It glided up the slope of her neck coming to rest at her nape. She turned to see Brent gazing at her, sympathy in his eyes. She'd almost forgotten he was there.

Almost forgotten everyone was there, busying themselves with the cleaning and trying not to listen to the conversation between Tash and Grace. But the sudden shocked silence spoke volumes.

Grace looked at Tash, her heart breaking as tears trekked down her niece's face. 'I think we both know, that's not true, Natasha.'

'How do you know?' Tash yelled. 'You were never around anyway.'

'Natasha!' a shocked Trish gasped.

Tash glanced guiltily at her grandmother before looking back at Grace. 'Oh, forget it,' Tash snarled, dashing the tears away with angry strokes. 'Just forget it.' And she stormed past them both heading to the tree house.

Brent placed a restraining hand on her arm as Grace turned to follow her. 'Leave her to cool down,' he urged.

Grace was shaking on the inside from the confrontation, from the venom in her niece's accusation. 'But she's crying. I can't bear it when she cries.'

The anguish in her eyes was evident. 'I know,' he said, his thumb circling against the skin of her upper arm. 'Just give her a bit of space. Half an hour. Then talk to her.'

'He's right, darling,' Trish said.

Grace knew they were right but it didn't stop her wanting to go to Tash anyway. 'Okay.' She sighed. 'I'll help clean up then I'll go to her.'

CHAPTER SIX

THREE quarters of an hour later, Grace drained the dirty water from the sink, her gaze flicking beyond the window to the darkened tree house for the hundredth time.

Dread at the conversation she needed to have was churning in her stomach like bricks in a tumbledryer.

How was she supposed to handle this?

'That's the last one,' Brent said, as he dried the sole remaining plate.

They were the only ones in the kitchen, standing side by side at the sink. The others had all left in a noisy flurry and he'd shooed Grace's parents out, picking up a tea towel and ordering them to relax. Benji had been out on his feet and had gone to bed half an hour ago.

So he'd been left to prattle on with what turned out to be a very one-sided conversation.

He placed the dried plate on the bench and moved to stand behind Grace, his hands sliding to the taut muscles either side of her neck. He looked out at the tree house, rubbing absently at the knots in her traps, his chin on her head.

'Why don't you let me go and speak to her?'

Grace stirred from her reverie. As nice as it was to lean into him, to have his heat at her back, she couldn't shirk this responsibility—no matter how much she wanted to. 'No. I'll do it.'

She sounded like she was about to walk in front of a firing squad. 'I'm serious. Sometimes it's easier to talk to someone who isn't so close.'

Grace was tempted. So tempted. To abdicate this to someone else…

Could she?

'At least let me try. I might be able to break the ice.'

Grace felt a wave of gratitude swamp her as she let go of the must-do-it-myself ideal. Maybe Brent was right.

'Okay,' she murmured, pulling away from him.

A few minutes later they stepped out into the brisk night air. Grace was pleased she'd donned a cardigan. She headed for the old wooden swing that hung beneath the tree house as Brent climbed up the ladder. The swing creaked a little as she sat on the wooden seat.

The smell of aged hessian filled her nostrils as she leaned her cheek against the thick roughness of rope. It mingled with the lingering aromas of cooked meat and wood smoke and transported her back to her childhood. If she shut her eyes, she could be fifteen again.

Tash's age.

Her heart gave a painful squeeze as a jumble of emotions took hold. Helplessness, anger, frustration.

Overwhelming sadness.

Poor Tash.

She heard the tread of Brent's foot on the wooden ladder that was as solid today as it had been the day her father had built it when they'd first moved to the house. Grace had been six years old.

Then she heard a knock from above and Brent asking if he could enter. His voice carried easily through the tree house's open windows and out into the stillness of the night.

Tash murmured something unintelligible and Grace heard Brent's steps and a shuffling as he settled somewhere.

She crossed her fingers.

Brent, his eyes adjusting to the dark, sat on the floor opposite Tash in the large hexagonal structure. It was strewn with pieces

of plastic furniture—tables, chairs, a large plastic kitchen en-
semble, free-standing shelves and cupboards pushed against
walls—and kids' toys.

He placed his palms on the floor as he lowered himself down
and felt something gritty scratching him. Sand from the sandpit
below, no doubt. He wiped his palms absently on his jeans.

Tash, her legs drawn up to her chin, had a big crocheted
blanket thrown over her knees, one of many, by the looks of it,
stashed in a beat up old cupboard beside her.

'I suppose you're here to *express your disappointment*,' Tash
said after a moment or two, raising her hands in the air and
mimicking quote marks.

'Nope.'

'Going to give me some lame you'll-get-over-it speech?'

'Nope.'

'Not even "I'm sorry for your loss"? Or "Things will get
easier"?' Tash gave a harsh laugh. 'God, I hate hearing those
trite, unoriginal words. Don't people realise how underwhelm-
ing they are? Like I lost a bloody library book or my mobile
phone.'

'Nope.' Brent shook his head. 'Not going to say that either. I
think this whole thing sucks. Big time. That you and Benji got
a raw deal. I wish I could make that better for you. Everyone
does. I know Grace does. But unfortunately you've got to do
all the hard yards yourself.'

Tash squinted at him. 'You're not a psychiatrist, are you?'

Brent laughed. 'No.'

'Good. Cos you really suck at it.'

Brent chuckled again and they lapsed into a short silence.

'It just doesn't feel right without them,' Tash said. 'Being
here, all together.'

Brent nodded. 'I imagine it's going to feel like that for a long
time. Maybe it always will.'

Tash drew the blanket up to her chin, observing him for a
while. 'Do your parents live in Melbourne?'

Brent shrugged. 'I don't know. I've never known my parents. I was abandoned as a child and spent all my life in foster homes.'

Tash sat up, the blanket falling down to her knees. She stared at him. 'Really? Oh, God, I'm so sorry...'

Brent raised an eyebrow. 'For my loss?' He smiled.

Tash started to say something else and then stopped, realising that Brent was teasing. 'Yeah, yeah.' She smiled and pulled the blanket back over her shoulders again.

They sat in more silence, which was eventually broken by Tash. 'Tell me a memory.'

Brent frowned. Did she want one from his childhood? Such as it was? He could, of course, tell her his one abiding memory of this tree house but it was hardly appropriate. 'Care to narrow that down?'

'You knew my mum, right? Tell me a memory.'

Ah.

Brent sifted through myriad images in his mind, twisting them and turning them over like an emotional kaleidoscope, trying to find one that best captured Julie's essence.

'I remember us all heading down to Bells Beach the week after she finished her final grade-twelve exams. Grace and I and Doug and Julie—'

'You knew Dad too?' Tash interrupted.

Brent nodded. 'Grace and I had been together for about six months when Doug came on the scene.' A tear spilled down Tash's cheek and he watched as she dashed it away. 'She was so happy that day. To be done with school. To be free. She kept saying, "I can't believe I'm free." She hit that beach and she cartwheeled all the way down to the ocean.'

Brent smiled at the image of Julie making Doug's day by bouncing around in that itty-bitty bikini. 'The water was absolutely freezing but she dived straight in. She didn't come out for hours.'

Tash smiled through her tears. 'She loved the ocean.'

Brent nodded again. 'Yep. She did.'

'She used to say if we won lotto we'd get a house right on the beach.' She wiped at another tear. 'Did Dad go in the water too? He was never a huge fan.'

Brent heard the hunger in Tash's voice. Her thirst for memories was so tangible it parched his throat. He chuckled. 'A little. He was just happy to watch your mum prance around in a bikini.'

Tash screwed up her nose, trying to look put off and murmuring a quick 'Eww!' But a laugh bubbled out quickly after. 'He was always such a perv.'

She laughed again and Brent joined her. When their laughter had settled, he decided to push a little. 'You know Grace and your other aunts and uncles, your grandparents, they'd share their memories too…'

Tash sniffed. 'It hurts them. To remember. I don't want to hurt them.'

Ah.

Tash wanted to spare them pain.

Brent shrugged. 'You might be surprised.' And then, because he could feel Tash was receptive, he pushed some more. 'You know Grace is just trying to keep you safe, right? She's worried about you, Tash.'

The teenager averted her gaze, taking great interest in the crocheted holes, poking her fingers through them.

'Tash?'

'I know. I just get…so angry sometimes. It's just so…unfair, you know?' She didn't wait for his acknowledgement as she stabbed all her fingers into available holes. 'And she's always trying to talk to me about Mum and Dad, trying to get me to talk about them. She thinks it's unhealthy not to. But I don't know what to say…'

'Have you told her that?'

Tash paused. 'She won't listen to me.'

Brent doubted that very much. He also doubted that was the

real reason for Tash's beef with Grace if the teenager's continuing avoidance of eye contact was any clue.

But he figured he'd probably pushed enough for one night. And Tash obviously agreed. She stood abruptly, letting the blanket fall to the floor. 'I'm going in now.'

Brent stood also. 'Okay. It was nice talking to you.'

Tash gave him a stiff nod and headed for the door. She turned awkwardly at the last moment. 'Thanks for the memory.'

Brent inclined his head. 'Any time.' And Tash disappeared down the ladder.

Grace sat motionless on the swing, unnoticed by her niece in the dark shadows of the tree house. A tear fell unchecked down her cheek. The back door opened and a shaft of light illuminated Tash's features.

Despite her attempts to look otherwise, the yellow glow softened Tash. Her grief was there in sharp relief but the beam of light also captured a sweetness, an innocence lost.

Grace would give anything to find it again.

Brent slid back down the wall, drawing his knees up, resting his hands on his thighs. He hoped he'd said the right things. Hoped he hadn't pushed too much. In a lot of ways he related to Tash. He knew what it was like to grow up with a big part of your life missing.

He heard steps on the ladder and turned his head in time to see Grace's appearing over the lip of the doorway. Their gazes locked.

'Did you hear all that?'

Grace paused where she was on the ladder and nodded. She'd heard every word—or most of them anyway. And each one had sliced into her heart with all the surgical precision of a scalpel blade. 'I feel like such a failure,' she whispered.

She looked utterly dejected and Brent's heart swelled in

his chest. Grace, the high achiever, the go-getter, was at a total loss.

'Come here.' He patted the floor beside him.

Grace hesitated only briefly before climbing the rest of the way in. She remembered all the times they'd laid together staring into the dark, talking. She talking. Him listening. Letting her vent about something at uni or some babysitting her mother wanted her to do or whatever had been bothering her at the time.

Giving her perspective.

He'd been her confidant as well as her lover.

She hadn't realised until this very moment how much she'd missed that about him. Brent had always been a great listener.

She crawled over to him on her hands and knees. It was darker inside than out but her eyes had adjusted. She sat down. Not too close. She left a respectable distance between his thigh and hers, his arm and hers.

'Yuk,' she said, rubbing her hands together. 'There's enough sand up here to open a beach.'

Brent chuckled. 'Yes, it is a little gritty, isn't it?'

Grace rolled her eyes. 'Still king of the understatement, I see.'

At one time he'd driven her nuts with his economical use of adjectives. It wasn't until she'd known him for a while she's realised that it was a trait born of his upbringing. He hadn't led a flowery life.

Listening to him talk to Tash about being abandoned as a child had released all her old feelings of impotence and sorrow. She'd been incensed on his behalf when he'd first told her about his bleak childhood. He hadn't been mistreated but he had been passed around. No chance for him to settle anywhere. No stability. No routine.

Her heart had bled for the lost little boy he'd been. But he'd just shrugged. *It is what it is.* That's what he'd said. And she'd wrapped her body around him and vowed to love him even more.

A silence settled around them as they both got lost in their own thoughts. Sounds of the night invaded the hush surrounding them. The distant noise of a car starting competed with a nearby barking dog and, somewhere in the neighbourhood, a crying child.

Brent rolled his head to the side. 'She's going to be all right, you know.' He didn't know how he knew, he just did.

He reached for her hand and entwined it with hers. It was cold and he used his other hand to encase hers completely, rubbing at it absently.

Grace looked down at their linked hands. It had been twenty years since he'd held her hand and it felt like just yesterday as the warmth from his hand travelled up her arm and reached into all the places that were cold with fear and doubt and worry.

His calm reassurance was comforting and she wanted to lay her head on his shoulder and have him tell her that over and over again.

'I hope you're right.'

Brent squeezed her hand. 'I usually am.'

Grace gave a half-laugh but felt absurdly like crying. She hadn't spoken any of her doubts out loud to anyone in eighteen months. And here she was dumping it all on an old boyfriend.

Who was now, technically, her boss.

And she didn't have a clue why.

'I can't believe the way she…' Grace's voice cracked on a jagged block of emotion that tore at her throat. She sucked in a breath to steady herself. 'The way she opened up to you.'

To her horror she felt a burning behind her eyes and a prickling in her nose. 'I mean,' she continued as the pressure built behind her eyes and in her nose and bloomed in her chest as well, 'I've been trying to get her to talk. To share things with her. Talk about Julie and Doug and…'

More emotion welled up, making it hard to talk, making her voice husky and useless. And then a tear fell, slipping under her glasses, and she dashed it away. She looked up at him.

'I have been listening. I have. I have a thousand memories I could tell her. I've tried to tell her…'

Brent ached to reach for her. Tash and Grace were both hurting so much. 'She's trying to spare you from the pain of them, Grace,' he said gently.

Grace felt another tear well. 'She's a kid. She shouldn't have to feel responsible for my…' Grace took a breath as a great big sob threatened and her face fought the urge to crumple. 'She's not supposed to worry about me. I'm not her… responsibility.'

'Oh Gracie,' he whispered, lifting a hand from hers and catching a tear with his thumb, wiping it across her cheekbone.

And that did it. Her face did crumple. In fact, her whole body seemed to fold in on itself and before she knew it he was hauling her close, his arm around her shoulders, tucking her into his side, stroking her arm with his fingers.

Grace pressed her face into the solid warmth of his shoulder as great heaving sobs tore through her chest. They ripped open the raw jagged edges of her grief and consumed her with their ferocity.

Later she would feel embarrassed. She'd want to snatch back time and erase the entire scene. But for now she clung to his stability like he was a lighthouse and she was being tossed about in a stormy sea. And strangely it didn't seem weird. They'd been apart for twenty years and yet turning to him still seemed so natural.

Grace hadn't cried like this since the day Marshall had shown up at her work in Brisbane with the bleakest eyes she'd ever seen. The family hadn't wanted to tell her over the phone.

Not even at the funeral. Because suddenly she had two children depending on her. Looking at her with bewildered eyes for comfort and direction. For someone to tell them it was going to be okay. They'd needed her to be together.

Sure, there'd been tears, but not like this. This seemingly bottomless well of grief.

Brent held her while she wept. She'd curled into his side and was half-draped across his chest, her arm flung around his neck. He ran his fingers down her arm and her back in long, smooth strokes as his shirt absorbed her tears and his body absorbed her almost violent sobs. She rocked against him as each one squeezed the anguish from her body like a contraction and he held her tighter.

'I'm s-so s-sorry,' Grace hiccoughed between sobs.

'Shh, it's okay,' he murmured, rubbing his chin against her hair. 'Julie died. You're allowed to be sad too.'

Grace shook her head. 'I'm usually s-stronger than this.'

Brent squeezed her shoulder. 'I know how strong you are.' She'd broken up with him, hadn't she? 'You don't have to be strong around me. Just get it all out.'

Grace nodded as more emotion welled in her throat and more tears fell unchecked. She scrunched his T-shirt in her hand and took his advice.

She let it all out.

Time passed. Grace wasn't sure how long. Twenty? Thirty minutes? Her sobs eventually became sniffles and the tears slowed and then dried up. She started to become aware of other things. The warmth of a solid pec beneath her cheek, the feel of wet cotton, the steady thud of his heartbeat in her ear, the luxurious stroking of his fingers against her back.

And the intoxicating aroma of man.

She found herself inhaling deeply, sucking it into the bottom of her lungs, savouring it like an addict. She scrunched his shirt a little tighter as it made her feel slightly dizzy.

'Better now?'

His voice rumbled through his rib cage and connected with

her ear. She stirred, lifting her head. She felt weary to her bones. Utterly exhausted. Wrung out. She felt like she could sleep for a week.

But, yes, she did feel better.

'Thank you. Yes.'

She straightened up. Uncurled her body from his side, supporting herself against the wall next to him. She readjusted her glasses. Their arms brushed. Their thighs were separated by the narrowest of distances.

Grace looked at him. 'I'm sorry to—'

'Don't.' It probably came out more fiercely than he'd meant it to by the look on her face, but he couldn't bear to hear her apologise again. He looked down at her and placed his hand against her mouth. 'There's nothing to apologise for.'

She blinked up at him owl-like through her glasses and he became aware of the texture of her lip gloss beneath his fingers. He could smell it also, sugary sweet. And suddenly the memory of him kissing that gloss off her mouth in this very structure pushed into his mind.

Sneaking in here with her late one night and laying her back on a sleeping bag and loving her. Stifling her climactic cries with his mouth so they didn't wake the entire neighbourhood. Especially her parents.

Their gazes locked.

He slowly withdrew his hand.

Grace held her breath. She wondered if he was thinking what she'd been thinking. About that night…

She was aware of his arm against hers, the heat of his thigh aligned with hers, his mouth so very, very close. Grace watched as his gaze dropped to her lips. She swallowed.

They shouldn't be doing this. 'Brent…'

The huskiness in her voice, the way she said his name went straight to Brent's belly. The urge to pull her into him, to drop his mouth to hers roared in his head and he struggled to deny it.

Her mouth shimmered in the darkness. Like a great beacon. 'Is that still the same lip gloss you used to wear?'

Her breath stopped in her lungs. 'Brent.'

'Honey something it was called. I've been trying to remember since the day of the interview.'

'Honey Jumble,' she whispered.

Brent nodded. Honey Jumble. That was it. 'Does it still taste the same?'

Grace felt her pelvic floor clamp down hard. 'Brent, I—'

He didn't give her time to voice her protest as the urge to reacquaint himself with the taste of the gloss, the taste of her, overcame him. Overcame all the reasons why he shouldn't.

It had been so long and she was so close.

So Gracie.

His hand reached for her face, cupping her jaw as his lips closed the distance from hers. Honey Jumble teased his taste buds and he licked at it like it was the elixir of life.

Grace felt only a second's resistance then she was groaning against his mouth, turning slightly to wind her arms around his neck, her surrender immediate. She opened to him deeper, angled her head, pulled him closer.

It felt so very good, being in his arms again. Being kissed by him again. So familiar. It fizzed through her veins and sparked at her nerve endings. So much of her life was foreign right now but this, this was, oh, so familiar.

Brent twisted, grabbing her arms and pulling her up and over him. She went eagerly, needing no urging to open her legs, to straddle him. He ploughed one hand into her hair as the other gripped her hip, his fingers digging into a rounded buttock. His tongue pushed into her mouth as his hips pushed up against hers.

He moaned deeply as hers pushed right back.

Heat licked at him. Everywhere. His belly, his thighs, his

groin. Flame rolled through his veins and arteries and burned behind his eyes. He was so damn hot.

So damn hard.

He pushed his hand up from her hip under her T-shirt, feeling the dip of her back and the smooth warmness of her skin in contrast to the ridges of her spine. He wanted to touch her everywhere. Feel her touching him.

'Grace? Grace?' A distant voice from the direction of the house broke into their intimacy. 'Benji's woken up. He's crying. He's asking for you.'

Brent pulled abruptly away as if Trish had thrown a bucket of cold water over him. Grace whimpered softly in protest and he almost groaned out loud.

'Shh,' he murmured, their foreheads touching, his thumb stroking her moist lips smeared with honey and him. His breathing was rough and loud in the confined space. As was hers.

Her chest heaved against his as they both struggled for air. Squashed against him, the evidence of his arousal was distracting as hell. It was tempting. So tempting to ignore her mother's call and just reach down and unzip him.

A few seconds was all it would take to reacquaint herself with all his glorious length.

But it wasn't just about her any more.

She lifted her head from Brent's. 'I'll be right there,' she yelled in the direction of the nearest window.

Grace heard the kitchen window shut and she looked back at Brent. His mouth was moist and his hair was well and truly ruffled.

'You should go.'

Grace nodded. 'You're angry, aren't you?'

'Nope.' Not at her anyway. At himself. He didn't want this. She'd walked out on him years ago and he was over her.

Grace shifted off him. 'This is my life now, Brent. I don't have room for any of this.'

'I know,' he said.

Then he hauled his butt off the floor, holding out a hand to help her up.

CHAPTER SEVEN

HALF an hour later Grace eased herself off Benji's bed. She'd cuddled him and read him a book and stayed with him until he'd fallen asleep. He was breathing evenly now and she stroked his forehead, pushing his fringe back off his face.

He had bad dreams about a car on fire and Julie's voice calling his name from somewhere amongst the flames.

The counsellor said it could take a while for them to become less frequent and that it was possible he could have them for ever.

Grace shuddered at the thought. Poor Benji. He was so little. Too little for all this.

She left his lamp on and switched out the overhead light as she wandered towards the lounge room. Her thoughts returned to Brent and what had transpired earlier in the back yard.

A momentary aberration.

A mistake.

She was surprised to hear the low rumble of Brent's voice as she approached the lounge room. He was supposed to be gone. She stood in the doorway unannounced for a moment. Brent and her father were sitting in the recliners, their backs to the door. Her mother and Tash were sharing the three-seater.

They were all chatting away like Brent had never left their lives. Like the intervening twenty years had never happened. Her mother said something. Brent laughed. Tash joined in.

It was way too cosy for her liking.

'Oh, there you are, darling,' Trish said, suddenly noticing Grace leaning against the doorjamb.

Brent looked over his shoulder. Grace was frowning and he didn't need his medical degree to figure out why. He rose quickly.

'Right, well, I'd best be off, then,' he said.

The family stood, all talking at once, urging him not to be a stranger.

'He can come to our house-warming, right, Aunty Grace?'

Grace blinked. 'We're having a house-warming?'

'Of course,' Tash said. 'I can invite my friends over—that way you'll get to know them.'

Grace slid a sideways glance at Brent. Was this progress? She looked back at Tash and saw the plea in her eyes.

'Well, I suppose so...but you'll want to do the renovations to your bedroom first, right? Don't want anyone seeing that hideous wallpaper.'

Tash agreed quickly. 'Oh, God, no. But that should only take a weekend once we're in. Hey...' she turned to Brent '...maybe you could help—'

'Tash!' Grace admonished quickly. 'Brent is a very busy person. With his own life.'

Brent chuckled for Tash's benefit but got the not-so-hidden message. 'It's all right. I'm pretty sure I can help out with a bit of DIY.'

Tash grinned and Grace rolled her eyes. 'Well, we'll see,' she said. 'Say goodbye, Tash.'

Brent made his farewells and followed Grace to the door, stepping out as she opened it, his brain fixated on their kiss. What had happened in the tree house had been an anomaly, he reminded himself. The result of an overwrought Grace colliding with a hefty dose of nostalgia. That was all.

He turned to face her.

'Thanks for taking the time with Tash today. I really *do* appreciate it. I understand that the dramas of a fifteen-year-old girl probably aren't in your field of expertise.'

Brent shrugged. 'It was no bother.'

Her breath caught in her throat at the husky note in his voice, which did crazy things to her pulse. She could almost feel his hand beneath her T-shirt again, his erection pressing into her.

God, what must he think of her instantaneous surrender? That she'd been pining for his touch for two decades? She took a step towards him, flicking a quick glance over her shoulder for any nearby flapping ears. Maybe she could explain?

And then she could explain it to herself!

'About before. In the tree house—'

Brent held up a hand. 'Don't worry about it. I understand. It was… There are a lot of memories up there. It was a slip, that's all.'

Grace nodded. A slip. Yes, that's what it was. 'Absolutely.'

'So, let's just forget it, okay?'

'Oh, yes, please.' Grace nodded again, relief flooding through her veins at his casual dismissal of what had transpired between them.

Brent chuckled at her palpable relief. 'Good. See you in a few days.'

He didn't wait for an acknowledgement and she watched as he turned away and trudged down the path.

Three days later Grace was behind a cubicle curtain, demonstrating to Adam Mather how to reduce a dislocated shoulder, when Brent tracked her down. Her eyes met his when he stepped in and she caught a glimpse of something raw and unguarded in his hazel gaze as the memory of their kiss slithered into the space between them before they slipped into their professional guises.

'Can I help you, Dr Cartwright?'

Brent shook his head. 'Ellen said you needed me?'

Grace blushed at his choice of words after their passionate clinch on Sunday night. She looked away quickly. She had asked the NUM when he'd be in but she hadn't meant for it to be a thing.

She'd thought she ought to take the temperature of their relationship after Sunday night but now Abby, the nurse who was assisting them, was looking at her curiously and she was annoyed at herself for saying anything at all.

'Oh, yes. I just needed a quick word.' For Abby's sake she added, 'It wasn't anything important.'

Brent nodded briskly, ignoring the stirrings caused by her Honey Jumble lips. 'What have you got?'

'Dr Mather?' Grace prompted.

'Forty-five-year-old male cyclist came off his bike, falling heavily on his left shoulder.' Adam slipped into presenting mode with ease. 'The position indicates a complete dislocation and the X-ray confirms it.'

Brent crossed to the illuminated viewing box onto which the X-rays were clipped. He studied them, noting immediately the obvious dislocation of the humeral head but paying closer attention for the presence of any fractures that would complicate the reduction process.

'The X-ray, as you can see, is clear of fractures,' Adam continued, 'and this is the patient's first presentation with this type of injury.'

Brent crossed back to the patient and smiled at the very fit, middle-aged man half out of his Lycra cyclist's gear. His face was tense and looking at the gross deformity of his shoulder Brent didn't blame him.

'Hi…' Brent looked at the patient's chart. 'Graham. Pain bad?'

Graham nodded. 'Terrible. Worse than my wife's three labours. But don't tell her that.'

Brent chuckled. 'I'll keep it between us. Sit tight. It'll all be over in a couple of minutes.'

Brent looked back at Adam and he continued. 'The ambulance gave him Penthrane. We've inserted a cannula and are about to administer midazolam for the procedure.'

'All right, then, I'll leave you to it.'

The curtain flicked back and Ellen appeared. 'Abby? You were supposed to go on your lunch break ten minutes ago.'

'Sorry,' she said, indicating the tray of drugs she'd drawn up ready to administer. 'I got a little held up.'

Brent looked sheepishly at the harassed-looking NUM. 'Sorry, that's my fault. You go to lunch, Abs. I'll give the drugs.'

Abs? Grace kept her face impassive at the easy familiarity. Did he make a habit of giving all the women he knew pet names?

Abs. Gabs.

Gracie.

'Thank you, Brent,' Ellen said. 'The least you can do,' she said with mock severity, before snapping the curtain back in place.

Brent chuckled as he took the green plastic tray from Abby and read the colour-coded labels attached to the drugs.

'Okay.' He nodded. 'I'm ready when you are.'

Grace indicated to Adam to take up position beside Graham. She nodded at Brent to administer the drugs.

'Okay, Graham, you'll feel sleepy and a little bit drifty for a while and that's when we'll pop this sucker back in. Let us know if you feel any pain during the procedure and we can top you up, all right?'

Graham nodded. 'Just do it,' he said, his words slurring. 'Just get it ov…'

Within seconds Graham had drifted into a light sleep, his eyes fluttering shut. 'Okay, Adam, you're on.'

Brent watched as Grace stood behind the resident, talking him through the procedure. He was impressed. A lot of doctors would have taught through example, through demonstrating the actions themselves, but Brent knew the best way to learn, the only way really, was by hands-on experience.

She showed Adam where to place his hands and how to apply traction while abducting and performing external rotation at the same time. She also warned him that, despite his sedated state, Graham might cry out when the humeral head slipped back into place.

Brent had known since the first day, when she'd cracked open that chest, he'd made the right decision in employing her, but this was the first time he'd seen her in a teaching role and his conviction was only strengthened. The Central was a major teaching hospital and she was a tremendous teacher.

Adam was nervous—having not one but two consultants watch you perform a procedure for the first time would give even the most confident resident the jitters—but she set him at ease. She didn't rush him or try to take over when he fumbled, and she congratulated him when he got each step right.

And when the joint finally clicked back into place and Graham cried out briefly in pain, giving Adam a scare, she clapped and grinned at him. As Brent gave some pain relief Grace said 'You did it. Congratulations, Dr Mather, you just reduced your first shoulder.'

Adam's answering smile said it all. 'Thanks, Grace. That was… Wow…' He ran his hands through his hair. 'That was amazing.'

Grace poked his chest playfully. 'You were amazing.'

Brent watched as they grinned at each other, feeling curiously left out. Then Graham stirred and Grace got back to business.

'We'll need a check X-ray,' she said to Adam, 'and then we'll pop it in a sling for discharge.'

Brent slipped away as the teaching continued.

Twenty minutes later Grace found Brent in his office, talking on the phone. He looked up as she stood in his doorway and he gestured her in. Grace took a seat, waiting while he finished his call. He looked very autumnal in his rusty gold shirt and a tawny tie the colour of an eagle's eye.

With his stethoscope slung around his neck, drawing attention to broad shoulders, he looked like a television doctor—sexy and god-like.

Brent ended the call and smiled at her. 'Great job with Adam,' he said. 'You're a good teacher.'

Grace felt her cheeks warm at his compliment and she smiled. 'Thanks. I enjoy it.'

He inclined his head. 'I can tell. Have you ever thought about lecturing?'

She nodded. 'I've toyed with it. Particularly when the kids came to live with me—better hours, all school holidays off. But I'd miss the vibe of the hands-on stuff.'

Brent completely understood. 'Yep. Totally.' He'd be bored in a minute with no patients to treat, no lives to save.

They sat for a moment in mutual agreement. 'So…you wanted to see me?' he prompted.

Clunk. The glow from Adam's successful performance disappeared and it was back to real life. She sat up and smoothed her trousers over her knee.

'Yes.' She looked over her shoulder at the open door. Why hadn't she shut it?

Because she hadn't wanted anyone to think anything untoward…

'I…I just wanted to check we're okay after the ki…after the other night.'

Brent felt the tempo of his heart rate pick up. Okay? Not really. He'd replayed that scene over and over in his head a million times. Dreamt about it.

'Cos I've been thinking,' Grace proceeded into the silence. 'It's like you said, it was a…slip. It was probably bound to happen really…given our history. Maybe we needed it to happen. To, you know, get it out of our systems.'

Brent was pretty damn sure from four nights of erotic dreams, all disconcertingly taking place in a tree house full of kids' toys, that nothing but full head-banging sex was going to *get it out of his system.*

'But I want to assure you that it won't happen again. I was a bit of a…mess, really. Well, I don't need to tell you that, do I? You just caught me at a really low point and it was easy to slip back into…old habits.'

Brent nodded. It hadn't taken his psychology major to figure out the kiss had been something familiar for her to reach for. Like an old teddy bear. He was just grateful she hadn't said bad habits.

'I'm aware though that my actions…my kissing you so… passionately…could be misconstrued. So I really need you to know that I'm not in the market for a relationship. I just don't have the time or space, emotional space, in my life for another human being. As you saw on Sunday night, I have my hands very full with two grieving kids and they need my undivided attention.'

Grace had no idea how garbled this was all coming out, she just knew she had to get it out. Put it all on the table. So she ploughed on.

'With everything so chaotic in my personal life and you know how much I hate chaos, it's important to me that one aspect of my life is stable. And for me that's work. Coming here gives me much-needed respite from home. I get to feel in control for eight hours. And I need that. So I don't need any… weirdness here at work. I don't want anything to affect our work relationship. I know we'd talked about being friends but first and foremost this relationship…' she pointed back and forth between them several times '…our professional relationship is paramount.'

Grace looked at a continuing silent Brent. 'Oh, God, please say something.'

Brent exhaled loudly. 'You haven't really given me a chance.'

Grace castigated herself for prattling. 'Sorry.'

Brent collected his thoughts for a moment. 'I agree that

our professional relationship is important and also don't want anything to jeopardise it either so please don't worry.'

Grace sagged against the chair, the relief overwhelming. It flooded through her entire body like a heroin high. 'Good.'

'As for me reading anything into our kiss…' He saw Grace tense and felt a corresponding tension in his neck and shoulders. 'I understand that Sunday night was a physical manifestation of an emotional day. I hadn't read any more into it than that.'

The high spun through Grace's head until she felt almost dizzy. She smiled at him. 'Good. I'm glad. I've been worried about it.'

Dazzled by her full-wattage smile, Brent found her obvious relief perversely irritating. It was time for him to lay some cards on the table.

'As we're being frank I'd like to say something too.'

Grace nodded. 'Sure thing.'

'It took me a couple of years to get over you, Grace. But I did. I moved on. Hell, I got married twice. And, please, don't think me rude when I tell you this, but I really need you to know that I would never make the mistake of falling for you again.'

Grace's smile slipped a little as his statement had popped the bubble she'd been floating in. *Had he considered falling for her the first time a mistake?*

'Yes, I'm still attracted to you. Yes, I'll probably want to kiss you again. But please do me a favour and resist, okay? Because you're obviously no closer to committing to someone than you were twenty years ago and I don't make the same mistake twice. Believe it or not, there are plenty of women who *do* want a relationship with me. In fact,' he lied, 'I have a date tonight.'

Grace was surprised at how much his words disconcerted her. The buzz had certainly died a quick death. In her first few days at the Central she'd heard all about his playboy reputation but to hear him confirm it elevated it above the gossip that she'd pegged it as.

'So, just to be completely transparent, I'm good with being

friends and colleagues and have absolutely no interest in anything else, okay?'

Grace swallowed. It seemed so much harsher coming from
him. But he was right, she wasn't in a position to commit
and rekindling what they'd had didn't benefit either of them.
'Okay.'

Grace's pager beeped loudly and she started. She checked
the message. 'I'd better get this.'

She stood and turned to leave. 'Oh, by the way, please don't
feel that you have to help with the renovations or come to the
house-warming party. Tash is really very good at emotional
blackmail.' She shrugged. 'I love her to pieces, but it's true.'

Brent stood also. 'Maybe. But I think it's important to her
that I come. And I'm more than happy to.'

Grace swallowed. He was such a good guy. He'd always been
a good guy. They'd just wanted different things and she'd been
terrified that she'd loved him so much she'd end up sacrificing
her things for him and she'd be swallowed up again.

'Okay. It'll probably be a couple of weeks before anything
gets started.'

He shrugged. 'Fine. Whenever. Just let me know.'

The beeper rang out again. 'Gotta go,' she said, and backed
out of his office.

Brent watched her go, pleased with the outcome. They both
knew where they stood. The memory of Sunday night's kiss
would probably make them awkward for a bit but they'd soon
get into the swing of it.

Now all he had to do was extinguish her and her Honey
Jumble mouth from his dreams.

And find himself a date for tonight!

Two weeks later, Grace found herself in the middle of the shift
from hell. The department was frantic and everyone, including
Brent, was pitching in.

Grace was examining a thirty-two-year-old woman who

had taken a tumble down her front stairs at home and fractured both the bones in one of her lower legs. Her mobile phone had slipped out of her pocket during the impact and had landed in a garden bed that lined the front path.

With her eight-month-old baby feeling abandoned and crying inconsolably in the house, the woman had dragged herself over the rocky path and in severe pain to retrieve the phone, which had landed beneath some shrubs, so she could ring for an ambulance.

It had taken her half an hour. She looked like she'd been dragged through a hedge backwards as she apologised to Grace for the third time about her clingy little girl. Grace was trying to examine the woman's bruised ribs without much success.

'I'm so sorry,' she said, wincing as she jiggled the baby a little. 'My husband should be here soon.'

Grace smiled at the harried-looking woman, who couldn't even give in to the pain of her tib and fib fracture that was so bad it had broken the skin. Not to mention the likelihood of a rib or two. Her patient was doing what mothers did—putting her child's needs first.

'It's fine, Linda,' Grace assured her. 'This little one had a major fright too today.'

Grace ruffled the baby's hair and watched as the baby shied away, bursting into tears again as she buried her face in her mother's neck. 'I think young Penny will be sticking to you like white on rice the next few days.'

Brent was passing the cube when the baby's cries pulled him up short. There was something gut-wrenching about the noise that tugged at primal instincts and he was pulling back the curtain before his brain even registered the action.

He spied Grace immediately and allowed his body the inevitable leap it took every time he saw her. His pulse kicked up a notch and his senses became sharper as he homed in on the tiny flutter at her throat and the glisten of her lips. His mouth watered, remembering how good she tasted, and he gave himself a mental shake.

His reaction to her didn't seemed to be lessening, as he'd hoped.

Sure, their relationship had normalised considerably. They were developing a good collegial routine. Professional and courteous. And he was going to her place this weekend to help out with the kids' bedroom makeovers.

But this unchecked response of his body to hers whenever they were near was a damn nuisance. Something he didn't want and could most definitely do without. Still, no matter what he did, no matter what he told himself, it was always there. So he was going to have to learn to live with it.

He'd loved her once. There was bound to be residual... attraction.

It wasn't going to kill him.

'Well, now,' he said, his gaze shifting to the woman on the gurney and the bawling baby. 'Someone's not a happy camper.'

Grace sucked in a breath as Brent filled the small cubicle with his breadth and his deep, rumbly voice and his sheer unadulterated maleness. Her heart did a quick two-step as his charisma reached out and brushed gossamer fingers over her breasts, her thighs, her belly.

She cursed her reaction to him. How did he still have such an effect on her? She was at work with a baby screaming merry hell at her elbow, for Pete's sake. How long would it take for this unwanted surge of lust to die a natural death?

She watched as Brent cooed at the little girl, flashed his penlight at her and, as she reached for the light, plucked the unprotesting bundle into his arms.

Grace's heart went thunk, thunk, boom.

'She likes you.' Linda smiled.

'Of course she does.' Brent grinned at the baby and handed

over the torch, which she promptly stuck in her mouth. 'What's not to like?'

He turned to face her and Grace nodded her head absently. *What indeed?*

Certainly not seeing him with a baby. She caught her breath as Penny smiled up at him around his pen. She made a grab for his ID, which hung from a lanyard around his neck, and transferred her dribbly attention to it.

And suddenly sexy went to a whole new level.

Watching him with the babe was like a sucker punch to Grace's solar plexus and she had difficulty breathing. He looked amazing with a baby—he was so big and broad compared to the wee little sprite in his arms and it magnified his masculinity tenfold.

Grace remembered how desperately he'd wanted his own family. Children to love and spoil. To give a life he'd always craved and never known.

Looking at him now, she had no doubt he would have been an excellent father. In fact, she'd never had any doubt. Visions of him piggy-backing a squealing, giggly four-year-old Barry around their house during babysitting episodes came back to her. He'd always been excellent with kids.

A funny niggling feeling teased at the periphery of her consciousness as she glimpsed a life she could have known. He looked so confident with Penny, so at ease, she could imagine him with their daughter smiling up at him like he was the centre of her universe.

Grace's breath caught in her throat as the sheer beauty of the vision pierced her to the core. An emotion she couldn't identify—didn't want to identify—welled in her chest.

But it felt eerily like melancholy.

He'd already told her that he'd never found the right person. That it *just hadn't happened*. But looking at his big hand spread securely across the baby's back it made her wonder.

Late at night, when he was lying alone in his bed, did he have regrets?

Like she was having now?

But thoughts of him in bed, alone or not alone for that matter, were not good for her equilibrium and Grace was pleased when Linda said, 'Now's your chance, Dr Perry, I'm not sure how long peace will reign.'

CHAPTER EIGHT

EVENING had darkened the sky to a velvety blush several hours later when Brent popped his head into the minor ops rooms to find Grace stapling a head laceration from a workplace accident. Ellen was assisting.

'Ah, good, Ellen, you're a hard woman to track down.'

Grace looked up, her steady hand suddenly slightly shaky, and she thanked her lucky stars she was holding a stapler, not a curved blade with a suture attached. She looked beyond his shoulder and saw Donna, an agency nurse who'd been doing a lot of work in the department lately, hovering closely behind, obviously not dressed for work.

Dressed for fun.

A swift, hot dart of emotion jabbed at her diaphragm and her breath hitched.

Ellen looked up too, also not missing Donna. 'You've got me,' she said, flicking her gaze back to the job at hand, using forceps to bring the jagged edges of the head wound together for Grace to staple in place.

'Just letting you know I'm off for the night.' Brent frowned. 'Grace, shouldn't you be done by now? I'd thought you'd already gone?'

She didn't bother to raise her head again. Didn't want to see him all cosy with a woman dressed for fun. 'Just doing this last job.'

Brent felt Donna's hand on his shoulder and for some reason he tensed. 'Good.' He checked his watch, the action displacing his date's hand. 'What time on Saturday?' he asked.

Grace gripped the instrument in her hand a little tighter. 'Whenever you can get there,' she said casually. 'If something comes up, no sweat.'

'I'll be there,' he said.

The finality in his voice was unmistakeable and this time she did look up. 'Okay, see you then.'

He nodded and Grace just caught a glimpse of Donna slipping her hand into Brent's as he turned and walked away.

Her diaphragm twinged again.

Grace looked at the empty hallway for a moment before returning her attention to the patient, whose head was obscured by several green drapes. 'How are you doing under there, Jock?' she asked.

'I'm fine, lassie.'

Grace smiled at the broad accent. Jock had called Australia home for thirty years but hadn't managed to lose any of his thick Scottish brogue.

'Okay. I'm about halfway,' she said, inspecting the laceration that went from occipit to temple. 'We'll have you done in a jiffy.'

Jock grunted. The wound had been inflicted by falling debris at a work site and the Scotsman had been very lucky not to have sustained a more serious injury. It hadn't affected his gift of the gab, however, and Jock had been having a fine time flirting with every female in the department.

Even Sophia had been included in Jock's harmless banter.

Grace had completed two more staples when Ellen opened her mouth. 'That's three times with Donna in the last fortnight,' she mused. 'He must really like her.'

Grace's hand faltered slightly as she flicked her eyes up into Ellen's deadpan gaze. It was too shrewd by far and Grace looked back to where she'd lined up the wound for the next staple. She depressed the stapler.

'That's unusual for him?'

Grace kept the question light but seeing him with Donna had

made her skin itchy, as if there were prickles in her bloodstream, and she couldn't stop the words from tumbling out.

She knew the gossip about him. She'd like to know the truth. And Ellen was a straight shooter.

Ellen nodded. 'I've known him a long time. A week with one woman is a long-term relationship to him.'

Grace's gaze flew to Ellen's face. 'A week?' She hadn't meant it to come out as a squeak—but she was pretty sure it had anyway.

She nodded. 'Brent's always dated like it's an extreme sport.' Grace swallowed as Ellen held her gaze. 'Rumour has it he was rejected by a woman a long time ago. She ruined him for all other women.'

Grace, her hand poised above the wound, had forgotten all about the task. 'Well, he is twice divorced.'

Ellen shook her head. 'No. Before that. I know his first ex-wife, Serena, and she reckons it happened back in his uni days… You knew him back then didn't you?'

Grace dropped her gaze quickly. 'Only for a couple of years,' she prevaricated, inserting another staple.

'Such a shame,' Ellen said, 'he's such a great bloke. Great doctor. So compassionate. He must have really been something in uni.'

'Er, yes.'

Grace could feel Ellen's razor-sharp gaze heavy on the top of her head as she pictured Brent's youthful physique, stretched out naked beside her. She was pretty sure Ellen hadn't been referring to Brent's body so she suppressed the sigh that rose to her lips.

'Whoever he is, he's a blind fool if he knew you back then and didn't snap you up, lassie. If I were twenty years younger, I'd make a play for you myself.'

Ellen and Grace looked at each other above their draped patient's head. Ellen winked and Grace had to stop a bubble of laughter escaping.

'If you were twenty years younger, Jock, I might just let you.'

Jock roared with laughter. 'If I'd known that, lassie, I would have taken my hard hat off years ago.'

Ellen and Grace laughed with him. 'Okay now,' Grace said when their laughter had settled. 'Hold still, another dozen or so to do.'

Grace resumed her work, concentrating on the job at hand. *Had she ruined him for other women?* He'd certainly ruined her for other men.

No one had ever matched up to him.

'Funny thing is, though,' Ellen mused, her eyes firmly on the laceration, 'until a couple of weeks ago he'd gone a good few months without any dates. Just seemed to stop cold turkey. None of us could figure that one out at all. In fact, a friend of mine had a date with him the night he'd gone for the interview for the director's position and he rang and cancelled. Hasn't been on a date since as far as any of us know. And now Donna.'

Grace let Ellen's revelations sink in. Had their meeting up again on the day of the interview after twenty years apart caused Brent to cancel his date?

And, if so, what the hell did that mean?

Brent arrived at nine on Saturday morning. Tash had been prowling around the house for two hours and wrenched open the door even before Brent had a chance to land his first knock.

He handed over a bakery packet to Tash. 'I bought croissants,' he said.

Tash wrinkled her nose. 'Are they chocolate?'

Brent shuddered. 'Absolutely not.'

'I prefer chocolate,' she said, peering into the bag.

Brent grinned. 'I'll remember that for tomorrow.'

'Aunty Grace is just in the shower,' she said, indicating for him to enter. 'She said to feed you coffee if you arrived.'

Brent shut his eyes momentarily as images of a wet, naked

Grace slipped into his brain. Water sluicing off her hair, running over her breasts, down her belly, her thighs. Soap bubbles clinging to her pale pink nipples. Or maybe they weren't pale pink any more. Maybe they'd darkened over the years?

'Brent!'

His eyes flicked open and Tash came into focus. 'Sorry. What?'

'I said, do you want coffee?'

'Yes, please,' he said, shutting the door behind him.

He was going to need a lot of coffee.

Grace stepped out of the shower, patted her face dry and then slipped on her glasses. She reached for her knee-length black satin robe, wrapped herself up and belted it firmly around her waist. She opened the bathroom window and peered out at the street view. No Brent.

She cleared the fog from the mirror and gazed at her reflection. She rubbed at her hair with a towel and finger-combed it into place, tucking it behind her ears. She patted at the lines around her eyes wishing they weren't there. But nothing distracted her from Brent's absence.

Maybe he wasn't coming today after all? Maybe he'd spent all night in bed with Donna and planned to spend all day there as well.

She sank her teeth into her bottom lip as she clamped down hard on the unproductive images that simmered through her brain and prickled beneath her skin. According to Ellen, Brent had gone a while between dates—he was probably having wild animal sex right at this minute.

A tidal wave of something very akin to jealousy washed over her and she frowned at herself.

The man could sleep with whoever he damned well wanted—it was none of her business.

But Tash would be very disappointed. She'd been planning

her bedroom redecoration since they'd moved in three weeks ago. A no-show would be potentially calamitous.

Things between Tash and herself hadn't shown any sign of improvement since the move. Grace had felt sure that having her own space, one that was truly hers—not Grace's, not her grandparents, but hers—would help. And it had certainly given Tash a focus, a project. But Tash was still keeping her at an emotional distance.

There was a coolness, a politeness, in the way her niece spoke to her. A way Tash had of excluding her from information she shared easily with Benji or the rest of the family. Hell, even with Brent. She wasn't overtly rude, she just wasn't inclusive, and Grace was left in no doubt that Tash was keeping her firmly on the outside.

The aroma of freshly brewed coffee wrapped her in a seductive embrace as she opened the bathroom door and Grace breathed the heavenly fragrance deep into her lungs. Deciding her caffeine need was more important than clothes, she went in search of a quick hit.

Grace entered the empty kitchen and poured herself a mug of coffee. She took a sip of the black liquid and sighed as she felt it hit her system. And then another smell assailed her—warm flaky pastry. She looked around for the source as her stomach growled loudly.

Her gaze fell on the nearby bakery bag. *Croissants?* Grace's pulse rate shot up. And it had nothing to do with the caffeine.

There hadn't been any croissants when she'd climbed into the shower fifteen minutes ago.

Brent?

Brent was here?

She looked down at her attire. Her old faithful robe that she'd owned for too many years to count and not a stitch on beneath. She turned to flee the kitchen but it was too late. Brent was lounging in the doorway.

'Morning.'

'Er…' she said rather inarticulately, clutching the lapels that tended to gape a little too much with one hand as she gripped the coffee mug hard with the other.

The man looked good enough to eat. All casual and relaxed in jeans and an old T-shirt that stretched over a taut chest and flat belly. Her innards did a strange flip-flop at his magnificence. His gaze, zeroing in on all the places where the robe clung, made her feel even more naked.

'I'm sorry…' she said, feeling at a distinct disadvantage. 'I didn't realise you were here.'

Brent nodded. That much was obvious. He opened his mouth to say words to that effect but coherent thought was difficult when her breasts were perfectly moulded by black satin and her nipples were hardening before his very eyes.

She was naked beneath the gown. *Very naked.*

A stray bead of water trekked from her hair down the side of her neck, inexorably heading for her collar bone. Every fibre of his being wanted to lick it.

'You're wearing my robe.'

It took a moment for Grace to comprehend his words. She looked down at the clothing in question, her brain slow to compute. And then it dawned on her. It *was* his gown. She'd claimed it years before, loving its silky coolness and how it had smelled just like him.

She'd kept it after they'd split. Her one tangible reminder of him. She hadn't washed it for weeks afterwards, greedily hoarding the ingrained aroma of him.

How could she have forgotten that?

'Oh…yes.' She shrugged. 'I'd forgotten.'

Brent lowered his eyes. *He hadn't.* He could see the juncture of her thighs clearly outlined by the clinging satin and he shoved his shoulder harder into the doorjamb as the urge to cover the distance between them built like a thunderstorm with every erratic thump of his heart.

How often had he peeled that damn thing off her? Slipped

his fingers under the hem and stroked right where the satin now dipped to form an intriguing channel between her thighs?

He returned his gaze to her face. 'It still looks way better on you than it did on me.'

Their gazes locked. Grace didn't know what to say. He used to whisper those words just prior to pulling the cord at her waist and sliding his hands inside.

It looks better on you than on me.

Luckily, at that moment her stomach let out an enormous rumble that could have possibly registered on a Richter scale somewhere. Grace pressed her palm against the noisy organ.

'Sorry.' She blushed. 'I'm starving.'

Brent chuckled despite the fact that her hand was no longer holding her lapels together and a tempting view of creamy cleavage was now on display.

He really had to stop ogling her like a horny teenager. She wasn't his to ogle.

They weren't together any more.

He inclined his head in the direction of the kitchen table to indicate the offerings. 'I bought croissants.'

Grace followed his gaze. 'My favourite,' she murmured.

Brent nodded and looked back at her. 'I remember.'

Grace sucked in a breath at the intensity of his tawny gaze. She remembered too. Croissants in bed from the bakery near campus. Brent deliberately using her naked body as a table, leaning over her as he sank his teeth into the moist flakiness and then slowly licking the flakes off her after he'd finished.

She returning the favour.

She'd eaten so many pastries in those days it was a wonder she wasn't as big as a house.

The phone rang and Grace almost leapt out of her skin. Tash yelled, 'I'll get it!' as she thundered down the hallway.

It was exactly what she'd needed. Grace straightened immediately. 'Ah…I'd better get dressed.' She pushed off the kitchen bench, coffee mug and lapels firmly in hand.

Brent stood aside as much as the doorway allowed, stuffing his hands into his pockets as she slipped past him. He would not reach for her. Not stop her and turn her and back her against the doorjamb and kiss her and slide his hands beneath her robe.

His robe.

It didn't matter that she smelled liked soap and shampoo and black satin. And about a thousand memories.

He knew from bitter experience that down that road lay no good.

Despite their rather shaky start the day progressed without further incident. The fact that Grace was dressed in a pair of tatty old jeans, almost completely enveloped by a huge, shapeless, paint-stained workman's shirt, definitely helped. Thank goodness for her father's cast-offs and that her mother never threw anything out.

The division of labour also helped. Tash had taken command and Grace had been relegated to helping Benji with his room while Tash shamelessly monopolised Brent.

Not that it bothered Grace. After this morning's awkwardness, it was probably best to not be in each other's pockets and it was good to spend time with Benji. She seemed to spend so much time dealing with, and worrying about, Tash that it was nice to hang out with her nephew.

He was so low maintenance compared to his sister that it was easy to forget that he was also bereaved. If it wasn't for the nightmares, Benji's suffering could easily go unnoticed.

They chatted about school. He bombarded her with facts about the gold-rush era, their current unit of learning, and chatted excitedly about the camp that was being held at the end of the year. She found out that his teacher, Miss Sykes, was allergic to strawberries and how Mr Riley from the next-door classroom yelled all day.

It was a very pleasant morning indeed. Between she and Benji bonding and the low murmur of voices she could make out from Tash's room, Grace actually felt optimistic. It was especially good to hear Tash chatting away. It was nice hearing her be natural and not stilted and guarded, as she so often was around her.

Brent popped his head into Benji's room around lunchtime to let her know that he and Tash were going to the hardware store to hire a wallpaper steamer as the current revolting wallpaper was just one of several hideous layers and that they'd bring something back for lunch.

'I think Dad has one somewhere. He did offer it so you might like to pop in there first,' she said, barely looking up from the scraping she was doing.

Brent nodded at her back. The oversized shirt had fallen off her shoulder to reveal a black bra strap and an image of her breasts encased in black satin rushed out at him.

He shook his head. The sack she was wearing should have been guaranteed to stop lustful thoughts. It didn't.

'Come on, Tash,' he said, turning away.

Grace and Benji continued. She actually found the repetitive, laborious process quite therapeutic. There was something satisfying about scraping walls. Watching the outer skin peel off in satisfying sheets, revealing the true wall beneath, the one that had been there since the house had been built.

She wished she could do the same to Tash as easily. Peel away her anger and find the grieving girl beneath.

Another flake of cartoon superman wallpaper fell victim to her scraper and Grace was pleased she'd refused the offers of help from her family. She and the kids had needed something to make this place theirs and doing it together was a step in the right direction.

Besides, Saturdays were always bedlam with the extended Perry clan when the various progeny were shuffled from one sporting or extra-curricular activity to the other. And her father, who had retired a few years ago, played golf with some friends every Saturday.

Her siblings and parents already did so much for her, helping out with the kids—she was adamant they could scrape a little wallpaper and manage a bit of painting themselves. Her father had been sceptical about her abilities but when Tash had said that Brent was helping, he'd acquiesced.

Grace should have been annoyed over the inherent sexism—like her father didn't know already she could do anything she set her mind on—but she was too grateful for his sudden about-face that she let sleeping dogs lie.

Brent arrived back an hour later with the steamer and a platter of fresh sandwiches that would feed an army. Her mother had insisted he take them. Grace bit into an egg and lettuce one and was grateful that her mother had paid no heed to Grace's protests about managing by herself.

Sandwiches on fresh white bread were just what they all needed.

They ate lunch at the kitchen table, chatting about neutral subjects. Grace watched Brent surreptitiously as he talked with the kids. Even though Tash and Benji were seven years apart in age he seemed to be able to effortlessly adjust his interaction so he was right at their levels. He joked with them and they seemed to genuinely enjoy his company.

She remembered how he'd picked up Linda's grizzling baby just a few days ago and had seemed to know instantly what would work with her. How to calm and engage her.

He was like some kind of child whisperer!

She didn't like how it made her feel. How it made her doubt the choices she'd made all those years ago. Sitting here around a table with the kids and Brent, she'd started to wonder if she'd been wrong back then. Maybe she could have had it all? Brent, kids, a career.

The irony slapped her sharply in the face. She'd turned her back on Brent because she hadn't wanted the same things he had. And yet here she was, twenty years later, with exactly the things she'd avoided.

The only difference was she was doing it alone. Without him.

Was the universe punishing her?

The conversation drifted to sport and Benji, Tash and Brent had an animated conversation about their beloved Aussie Rules team, Collingwood. 'Are you playing on a team, Benji?' Brent asked.

Benji shook his head. 'I did in Brisbane but the season was half-over when we got back to Melbourne so I can't join the local club till next year.'

Brent could have been blind and deaf and he still would have picked up on Benji's disappointment. Not that he could blame the child. He remembered his own youth and how a game of football had been one of the few things that had been able to completely take his mind off all his problems.

What wouldn't he have given to have had enough continuity of care to play full time? To have had a father figure to kick a ball around with, to go down to the MCG and watch a game together.

In a lot of ways, he and Benji were similar and the boy's obvious disappointment resonated deeply.

A boy needed his footy. And Grace had never been a fan.

He glanced at Grace then back at Benji. 'If it's okay by your aunty, you could join the team I coach.'

Grace's eyes met Brent's. *Where had that come from?*

Benji jiggled in his seat, his eyes growing as large as soccer balls. 'You coach a team?'

Brent dragged his gaze from hers and nodded at Benji. 'It's not a club or anything. Just a bunch of kids at a local oval. We train together Sunday mornings and then play a game. You can come and see if you like it tomorrow morning.'

'Wow!' Benji bounced in his seat again and turned to face her. 'Could I, Aunty Grace, please?'

Grace could feel her nephew's excitement right down to her toes. Poor Benji, she'd tried to be both mother and father to him but she knew there were certain things that a man, a father, was better equipped to fulfil.

And football was just the beginning…

Doug and Benji had shared a passion for AFL. It wasn't until right now, with excitement radiating from Benji's eyes and vibrating through every cell of his body, that she realised how much Benji needed that connection.

For his future adjustment.

But also to help him stay connected with his past.

'I can pick him up and drop him back,' Brent prompted quietly, when a misty-eyed Grace hadn't said a word.

'Please, please, please, Aunty Grace,' Benji wheedled.

Grace smiled and blinked furiously. How could she say no? She'd been to every club in Melbourne, trying to get Benji into a team, and here was Brent offering her a perfect solution. If it pushed them together more, that was a small price to pay for Benji's happiness.

'Of course. As long as you're sure…?'

Brent nodded. 'Absolutely.'

Benji whooped, his face splitting into a huge grin. He leapt off his chair and raced around to Grace. 'Thank you, thank you, thank you,' he said, dropping a kiss on her cheek after each 'thank you'.

Grace laughed. 'Okay, okay. Don't get too excited. We've still got acres of wallpaper to go before then.'

Brent laughed too, swept up in Benji's enthusiasm. He winked at Grace and sucked in a breath as she blasted him with a one-hundred-watt dazzler.

'Okay, let's get back to work,' he said.

Before he did something insane like reach across the table and kiss that Honey Jumble smile.

CHAPTER NINE

BRENT knocked on Grace's front door at ten o'clock on Sunday morning for round two of Temptation Island. An exhilarated if somewhat muddy Benji was by his side, chatting away ten to the dozen.

To say Grace's nephew had enjoyed his morning was a massive understatement. The other kids, used to the flux nature of the team, accepted him without question and Benji, whose ball skills were impressive, had fitted right in. He was already talking about next week.

Tash answered the door again and Brent handed over another bakery bag, this time with chocolate croissants. Benji dashed off to get changed and Brent found himself hoping as he entered that Grace was not back in her baggy shirt.

She'd been in a thick woollen dressing gown that fell to her toes that morning when he'd picked Benji up and they'd had a brief thirty-second conversation. It had been a vast improvement on the short black robe.

The robe had featured in his dreams all night—elusive dreams, a mix of old memories and new fantasies—and he wasn't sure he could see her in it again and not have it off her in seconds.

He may have steeled his heart to her, shut down all possibilities other than friendship, but he *was* only flesh and blood.

He entered the kitchen to find her, hip propped against the sink, staring out the window into the back yard, a mug of coffee cradled in her hands. Denim encased her butt and hugged her legs. A spaghetti-strapped singlet-style top, covering her more than decently, clung to the hollow of her back, the slight swell of an almost flat belly and the sweet peaks of her very female chest.

Her hair was damp again and he could smell clean, soapy skin.

Oh, hell.

'Morning,' he said, propping up the doorway again.

Grace turned her head and felt the hitch in her lungs, the skip of her pulse as a slow burn ignited in her belly. She suspected she was always going to have that hitch in her breath, the catch in her pulse whenever he was near, so it was long past time she disregarded it.

The man was gorgeous.

It was just dormant chemistry.

She nodded. 'Morning. How was it?'

Brent grinned. 'Great. Benji was a hit.'

Grace smiled. 'He's a likeable kid.'

'He wants to join. I told him he'd have to okay it with you first.'

'It's fine by me as long as you're sure…'

'Of course,' he said. 'The more the merrier.'

Grace took a sip to hide the rush of gratitude as it trembled through her fingers. 'Thanks, Brent. He's rapt. It means a lot to him…to me… There are some days when not having a Y chromosome puts me at a distinct disadvantage.'

He wanted to say that from where he was standing her chromosomes were put together just right, but he shrugged instead. 'What are friends for?' he murmured, as much to remind himself as her.

Their gazes locked for a moment that seemed to drag interminably. Then Tash entered the kitchen.

'Croissants,' she announced, throwing the packet on the table and dragging out a chair. 'Chocolate.'

Grace couldn't think of anything she felt like doing less than eating but she was grateful for the interruption. 'Coffee?' she said to Brent, pouring him one without waiting for an answer.

They sat for a while, eating croissants and drinking coffee while Benji regaled them with his antics on the footy field. Grace concentrated hard on every detail, determined to ignore the fact that Brent was sitting next to her all big and warm and solid.

His laughter brushed down her side and the low sexy rumble of his voice stroked all those places his hands, his mouth knew so well.

Tash finished the last croissant and Grace leapt to her feet. 'Right, let's get this show on the road.'

After a combined effort by the four of them they'd finished scraping the multiple layers of wallpaper off Tash's room by eight o'clock last night. And both rooms stood ready for two coats of paint.

Grace escaped to her room for a mental breather before joining Benji. She needed a moment to bring her hormones under control. Being in close proximity to the man she'd once loved had been more difficult than she'd imagined. Especially when he still looked as fine as Brent did.

She really needed to get a grip!

When Brent tracked her down ten minutes later she was donning her baggy shirt. He caught sight of bare belly as Grace's singlet rode up with the action of pulling the shirt over her head.

He swallowed hard.

'Have you got drop sheets?'

Grace, appearing from the folds of fabric, almost had a heart attack as her head whipped around to locate him. Lounging in her doorway. It took a moment for her to find her voice.

'No need. Dad's arranged for some tradie friends of his to come in next week and rip up all the carpets and polish the floorboards so you can spill as much paint as you like.'

He nodded. 'Okay.' Yet he didn't seem to be able to move from the jamb. He looked around her room. Noted the unmade bed with the tangled sheets. Had her sleep been as restless as his?

'Looks like this room could do with a make-over next,' he said as he averted his gaze from the temptation of the bed to the aged flocked wallpaper decorating—dating—the walls.

Grace shook her head. If he thought he was going to be standing in here all warm muscles and capable man then he had another think coming. She had enough ammunition for her dream life without adding *Brent the Handyman* to her repertoire.

'Low down on my list of priorities,' she said briskly, walking towards him with purpose in her stride. 'Let's get to work.'

Brent took one last look at the bed, an image of rolling her over in it firmly implanting itself into his subconscious, before retreating from the doorway. He heard the firm click of her door as he headed towards Tash's room.

The click spoke volumes. *Stay out. Don't even think about it.*

His head and heart heard it loud and clear.

If only his libido wasn't profoundly deaf.

At lunchtime Grace left Brent with the kids while she dashed down to the local hardware store to buy a couple of smaller paintbrushes to do the finicky work. The rooms had each had an undercoat and should be dry enough after lunch for their top coat.

It was a good thing too. Watching Brent make himself at home in her kitchen—opening her fridge, retrieving plates from the overhead cupboards, getting a glass of water from the tap at the sink—was a little too cosy for her liking.

It was all a little too happy families. This was her house and it was dangerous to get used to having him in it. No matter how good he looked in her kitchen. No matter how much it took her back. Nothing was the same as it had been then. She had two grieving kids who were her main priority. They needed routine and security and roots.

They needed her focused.

Grace made it back to the house in thirty minutes. She could hear the chatter coming from the kitchen and smiled as she heard Benji and Tash laughing at something Brent had said in his deep, rumbly way.

She was approaching the kitchen when Tash's 'Tell us a memory' pulled her up short.

There was a moment of silence where Grace's heart all but filled her mouth. The merest hint of longing in her niece's voice was heart-wrenching. Grace pressed herself back, her palms flat against the wall.

A spike of jealousy lanced her through the middle. *Why did Tash never ask her for a memory?*

Brent looked at the two expectant faces. He'd spent all weekend with them and they'd talked and laughed and acted like two normal kids. But under the surface they were still two children whose parents had been cruelly snatched away and they were hungry for connection.

Brent understood that hunger for connection probably better than anyone.

'I remember your mum's grade-twelve graduation.'

He smiled at them as a snapshot of Julie descending the stairs in her frock came into sharp focus. 'She wasn't really a girly girl—before she met your dad anyway... I don't think I'd ever seen her in a dress before that night.'

'How come you were there?' Benji asked, his mouth full of biscuit.

'Grace and I were babysitting. I think your grandma and grandpa were going out to dinner with some other grade-twelve parents.'

'Oh, that's right,' he said, cramming another biscuit in his mouth in a display the cookie monster would have been proud of. 'I keep forgetting you used to be Aunty Grace's boyfriend.'

Brent nodded absently, wishing he could. Wishing the memories from that day hadn't stirred all the other memories.

'Was she beautiful?'

Grace heard the catch in Tash's voice and tears misted her eyes. She turned and walked the two paces to the open doorway in time to hear Brent say, 'She was gorgeous. She had on this purple floaty dress and your Aunty Grace had plaited these little white flowers in her hair.'

Brent heard a noise and looked up to find Grace in the doorway, her eyes shimmering with moisture. She looked like she was about to break.

Unbreakable Grace.

It was unbearable.

'She was so excited, wasn't she, Gracie? Doug was picking her up in a limo. She almost floated down those stairs.'

Tash and Benji's faces also sought her out and she furiously blinked back tears. 'Yes.' She smiled, moving her legs automatically, feeling like a robot as she made her way to the table and sat down.

She reached her hands across the flat tabletop palms up, reaching for their hands. Benji took hers eagerly. Tash moved her hands away, placing them on her lap. Grace tried not to feel the snub all the way down to her bones.

She pulled her empty hand back and placed it over top of her and Benji's linked fingers. 'She could barely sit still. It took me ages to weave those flowers through her hair.'

Brent saw the emotional flinch as Tash's silent rejection hit Grace hard. He'd hoped by including Grace in the memory that Tash might open up a little towards her aunt.

Apparently not.

He wanted to place his hand on top of Grace's, give it a squeeze, but it was important that he didn't allow even the slightest chink in his heart.

The chink in his libido was bad enough.

'What was that flower called?' he asked.

Grace bit hard on her lip at the memory of the tiny white buds. 'Baby's breath.'

'Baby's breath?' Benji asked, pushing his chair back and not waiting for a reply as he raced out of the room.

They barely had time to blink before he was back again, carrying the photo frame that sat on Grace's dressing table. Benji had asked her ages ago what the flowers in his mother's hair were called.

'Is this from then?' he asked, thrusting it at Brent.

It was a snap from that night. Julie, all dolled up, grinning madly at the camera, with her arm slung over Grace's shoulder. Grace also laughing into the camera. Happy for her sister. And madly in love with the photographer.

Brent nodded, his thumb sweeping along the thick ceramic border. 'I took that photo.'

'Really?' Benji did an excited little jump. 'Isn't that amazing, Tash?' Benji said, shoving the photo at his sister. 'Brent took this picture all those years ago.'

Grace watched as Tash looked at the picture. For a moment Grace thought her niece was going to burst into tears and then her mouth tightened and she looked up like nothing in the world was bothering her.

'It's a small world, Benji boy,' she said, ruffling her brother's hair, avoiding the two adult gazes. 'Now, come on.' She stood and started clearing the table. 'We've got another coat of paint to do.'

Brent raised an enquiring eyebrow at Grace as Tash retreated to the sink. Grace shrugged. It was no use asking her—she didn't know what went on inside her niece's head any more.

By seven o'clock both rooms' paint jobs had been completed. Tash now had three bright purple walls and one burnt orange one that somehow seemed to work. All Benji's walls were one colour—mint green with darker green trim.

They looked fresh and modern and a far cry from the wall-papered monstrosities of two days ago.

Brent was cleaning the brushes in the laundry when Grace tracked him down. 'We're getting pizza—are you in?'

Brent looked up from his task. She'd taken off her baggy shirt and was back to the singlet top. She looked so damn sexy standing in the doorway looking at him, hand on hip, through her black-rimmed glasses, her feet bare, her short, shaggy hair framing her face. Her Honey Jumble lips glistened in the half-light.

Frankly she was a sight for sore eyes.

He was tired from two days of physical labour—his neck and shoulder muscles ached—and a fitful night's sleep.

He didn't feel like being her friend tonight. His resistance was at a very low ebb.

'You don't have to feed me,' he said, returning his attention to the brushes.

'It's the least we can do,' she dismissed. 'Besides, the kids won't be impressed with me if I just let you run off home.'

She smiled, trying to keep it light, but she knew that Tash and Benji had just assumed he would be joining them and she didn't want to disappoint them.

Brent closed his eyes for a second, fighting the urge to turn off the taps, take two strides towards her and yank her into his arms.

She frowned at his hesitation and then it dawned on her. 'Oh, sorry.' She raised her palm to her forehead. 'You've got a date…' She dropped her hand to her side. 'Look, don't worry, the kids will understand… Please, you've already done enough this weekend—'

'Grace!' He didn't mean it to come out as forcefully as it did but her assumption had rankled. Apart from a few recent dates with Donna, which had been more for distraction than anything else, he hadn't dated since Grace had barged back into his life.

He couldn't even remember the last time he'd had sex.

'I *do not* have a date. Thank you, I would love to eat with you. And Tash and Benji,' he quickly clarified. He patted his belly. 'I'm starving, actually.'

Grace's gaze dropped to where his hand rested against his flat stomach. The sudden urge to see it again assailed her and she gripped the doorjamb hard in case her hands decided to follow through.

Perhaps Brent staying for dinner wasn't such a wise idea after all...

'Good. I'll go and order, then.'

Half an hour later they were all spread out in the lounge room in front of the television, shovelling pizza into their mouths and watching the Sunday football game that Benji had recorded.

The kids had taken a single lounge each, leaving the triple-seater for Grace. Brent had chosen the floor, propping his back against the three-seater a respectable distance from Grace.

It didn't mean that he wasn't excruciatingly aware of her denim-clad thighs in his peripheral vision or of every single movement she made. Or that the lounge wasn't big enough to stretch out, push her back and reacquaint himself with her body.

But she was out of reaching distance. All he had to do was eat, drink and keep his gaze locked on the television.

'Oh, no,' Benji groaned just prior to half-time when the referee called a penalty against his beloved Collingwood. 'The Cats were offside, not us,' he called to the television.

Brent took a deep swallow of his beer. 'I think the ref needs glasses, mate,' he said to Benji.

'Maybe he can borrow Aunty Grace's.' Benji laughed.

Brent joined in. 'I don't think they'd suit him.'

Grace smiled. She was pleased that Brent had agreed to stay. Her interest in and knowledge of football was minimal but as both kids were dyed-in-the-wool AFL fans, she'd been making an effort.

And now, like it or lump it, she was also a Collingwood supporter.

Brent missed the next goal as Grace shifted in the chair, tucking her left foot up under her right knee. Her breasts bounced enticingly with the move and he took another deep swallow of his beer.

'I'm taking the kids from the footy team to the match next weekend,' he said, desperate to distract himself. 'Would you guys like to come?'

Tash and Benji looked at him like he'd just bought the Collingwood football team for them. 'Seriously?' Tash demanded.

'Really?' Benji asked.

Brent chuckled. 'Really. Seriously. Even your aunt can come.'

Benji turned pleading eyes on his aunt, his little hands clasped together. 'Oh, can we, Aunty Grace? I know you don't like football, but can we? Can we, can we, can we?'

Grace laughed. 'Ah, yeah, I guess.' She looked at Brent. 'Are you sure?'

Sure? No. But at least he'd have a whole bunch of kids to distract him. And nowhere handy to lay her down.

An hour later the game had ended and Grace rounded up two unprotesting kids. Not even Tash gave her grief about going to bed at eight-thirty. They said goodnight to Brent and Grace herded them into her bedroom.

The paint fumes in their own rooms were still a little too toxic for safe sleeping so they were spending the night with her. With both bedroom windows open and fans on low, the fumes should be non-existent by the morning.

'I'll lie with Benji until he goes to sleep,' Tash said, climbing in next to her brother. 'Then I'll sleep on the mattress.'

Grace looked at Tash's mattress, which was made up on the floor next to her bed. 'You can sleep with me too,' she said. 'The bed's big enough. You'll probably be more comfortable.'

Tash stiffened and shook her head. 'No, thank you.'

Grace felt the icy blast from her polite rejection deep inside and steeled herself not to react. 'Okay.' She nodded. 'No probs.'

Still, feelings of alienation shadowed her as she walked back to the empty lounge room and she hugged herself. Brent entered from the kitchen, juggling two full rubbish bags, several empty pizza boxes and his keys.

'I'll be off too,' he said, not giving himself time to think or feel or analyse why the hell he was getting out of this house— fast. 'I'll dump these in the wheelie bin on the way out.'

Grace nodded. 'Here,' she said, relieving him of the boxes. 'I'll give you a hand.'

She followed him out the front door, her mind still preoccupied with Tash. The coolness of the night air didn't register, not even the way Brent's denim-clad butt strutted in front of her registered.

They dumped their cargo in the bins that lived beside the garage and Brent headed for his car parked in the driveway. He pressed the unlock button on his key and four lights flashed momentarily, illuminating the relative darkness.

He stopped by his door. 'Well, I guess I'll see you at work. When are you on next?' he asked.

Grace, still preoccupied with Tash, had to think for a moment. 'Tuesday.'

Brent nodded. His heart was thumping in his chest like a teenager on a first date trying to work up the courage to steal a kiss.

He was not going to kiss her.

He pulled the handle and the door opened. 'Until Tuesday, then.'

The soft snick of the door opening pulled Grace out of her

reverie. Where were her manners? 'I'm sorry,' she apologised. 'I'm a little distracted.'

A little distracted? Brent almost groaned out loud as she propped her hip against the back passenger door and vanilla wafted towards him from her Honey Jumble mouth.

He was very distracted.

'I don't know how to thank you for the last couple of days. The job would have been a lot slower without you, and the kids have really enjoyed your company. You've really clicked with Tash, and inviting Benji to join your footy team was the icing on the cake.'

Brent knew exactly how she could thank him. *It involved hands and mouths and lots and lots of naked skin.*

Grace looked up at him, all solid and warm in front of her, but the streetlight was behind him, cloaking his eyes in darkness, and she couldn't read his expression. Still, the urge to unburden was overwhelming.

Just like old times.

'You're so good with them.'

Brent heard a trace of anguish in her voice. *Damn.* 'You're good with them too.'

Grace desperately wanted to believe but she knew it wasn't true. She shook her head. 'No, I'm not. Benji, sure, but Tash…' Grace grasped her upper arms as the cool night air finally began to register. 'I don't know about that…'

Brent gripped his door harder. *Please don't do this.* Please don't look at me with big, lost eyes. 'She's been through a lot—'

'No,' Grace interrupted earnestly, taking a step towards him. 'It's more than that—she's angry.'

'Her parents died, Grace.'

Grace shook her head and moved closer still. 'No. Not at that. At me. She's angry with me for some reason.'

Brent didn't know what to say, what to tell her. She was so close. When he breathed in, his lungs filled with her. Every rational thought flew from his head as the desire to pull her into his arms and kiss her until all the anguish went away consumed him.

Grace shook her head as his growing silence brought her out of herself. 'I'm sorry.' She took a step back and rubbed at her arms. 'I'm keeping you.' She might not have been able to see his eyes but she could sense his reluctance to be there.

Like he couldn't wait to get away.

Well, duh! Just because he'd said he didn't have a date it didn't mean he wasn't hooking up with someone later. Maybe he was up for a booty call somewhere?

'Go. You go,' she said, rubbing at her arms more vigorously, suddenly feeling cold on the inside as well. Cold down to her bones.

Oh, hell. 'You're cold,' he said.

And then he stepped closer to her, knocking her hands aside as he took over the job. Her skin was cool. But as soft and smooth as he remembered. 'You should have a jumper on,' he chided, as each pass of his hands wafted more of her sweet aroma towards him.

Grace felt his brisk, completely impersonal touch fan across her pelvic floor muscles. Her nipples tightened and she tried to tell herself it was the cold but she knew it was a lie.

'I'm sorry,' she whispered, because she couldn't think of anything else to say.

Brent looked down into her face. Light from the streetlight slanted across her cheekbones, illuminating her glistening, slightly parted lips. And the confusion in her grey eyes.

His hands stilled on her upper arms.

'Oh, hell,' he muttered, as the last of his resistance melted away and he pulled her towards him, his mouth swooping down to cover hers.

CHAPTER TEN

GRACE went to him willingly. He was so big and solid and warm, and in ten seconds flat she was hot. Hot all over.

For his touch. For his kiss. For him.

She groaned against his mouth as his palms slid up her neck and cradled her jaw, locking her head in place as his tongue plunged inside her mouth. She bunched his T-shirt in her hand, pulling him closer, needing him nearer.

Brent turned, pushed her back against the car door, swallowing her gasp as the tastes of Grace—honey and vanilla—filled him up. He opened his mouth wider, pushed his tongue deeper, wanting more of her taste, needing more.

Grace felt the cold metal of the passenger door brand like fingers of arctic ice on her fevered skin. There was fever in her blood as well, licking like flame through her body, flushing heat over her skin and scorching her insides.

Her nipples, already unbearably erect, tightened further. Her belly contracted. Her thighs quivered. A tingling between her legs intensified until it itched and burned and she rubbed herself against him, against his hardness, to relieve it.

Brent dug his fingers into her hips as her frustrated growl and agitated grinding against his aching erection drove him a little closer to insanity. He wanted more.

To be horizontal.

To be over her.

In her.

To look down at her as she came.

He dragged his mouth from hers, pulling her off the cold

metal as he reached for the car door. 'In,' he gasped, as the door opened and he manoeuvred her backwards.

Grace didn't argue, somehow managing to back into the back seat without injuring herself and pull him in with her too. She drew up her knee and let it fall against the seat. Placed her other foot in the footwell, opening her denim-clad legs wide, forming a perfect cradle for his hips.

The back of his sporty convertible was cramped and the cold night air was pushing inside from the open door where both of Brent's legs hung out. But his weight was pressing her into the seat and his mouth was back on hers and nothing else mattered.

She grabbed a handful of his T-shirt where it covered his shoulder and tugged, ruching it up and dragging it over his head. Her greedy hands revelled in the solid warm muscles of his back as she kissed his jaw and his neck and his collar bone. Then his greedy mouth demanded her attention again.

Brent couldn't get enough of her mouth. Every sweet curve held a memory and he wanted to plunder them until he'd re-membered every one. But her nails dragged down his back, dug into his backside, slipped under his waistband and squeezed his bare buttocks, and kissing her mouth was no longer enough.

He wanted to kiss her everywhere. Lick all the places that made her shiver.

Taste her.

His hand reached for her singlet top and pushed it up. His palm felt the ridges of her ribs and then his fingers touched the edge of cushioned satin. She moaned as his hand moved to claim all of her breast and his thumb flicked over her taut nipple.

He dragged his mouth from hers, ignoring her hoarse whim-per. He needed to taste the tight little berry grazing his finger-tips. Lave it with his tongue, suck on it until it grew large and engorged in his mouth.

He yanked her bra cup aside, remembering how sensitive

her breasts had been, how crazy it had made her when he'd worshipped them.

Grace bucked against him, biting her lip to prevent the expletive as Brent's hot tongue swiped across her tortured nipple. She dug her fingers into his shoulders and arched her back.

How had she ever erased this from her mind? This bliss that he created. This erotic havoc that scrambled her brain and turned her into a pleasure-seeking android with no question of sense or protest or denial.

He pulled her other bra cup aside and sucked that nipple straight into his hot, hot mouth. She cried out. Was it possible that he'd got even better?

What else had changed?

What else was better?

Suddenly she needed to see all of him. Touch all of him. Reconnect with what had once been very familiar territory.

Hoping she had enough functioning brain cells left while Brent continued to lave her breasts with his tongue, she reached between their bodies for his fly. Her hand brushed the bulge beneath and her fingers shook in anticipation.

She breached his zipper and underpants within seconds and a guttural sound of triumph escaped her lips as she wound her fingers around his thickness. It filled her palm, just as she remembered, and she ran her hand up and down its length.

Brent reared back as sensation ripped through his groin and spasmed through his buttocks and belly. He felt as if he'd been struck by lightning and he released her nipple as a deep groan tore from his mouth.

His whole body bucked. His head hit the armrest and his shin banged hard against the metal framework of the door.

It was just the dose of reality he needed.

What the hell was he doing? Making out in a car with Grace like a horny teenager while her sister's bereaved kids were asleep in the house.

Grace, who hadn't wanted him twenty years ago and certainly didn't have time for him in her life now.

Other than a quickie in the back of a car.

'Are you okay?' she whispered stroking her hand against him again. Once, twice, three times.

Brent fought the urge to let his eyes roll back in his head, to push himself further into her palm, to rock his hips.

'Wait,' he said. 'Just wait.'

He placed his forehead on her chest, trying to think over the roar of his pulse and the gasp of his breath as he fought to get more oxygen into his lungs.

Grace, still dazed and foggy, her own pulse loud in her ears, her breath ragged, struggled to understand his command.

Wait?

She fought the whimper that rose in her throat.

What? No. She moved her hand again.

Brent squeezed his eyes shut tight. 'No.' He angled his hips away, dislodging her hand, breathing hard into her chest.

They lay there for a moment or two longer before Brent eased back, bending his knees then lifting himself off her. Grace, stunned at the sudden turnaround, fixed her bra, pulled her shirt down, drew her legs up and swung them round until she was sitting where moments ago her head had been.

She ran a shaky hand through her hair as Brent sat on the seat next to her and retrieved his shirt from the floor. Her face was still flushed, hot. She was still burning up, still hot for him everywhere.

'I'm sorry,' he said as he pulled his shirt back over his head.

Grace dragged in a breath. 'It's fine.'

Brent raked a hand through his hair. 'I can't…do this with you again.'

Grace felt her second rejection tonight like a sledgehammer to her heart. Even though she knew he was right. Knew stopping what had just happened had been the best move. Even if her body did feel like it had been denied something she'd been craving for twenty years.

'I know.'

Damn it, why was she being so bloody reasonable when he wanted to smash things? They could have been doing this for the last twenty years. They'd had something good and she'd ruined it.

'You can't just waltz back into my life and expect to pick up where we left off, Grace.' He wasn't sure if he was saying it for her benefit or for his.

She placed her forehead against the seat back. 'I don't.'

Brent glanced at her sharply. 'Yeah, well, it sure didn't feel like it just now.'

'Hey.' Her head snapped up and she glared at him. 'You kissed me.'

Brent glared back, his breath sawing in and out of her lungs. She was right. He was angrier with himself than with her. It was just easier to blame her than take responsibility.

He sighed, throwing himself back against the car seat. 'I'm sorry. I'm just…I hate how you still get under my skin. I wish I still didn't…want you so much.'

Grace felt her anger deflate just as quickly. 'Same here,' she murmured. 'But we've got a lot of history. It's to be expected, I guess.'

They sat for a moment or two in silence, each contemplating the enormity of the admissions they'd made tonight. It wouldn't make it go away but it might make it easier between them.

Grace turned, her hand on the doorhandle. 'See you next week.'

'Can you just answer me one question?' he asked.

Grace paused, one leg out of the car. 'Sure.'

Brent leaned forward, his elbows on his knees, his hands in his hair. 'Why did you agree to marry me? Why say yes, why put my ring on your finger only to break it off two months later?'

I don't believe it was ever about me distracting you from your studies. What's the truth, Grace?'

Grace felt her heart slow for a moment before it kicked back in with a painful thump. 'Because I loved you, Brent, and you wanted it so much. I wanted to make you happy.'

'Sounds like good reasons to stay together.'

'But I didn't want what you wanted. I didn't want babies and the whole white-picket-fence thing. I wanted to be a doctor, I wanted a career.'

'I told you I didn't need that.'

Grace gripped the handle hard. 'Yes, but I knew you wanted it. And I knew you'd be miserable without it. You'd had a miserable childhood and it was your time to be happy, Brent. I wouldn't have made you happy.'

'There's more than that, Grace. There has to be.'

Grace nodded. He was right. She'd never told him before because it had always seemed so selfish, but maybe she owed it to him now. 'I was afraid I'd give in to you because I loved you too much. And then I'd have been miserable.'

And there was more but she just couldn't say it out loud. *I was afraid that I loved you so much that I'd start to want it all too. That I'd give up my dreams without blinking an eyelid.*

Brent dropped his hands and turned to look at her. 'And we're both so happy now, right?'

The irony was not lost on Grace. They were both living a life neither of them had wanted. The only difference was that they were doing it without each other.

But what was done was done.

'See you Tuesday,' she said, climbing out of the car and shutting the door after her.

Grace headed straight for the shower, stripping off her clothes, plunging herself beneath the spray, trying to wash away his smell, his touch, his taste. Her body still craved them but deep in her soul she knew she had to expel every last trace of him from her body.

Or lie awake all night, going slowly mad.

As the water drummed against her face his words repeated themselves over and over. *You can't just waltz back and pick up where we left off.* She let it replay. Let it chase round and round her head on continuous loop. Because she needed to remember. She needed her body to remember.

They weren't together any more.

Things between them were still complicated. Different complicated sure, but complicated nonetheless. And she would not allow herself to mess up a relationship with him the second time around because of some misplaced sense of nostalgia. Or latent chemistry.

They weren't together any more.

After a couple of minutes Grace shut off the taps briskly, shutting off the voices in her head just as decisively.

She got it. *They weren't together any more.*

She dried herself briskly. Time to start thinking about what she did have, the here and now, not the things she couldn't have.

The kids, her home, her family.

Her job.

She wondered, as she headed to her bedroom, when medicine had become such an afterthought.

The answer greeted her as she crossed the threshold to her room. Tash and Benji lying in her bed, sound asleep. Her troubled thoughts ceased as her heart filled with love for these two bereaved kids. They looked so sweet and innocent like this—how could life be so cruel?

They were her priority now. Everything else was secondary.

Still, despite lecturing herself about priorities, Grace spent the next few days obsessing over the back-seat incident. Reliving it *ad nauseam.* Wondering how it might have ended if Brent hadn't put the brakes on. Alternating between embarrassment at their teenage behaviour and supreme sexual frustration.

And as Tuesday inched closer she grew more and more nervous about what they'd say to each other. About how it would be between them.

She needn't have worried.

Tuesday started with a bang and didn't get any better. There certainly wasn't any time for psychoanalysis.

Her sister Wendy rang at about seven-thirty as Grace was packing the kids' lunches to let Grace know that her daughter, Kelly, had seen Tash and some other girls hanging around a local park smoking after school the previous day.

Grace confronted Tash. An argument ensued. Grace struggled to keep her cool—Tash felt no such compunction. She loudly denied it as Grace snatched her niece's bag from her and searched it for contraband. She found nothing but she could detect a faint trace of tobacco and she confiscated Tash's iPod and grounded her for a fortnight.

Tash slammed out of the house, tears streaming down her face, yelling about living in a prison.

And then at work there was no time for awkwardness or talking the situation to death. Grace had barely been at work for an hour when the hospital was plunged into chaos.

A light aeroplane had crashed onto a nearby high school oval, ploughing into the crowds that had had been enjoying their annual sports carnival. Both Melbourne Central, the Royal Melbourne and the Children's Hospital had activated their external disaster plans and were expecting mass casualties.

After an initial gut-wrenching moment when Grace had to be reassured that it wasn't Tash's high school, she clicked into her doctor zone. She'd been involved in many mock disasters in her time and knew the routine back to front.

To be able to deal with situations like this, hospitals—emergency departments particularly—had extensive protocols in place. Planning and practice for such incidents was a must and all hospital departments trained for this kind of eventuality.

She knew the Central would be no different.

Brent assured her that the hospital maintained a high state of preparedness for this kind of situation and had the staff, the skills and the capacity to cope.

External disasters also required leadership, communication and collaboration with all emergency services—police, fire and ambulance. When Brent received the request from the field command to send two senior doctors and nursing staff to the scene to help with triage, he didn't hesitate in calling on Grace.

'Let's go,' he said, their necking session in the back seat of his car on Saturday night unimportant in the face of the potentially dire situation not two kilometres from their doorstep. 'They need us for triage.'

Grace nodded. 'Everything's ready to go here. ICU and OT are on standby. All wards and medical teams have been notified. We have a dozen registrars and Ellen has arranged to pull extra nursing staff from the wards.'

'Good.' He nodded. 'We'll grab her and two other nurses as well.'

Ten minutes later they were all piling out of Brent's car at the accident scene. They were dressed in navy-blue overalls and laden with equipment. Grace and Brent had *Doctor* emblazoned front and back. The nurses' overalls were marked *Nurse*.

Grace's nostrils flared at the pungent smell of burning Avgas as she took in the carnage. The oval looked as if it was a scene from a post-apocalyptic movie. People milled everywhere as they were directed to medical stations. Some crying, some shouting, others bloodied and obviously injured or looking frantically for others.

Emergency services vehicles were parked haphazardly all round the oval—fire trucks, police cars and ambulances. They looked like toy cars amidst the enormous scale of the destruction. Sirens pealed everywhere—in the distance and nearby. News helicopters swarmed overhead.

Black smoke rose from the smouldering remains of what she assumed was the aircraft. It was being continually doused by a team of firemen. It seemed to have torn up half of the oval, scorching the earth in its wake as well as upending various stands, ploughing into a packed wooden grandstand, collapsing it and setting it alight.

'Let's report to the central command post,' Brent said, rousing them all out of their momentary stupor.

The officer in charge, Dr Jennifer Warner, was pleased to see them. 'Most of the triage is complete. The casualties have been grouped in red, green and yellow.'

She pointed to the make shift 'stations' where people either sat or lay.

'We have seven black tags over there. Two students. Five adults. That doesn't include the pilot, who is presumed dead.'

She indicated with her thumb over her shoulder to the deceased, who were covered in sheets. Two police officers were constructing a canvas screen to block the morbid sight from the eyes in the sky and the gathering press contingent that were like hounds baying for blood behind the police tape cordon that had been erected to keep non-emergency personnel out of the area.

Grace shivered. Seven dead. Plus the pilot. She glanced back at the twisted, charred shell. Surely no one could have survived that impact?

'Could you all head towards the red tags and get as many treated and transported as possible?'

'On it,' Brent said.

And then it was all go, go, go.

Grace knew as she headed into the fray that all the victims sporting red tags around their wrists would have been assessed as requiring immediate medical attention because they had life-threatening injuries. If they had difficulty breathing, lacked a radial pulse, were in shock or unable to follow simple commands, they would have been tagged as red.

As they pushed through the crowds of dazed people Grace noticed many of them were being ushered to the green area and had green tags dangling from their wrists. They were essentially the walking wounded who had suffered minor injuries only and wouldn't be seen until after the high-priority casualties had been evacuated.

Just before reaching the red area they passed the yellow station, which seemed inundated with victims. A yellow tag indicated injuries that were not fatal or life-threatening. These people would have a good pulse and would be able to follow simple commands, but couldn't sit or stand because of injuries.

Grace knew that these patients, though not requiring immediate attention, would need treatment within the next few hours.

It was going to be a long day.

'Doc, here!' A paramedic indicated frantically at them and it was all hands on deck.

Grace didn't know how many people she treated in that first two hours. Kneeling on the ground beside stretchers, putting in lines, controlling haemorrhages, splinting fractures. Evacuating the critical into a seemingly endless convoy of ambulances. Pulling off her gloves, snapping on a new pair and starting again with the next one.

It was automatic.

She and Brent, working side by side, the sun beating down on their heads, as if they'd been working together for the last twenty years. Royal Melbourne doctors working with them too. All being methodical and thorough. Complementing each other.

Blocking out the extraneous noise of the ebb and flow of people all around them. Adults, students who'd been on the oval walking around dazed or sobbing, comforting each other.

Emergency personnel going about their jobs with grim efficiency. Panicked parents arriving at the school, frantic for their children.

Someone handed them water to drink and a chocolate bar to eat every half an hour. They gulped them down without protest and then turned their attention back to the task at hand. Treating the wounded.

'Got one for you, Doc.' A paramedic and a fireman arrived with a man on a field stretcher. 'He's just been pulled from under the grandstand. He's critical. No radial. Weak carotid. Gurgly airway. Blown left pupil.'

Brent and Grace made way for the stretcher. The patient was unconscious with a large head wound. Brent felt the faint flutter of a pulse. Grace reached for the nearby portable suction unit, opened a new Yankeur sucker and pushed it onto the end of the tubing. She inserted into the man's mouth and cleared his airway. Blood filled the tubing.

'Two minutes of CPR,' Brent said.

Grace reached for the ambu-bag and administered the breaths, the patient's chest rising and falling in sync with Brent's compressions.

At two minutes the paramedic called, 'Time.'

Brent stopped, felt for a pulse, waiting many seconds longer than was necessary. Nothing. Maybe he could have saved this man, this stranger that had been in the wrong place at the wrong time, if he'd had two hours, a neurosurgeon and a hospital full of equipment.

But he didn't.

He could, however, with any luck, save the twenty more people with red tags lined up for them on stretchers.

And that, unfortunately, was what happened in mass casualty situations. Priorities. Treating quickly and efficiently and evacuating the living to a tertiary centre. Not spending precious minutes on someone that couldn't be saved.

Brent snapped off his gloves. 'Tag him with a black and put him with the others.'

There was a brief pause amidst the activity all around them, shared by the four. Staring down into the dead man's face, Grace felt a surge of impotence as the futility of the situation overwhelmed her almost more than the pervasive smell of Avgas.

What was his name? Was he a parent? A teacher? What could he have possibly done in his life to deserve dying today in this way, surrounded by strangers?

It helped put things into perspective. Life was fragile. Grace knew she should know that better than anyone. Between her job and losing Julie. But it was easy to forget amidst the hustle and bustle of it all. It was easy to let the continuing juggle with life and problems with Tash overwhelm her.

She was all right. The kids were all right. She and Brent would be all right.

Her life wasn't perfect. It wasn't all neat and controlled, as she would have liked.

But she was doing all right. And she'd get there.

Then the guys who had brought the patient to them, whose names she also didn't know, were picking up the stretcher and carrying it away.

'Well, that sucks,' Grace said as her gaze tracked their progress.

Brent nodded, dragging his eyes from them as well to look down at her. 'You okay?'

She looked at him. 'Yep.'

And she turned to her next patient.

CHAPTER ELEVEN

ON SUNDAY Grace drove Benji to the oval with a recalcitrant Tash. Her niece was still incensed over losing her iPod and the grounding, so things were tense. Benji was oblivious but Grace's gut was churning madly.

Brent, looking all tall, dark and handsome, was a powerful antidote.

Or was that aphrodisiac?

He was wearing tatty old jeans and a Collingwood hoodie and was so sexy she wanted to tackle him to the ground and pash him in front of twenty impressionable children who obviously hero-worshipped him.

However his *You can't just waltz in and pick up where you left off* beat like little frantic bird wings in her grey matter and she just managed to bring her body under control.

Even though kissing him seemed much more preferable to talking with a stony-faced Tash. And way more pleasurable.

Half of her extended family arrived to watch Benji play, which not only swelled the spectator ranks considerably but made it easier to be around Brent.

Sort of.

It certainly gave her something else to focus on. But every word of praise from the sidelines, every whistle blow from Brent drew her gaze and dug the well of longing a little deeper.

It seemed their passionate clinch in the car had popped the cork on her repressed libido and his pure physicality on the field was stoking it ever higher.

But even more so, his interaction with the kids.

He was marvellous with them all, Benji included. He laughed and joked. Cajoled and encouraged. Praised and advised. And he didn't mind a bit of rough-housing. More than once he stole the ball and ran with it and a dozen kids chased after him, laughing and yelling, 'Get him!' all the way.

He let them catch him and he let them tackle him to the ground and jump on him. He came up laughing and roaring, dragging as many kids clinging to his arms and legs as he could as he strode towards the goal line.

They plainly adored him.

And it was easy to see why.

When the game was over for the morning and the kids had been taken home by their foster-parents, the Perry clan decided to keep the game going. Everyone, including Grace, got dragged into the fray and much hilarity ensued. Even Tash forgot her bad mood and got into the spirit of it all.

Brent led the kids' team and Marshall led the adults. Some would have said that was unfair but the kids disagreed and Brent was their champion. Grace spent most of the time running around without a clue of what she was doing, mainly just ogling Brent as he whizzed past, throwing and kicking and diving.

He was a sight to behold.

So distracted was she that it was a complete surprise at one stage to end up with the ball. She stared at it dumbfounded for a moment. Then Benji yelled, 'Get her,' to a nearby Brent. Grace looked up as a look of pure devilish fun lit Brent's tawny gaze and he started towards her, bellowing like an Apache on the warpath.

'Run!' Marshall yelled.

Grace took one look at the mischief in Brent's gaze and didn't need to be told twice. She gave an inhuman squeak, turned and ran towards the goalposts, a cacophony of cheers and screams propelling her.

But she was no match for Brent's superior prowess and she hadn't gone far before he swooped in and bundled her up close to his chest, spinning round and round, the sky and clouds and treetops twisting and turning like the multi-hued petals of a kaleidoscope.

'Stop, Brent,' she begged, clutching the ball with one hand and his shirt with the other, hanging on for dear life, her head spinning and her side hurting from laughing harder than she had in a very long time.

'Put me down. Put me down. I'm getting dizzy.' Everything spun and moved, including her crazy silly heart, flopping in her chest like an epileptic fish.

Brent laughed, dizzy himself. 'Okay, you asked for it,' he murmured, falling to his knees and half dropping, half placing her on the ground as the earth spun. Her arms clutched at his neck as she fell backwards, pulling him down, pulling him across her.

'Oomph!' The inelegant noise escaped from Grace's mouth as Brent's big, warm body squashed hers into the cool grass.

He chuckled. 'Sorry.'

Grace laughed too. 'Mmm,' she said, shutting her eyes. 'Everything is spinning.'

Brent levered his knee between her legs and half pushed himself off her, looking down into her face, her mouth so very near. She looked so beautiful his breath became momentarily trapped in his lungs. 'I see you just fine.'

Grace opened her eyes, still smiling. And then awareness kicked in.

Of him.

Everything else faded into the background. Her family racing towards them, their claps and cheers and wild laughter. The cars on the nearby busy-for-a-Sunday road. Even the plane overhead.

Instead she could feel his heart beat beneath her palm, feel his warm breath on her cheek, hear the harsh suck of oxygen as it sawed in and out of his lungs, see the dilation of his pupils.

Brent shook his head, trying to clear the roar of the blood coursing through his ears. 'This is crazy,' he muttered.

Grace watched his mouth as it formed the words. It was so very close. 'Yes.'

She didn't need to ask him to clarify. She knew what he meant. This thing still between them *was* crazy.

And then Benji leapt onto Brent's back crying out, 'Geronimooooo!'

'Oomph,' Grace said again, as Brent and Benji's combined weight pressed down on her. The action zapped her back to the present with the startling force of a cattle prod.

Her family crowding around, reaching for them, laughing, helping them up.

The cars, the plane, the noise.

'Got it!' Tash exclaimed as she wrestled the ball from Grace's unprotesting fingers and ran with it.

Benji whooped and ran after his sister. Brent, trying and failing to compute those few cataclysmic moments pressed against Grace, dragged his gaze away from the woman in question.

'Run, kids, run,' he shouted. 'Faster,' he said, as he took off after them, needing to get away from Grace, Far, far away. She had grass in her hair and he wanted to lay her back down and kiss those Honey Jumble lips until they both forgot their names.

He ran and ran, hoping he could run away from the craziness. 'Faster,' he called, gaining on the kids and then reaching them.

Without breaking stride, he grabbed for their waists and swooped them both up, carrying them effortlessly, holding one under each arm—a teenage girl and a seven-year-old boy—like they weighed no more than footballs. Tash and Benji giggled and screamed all the way until Brent reached the goalposts and they all collapsed in a heap.

The Perry family clapped and cheered. Marshall let out an almighty whistle that would have done any sheep farmer proud.

Benji, Tash and Brent all sprang up. They jumped up and down, high-fiving each other.

Grace watched with a lump in her throat as Brent put an arm around each of the kids' shoulders and pulled them against his sides, all of them laughing.

He didn't look like an important emergency care physician, standing there, laughing with her kids.

He looked like a father.

She smiled through the lump as it grew larger, threatening to choke her as a sudden awful certainty settled into her bones.

She loved him.

She'd never stopped loving him.

Grace couldn't sleep that night. She tossed and turned, the sheets twisting around her legs, tangling her up as euphoria battled with despair. The realisation that her epiphany earlier in the day was worthless had come swiftly to her in the silence of the night.

You can't just waltz back in and pick up where you left off.

The finality, the power, of those words echoed endlessly around her head, chasing each other through the long dark hours. They vanquished any fledgling hopes of dozens of dormant fantasies that tried to rise above them.

You can't just waltz back in and pick up where you left off.

Sure, he still found her attractive, still desired her. A few magical moments in the back seat of his car and an intense moment in the park were testament to that.

They had undeniable chemistry.

But what about his heart?

Did he still love her?

Could he?

Or had he shut himself off to a second chance with her? Had she hurt him too badly? When she'd *ruined him for all women*, had she blown it for herself too?

Because after twenty years without his love she needed more than sexual attraction.

She didn't want to be just two bodies slaking a two-decade-old thirst. Although, God knew, as she balled her hand into a fist and stuffed it between her legs, she wanted to feel him inside her again so badly it was a physical ache.

Which grew fiercer by the second.

She wanted to love him.

Wanted him to let her love him.

Could she just go to him and tell him what a fool she'd been? That she'd been wrong about all the things she'd said she hadn't wanted because she had them now and the world hadn't come to an end and she still had a career.

The only thing she didn't have was him.

Could it be that simple?

You can't just waltz in and pick up where you left off.

She groaned into her pillow. She'd stuffed up—big-time.

What if he never let her back in?

She'd have to fight for him.

Fight to make him see. Fight to convince him that she'd made a mistake. That she wanted to try again.

But she was so tired of fighting.

Battling with a teenager was hard enough. She didn't want to go into another battle she wasn't sure she could win.

Besides, nothing had changed. She was still in a situation where she couldn't commit to him. Her life was on hold for the foreseeable future and he deserved more than crumbs.

Sure, Brent had always wanted a family—but wanting one from scratch, one that was all shiny and new, and inheriting one were two different things. The Brent she'd known had wanted a handful of kids and a house in the suburbs complete with the white picket fence.

He'd wanted perfection.

Would he want this family? This out-of-control, dysfunctional, grieving, far-from-perfect family?

Grace pulled her pillow over her head and rubbed her face into it hard.

Brent was right. This was crazy.

A miserable, sleepless week followed. Grace tried to avoid Brent at work but the harder she tried, the more she ran into him. He seemed to be around every corner. Smiling and chatty and being so damn nice to her, her whole body ached.

Her face ached from her fake smile, her head ached from being perennially pleasant and her heart ached from the constant cramp it seemed to contract into whenever he was near.

But she smiled and chatted back, acted like everything was fine, pretended her whole house-of-cards existence hadn't just had several cards removed. The ache that had dulled and which she'd trained herself to ignore over the years was back, and she was going to have to learn to live with it all over again.

Breaking it off twenty years ago had been one of the most difficult things she'd ever done. Deciding to stay away, deny her love, trumped that tenfold.

But it was the only way.

And in a strange sort of way she almost welcomed the pain. It was her punishment. For leaving him in the first place. Her comeuppance. Her due.

It was bitter, bitter irony.

It was exactly what she deserved.

By the time Sunday came around again she was a wreck. She'd barely slept, she had a giant headache and her hands trembled from the multiple cups of coffee she'd been existing on just to get through the week.

And to add to her woes she and Tash had a massive argument just before leaving for the oval for Benji's footy game. Her niece announced she was going to a friend's house for the day and wouldn't be attending the game.

Grace saw red.

She yelled. Actually yelled. She'd always been so calm and measured before, reining in her temper, preferring to use un-ruffled reasoning. To treat Tash like an adult. She'd never tried to be Julie, knowing instinctively that Tash would react very badly to any attempts to be mothered.

But this was the last straw.

Tash was grounded. And Grace discovered that calm and reasoned could last only so long in the continuing face of a badly behaved teenager hell-bent on self-destruction.

When they arrived at the oval an hour later Grace added a sore throat to her list of physical ailments. And one sulky, rebellious teenager.

Benji bounced over to his team the second he alighted the car and Grace watched with an aching heart as Brent squeezed her nephew's shoulder and grinned down at him.

Grace joined the huddle at a more sedate pace, needing time to suppress her body's reaction to Brent looking all big and broad and sexy as hell surrounded by a group of kids who plainly hero-worshipped him.

Surrounded by his urban family.

Brent smiled as she approached. 'Are you okay?' he asked. She looked tired. Sexy tired in jeans and a skivvy that hugged all the right places, but tired nonetheless.

Grace nodded and diverted her gaze from the concern in Brent's tawny eyes to Benji high-fiving his teammates. 'Fine,' she said. 'Just had a…difference of opinion with Tash.'

Brent glanced at the teenager, who hadn't moved from the car. Her deep scowl and furrowed brow were plainly visible even from this distance. It wasn't a face that would have launched a thousand ships.

'She doesn't look happy.' Neither did Grace.

Grace shrugged. 'Let's just say I'm not her favourite person this morning.'

The note of defeat in Grace's voice grabbed at his gut. He tossed the football from one hand to the other as he searched her face. It was free of make-up except for the usual coating of Honey Jumble lip gloss, the smell of which wafted towards him, trumping the aroma of cut grass.

The last week, no matter how many times he told himself it was crazy, the idea that they could start over had slipped beneath his defences.

He smiled at her. 'If it helps, you're one of my favourite people.'

Grace glanced at him, startled by words that sounded utterly sincere. She looked for a sign he was being disingenuous, maybe even joking, but his steady, smiling face was reassuring.

'Yes, actually,' she admitted with a half-smile. 'It probably seems a bit pathetic, but it does.'

Brent grinned, their gazes locking. 'Good.'

Suddenly she found herself grinning back, the weight on her shoulders easing as her heart bloomed beneath the warmth of his smile, her love growing bigger again.

And for a moment it felt like they were the only two people on earth.

'Come on, Brent,' Benji said, relieving Brent of the ball. 'Let's play.'

Brent dragged his gaze from Grace's and looked down at the kids. 'Okay, team. Line up over at the posts.' He winked at Grace. 'Catch you later.'

Grace nodded silently and finally remembered to breathe.

A few hours later they were nearing the end of the Perry family friendly when Grace noticed that Tash, who had refused to participate and had sat on the sideline, texting, for nearly an hour, was now notably absent.

Her heart began to beat a little harder as a prickle of dread mixed with the bead of cold sweat that was trekking slowly down her spine. She craned her neck, letting her gaze sweep the greater area of the park in ever-widening circles. Finally she spotted a few forms behind a clump of gum trees at the furthest reaches of the park.

She couldn't actually tell if one of them was Tash or even if there were three or four of them, but Grace knew in her bones that her niece was among their number.

'I'm out,' she called as she stalked off the field and headed towards the gum trees.

No amount of lecturing herself about staying calm helped the spike in her blood pressure when the distinct aroma of tobacco smoke assaulted her as she drew nearer.

In fact, Grace was pretty much near boiling point as she bore down on the oblivious teenagers. Three girls and a boy.

'Natasha!'

Four startled faces almost choked on their cigarettes as they whipped round to face her. Before her niece had a chance to do or say anything, Grace pulled the offending item from her lips, threw it to the ground and stomped on it hard.

The others all dropped their cigarettes too.

'Do your parents know you're down here, smoking behind their backs?' Grace demanded, looking hard at each teenager.

'Aunty Grace!'

Grace ignored the horrified plea from her niece. 'Go home,' she said, lowering her voice to a growl as she continued to eyeball them. 'Right now!'

'Aunty Grace!'

'Its okay, Tash,' the boy said, his eyes darting nervously between Tash and Grace. He gave her a quick hug, as did the girls, and they took off without a backward glance.

'That was so not cool,' Tash said, shaking her head at her aunt, her mouth a thin, bitter line.

Grace gave her an incredulous look. 'Do you think I give two hoots about being cool?'

'Obviously not,' Tash threw at her.

Grace ignored her and held out her palm to her niece. 'Give them to me,' she demanded. 'The cigarettes.'

Tash shook her head, mutiny in her eyes. 'I don't have any.'

Grace kept her hand out. 'I don't believe you.'

Tash gasped. 'You can't treat me like this.'

Grace kept her hand out but sucked in a breath, reaching for patience. 'If you're endangering your life, I can.' She waggled her fingers. 'If I have to wrestle you to the ground, I will.'

Tash shook her head as tears filled her eyes, looking at her aunt as if Grace had just grown a second head. 'I can't believe this,' she said, opening her bag, reaching in and pulling out the packet. She slapped it into Grace's palm.

Grace opened them and pulled one out. She ripped it in half and threw it in the dirt. 'Are you trying to kill yourself?' she demanded, as she pulled out another, tore it in half as well, throwing it down to join the other.

'Lung cancer.' She pulled out and tore one more. 'Emphysema.' Another one hit the ground. 'Heart disease. Nicotine addiction.'

By the time Grace got to the end of the long line of smoking-related medical conditions, every one had been broken and was lying in the dirt at their feet.

Tash was staring at her aunt, open-mouthed, shaking her head. 'Are you crazy?' she yelled.

'Crazy?' Grace yelled back, her head ready to explode right off her shoulders. 'I'm not the one who's smoking. Who's polluting pristine lungs.' She poked Tash in the chest. 'See this picture?'

Grace pointed to the graphic image of a cancerous lung that the government decreed all cigarette packets must display.

'Do you have some kind of death wish? Do you think your parents would approve of you smoking?'

Tash balled her hands into fists by her sides. 'You are such a…bitch!'

Grace gasped as if she'd been slapped. Had Tash really just called her *that* name? Had she heard right?

'What is the matter with you?' she demanded, grabbing Tash's upper arms and giving her a shake. 'Why are you acting like this?' This wasn't the Tash she'd known. 'This isn't you, Tash. I know things are hard for you at the moment but they will get better, I promise. This isn't the way to go about it.'

'Leave me alone,' Tash said, wrenching herself away. 'Just leave me alone.'

'No, Tash,' Grace said, shaking her head. 'No. You mightn't like me very much right now but I'm not ever leaving you alone. I love you.'

Brent could hear the raised voices from quite a way away and he quickened his pace. Grace's mother had asked him to go and investigate after the game had ended and he'd been happy to oblige.

But did he want to get into the middle of this? It was obviously personal and he wasn't sure it would be appreciated.

All of this week the insidious thought that maybe he and Grace could make another go of it had been insinuating itself into his grey matter. But this was the stark reality of Grace's life. She came with two orphaned kids—one of them a very angry teenager.

It was a reality check he wasn't sure he wanted when the fantasy was much prettier.

But then he saw Grace grab Tash and something deeper, something primitive overrode his hesitation and spurred him on.

'Everything all right here?' he asked moments later.

Grace and Tash, both obviously engrossed in their slanging match, looked at him like he'd just landed from Mars.

'Brent,' Grace said. He looked so good and capable and she just wanted to go to him and sob all over his shirt, absorb all that strength that seemed to ooze from his every pore.

Brent took one look at the scene—the smell of smoke, several shredded cigarettes in the dirt, a furious-looking Grace, a tearful Tash—and summed it up in a second.

He looked at Grace and then at Tash. 'Come with me,' he said.

CHAPTER TWELVE

TEN minutes later they were in his car and a tense silence had descended. Tash was in the back, staring stonily out the window. Grace, sitting in the front seat, her stomach churning and her brain tumbling, turned to face Brent.

'Brent?' she asked quietly.

He glanced at her briefly, before returning his eyes to the road. 'Trust me,' he murmured, reaching out and giving her knee a quick squeeze before returning it to the steering-wheel.

The action was so comforting that Grace almost covered his hand with hers but it was so brief his hand was gone before she had the chance.

She did trust him. *Implicitly.*

Ten more minutes and they were pulling into Brent's car parking space at the Central.

'What are we doing here?' Tash asked.

Brent ignored the huffy note in the teenager's voice. 'I have someone I want you to meet.'

Tash looked like she was about to object but Grace shot her a my-patience-is-running-out look and she climbed out of the car.

They walked through the emergency department, greeting staff as they went but not stopping as Brent ushered them into the lift and pushed the fifth-floor button. No one spoke for the brief ride and then they were out and Brent was shepherding them into ward 5C.

He walked down the hallway until he found room nine and strode in, with Grace and Tash following. A man was sitting hunched on the side of the bed, his legs dangling over the edge. He was grey and breathless, with plastic oxygen prongs in his nose.

'Hi, Bill,' he said.

Bill looked up and smiled. 'Hey…Doc,' he murmured, his pursed lips grabbing for air between the words.

Grace recognised the man instantly. William Loch. She'd admitted him a couple of days ago for exacerbation of his chronic obstructive airways disease.

'I've brought you someone to meet, Bill,' Brent said. 'You know Dr Perry, of course, and this is her niece Natasha.'

Bill nodded at Grace and smiled at Tash. 'And to what…do I…owe the…pleasure?' he puffed.

'Tash here has taken up smoking,' Brent said.

'Ah,' Bill said. And then laughed. It wasn't the first teen smoker that Brent had brought his way and he was more than happy to oblige with a little public health education—anything to get the message out to kids.

Bill's laugh stimulated a cough. And then another and then he couldn't stop. Great hacking coughs that tore at his throat. He held his chest and pointed at a Styrofoam cup on his bedside table, indicating for Tash to pass it to him.

She picked it up, looking down as she passed it on, recoiling from the yellowy-green slimy substance in the bottom flecked with blood. Tash dropped it quickly into Bill's hand and watched in horror as he coughed up another disgusting-looking globule of gross-coloured sputum.

'Thanks,' he said, when the coughing fit had passed.

'Mr Loch is a respiratory cripple,' Brent said to Tash. 'Thanks to smoking.'

Bill nodded. 'Started when I…was your age… Stupidest thing I…ever did.'

He looked down at his hands and held them up so Tash could see the unsightly orangey-yellow stains on his fingers. Tash took them in along with the shocking state of Bill's heavily yellow teeth.

'Take my advice, girlie…don't start…choose life… This is no…no kind of life.'

Bill tired quickly and they left the room a couple of minutes later with a rather subdued Tash. Neither of them said anything to her. They knew that the message had been well and truly taken on board.

They rode the lift back to the emergency department. Tash needed to use the toilet and Grace showed her to the staff facilities. 'We'll just be in there,' Grace said, pointing to the door of the staffroom just down from the loo.

She joined Brent in the deserted staffroom, the door swishing silently closed behind her. He was lounging against the sink, drinking a glass of water. 'Want one?' he asked.

She nodded. 'Thanks.'

Brent pulled a glass down from the cupboard above the sink and filled it at the bench-top bubbler. He passed it to her, settling back against the sink again, crossing one ankle over the other. He clinked his glass against hers. 'Here's to Bill.' He smiled.

Grace laughed. She felt like she hadn't been happy for a week and it was good to at last have a reason to laugh. 'That was ingenious, thank you.'

'Bill and I have an arrangement. Quite a few foster-kids have found themselves passing Bill's sputum cup.'

Grace laughed again, remembering Tash's look of disgust. 'I guess it's handy to have a respiratory cripple up your sleeve.'

Brent grinned and Grace felt her breath hitch as tall, dark and handsome morphed into sublimely sexy. She sipped at her water to hide the sudden rush of lust blooming from her core. Her gaze dropped and centred on his throat as he took another deep swallow of his water.

The bloom rippled ever outwards and her nipples tightened just thinking about laying her lips against the heavy pulse that thudded at the base of his throat. She remembered how good he smelled right there.

Brent swallowed, his throat suddenly parched. His gaze locked on her mouth, watching as it pressed against the glass, her lips moist. They'd be cool against his throat, at the spot where she was staring. And wet. Maybe they'd even sizzle on contact.

He flicked his gaze upwards and their eyes met. Hers looked large behind the frames of her glasses. And hot. Like steaming thermal pools.

The heat radiated towards him and he felt a corresponding warmth seep into him. They were close, close enough for him to pull her towards him.

Maybe they *could* pick up where they'd left off?

'Maybe,' he said, reaching for her, their gazes still locked as his finger hooked through a loop on her waistband, 'this isn't so crazy.'

He tugged and pulled her slowly towards him. She didn't object.

Grace's heart gave a little leap as their bodies touched. He shifted, settling her against him as his breath fanned her cheek. She held his gaze, watched it shimmer with desire.

Brent lifted a lock of her fringe with a finger and tucked it behind her ear. 'I want to kiss you,' he murmured. 'Is that crazy?'

Grace heart pounded like a freight train in her chest, thrumming through her ears. His fingers stroked down her cheek and his thumb teased the corner of her mouth. She swallowed. 'Probably.'

Brent smiled. He held her gaze for a moment longer and then slowly inched his mouth towards hers.

Just as his lips brushed hers a loud knock followed by 'Aunty Grace?' burst into their sexual bubble, and they leapt apart like a couple of teenagers being sprung by their parents. Brent turned to face the sink, emptying his glass, and Grace took two paces away from him and faced the door.

'In here,' she called.

Tash opened the door. 'Can we go?' she asked. The abruptness of her request was tempered by the contriteness of her tone.

Grace cleared her throat. 'Sure.' She glanced at Brent and then quickly away. 'Let's go,' she announced, making a hasty exit.

Brent followed Grace at a more sedate pace, still rattled, needing time to recover from their near kiss.

If only Tash had waited another minute...

But it was a good reminder that with two kids in the mix Grace's life was full of interruptions. It wasn't just her any more. And as much as he'd like to think they could recapture what they'd had, it plainly wasn't possible.

Things seemed to settle with Tash over the next couple of weeks, which freed Grace's head space up for other more pleasurable things—like daydreaming about the Brent possibilities.

His *maybe this isn't so crazy* fuelled an avalanche of fantasies and she let them have free rein.

Maybe he would fall in love with her again? Maybe they could be together.

Working with him became the highlight of her days. Even though they didn't touch and they didn't talk about Brent's *maybe this isn't so crazy*, there was a vibe between them now.

They stopped in the corridors to chat to each other. They ate lunch together. They joked. They reminisced about their uni days. His gaze would often drop to her mouth when she was talking or eating, and occasionally she'd be checking out his butt as he walked away and he'd turn and wink at her.

She felt all warm and delicious inside for the first time in a long time instead of edgy and anxious.

She sprang out of bed on work days and thoughts of him filled the non-work days. And the Sunday footy match was heavily anticipated by more than Benji.

It was a good opportunity to be near him and not have to be professional. Where they were just Brent and Grace. Not Dr Cartwright and Dr Perry. To able to laugh and play and flirt and build on their relationship outside the confines of work.

Neither of them broached the subject of the future but, with two weeks of exemplary behaviour from Tash, so much seemed possible.

Until at two one morning her mobile rang and changed everything.

Grace sat bolt upright in bed, completely disorientated, groping for her phone, the light, her glasses as the ring pealed insistently. It was raining outside, drumming on the roof, a good foil to her drumming heart.

Grace was all fingers and thumbs at this hour, trying to find the damn thing quickly so as not to wake the kids. The lamplight blinded her as the possibilities stomped through her brain like stampeding elephants. A ringing phone at this time of night was never good news. She wasn't on call, so what was it?

Had something happened to her parents?

Please, dear God, no, she couldn't bear another loss.

At last, through a combination of cramming her glasses on her face and squinting, she located her phone and hit the answer button, her heart pounding.

'Hello?'

'Grace? It's Brent.'

It took a few seconds for Grace to recognise the voice on the other end was Brent's, even though her body recognised the deep rumble on a completely primal level.

'Grace?'

'Sorry—yes, I'm here.'

She snuggled down beneath the covers, her heart rate settling. She didn't know why he was ringing her at this hour of the morning but his voice sounded all sleepy and sexy and she wanted to curl up and listen to him as the rain kept up its steady beat on the roof.

Maybe he'd rung to talk about the thing growing between them? Maybe he'd been lying awake night after night too, fantasising about them?

'I'd forgotten what a sexy voice you have,' she murmured, her inhibitions blunted by drowsiness, her eyes already shutting as she yawned.

'Grace, I need you to listen. Are you awake?'

'Mmm.' She sighed, snuggling further under the covers.

'Grace!'

Grace opened her eyes at his abrupt command. 'What?' she said crankily.

'I'm at work—'

That's right. He was on call. 'You want me to come in?'

He was ringing about a work matter? She sat up a little, the bubble created by the darkened room, the rain and his sexy voice well and truly bursting. 'I can't, Brent. The kids are asleep.'

'Grace, Tash is here. She's all right but she's been in an accident.'

Grace frowned and sat up even higher. She gave a half-laugh, 'What? No. She's in bed sound asleep.'

'Grace…'

Grace was silent for a moment then she was kicking aside the bed covers. 'She's in bed,' she insisted, padding through the house, picking up speed as she got closer to her niece's room.

Empty.

The bed was empty.

Grace pushed a hand into her hair, her heartbeat thundering in time with the rain again. But she'd checked on Tash before she'd gone to bed at ten. She'd kicked the covers off and Grace had pulled them back up.

'Oh, God. Is she injured?' Panic slammed into her. White hot, burning. Grace stalked to her bedroom, dragging on jeans. 'What? Tell me what?'

'She's fractured her ankle. It's a simple fracture and won't need surgical intervention. There's a lot of swelling so we've put it in a backslab for now and we'll admit her overnight for observation.'

'Oh, God,' Grace wailed. 'I don't believe this. How? She was asleep five hours ago!'

'They were all very lucky.'

'They!'

'Just get here Grace, okay? I can tell you the rest when you get here.'

Grace sucked in a breath. His voice was calm and she latched on to it. 'That's it, right? You're not trying to sugar-coat this? That's all?'

'Just some bumps and bruises…that's all. No other…physical injuries.'

'Right,' Grace said, her mind racing ahead in time with the gallop of her heartbeat, deaf to the hesitation in Brent's voice. 'I'll be there in…' Hell! How long would it take to get her mum here? She couldn't think. 'I don't know, half an hour.'

'Drive carefully, Grace, please. There's no point having you both in hospital.'

Grace made it in forty-three minutes. She screeched to a halt in the ambulance bay, uncaring that it was for emergency vehicles only. Brent greeted her at the sliding doors.

'Where is she?' Grace demanded.

He placed a restraining hand on her arm as she stormed inside. She was wearing jeans and a V-necked skivvy with a hoodie and, even frantic, with no make-up on except her regulation lip gloss and a blanket mark still visible on her face, she looked beautiful.

'Just wait for a moment,' he said. 'I need to talk to you.'

'Oh, God—what?' Grace clutched her stomach, grabbed his arm. 'What's happened?'

Brent slid his palms up her arms and gently grasped her upper arms. 'Nothing's happened. She's exactly the same as I told you on the phone. But there's something you need to know before you go charging in there.'

Grace looked at him sharply. There was something he wasn't telling her, she could hear it in his voice. She was torn between demanding to know and burying her head in his chest and bawling her eyes out.

Brent could see he had Grace's full attention now and he took a breath before imparting what he was fairly certain was going to be very unwelcome news. He wished he could shelter her from it but it had to be said.

'She's drunk, Grace. Her blood-alcohol level has come back at double the legal limit.'

Grace felt an instant denial rise to her lips. 'It must be wrong.'

Brent shook his head. 'She's pretty wasted.'

Grace stared at him in disbelief. Was this truly happening? But looking into Brent's steady tawny gaze, she knew this was very, very real.

A surge of anger joined the volatile mix of fear and anxiety that had been rampaging through her system. Apart from a couple of notable incidents, she'd been pussy-footing around Tash for ages now, trying to give her space and show her faith and trust, and this was what she got?

First smoking and now sneaking out and drinking and getting into car accidents?

Grace looked at Brent in utter dismay, finally truly broken. Was this what happened when she took her eye off the ball? When she dared to start thinking about herself?

'Tell me all of it.'

* * *

Tash was asleep when Grace flicked back the curtain and she felt all the anger and frustration melt away at how small and fragile Tash looked on the gurney. She looked twelve, not fifteen.

So young and innocent.

Tash's eyes fluttered open, taking in the two grim-faced adults looking down at her. Her lips twisted. 'I told you not to call her,' she said, ignoring Grace and glaring at Brent. Belligerence dripped from her slurred voice.

'Tash!'

'Oh, what?' the teenager demanded. Her mascara had run and big round panda eyes stabbed hostility towards her. 'What do you care anyway?'

Grace felt as if Tash had slugged her with a knuckleduster. She sucked in a breath, fighting to stay calm.

It didn't work.

'What do you mean?' she asked, crossing to stand beside the gurney. 'Of course I care, you stupid girl,' she yelled. 'You think it doesn't worry me sick that you're sneaking out in the middle of the night, getting drunk, getting in cars with drunk people, running into power poles?'

Grace could feel her fingers trembling and she wrapped them around the gurney's metal safety rails. 'You could have been killed,' she snarled. 'You all could have been killed.'

'Yeah, well—at leasht I'd be wiv Mum.'

Grace felt cold fingers clutch her heart. Did Tash have some kind of death wish? She'd asked her that a couple of weeks ago during the cigarette incident but what if her niece really was suicidal?

'Do you think that your mother would want you dead at fifteen? Do you?' Grace demanded, her voice getting higher. She could feel her tightly wound control unravelling. 'Because I can tell you for absolutely bloody certain that she wouldn't. She'd be horrified.'

Tash reared up. 'Don't you talk to me about my mother,' she shouted. 'How would you know? You were never here.'

Grace blinked as alcohol fumes and spittle from her niece's impassioned tirade sprayed her face. More black tears flowed down Tash's face and Grace felt her own building.

'Where were you when she needed you the mosht? You the great docter! You could have saved her.' Tash stabbed her finger at Grace's shoulder. 'But you were too bishy wiv your great important life. You didn' love her. She needed you and you let her die.'

'Natasha! That will do!' Brent's voice sliced through the teenager's hysteria as he stepped forward and placed his hand on Grace's shoulder. 'Your aunt is not to blame for your mother's death.'

Tash burst into tears and turned on her side away from them both, loud sobs echoing around the cubicle.

Grace sucked in a breath, disbelief pounding through her skull. She was pleased for Brent's solid presence behind her as her entire world tilted around her. Hot tears welled in her eyes and slipped down her cheeks.

She'd known Tash was angry, but not over this. Tash blamed her for not being around? For not being at the Royal Melbourne Hospital that night, working, when her sister had needed an emergency physician?

How could her niece know that she blamed herself for the same thing? That the guilt about being so far away from Julie, from her family, when it had happened had been so profound it still lingered to this day?

She looked at Tash's back, watching the heaving of her shoulders, desperately wanting to reach out and touch her despite still reeling from her vitriol.

But knowing Tash would never accept it. Not at the moment.

The gap between them had never felt wider.

Brent felt Grace sag back against him and he gently stroked his thumb up and down the vertebral ridges at the back of her neck. He'd watched with dismay as Tash's barbs had hit Grace square in the chest.

The two Perry women were hurting—their pain was like a force-field in the cubicle, arcing between them, pushing each other apart like two opposing magnetic fields.

He wished he could take away their pain.

Gabi stuck her head behind the curtain, looking uncertainly at Brent and Grace. 'The ward's ready for Natasha now.'

'Thanks, Gabs. Let's get her transferred.'

Twenty minutes later Tash was ensconced in the orthopaedic ward, her lower leg in a half-plaster at the back to support the fracture but allowing for more swelling. It was elevated on two pillows.

She complained of pain and a nurse administered some intravenous pain relief.

Grace wasn't surprised. She felt ill, looking at the blue and purple joint, which was puffed up to the point of being unrecognisable as an ankle. What if it had been her head?

She shuddered at the hundreds of horrifying possibilities—the things that could have happened.

In fact, Tash, sitting in the front passenger's seat, which had been the point of impact, had come off worst. The driver and other passenger, girls from Tash's school, had suffered only minor injuries. Seat-belt bruising—which luckily hadn't damaged the spleen—and a head laceration from hitting the steering-wheel.

Tash and Grace hadn't spoken in anything more than a perfunctory manner since their earlier argument, and when the nurse left the room there was just the two of them and the things that had been said lying large and loud between them.

Tash settled herself against the pillows. 'You should go home,' she said to the ceiling. 'I'll be fine.'

Grace didn't take her eyes off her niece. 'I'm staying.'

Tash rolled away—as much as she could with her injured leg elevated—and Grace was left to stare at the back of Tash's head.

And worry.

CHAPTER THIRTEEN

AN HOUR later, Grace stood. She couldn't sit a minute longer in the uncomfortable plastic chair, listening to the continual treadmill of her thoughts. Tash's anger had been shocking. Even more so on continuous loop through her head. It was terrible to realise that her niece had been harbouring such thoughts for the last eighteen-plus months.

You let her die.

No wonder Tash had been treating her so disparagingly.

Grace paced around the small single room for a while, staring out the window at the wet streets of the car park and beyond, the reflections of traffic lights in the puddles making the streets look all shiny and new.

A great night to be tucked up in bed.

She looked over her shoulder at Tash. She was sleeping soundly, her panda eyes making her look even more disconsolate. There were times she looked so much like Julie it was spooky.

Grace was reminded again of the incident when she and Brent had had to rescue Julie from imminent alcohol poisoning. Her sister had looked just as wretched that night. And if memory served her correctly, she'd felt even more wretched the next day.

Tash was going to have one hell of a headache in the morning.

Grace turned back to the window, her gaze falling on Brent's sporty little convertible in the car park. The one they'd made out in like they had both still been eighteen.

Before he'd told her they couldn't pick up where they'd left off.

Before she'd realised she still loved him.

Before his *maybe this isn't so crazy*.

Before he'd had to ring her and tell her that her inebriated niece had been in a car crash.

She pressed her forehead against the window pane, the moist coolness like soothing balm. She recalled his hand on her shoulder, the stroke of his thumb at her nape. Giving her an anchor, something to lean on. Thank God it had been him on duty tonight. Someone who knew. Who cared.

It seemed like he was always there for the Perry women and their alcohol-related crises.

She'd give anything now to be held by him. To bury her face in his shirt and have him tell her it was all going to be all right. That he loved her. That he'd be by her side.

But if tonight had demonstrated anything to her, it had demonstrated that Grace had failed in her responsibility as Tash's guardian. That while she'd been building an imaginary castle in the air, Tash had still been feeling wretched enough to sneak out of the house and put her life in danger.

How had she missed that?

She wouldn't let her attention be hijacked again.

So she couldn't go to him for comfort. But she could go and thank him for tonight. For not listening to Tash and ringing her. For coming to her defence during Tash's drunken tongue-lashing.

She turned. Tash was fast asleep and between the medication and alcohol probably would be for hours. Her gaze wandered to the uninviting contours of the hard plastic chair.

Stretching her legs seemed a much better option.

Brent had just laid his head on the couch when the knock sounded on the door. He sighed. So much for sleep. He threw the blanket off, rose and padded across to the door, unlocking it and pulling it open.

'Oh,' he said as he took in Grace, her hands shoved in the front pockets of her jeans, an uncertain look on her face.

He'd fought the urge to go and visit her up on the ward before crashing in the on-call room. Grace had seemed so defeated by Tash's accusations, so...lost that he hadn't been sure he wanted to put himself in the midst of that.

Visions of that night in the tree house and in his car had been powerful reminders that a vulnerable Grace quickly slipped under his skin. Neutralising his resistance.

And the last thing she needed now was him complicating things further.

He'd planned instead to go visiting in the morning before he went home. With some sleep under his belt. And a modicum of perspective.

'Hi.'

'Hi,' he said. 'Is everything okay...with Tash?'

'Oh, yes.' Grace nodded vigorously. 'She's sleeping soundly. I just...'

She just what? Brent was standing at the door, looking all solid and warm, and she'd been fooling herself that coming to see him had been about gratitude. He looked weary and wary; his hand high up on the doorframe was not an inviting gesture. It quite clearly said, *Do not enter.*

Obviously this incident with Tash had been a wake-up call for him. He had probably suddenly realised what he was getting himself into with his flirty eyes and sexy laughter these last couple of weeks.

Tears pricked at her eyes as the enormity of this lost opportunity to love him slammed into her.

'I'm sorry...' Her voice was husky as a lump of emotion welled in her throat. She sucked in a ragged breath as she blinked back tears. 'You're trying to sleep. It doesn't matter.'

Brent sighed. Keeping his arm up high, he pulled the door open a little further. 'Come in.'

Grace knew it was her chance to be strong. To tell him to go to bed, that she'd see him later. But she was tired of being strong. She wanted to suck up some of that Brent confidence, if only for a little while.

She'd just stay for a little while.

She ducked in under his arm, his familiar scent embracing her, confirming the rightness of it all.

Brent shut the door quietly, pressing his forehead against the wood briefly, taking a moment to breathe as he flipped the lock. He turned and walked towards her, his heart rate picking up, his senses on high alert.

Grace fought to bring her overwhelming emotions under control, twisting her hands. Fingers of light from the outside corridor filtered through the blinds, illuminating the edges of the otherwise darkened room.

She stood in the middle, searching for the right words.

Words that did not start with L.

'I wanted to th-thank you,' she said. 'For everything tonight. I'm so glad it was you who was on. This whole thing with Tash…'

Grace stopped as a king tide of grief surged over her. She couldn't go on. She ducked her head as her eyes misted and a tear spilled down her cheek.

Brent's first instinct was to reach for her. He resisted. It was just too dangerous. He wanted her too much. But standing here, watching her cry, he felt so helpless. He hated seeing her cry. Always had.

His blood beat through his veins, thick and sludgy, thrumming through his head to a primal rhythm.

Grace looked up at him. 'She hates me.'

Brent sucked in a breath at the anguish in those three simple words. In her gaze.

Oh, hell.

He couldn't bear it. Watching her like this was too hard. And suddenly he knew why.

He was still in love with her.

The admission opened the floodgates and the emotions he'd held in check since she'd been back, the ones he'd buried all those years ago, rushed out at him, filling every cell and sinew of his body. They washed through his chest and flowed through his heart. They couldn't be denied any longer.

He loved her.

It wasn't a time for joy. If anything it was a complication so unbearable that for a moment he wanted to run far, far away. As far from her as he could. Thinking and wondering and fantasising about *being* with her again was a totally different prospect to *loving* her again.

Yet again, he loved this woman. And yet again, the gap yawned between them.

She was looking at him, waiting, with tears running down her cheeks. And he had nothing. Except the overwhelming imperative to keep her at arm's length lest he succumb to the potent dictates of his love.

But she was crying.

So he reached for her hand and tugged her towards him. She needed comfort. He couldn't deny the woman he loved that most basic human need.

It was just a hug.

'No, she doesn't.' He shut his eyes as she settled against him, honey and vanilla wrapping him in a hundred dangerous memories. 'She's drunk and I suspect angry with herself over her stupidity. She's just lashing out.'

Grace dropped her forehead onto his chest and leant into him, more hot tears falling. 'Yeah, but she's right, isn't she? If I'd been there...'

Brent looked down at her. He could see the doubt and the guilt and he couldn't bear the thought of her blaming herself for her sister's death. She'd been two thousand kilometres away, for crying out loud.

He slid his hand to her jaw and cradled her face. 'I've seen her file, Grace.' Brent had called in a favour at the Royal and read Julie's chart. 'Her injuries were fatal. No one could have saved her.'

'But—'

'Shh.' Before he knew what he was doing he dropped a kiss on her forehead. It came so easy. Felt so natural.

Grace blinked up at him. 'I miss her,' she whispered.

Brent heard a whole spectrum of emotions in those three simple words. Pain, sadness, regret, longing. More hot tears welled in her eyes and he felt his resistance melt as each one fell.

His pulse boomed in his ears, thundered in his chest as he came to a decision.

'I know,' he murmured, pulling off her glasses and kissing her tears away.

Between the tears, the dark and losing her glasses, the world went very blurry. 'Brent I…I can't see,' she protested half-heartedly, as his lips brushed her cheeks with infinite softness.

'Shh,' he murmured, dropping a kiss on the side of her mouth. 'Shut your eyes, you don't need them.'

Grace sighed, her eyes fluttering closed as surrender stole through her body. She whimpered as his breath fanned her lips. She bunched her fingers into his shirt as her legs threatened to give way. His arm slipped around her back, anchoring her to him.

His lips were tender when they brushed against hers. Gentle, like rain. And she soaked them up like parched earth, content for a while with light and tender. But then his tongue stroked along the soft pillow of her bottom lip and the slow fizz in her blood turned to a sizzle, burning bright and hot, and she opened her mouth wide and demanded he follow.

Brent groaned as the taste of honey taunted his taste buds and a surge of pure undiluted lust roared through his body. There was no thought of resistance now. This was Grace and he loved her and he might never be able to say the words but he could show her.

He could love her with his body tonight.

Cherish her.

Show her she was his everything.

His tongue plundered her mouth, his hand in her hair holding her head fast. His thumb tilted her chin back more, angling her head further, letting him go deeper, harder, with the kiss. She moaned against his mouth and he went deeper still.

He dropped his hand to her neck, stroking his fingers down her throat, rubbing his thumb over the frantic beat at the base. He dragged his mouth from hers, following the path of his fingers—across her jaw, down her throat, along her collar bone.

He felt her hands beneath his shirt, exploring the planes of his back, pushing beneath the waistband of his jeans, grasping his buttocks. He shut his eyes momentarily as his erection twitched, straining against the confines of cotton and denim.

Then he was nuzzling her cleavage, swiping his tongue across the rise of her breast. He held her close, his hand splayed between her shoulder blades as he dragged aside her shirt, her bra, his mouth seeking her nipple, finding it. She gasped and arched her back as he sucked it into his mouth, laved it, felt it grow taut and puckered against his tongue.

Grace almost fainted from the exquisite torture his mouth was dishing out. 'Brent,' she murmured, holding his head fast to her breast with one hand, fumbling with his fly with the other. Needing to touch him again. Wanting to grasp all that hardness. Desperate to feel it inside her again.

It had been too long. Twenty years without this. Without Brent. Without touching him, kissing him. Needing him.

Finally her hand lowered his zipper, his undies and she was freeing him, touching him—big and hard and hers.

Even if it was just for now.

Brent groaned against her breast as she swiped her thumb across the swollen tip of him. He lifted his head, sought her mouth again, sucked her lips against his, pushed his tongue inside her.

His eyes rolled back as she ran her hands up and down his shaft and he broke the kiss off. He grabbed at his shirt, pulling it over his head. 'Naked,' he gasped. 'Now.'

He grabbed her shirt, yanking it upwards, kissing her hard on the mouth once it cleared her face. His fingers found her bra clasp and made short work of it. He stared at her for a moment, his breath heaving in and out, distracted by the beauty of her bare breasts.

But then she was unzipping her jeans and wiggling out of them and he did likewise and then they were totally naked together for the first time in twenty years and then somehow they were on the couch, Grace propped against the cushioned leather arm, her legs locked around his waist as he kissed down her neck, to her breasts and lower.

'Brent, no,' she panted as his overnight growth scratched her belly and muscles deep inside tightened to an unbearable ache. She pulled at his shoulders. 'I need to feel you inside me. Now.'

She wanted to be consumed by him. Branded. Connected to him in the most intimate way two humans could be. She didn't want foreplay.

She wanted possession.

Brent felt her hips move restlessly against his and saw fever in her gaze. Felt the answering call in his blood. His gut. His loins.

He was powerless to resist it.

He reached for the chair arm and dragged himself back to her as her legs locked him in place again. Then he was positioning himself, one forearm resting on the arm next to her head, the other grasping her hip, his engorged head nudging her hot slickness.

And with one push he was buried to the hilt and she was crying out, her head flung back, her mouth open, and he covered her mouth with his as he reared up over her with each thrust.

They set a rhythm that was uniquely theirs. Building and building with each thrust, each kiss, each groan. Deeper and deeper. Higher and higher. Their bodies telling each other things their mouths could not.

Reaching for the stars. Burning for each other brighter than any sun.

Grace dug her nails into his back as her climax built, rippling, undulating, twisting through her belly. She moaned against Brent's mouth.

'Yes,' he whispered. 'Yes.'

Grace whimpered. She clutched his shoulders, feeling them tremble, knowing he was near too, knowing he was as out of control as she was.

But for once she didn't care. She loved him. She was making love with him and it was the sweetest thing she'd known in for ever.

And then it broke over her and she screamed into his mouth as she clutched at his backside, holding him closer, deeper as she bucked and surged against him.

Brent felt her clamp hard around him and the slow, inexorable march to pleasure accelerated to warp speed and he was moaning into her mouth, bucking and grinding, thrusting wildly, pounding and thrashing and hammering. Pistoning in and out as he spilled into her high and hard, over and over, coming and coming and coming until he collapsed against her chest totally spent. Utterly exhausted.

They lay together for a while still joined, not moving, not speaking. Brent's weight pressed her into the lounge and she stroked his hair, his forehead, as their heart rates settled, their breathing slowed.

'I have to go back to Tash,' Grace said into the silence.

'I know.'

Another minute passed. A hundred other things she wanted to say tripped through Grace's head. But she didn't say any of them. She shifted and he moved off her. They dressed without looking at each other without saying a word, both too wary to speak at all in case the truth came out.

Grace slid her feet into her shoes and glanced at him. He was sitting on the lounge fully dressed, looking tired and handsome and very, very male. 'Thank you,' she said.

Brent gave a half-smile. 'My pleasure.'

Grace returned his half-smile with one of her own. 'I have to go.'

Brent nodded. 'I'll pop in and see Tash before I go home.'

Grace nodded back. Then she turned away and left the room.

Grace had a lot of time to think about the potential consequences of what had just transpired in the on-call room between her and Brent as she sat by Tash's bedside and dawn broke over Melbourne. But she didn't.

The implications needed a sharper brain to analyse them than the current state of her own, so there seemed little point. And she had no doubt that she'd think and rethink it *ad nauseam* in the days and weeks to follow.

For now, she refused to sully its perfection, refused to feel guilt. For now she was happy just to relive it. The magic of his kiss. His touch. The way he still filled her so perfectly. The way only he knew how to bring her to the heights of dizziness through penetration alone. How he seemed to know exactly what she needed at exactly the right moment.

It was probably going to be her only chance to love him so

completely. And if that was selfish then she refused to feel guilty about that too.

Tash shifted and frowned in her sleep and a little of that guilt raised its ugly head. Tash was what she should be thinking about. Maybe if she'd been thinking more about Tash and less about Brent they wouldn't be in this predicament now.

But it was much easier to relive those thirty minutes with Brent than face the conundrum that was Tash.

Grace yawned as tiredness swamped her body. It had been a momentous night. Both physically and emotionally. An abrupt awakening combined with fear, stress, tears and a mind-blowing orgasm had taken its toll.

Suddenly, she was so, so tired.

She laid her head on Tash's bed, sliding her hand up the crisp white sheet to cover Tash's hand. Grace waited for her niece to move it away but when she didn't Grace relaxed and her eyes fluttered closed.

She'd just rest her eyes.

Just for a moment or two.

CHAPTER FOURTEEN

THE sun was streaming through the window when Grace woke to a noise a couple of hours later. She sat up abruptly, her neck and shoulders instantly protesting, her fingers numb and tingly from sleeping on her hand.

The noise came again and she turned quickly to face it. Tash was holding her head and groaning.

Grace stood and moved closer to her niece. 'Head bad?'

Tash nodded, cracking open an eyelid to look at Grace. 'I feel like someone's put my brain on the rack. It hurts worse than my ankle.'

Grace was tempted to give her a lecture about the perils of alcohol and let her suffer for a bit. But she'd never been the tough love kind of aunt and she knew she couldn't start now.

'I'll get some Panadol from the nurses. In the meantime,' she said, pouring a glass of water from the pitcher on the bedside table, 'drink this.'

Grace returned ten minutes later with two pills in her hand. She shook Tash's shoulder and Tash woke and downed the pills with another glass of water. Grace poured a third and insisted that Tash drink it.

'Alcohol dehydrates you. That's how come you have a headache,' she said, keeping it factual and non-judgmental. 'Rehydrate yourself and it'll help with the headache.'

Tash gulped it down without argument then sagged back against the pillows. 'Thanks,' she muttered.

Grace raised an eyebrow. *Progress.* 'How's the ankle?'

Tash looked down at her elevated limb. 'It's sore. But bearable.'

Grace nodded. She lifted her hand and felt lightly for the pedal pulse on top of Tash's foot. It had been marked with an X by the nurses for ease of finding it as they'd monitored it throughout the night.

Grace located the strong beat easily. It was good to feel the foot was warm, and when she lightly pressed on the skin the capillary refill was brisk. 'Can you wriggle your toes?' Tash wriggled. 'Any numbness?'

Tash shook her head. 'No.'

Grace sat down, satisfied. Her niece was lucky the swelling hadn't caused nervous or vascular compromise to her foot. They'd get another X-ray in a few days once the swelling had started to subside then a full cast would be applied.

Grace and Tash sat in silence for a few minutes. Grace came up with and discarded a variety of ways to talk about the previous night. Tash's eyes were closed but they did need to talk. Better here, while it was all still fresh, than at home in front of Benji.

'I'm sorry.'

Grace was startled out of her mental gymnastics by Tash's almost whisper. She looked at her niece. Her eyes were still closed. Had she imagined it?

Tash opened her eyes and looked at Grace. 'About the things I said last night. I'm sorry.'

Grace was stunned. She hadn't expected an apology. She'd expected excuses and more belligerence. More finger-pointing.

This was most definitely progress.

'Thank you,' Grace said. 'I appreciate that.'

She debated leaving it at that for now. Waiting for Tash to talk to her about things. But it wasn't a strategy that had worked thus far and her niece had given her an opening. Grace knew it would be foolish not to take it.

She drew her chair closer to the head of the bed. 'It's

obviously how you've been feeling, though,' she said tentatively. Tash opened her mouth to deny it but Grace waved her quiet. 'There's nothing quite like drunk honesty.'

Tash dropped her gaze to the bed covers. She sucked in a shaky breath. 'It makes it easier to have someone to blame.'

Grace nodded. 'Of course it does. I just wish I'd known earlier it was me you blamed. We could have talked about this instead of you bottling it up.'

Tash sniffed. 'I don't really, you know. Not deep down. I know rationally that you couldn't have saved her, that you lived thousands of kilometres away…'

Grace watched a tear trek down her niece's face as she struggled with her emotions, struggled to find the words. She covered Tash's hand with her own and gave it a squeeze. It felt incredibly good to have Tash squeeze back.

'I'm just so…so bloody…angry.' Tash balled her other hand into a fist and thumped it against the mattress. 'It's just not fair.'

Her voice cracked and she scrubbed at her face as more tears fell. 'And I do this thing with God, or whoever it is out there who's supposed to be in charge and doing a really, really lousy job…'

A sob tore from Tash's throat and she stuffed her hand against her mouth to stop any more coming out.

'Every night in bed I ask, beg, to be able to turn back time and have them safe at home with us that night and then, if I can't have that, I ask for you to be here in Melbourne and working at the hospital when she comes in and you save her.'

Grace swallowed against the lump in her throat, feeling useless and inadequate in the face of Tash's overwhelming grief.

'And every morning I wake up and they're still g-g-gone.' Her face crumpled and great heaving sobs tore from her mouth.

'Oh, Tash.' Grace pushed back the chair and threw herself on the edge of the mattress, dragging her niece towards her, hugging her close. 'Baby, I'm so sorry,' she whispered, rocking Tash back and forth.

'Why,' she sobbed into Grace's shoulder, 'do I keep thinking that tomorrow it will be d-different?'

Grace felt her own emotions spill over and she choked back her own tears—she wouldn't be any good to Tash if she also broke down. She eased back to look at Tash, wiping at her dirty mascara tears, pushing her fringe back from her face.

'You're grieving, darling. You're bargaining. It's normal and its natural and it's not anything I haven't done a thousand times also. Do you know how much I wish I'd been at the hospital that night? Do you know how many times I've asked to get those couple of hours back so I can change things?'

Tash shook her head vigorously at the doubt and agony on her aunt's face. 'No. No, please, I was wrong to say that. To think that. You loved Mum, she loved you. I'm so sorry, I didn't mean it. She missed you so much but she was so p-proud of you.'

Grace started to cry then. It was impossible not to. She pulled Tash back onto her shoulder and for the next few minutes the room was filled with the gut-wrenching sounds of two people grieving the loss of someone dear to them.

Someone they could never get back.

Tash eased away after a while and Grace looked at her. 'Better now?'

Tash nodded. 'Much.'

Grace squeezed her hand and sat back down in the chair.

Tash sagged against her pillows and shut her eyes for a moment. She opened them again and looked at Grace. 'Would you have come back sooner? If you'd known she was going to die?'

Grace didn't hesitate. 'Yes. Yes, yes, yes. A thousand times yes. I will always regret staying away for so long.'

She'd missed out on so much time with her sister. So much precious time. Her mind strayed to Brent. Maybe if she hadn't spent so much time away they'd be together again now.

Tash grimaced as she attempted to reposition her ankle and Grace helped adjust the pillows. 'You girls were so lucky,' she murmured as the ugly bruising made her want to shudder.

Tash gave her aunt a guilty look. 'I'm so sorry. I deserve to be kicked out for what happened last night.'

'Oh, Tash, I'm not going to kick you out,' Grace chided. 'But I want you to talk to me. I want to know what's going on with you. What on earth possessed you to sneak out of the house last night? To get drunk? To get in a car with a drunk driver? It could have ended so much worse than it did.'

Tash shook her head. 'Since Mum and Dad died…I've just felt so…straitjacketed. I mean, life's short, right?' She turned pleading eyes on Grace. 'Any one of us could be dead tomorrow. I…we…know that better than anybody. I want to live, to experience it. To say yes to adventures.'

Grace's heart broke for Tash. She was still hurting so much. 'Smoking, getting drunk…they're no adventure, Tash. I'm sure your head will agree.'

Tash grimaced. 'Oh, yeah!'

'Sweetie…there's adventure and there's just plain old unsafe.'

'I don't want to play it safe, Aunty Grace. You didn't.'

'Oh, darling, I followed my dreams, yes, but they were hardly daredevil. There's a big difference between playing it safe and outright risky.'

Tash's chin wobbled. 'I know. I know.' She sniffed again. 'But you know what? Mum played it safe all her life. They always talked about seeing the world one day when they retired. I think she envied you, you know. I think…sometimes…she regretted having kids so young.'

Grace stilled as the note of uncertainty in her niece's voice clanged a loud bell.

'Hang on a moment, sweetheart.' She leaned forward in the chair. 'We might not have lived in each other's pockets for the last twenty years but I do know this—your mum only ever wanted a family. A husband and kids. The minute she met Doug that's all she talked about. All they talked about. And the second she found out she was pregnant with you she was utterly besotted.'

Grace paused to check that it was sinking in. 'She might have talked about travelling one day, might have had the odd moment of the grass being greener, but you can be absolutely certain that she died with no regrets about what she'd done with her life because you and Benji and your dad were all she ever wanted.'

Tash's face crumpled again. 'I don't want to die with regrets either, Aunty Grace.'

Grace stood and sat on the side of the bed again, grasping both her niece's forearms. 'And you won't. You're going to grow up and have great adventures, *safe adventures*, and grow old enough to tell your grandchildren all about them.'

Grace leaned forward and swept Tash's fringe off her face, 'Sweetie, you can't live your life thinking every day could be your last. I know that's what those bumper stickers say but it'll drive you crazy, Tash. And I'm pretty damn sure Julie wouldn't want you to live like that.'

Tash gave a wobbly smile. 'Mum would have killed me over last night.'

Grace laughed. 'Well, if it's any consolation, killing you did cross my mind last night too.'

Tash gave a half-laugh then blew out hard a few times, raising and lowering her shoulders, trying to stem another batch of tears. 'I'll be better from now on, I promise.'

Grace smiled, hooking Tash's fringe behind her ear, wiping at her wet cheeks. For the first time in eighteen months she actually felt like it was going to be okay. It had been an emotional eight hours. Cathartic. And she finally felt like Tash had bared her soul. Maybe now she could move forward. They all could.

Oh, Grace wasn't foolish enough to believe that Tash would

be all sweetness and light from now on. She was, after all, still a teenager. There'd be battles won and lost. But she'd had a big scare and had finally unburdened herself.

It was a good start.

Grace kissed Tash's cheek. 'Good.'

Tash smiled and then grimaced. 'Ouch.'

'Ankle sore?'

Tash nodded. 'Very.'

Grace rang the call bell and within ten minutes the nurses had administered strong oral pain relief.

'Nod off for a while, Tash,' Grace said, straightening the sheet around her niece, fussing with the covers. 'I'll wait until you fall asleep and then I'll go home and pick up some toiletries and a change of clothes.'

Tash nodded, already closing her eyes. She made a grab for Grace's fingers and Grace was reminded of all the times as a child Tash had greedily monopolised her hand.

But it had never felt as sweet as it did right now.

'Tell me a memory,' she whispered.

Grace glanced at her niece's sleepy face, her heart thudding painfully in her chest, her throat tight with emotion. Grace swallowed the lump and opened her mouth.

'I remember one time when your mum was five and she wanted a skateboard…'

Ten minutes later Tash's fingers had slackened and her breathing was deep and even. Grace sat for another ten minutes just watching her niece sleep. She felt as if an enormous weight had been lifted from her shoulders and that she finally had Tash back.

Conscious of time slipping by, Grace eased her hand away. She had to go home and pick up some of Tash's things. She rose from the chair just as Brent strode into the room.

There was a moment of silence as they looked at each

other. The memory of the on-call room stirred the air between them.

'Hi,' Grace said, her voice husky.

'Hi,' he replied standing in the doorway, hands on hips, before striding into the room. 'I came to see—'

'Shh.' Grace cut him off. She put a finger to her mouth and indicated a sleeping Tash. 'She's just had some pain relief.'

'Oh, sorry,' he said, treading quietly as he came closer to the foot of the bed. 'How's the ankle?' he whispered as he felt for her pedal pulse, his fingers a mere flutter against the bounding vessel.

'Sore.'

He nodded. 'And the head?'

Grace smiled despite her internal tumult. 'I think it's on level pegging with the ankle.'

Brent flicked a glance at her from the end of the bed. 'Are you—?'

'Shh,' Grace chided as Tash stirred. Brent's voice seemed to boom around the room.

Or was that just her crazy heart?

She grabbed his arm and ushered him over to the far corner.

'Sorry,' he apologised.

Grace shrugged. 'Its fine. Let's just keep it low, okay?' His scent surrounded her as he crowded close. She could smell herself on his skin, just as she could smell him on her.

'You look like you've been crying,' he murmured, suppressing the urge to sweep a lock of her fringe back behind her ear. He'd noticed the puffy redness behind her glasses the second he'd laid eyes on her face.

'Oh, yes,' Grace said, touching her face, embarrassed suddenly over her appearance. In eight hours she'd yelled, cried, been scared half to death, thoroughly loved and fallen asleep on a hard, small, plastic chair.

She must look a complete wreck.

Distracted by his cross-armed stance, which emphasised the broadness of his shoulders and chest, Grace looked at her feet.

'Tash and I have been doing a lot of talking. And crying.' Grace gave a quiet half-laugh and then looked at him. 'I think she's going to be okay, Brent.'

She wanted him to know that. Needed him to know. Not that it would make a difference but she knew that he cared about her niece as well.

'I know there's still a long row to hoe. It's not going to be all plain sailing, but we made a real breakthrough.'

Brent could feel her relief, her hope, deep in his soul. He wanted to put his arms around her, place his hands on her shoulders and pull her close. But just because things were changing for Grace on the home front, it didn't mean anything had changed with them.

She'd just said there was still a long row to hoe. And he wasn't going to put his heart on the line again. He could live with unrequited love—he'd done it for ages after she'd left twenty years ago.

He couldn't live with her rejecting him one more time. Even if he understood her motivation.

'That's great,' he said, stuffing his hands into his pockets, keeping his voice low. 'Really great, Grace.'

Grace heard his genuine happiness and beamed at him. 'It's such a relief.'

He smiled. Joy shone in her eyes, sparkling like diamonds in mist from her grey eyes. 'I bet.'

They fell silent then, still looking at each other, their smiles slowly dying as the memories of their passionate encounter reared between them again and the smell of sex heated the air.

Brent sucked in a ragged breath as his body fought a war between two potent forces. Love and desire. If he didn't say something soon he would haul her back into his arms.

Or, worse, tell her he loved her.

He had to distance himself from her, both physically and emotionally. She had to know that what had happened between them in the wee small hours had been an anomaly.

For his own sanity he had to declare his intention of keeping her arm's length.

His old job back at the Royal Melbourne suddenly seemed very attractive. Working with her when sexual attraction had been the only issue had been difficult but doable. But now love was in the equation he didn't think he could see her every day and not eventually go stark, raving mad.

Then she'd probably get his job here, which was what she'd wanted all along.

It would be win-win.

Except he'd be miserable.

He took a small step back from her and cleared his throat. 'About earlier.'

Grace held her breath. His presence was intoxicating and she wanted to reclaim the step he'd taken away.

But *he* had taken the step away.

Could he be any clearer?

'I'm sorry, that was my fault,' she said quickly. 'I was upset… you were just trying to comfort me. I… Let's just forget it, okay? And you know, it's…this attraction thing…it's probably out of our system now, right? It's probably the purge we were meant to have.'

Brent nodded, even though he knew she would never be out of his system. That he would love her, dream about their on-call tryst, for ever. His hands still stuffed deep in his pockets, he rocked back and forth on the balls of his feet.

'Absolutely. I just wanted to check we're both on the same page.'

'Of course,' she rushed to assure him.

Brent felt her eagerness to be done punch him right in the gut.

He had to get away. He couldn't bear being near her, knowing he loved her and she couldn't be his.

'All right. So I'll see you around.'

Grace nodded, just wanting him to go so she could lick her wounds without an audience. Whoever had said that thing about setting love free knew nothing about being a two-time loser in the relationship game.

She watched him turn. Watched his broad shoulders and back retreat, watched his lovely butt sway closer to the door.

And she was stricken with a sudden sense of panic. A feeling that if she let the man that she loved walk out of this room she'd regret it for ever. That if she didn't tell him now, she never would.

She'd told Tash that she couldn't live her life thinking every day was her last. But what if this was *her* last—as Tash had pointed out, no one knew when their time was up.

Would she have regrets?

Damn straight she would.

She'd been so busy telling herself she didn't have time in her life for a man. For another single human being. Making excuses to keep them apart. She'd forgotten what her mother always said.

Love doesn't divide, it multiplies.

Eighteen months ago she'd thought there wasn't room for anyone in her life. But there was. Tash and Benji had fitted right in. Expanded it. Made her better.

How much better would it be with the man she loved?

There *was* room in her life for Brent—her heart was big enough for all of them.

And what kind of a carer would she be to Tash and Benji when so much of her focus would be on losing Brent? She had some tough years ahead and she didn't want to do it alone. Sure, she had her family, but she needed more. Wanted more. She wanted the man she loved by her side, helping her through it all.

But did he love her? Feel anything for her at all? Had she misread the signals the last couple of weeks? And if he did, would he want a part of her insane life?

He was in the doorway when she called out softly, 'Wait.'

Brent stilled, his hands gripped the architrave of the door-frame. His heart was pounding in his chest.

No.

No, no, no.

So close. He was so close to walking away with his secret intact.

Grace took a deep breath. 'I love you.'

Brent stood stock still in the doorway, his back to her, for a few moments.

What?

He was too confused to be elated. Too wary. He turned slowly.

'What did you say?'

Grace almost threw up. His face was so grim, his jaw set so hard she was afraid it was going to shatter.

Oh, God, she'd made a horrible mistake.

But it was out now. And giving voice to those three little words, even knowing there was so many more to come, had lifted an enormous weight.

'I said…I love you.'

She held her hand up quickly, not wanting him to speak until it was all out. Until she'd confessed it all.

'I'm sorry. I know it's not what you want to hear. And I really hadn't planned it. I wasn't going to say anything—truly, I was just going to quietly live with it. But Tash and I have been talking about regrets and I realised as you were walking away that I didn't want you to be my biggest regret.'

Brent shook his head. Had he really heard right? Or had his desperate, love-starved imagination just conjured it up? Was he hallucinating?

Not what he wanted to hear? Was she mad?

'I realised the day of that first footy match but I also knew I'd hurt you too much in the past. That I'd ruined any second chance I had with you. I knew that I'd have to fight for your love and, Brent, I'm sorry, but I'm so over fighting. I've just come out of this battle with Tash…I hope…and I'm too tired to fight with anyone else.'

Brent took a few paces towards her. *She loved him?* 'Grace?'

Grace shook her head. 'No, stop. Don't come any closer. Please. I can't think when you're near me.'

Brent stopped.

'Where was I?'

'You love me,' Brent supplied.

Grace nodded. 'Yes.' She gestured helplessly. 'I'm sorry.'

Brent was silent for a moment then he smiled. The smile turned into a laugh. She loved him and she was sorry? His heart had felt like lead in his chest just moments ago but suddenly it floated as light as air.

She frowned. 'What?'

Brent took a couple more steps towards her. 'Don't be sorry.'

'Why not?' He was smiling and laughing. She was confused, even as a little piece of her heart glowed with hope. 'It's a disaster.'

'No.' He shook his head. 'It would be a disaster if I didn't love you back.'

His words took a moment to sink in and even then she didn't dare hope as she cruelly snuffed out the little flare of light in her chest.

He moved so he was standing right in front of her now. Close. Very close. 'But I do.'

Grace eased the breath out of her lungs. 'You do?'

He nodded. 'I realised just before we made love. It was horrible. I'd spent all these months denying my feelings for you and suddenly it was so clear.'

Grace latched on to the one word she could understand. 'Yes, it is horrible.'

Brent chuckled again. 'No. It's perfect.'

Grace kept the wild leap of her pulse under control. 'But don't you see? It's not as simple as it was twenty years ago, Brent. I come with a lot of added extras. It's never going to be just you and me. And you deserve more than a woman with divided interests. You grew up on crumbs of people's love, you deserve more than that.'

Brent reached for her, put his hands on her waist, hooked his fingers through the loops of her jeans and dragged her hips forward until they were snuggled into his.

'Are you telling me that you're only going to give me crumbs?'

Grace kept her torso erect and as far from his as possible given the closeness of their hips. 'No, of course not.'

God, if she was given the chance she would love this wonderful man with every fibre of her being for all eternity.

'I keep thinking about that thing that Mum always says, you know? That love multiplies. I know I can expand my life to add you into it because I've already done that with the kids. But I think it's a lot to ask you to take on and I know you want kids of your own and I just don't know if that will ever happen. It'll probably just be the four of us. I know you always wanted the perfect family, Brent, and we are far from that. It's not going to be like it was the first time around.'

Brent shook his head. Sometimes this incredibly smart woman could be as dumb as a rock. 'You're my family, Grace. It's always been you. I spent a long time searching for what we had, searching for you in someone else, but I couldn't ever find it. Because it's right here.'

Grace didn't know what to say to that. She felt tears at the back of her eyes and couldn't believe there could actually be any more to shed after the events of the last few hours.

'So what, you guys aren't perfect.' He shrugged. 'I'll take

you however you come, Grace. Families come in all shapes and sizes. I know that better than anyone. Of course it's not going to be like it was,' he said, stroking her cheek. 'It's going to be better.'

He slid a hand up her back and urged her towards him but she resisted. She loved him, the mere thought that this might actually work out hummed through her blood. But she had to be sure he knew what he was letting himself in for.

'Better? A teenage girl and a little boy who will also, I should point out, be a teenager before we know it?'

Before *we* know it. Brent knew he'd won then. 'All they need is love, Grace. I can do that. Just let me. Let me love you. Let me love all of you.'

Grace felt his hand at her back, bringing her closer, and she almost gave in to that knowing look in his tawny gaze but still she resisted. 'My whole crazy, in-your-face, in-your-business family?'

'I love your family.'

Grace felt her heart fighting to be let free. 'Benji wants a puppy,' she said.

Brent leaned in and kissed her neck. 'I love puppies.'

Grace's eyes rolled back in her head as Brent's tongue lapped at the pulse fluttering madly in her neck.

She loved him so much. Could this really be true?

'Gracie,' he whispered in her ear. 'I love you. We'll work the rest out as we go along. Just say yes.'

Grace sighed, letting all her reservations fly free as she melted into his arms.

'Yes.'

SUDDENLY SINGLE SOPHIE

BY
LEONIE KNIGHT

MILLS & BOON®

First published in Great Britain 2011
by Mills & Boon, an imprint of Harlequin (UK) Limited,
Eton House, 18-24 Paradise Road, Richmond, Surrey TW9 1SR

© Leonie Knight 2011

ISBN: 978 0 263 88597 2

Harlequin (UK) policy is to use papers that are natural, renewable
and recyclable products and made from wood grown in sustainable
forests. The logging and manufacturing process conform to the
legal environmental regulations of the country of origin.

Printed and bound in Spain
by Blackprint CPI, Barcelona

Dear Reader

Inspiration for the novels I write sometimes emerges from the unlikeliest of places. The idea for the story of Sophie and Will's bumpy journey along the road to finding love originated from a TV documentary about a rundown, inner-city suburb destined for destruction. It was saved by a courageous and spirited group of people, determined to make better lives for themselves.

To outsiders, the residents of my fictional suburb of Prevely Springs have little hope of ever achieving that elusive *better life*. Will Brent—an overworked, brooding but devoted GP—tries his best to help, but it takes the addition of a bubbly socialite from the other side of the country, with a mission to *make a difference*, Dr Sophie Carmichael, to turn his hopes and dreams into reality and release him from his tortured past.

I wanted to show a community working together to overcome serious and sensitive problems as a backdrop to the unlikely romance between my hero and heroine, and their attempt to overcome their own inner demons. I believe the more difficult the journey, the greater the satisfaction at arriving at the final destination.

I hope you enjoy reading my story about Sophie, Will and the people of Prevely Springs as much as I enjoyed writing it.

Leonie

To my unfailingly supportive husband, Colin,
and my amazing writing friends, Anna, Teena,
Lorraine, Susy and Claire.

Thank you for your faith in me.

PROLOGUE

'YOU'RE better off without him.'

Sophie Carmichael's body-racking sobs began to subside as her best friend Anna put her arm around her shoulder and gave it a reassuring squeeze. Sophie reached for a handful of tissues and noisily blew her nose. Venting her distress in a tearful outburst definitely helped ease the rawness she felt. She took a deep breath and managed a wilted smile.

'I still can't understand how he could be so cold…and two-faced,' Sophie said. 'He didn't even have the courage to tell me to my face.'

'It could have been worse. He might have broken up with you with a text message. Vanessa's boyfriend—'

'I know, I heard. But they'd only been together for two minutes, not nearly two years.' Sophie wiped away the last of her tears and felt her fighting spirit begin to return. It made sense now why Jeremy had stopped pleading with her to move in with him. He apparently wanted a live-in lover, not a wife. And he'd found one—who was now pregnant with his child. She'd wondered if the two of them had planned the whole scenario.

Sophie clenched her teeth, not wanting to believe her ex was capable of such blatant and calculated cheating. She wasn't going to let a two-timing, deceitful rat like her ex-fiancé ruin her life, though.

'Didn't Jeremy make it quite clear he didn't want kids until he'd finished his training and set up in private practice?'

'That's right. And muggins me went along with it.' Sophie slumped back in her seat and sighed. She tried to stand back from her churning emotions and look at the situation objectively. 'You're right, you know. I'm glad I found out about Jeremy's unfaithfulness before we actually tied the knot. I *am* better off without him.'

The women sat in silent contemplation for a minute or two before Anna finally spoke.

'What are you going to do now?'

Sophie had asked herself that same question a hundred times over the past weeks since she'd found out about Jeremy's infidelity by overhearing a conversation at the hospital where he worked. She had naively believed it was purely unfounded gossip. When she'd confronted him, though, he'd not wasted words in telling her the brutal truth. It seemed everyone had known before she had. She'd never felt so humiliated in her life and was grateful the news hadn't spread to the staff of her father's general practice where she worked.

At least she'd been able to choose the time and place to tell her parents—but it hadn't made it any easier. Her father's attitude had left her firstly stunned and then outraged. Ross Carmichael still thought the sun shone from Jeremy's nostrils and seemed to believe they'd get back together again. She couldn't believe he could be so insensitive to *her* feelings. Her mother had hardly disguised her disappointment. She'd often reminded Sophie of her relentlessly ticking biological clock and didn't like the idea of the mob of grandchildren she so dearly wanted being put on hold. Of course Sophie still wanted a family but now, at thirty-one, unceremoniously dumped and unexpectedly single, she was in no hurry.

'I really don't know. I haven't had a chance to think about it but one thing I do know for sure.'

'And what's that?' Anna was stroking Sophie's cat, which had jumped up on her lap, probably sensing the calmer of the two women was Anna.

'I'm going to steer clear of men for a while.'

Anna smiled. 'They're not all rotten, you know.'

'I didn't say they were, but—'

'You need a break. I can understand that. It's early days.'

Max, Sophie's Burmese bundle of masculine feline charm, gracefully stretched, began purring loudly and rubbed his chin on Anna's thigh, as if defending the male of the species.

'Maybe you need a holiday,' Anna continued.

'A permanent holiday.' Sophie suddenly realised what she really needed was a working holiday; a complete break from her predictable life. She'd always had her father, or Jeremy, or the expectations of the high-flying social set she moved in to make the big life decisions for her. Or at least nudge her in a certain direction. It hadn't bothered her in the past, but now… She felt manipulated, controlled and wanted a taste of freedom. If she made mistakes, at least they would be her own.

'I might look at leaving Sydney for a while, maybe head north.' She paused and felt her heart pumping faster. It was a lightbulb moment and made a great deal of sense. She would only stagnate in her father's practice and was tired of listening to the woes of the affluent, worried well-to-do. She remembered when, as an enthusiastic new graduate, she'd wanted her work to make a real difference to her patients' lives. There was little chance of that happening if she stayed where she was. Her mind started to work in overdrive.

'Or even west. I've heard there's a shortage of GPs over in Perth.'

Anna looked only mildly surprised, as if she'd been expecting it.

'Well, good for you, Dr Sophie.' She lifted Max from her lap and dumped the protesting cat on the floor then added, 'How about we open that bottle of wine I brought?'

'Great idea. And I'll see if I can rustle up some comfort food,' Sophie said with a grin. She felt renewed, ready to take on whatever challenges life presented.

While Anna uncorked the Chardonnay, Sophie loaded generous serves of chocolate cheesecake on plates.

When they sat down again, Anna raised her glass.

'To your new life,' she said as they clinked glasses.

'Without the complication of men,' Sophie added.

CHAPTER ONE

'She's here. Come and have a look,' Caitlyn called from the tea room.

Dr William Brent didn't share his young receptionist's excitement at what he presumed was the arrival of the new doctor. It was barely twenty minutes since the last patient had left. Saturday morning clinics were supposed to finish at midday and today he'd particularly wanted to run to schedule. But it was already after two o'clock, the time he'd planned to meet Dr Sophie Carmichael.

She was late. Not an ideal start.

He was a busy man and didn't have spare time to waste on waiting. He had a house call after the interview and a meeting with a builder scheduled for mid-afternoon.

He dismissed his annoyance in the name of an urgent need for an assistant and hoped Caitlyn was right.

Sophie Carmichael's phone call, just over a month ago, had come at the right time and he'd invested a considerable amount of energy in getting the well-qualified Sydney doctor to relocate, even if it turned out to be for only a couple of months.

'Quick, you've got to see this, Dr Brent.' Caitlyn stood in the doorway to his office with a broad grin on her face and Will couldn't help but feel a sense of foreboding.

Why was Caitlyn so excited and, worse, why was she grinning?

He followed her down the short corridor to the tea room and peered through the small, grubby window.

'Oh, my God!' The words escaped before Will had time to check them and now he understood why his young receptionist was so insistent he have an advanced viewing.

Will glanced at Caitlyn, who was still grinning, but couldn't stop his eyes returning to the new arrival. His heart dropped. She was driving a nippy little sports car. He didn't usually trust first impressions but had the gut feeling this stern-faced young woman, whom he could see clearly in the open-topped vehicle, would be as at home in his practice as caviar at a sausage sizzle.

But he was truly desperate.

Working twelve-hour days, being on call weekends and after hours, as well as trying to find time to get his plans for the community centre off the ground was wearing him down to near breaking point. There just weren't enough hours in the day.

He had to keep an open mind.

'If that's the new doc, I hope she's better at fixing sick people than she is at parking her car,' Caitlyn said.

Will squinted through the dirty glass, watching the wine-red cabriolet being manoeuvred into a space that was way too small.

'Ouch.' He felt the scrape of metal on metal as the front-end passenger side didn't quite clear the carport post. If she was the new doctor, and Will had no reason to think otherwise, it was definitely not a good start to their working relationship.

But the show wasn't over.

The woman seemed to be having problems unfolding the roof to secure the vehicle. She huddled over the dash and first the windscreen wipers activated then the hazard lights flashed before the roof finally jerked into place. She abandoned the car and squeezed her petite frame into the gap between her fancy sports car and Will's elderly, slightly battered station wagon. She was in shadow so Will could no longer see her face, but her body language clearly conveyed frustration and anger. He was fascinated. Mesmerised, even.

'Look what she's wearing.' Caitlyn was obviously enjoying the spectacle but her tip-off was unnecessary. How could anyone *not* notice the woman's outfit? It was so out of place for a meeting, no matter how informal, with her new employer. She wouldn't last five minutes in this neighbourhood decked out in low-slung, skin-tight black jeans with lolly-pink high-heeled sandals and a top that was body-hugging, and exposing more skin than…

'Whoops. She's seen us.' The girl's attempt to duck away from the window wasn't quick enough, but at least she'd tried to look discreet. Will suddenly realised his jaw was gaping and he snapped his mouth shut the moment the woman's blazing eyes met his. But he couldn't take his eyes off her. He could see her more clearly now and there was something about the determined thrust of her jaw and the resolute expression on her fine-featured face that captivated him.

It didn't take her long to compose herself, though. She smiled and waved as she hoisted a large bag over her shoulder and headed towards the back staff entrance.

'I'll put the kettle on, then?' At least Caitlyn was thinking sensibly. He needed a coffee.

'Good idea. I'll go and meet her.'

He took a couple of deep breaths, ran his fingers through his too-long hair and smiled as he opened the back door.

Sophie Carmichael had finally arrived at the Prevely Springs Medical Clinic. She was tired, frustrated and wondering if she'd made a huge mistake. Not sleeping the previous night, coupled with an inconvenient run of bad luck, hadn't helped. She felt like getting on the first flight back to Sydney.

The move to Western Australia was supposed to be about taking control of her life but obstacles had appeared at every turn. She should have arrived in Perth in plenty of time to make it to the hotel she'd booked for the night. She'd planned to at least get a few hours' sleep and then shower and change before her interview.

But the best-laid plans…

Firstly her plane had been delayed and she'd been forced to sit in the airport lounge for most of the night. Then, on her arrival in Perth, she'd discovered her luggage had been lost. Now she was fifteen minutes late for her meeting with her future employer because the airport taxi driver had taken her to the wrong rail depot to pick up her car…the beautiful, brand-new sports car she'd bought only a week ago as a symbol of her new-found freedom. Which now had an ugly gouge down one side due to a momentary lapse of concentration.

She tried to focus on the positives.

She'd never been a quitter.

Leaving home hadn't been a mistake.

She wasn't running away from her problems, just taking a break to regroup.

Her objective while in Perth was to work, and learn, and prove to herself she wasn't afraid of leaping out of her comfort zone into the wild unknown.

She also planned to show her toad of a fiancé that she was quite capable of fulfilment…and independence…and happiness…without him.

She scowled.

Jeremy…her fiancé… Not any more.

It hadn't taken as much courage as she'd thought to relocate to the other side of the country, even if it was only for a couple of months. The last thing she needed was a holiday with endless empty time on her hands—work was definitely the answer, and work on the other side of the country was perfect. She needed time out without having to deal with the tattered remnants of her life; without the distraction of the opposite sex; without having to get approval for everything she did from her father or Jeremy.

'Things can't possibly get any worse,' she muttered as she locked the car. She glanced at the single visible window and caught a glimpse of two curious faces not quite pressed against the glass. One was a teenage girl and the other...

She instantly forgot her troubles.

The dark-haired man was half smiling, and even through the grubby glass she could see he was...absolutely gorgeous.

He waved and then ducked away from the window as if he'd been caught in the act of being nosy.

Then he reappeared.

When she saw him standing in the doorway, all mussed-up hair, baggy clothes and brooding dark, black-brown eyes, she *knew* she'd made the right decision in leaving Sydney.

If this man was Dr Brent, it would be no hardship to work with him but she'd have to be careful. He was too damned attractive for his own good and she'd bet her last dollar he had no idea he had all the attributes to turn women's heads.

Slinging her bag on her shoulder, she strode towards the ramp leading up to the back entrance. She still couldn't rationalise the preconceived image she'd conjured up of Dr Brent, with the man standing in the doorway.

On the phone he'd come across as kind, conservative, passionate about his job and desperate for a second GP to share his increasing patient load. He'd also sounded...weary.

She'd thought he'd be middle-aged and suspected he might be looking for someone young and fresh to share the patient load at the practice, if the wording in his ad in the widely read *Australian General Practice* magazine was anything to go by. He'd really wanted someone who was prepared to commit long term, with a view to partnership.

But it appeared that type of candidate was thin on the ground and she definitely wasn't that person either. She had no illusions that her escape from her failed relationship and the gossip of Sydney's heartless, egocentric socialites was anything but temporary. She just needed time to heal.

Sophie was totally realistic about her future. She had solid reasons to return to the city she loved. All her friends were in Sydney; she owned a beachside apartment at Collaroy she didn't want to give up; and had adopted a feisty feline named Max that she couldn't leave in her friend Anna's care for ever. She planned to go home as soon as the fallout from her broken relationship settled, and she'd made sure Dr Brent knew she wasn't planning on staying permanently.

And the reality of this man standing in the doorway had just made her decision to have a break much easier.

Could this seriously good-looking hunk possibly be her new boss?

She was about to find out.

For a moment Will Brent was spellbound by the woman's penetrating china-blue eyes, fascinated by the tilt of her cute, lightly freckled nose, captivated by her hesitant smile.

'I'm Will Brent and I assume you're Dr Carmichael. Can I take your bag?' he asked as he extended his hand in greeting.

She offered hers and it felt cool, soft and damp. Was she nervous?

'Yes. Please, call me Sophie, and, no, thanks. I'll be fine.'

'Come in,' he said in what he hoped was a welcoming tone.

She repositioned the bag on her shoulder as she stepped from the short ramp into the building. He suspected she could be just what the practice needed. So if her first impression of Prevely Springs Medical Clinic was to go as smoothly as he'd planned, he'd have to remain totally objective, professional... look beyond the attractively packaged woman standing on his threshold.

Attractive didn't mean dependable. It meant the pain of betrayal; it meant shallow; it meant priorities very different from his. What twisted lapse of judgement had let him fall in love all those years ago?

Will did a quick reality check.

He had no right to prejudge or compare.

Sophie Carmichael was simply a colleague, who happened to be beautiful.

And he mustn't think of her in any other way.

There was no way he could burden *any* woman with his problems. He still felt the hurt and disappointment of his past and the weight of the emotional debt he was struggling to pay. He had *chosen* to lead a solitary life in the rough inner-city suburb he'd grown up in. And he'd made a promise, nearly twenty years ago, to stay and in some way give back to this community.

Love, marriage, children… The fantasy just didn't fit with the dark reality of his life.

He'd caused the two people he'd loved most in the world so much anguish. There wasn't a day went by when his heart didn't fill with regret for those angry, irresponsible teenage years that had shaped his future. His devotion to his practice and the salt-of-the-earth people in the Springs was the only way he knew to repay his grandparents, and he often lamented that they weren't alive to witness his achievements.

He'd only recently admitted, though, that he needed help to keep going. The long hours he worked, being on call weekends and after hours, was wearing him down to near breaking point. He had high hopes for the woman standing in front of him.

Releasing Sophie's fingers from his grip, he did a lightning rethink of where he could conduct the interview but came to the conclusion every room in the building was in a similar state of disarray to his own.

Better the mess you know…

Usually it wouldn't bother him but he felt an unsettling compulsion to make a good impression and wished he'd chosen something more stylish to wear than his crumpled khaki chinos and faded short-sleeved checked shirt. But she'd find out soon enough that tidiness and fashion weren't high on his priority list.

He cleared his throat in an attempt to take his mind off Sophie Carmichael's creamy smooth shoulders and the soft curve of her neck. Somehow the inappropriateness of her attire didn't seem so important any more.

'We'll go down to my consulting room. It's the second door on the right,' Will said in a voice he hardly recognised.

She followed him down to his room and he stepped back to let her in first. Glancing around the cluttered office, he wondered if the hint of a frown on her face was due to disapproval. She was probably used to working in much more luxurious surroundings and he hoped she wouldn't be put off.

'Please, sit down.'

She sat in one of the patient chairs, legs crossed, hands resting in her lap, and he wondered what she was thinking. He'd done his best to prepare her.

The couple of times he'd talked to her on the phone he'd been totally honest with her, revealing Prevely Springs was an underprivileged area. But he'd told her the work was challenging and potentially rewarding. To her credit, she'd still seemed keen. Her agreement to commit to even a few weeks with him had rekindled a light at the end of what had recently become a very long, dark tunnel.

He didn't want her to change her mind.

'I've been looking forward to meeting you. Your CV was impressive, your references excellent.' He sent her what he hoped was an encouraging smile.

'Thanks,' she said.

Her credentials were almost too good to be true. But the phone conversation he'd had with her two days ago had allayed his concerns that the inevitable culture shock would be an obstacle for her.

She cleared her throat and Will wondered if the colour in her previously pale cheeks was a reaction to his praise.

'I…er…' She looked away as if composing her thoughts. *Was* she having second thoughts?

He knew she had a privileged background. She'd been educated at one of the most expensive ladies' colleges and graduated from medical school with top marks. He suspected her life choices had been easy and uncomplicated. He *had* wondered at her motivation in wanting to work in a practice so different to what she was used to.

She came from a medical family. Her father was a well-known and highly regarded GP in Sydney and Sophie had worked in his practice for the past two years. It had surprised Will that Dr Ross Carmichael had telephoned him a week ago and, in a roundabout way, had seemed to be checking *his* credentials. Will, in fact, had been annoyed at some of his questions and the cross-examination had struck him as being a little beyond normal protective paternal behaviour. Sophie seemed like someone who could look after herself quite capably.

He dragged his mind back to the task in hand. Sophie looked uncomfortable.

'I, um, owe you an apology.'

Now, that was something he hadn't expected.

A lock of Sophie's thick red-brown hair escaped from the clasp holding it in place, and as she tucked it behind her ear Will noticed an almost imperceptible tremor in her fingers

'An apology?'

She folded her arms across her chest.

'You must be wondering why I'm dressed like this.'

Yes, of course he was, but he didn't want to draw attention to her relaxed dress code. Well, not until he'd confirmed her commitment.

'I take it you're planning to wear something a little more conservative…' *less provocative* was another description that came to mind '…to work.'

Rosy colour swept into her neck and flooded her face.

'I'm sorry,' Will said, although he wasn't quite sure what he'd done to make her blush.

She took a deep breath.

'My plane was delayed so I didn't get here until this morning. Then it took another hour and a half for the airline to verify that my luggage had been mislaid. And the taxi driver who drove me to Wellesley to collect my car hardly spoke a word of English. So even if I'd had time to change—'

He'd heard enough, and doubted she could fabricate such an elaborate combination of misadventures. He understood why she had faint dark shadows under her eyes. She most likely needed rest rather than a grilling from him.

'Ah…I see. You've not had the best introduction to the west. You must be exhausted.' He thought of a dozen questions he wanted to ask but they would just have to wait. After all, he'd told her on the phone the job was hers and all he needed to do was discuss her duties, finalise her hours and sort out the paperwork.

'The interview is a formality, really. It's basically so we can introduce ourselves. You can ask me any questions about the work, the practice, anything you'd like to know, before you start next week.'

She leaned towards him, interlocked her fingers and placed her hands on his desk. The pose struck him as being assertive without being arrogant. Her anxiety seemed to have vanished.

Maybe she would be okay dealing with some of the rougher elements that were inevitably part of his practice.

'I'm looking forward to it,' she said. 'I haven't got any questions.'

'Great.' The interview was going well but there was one more thing he had to discuss and he didn't want to put pressure on her. 'We haven't talked about how long you're prepared to work here. I realise you're not planning on staying long term, but even a few weeks will be a great help to me.' He thought of the long-lost luxury of spare time. 'Does a period of six to eight weeks sound agreeable?' That would let him at least get the ball rolling with a time-consuming task he wasn't looking forward to—organising fundraising for the community centre. 'With the option of staying longer, of course.' He sent her what he hoped was a charismatic smile.

'That would suit me fine,' she said with a look that suggested relief.

At that moment Caitlyn appeared, cheerful as ever, with two steaming cups and a plate of biscuits.

'Thanks, Caitlyn.'

'That's okay, Dr Brent.' The girl cleared a space on Will's desk by pushing a jumble of referral pads to one side. She set down the cups.

'No problem. Have a good weekend.' She paused. 'Oh, and you told me to remind you about the home visit to Mrs Farris.'

'Thanks, I hadn't forgotten. See you next week.'

Six weeks was perfect, Sophie thought as she reached for one of the mugs filled with coffee she now felt sufficiently relaxed to drink. It was long enough to make her father understand she wasn't going to run back home after a week or two. She also thought of Jeremy and reminded herself she wanted to get as far away from him and his new girlfriend as possible, at least until the gossip died down.

And then she thought of Will Brent. How easy it was to like and admire him. She suspected he was close to burn-out and hoped she could give him the break he deserved. She felt certain she could learn a lot from him.

'Would you like a biscuit?' Will Brent's voice snapped her out of her reverie, but before she had a chance to reply there was a loud thumping on the front door.

'Is anyone there?' A man's voice boomed loud and urgent. 'Doc Brent, I need a doctor quick!'

There was no doubt about the genuine distress he conveyed and Will was out of his seat in an instant. He grabbed a large bunch of keys from a desk drawer, glanced briefly at Sophie with an expression that invited her to follow and headed towards the front of the building.

Through the frosted glass panels of the door Sophie could make out the dark shape of a man who appeared to be carrying a child.

Will opened the door and a stocky man wearing full football kit, including boots, stumbled in. A boy of about four or five, dressed in an almost identical outfit, lay limp and wheezing in his arms.

'Thank God you're still here.'

The child opened his eyes but barely had the energy to whimper as Will took him gently from the man Sophie assumed was his father.

'How long's he been like this, Steve?' Will voiced his first question with just the right mix of authority and empathy. He obviously knew the pair and was leading them past the reception desk into a well-equipped treatment room. He laid the child down, adjusted the examination couch so the boy was sitting and placed an oximeter on his finger.

'No more than fifteen minutes. Jake was with me mates at the oval, watching the game, and they called me off the field.' The man pulled down his son's sock to reveal an angry red swelling just above his ankle. Sophie could see similar, smaller lesions on his arms.

'Bee sting,' he added, as if that explained everything. 'We know he's allergic, but the worst he's had in the past has been a rash.' He took a sharp intake of breath. 'He's never been this bad. It came on real quick. He can hardly breathe. We were going to the hospital but I saw your car—'

Steve was close to tears and began hyperventilating.

The last thing they needed in a situation where the boy

should command Will's full attention was to have to deal with the father's panic attack as well.

Sophie felt her own tension climbing. The child was barely conscious and his breathing was becoming more laboured as each second passed. Will appeared remarkably calm.

'Sit down, Steve,' Will said coolly but firmly. 'Jake's going to be fine but I need to check him over.' He glanced in Sophie's direction. 'Can you organise a paediatric mask with high-flow oxygen?' He pointed to an emergency trolley next to an oxygen cylinder. Everything—medications, procedure packs, resuscitation equipment—was all labelled clearly and easy to find. 'And draw up…' He paused for a moment, calculating the crucial dose of lifesaving medication based on the boy's estimated weight. 'Point two of adrenaline for intramuscular injection.'

'Do you want nebulised adrenaline as well?' Sophie asked, trying to think ahead. She'd rarely treated emergencies in her father's practice but remembered the protocol from her hospital work. 'And an IV set?' she added as she positioned the mask on Jake's pale little face.

Will nodded. He worked incredibly quickly but gave the impression he was taking one quiet step at a time. Sophie drew up the medication, double-checked the dose and handed it to Will, who jabbed the needle into the boy's upper thigh so rapidly he hardly had time to respond. She could feel the tension decreasing in the room at about the same rate as the dusky grey colour in Jake's swollen lips began to turn the lightest shade of pink.

Will looked at the small device that measured oxygen levels in the blood. 'Ninety-four per cent,' he said as he placed a stethoscope on the little boy's chest and then checked his airway. The wheezing eased a little, but the movement of the muscles in Jake's abdomen and neck suggested he still had to work hard to get air in and out. Fortunately the risk of his larynx closing over completely had passed.

Will inserted an IV line while Sophie set up the nebuliser

and together they stabilised the five-year-old to the point where Will had time to talk to Steve. He pulled up a chair opposite him.

'Jake's over the worst, Steve, but he's not out of the woods yet. He needs monitoring in hospital and I'm going to call an ambulance. He also needs blood tests and will probably go home with an EpiPen, possibly an asthma puffer as well. Do you know what an EpiPen is?'

'Yeah, I think you told us about it the first time Jake was stung. It's the injection you keep with you all the time, isn't it?'

'That's right.'

'Do you want me to ring the ambulance?' Sophie offered.

'Thanks, the local number is on the wall above the phone,' Will said with a grateful smile. 'I'll put the kettle on.'

A short time later, while the adults sat drinking coffee, crisis over, waiting for the ambulance, Jake slowly and steadily improved. Sophie marvelled at how composed Will was as he chatted to Steve.

'Daddy,' Jake said suddenly in a clear, loud voice as he pulled off the mask and frowned. All eyes turned towards him.

'What's the matter?' Steve said, a look of panic returning to his face.

'That goal you kicked…just before three-quarter time.'

The adults exchanged glances and Steve smiled for the first time since he'd arrived.

'Yeah, what about it?'

'It was awesome.'

Steve grinned with obvious pride and Will chuckled.

'You think so?'

Jake took a couple of rapid breaths as he raised his hand for a high five with his father. 'The best.'

The ambulance arrived a few minutes later and after it had left with its two passengers, Will turned to Sophie.

'That was an impromptu example of general practice in Prevely Springs. Think you can handle it?'

Coping with the work wasn't a problem for Sophie. She was looking forward to the challenge. The predicament she faced was how she was going uphold her promise, the vow she'd confidently uttered when she and her best friend had made a toast to her new life...*without the complication of men.*

She had the feeling it wasn't going to be easy.

'I'll give it my best shot,' she said.

CHAPTER TWO

AFTER the ambulance left, Sophie experienced a satisfaction she hadn't felt since working in the emergency department as a raw, idealistic intern. She had no doubt in her mind that Will had, calmly, without fuss or wanting any praise, saved young Jake's life.

And she had been part of it.

'Do you deal with many emergencies?' she asked as she brought two mugs of fresh coffee into the treatment room where Will was tidying up.

He took one of the mugs and smiled.

'About one or two a week.'

'Across the full spectrum?'

Sophie perched herself on the examination couch and Will sat in the seat recently vacated by Jake's father.

'Pretty well. There's probably more than the norm of physical violence, drug overdoses, that kind of thing. The clinic operates a little like a country outpost, without the problem of distance and isolation. I do my best to stabilise patients who need hospital care before sending them on.'

Sophie thought of how different it was from her father's practice.

'Where I worked in Sydney, the patients are more likely to ring the ambulance first in life-threatening situations... To save time.'

Will's dark eyes clouded and he looked past Sophie into the distance before he refocused.

'A lot of my patients have had bad experiences with hospitals, and doctors who don't know them. And I don't blame the hospital staff making judgements on appearances. We all do it...'

The appraisal took only a second or two but Sophie felt Will's gaze flick from her high-heel-clad feet to the top of her tousled head, taking in everything in between. She suddenly became self-conscious about *her* appearance and the impression she'd made when he'd first seen her.

Before Sophie could think of a reply, Will had downed the last of his coffee and stood, stuffing his stethoscope into his pocket. He looked impatient to leave.

'I'll take you round to the flat. It's nothing flash but is clean, has the basics and is about twenty minutes' drive from here.'

Will's sudden change of subject didn't go unnoticed by Sophie, and she guessed her boss was just as tired as she was.

'Not in Prevely Springs?' She'd assumed she'd be staying closer to Will's clinic.

'No, Sabiston's the name of the suburb. I thought...' He hesitated.

'Yes? You thought?'

'It's a more...upmarket suburb than the Springs.'

More like what she was used to...

He smiled, a fleeting indication that he genuinely cared about her welfare, and it occurred to her how easily she could fall for this gentle, softly spoken, work-weary man. He was everything her cocky, self-absorbed ex wasn't.

No! Get a grip of yourself.

She hardly knew the man and it was way too soon. The painful sting of shame was still fresh in her memory and she didn't want to risk going through the indignity again.

'Don't worry, I'll manage,' Sophie said.

'I hope so.' He took his keys from his pocket. 'There's just one thing more, before we go to the flat.'

'Yes?'

'I need to make a quick house call. A woman with pancreatic cancer. I'm sure it won't take long. She only lives around the corner.'

Another surprise. Will did house calls…after hours…on top of what she calculated to be more than a sixty-hour working week.

'You'll like Bella Farris,' he added.

'And…well…the sooner I start, the harder it will be to chicken out.'

Sophie was determined to prove to her new employer she was prepared to tackle working in Prevely Springs head on.

Will knocked on the door of the tidiest townhouse in a shabby block of six and went straight inside without waiting for an answer. Sophie followed close behind, scanning the interior as she entered. The front door opened directly into a cramped living-dining area with a kitchen at the back. A boy of about thirteen or fourteen sat in front of a television screen connected to a games machine. He was overweight, pale, and his eyes didn't leave the screen. A couple of empty fast-food containers lay abandoned on the floor beside him.

'Hi, Brad. Is your mum upstairs in the bedroom?' Will's tone was cheerful and undemanding.

'Yeah.'

'How is she?'

'Same.' The boy's gaze left the screen, flicked to Will, hovered on Sophie for a second and then returned to the noisy, animated action on the screen. 'Aw, hell!' the boy added when some bloody tragedy terminated another of his virtual lives.

'Dr Carmichael and I will go up and see her, then.'

'Mmm.'

Sophie followed Will up the narrow concrete stairs, vestiges of mud-brown fibres the only indication they had once been carpeted.

'Bella, it's Will,' he called as he reached the dimly lit passage at the top of the stairs.

'In the bedroom.' The thin voice came from the only upstairs room with the door open. 'Come through.'

Sophie followed Will into a sparsely furnished room with a single small window overlooking a weedy back yard.

This family was struggling in more ways than one, Sophie thought as she smiled and nodded, acknowledging the woman propped up in a narrow bed near the window. Her spindle-like arms protruded from the bed cover and rested on her swollen abdomen. Her sighing breaths came irregularly.

'You've finally brought your girlfriend to meet me, have you, Dr Brent? About time too.' The woman smiled and a hint of colour advanced then rapidly retreated from Will's cheeks. She looked at Sophie and took a couple of deep breaths. Even talking appeared to be an effort for her. 'I told Will I wasn't going to leave this earth until he found a woman to replace me. He needs looking after.'

'Enough of your cheek, Bella.' Will put his medical bag down on the small table in a corner and sat on the end of her bed. 'This isn't my girlfriend. And you know that threat isn't going to work because you're not ready yet. Remember our little chat last week?'

He glanced over at Sophie, who was beginning to feel she was intruding in the relationship between these two people who were as close as a doctor and patient could be. Bella smiled with her eyes but her mouth remained in a grim line, suggesting she was in more pain than she let on.

'Who is she, then?'

'Dr Sophie Carmichael. She arrived this morning from Sydney to join the practice for a few weeks. Do you mind her sitting in?'

A look of disbelief flashed across Bella's face, as if the last thing she'd expected was for Sophie to be a doctor.

'Well, good for you, Sophie Carmichael.' She turned her head slightly to address Will. 'Of course I don't mind. Two heads are better than one.' She made a move to reposition herself on the pile of pillows behind her head, then grimaced and seemed to change her mind. 'You make sure you look after her and she might even stay more than a few weeks.' She turned to Sophie. 'Once you get to know him, he's not as bad as—'

'Enough, Bella. This isn't a social visit.'

Bella fixed her gaze back on Will and elevated an eyebrow. 'Of course not.'

'So what's been happening? How can I help?'

'Shelley insisted on calling you just to check. She thinks it's a blockage. I've not had a bowel movement for four days and I've got a new pain.' She pointed in the vague direction of her navel. 'And the nausea's a bit worse.'

Will got up and retrieved a file from the table where he'd left his bag and then returned to Bella's bedside. He looked across at Sophie. 'Shelley's one of the palliative care nurses.' He turned a couple of pages of the file Sophie assumed contained the nurse's notes. 'Your morphine dose has gone up in the last few days.'

'I vomited a couple of doses of the liquid yesterday and had to increase my night-time tablet.'

'What are you eating?'

'Not much.'

'How about fluids?' Will didn't labour the point.

'I'm keeping down a bit of water.'

Sophie admired Bella's uncomplaining courage, and as she watched Will examine his patient with large, gentle hands she felt admiration for him too.

'Well, what's the verdict?' Bella said when he'd finally finished. 'No beating around the bush.'

'I'm fairly sure the tumour is pressing on part of your intestine, causing a partial blockage.'

'What does that mean?'

'It means your food and drinks are passing through very slowly. It's probably why your pain and nausea are worse.'

'Oh.'

Sophie could see the stoic acceptance on Bella's face. She seemed to sense she didn't have long to live and trusted Will to do what he felt was best to make her last few weeks comfortable.

'I'll contact Shelley and ask her to organise for you to have your morphine by injection.' He went on to explain the device that would deliver a steady dose of the analgesic via a needle inserted into the fatty layer under the skin and a gadget called a syringe driver. It would overcome her problem of vomiting oral medication. 'One of the nurses reloads the medication daily. We can also mix in other drugs if needed, like an anti-emetic for nausea.'

Bella looked exhausted. 'Shelley said she'd come back this afternoon after you'd been.'

'Good. She can set up the pump. I'll also ask her to collect some dexamethasone from the pharmacy. If there's any swelling due to inflammation in the intestine, it should reduce it and might ease the blockage. It should help with the nausea too.'

'Okay. Best you two get on with enjoying the rest of your weekend.' Bella seemed to muster a last ounce of energy to wink and then she closed her eyes and sighed. 'Go on, then.'

Will and Sophie exchanged glances.

'I'll call in again Monday, Bella.'

The patient was breathing slowly. She appeared to be asleep, so the two doctors quietly left the room. Will made a quick phone call to Shelley before they went downstairs.

'Bye, Brad,' Sophie called as they let themselves out the front door.

The boy acknowledged their departure with a grunt and continued his game.

'How is Brad coping with his mother's illness?' Sophie asked as she buckled her seat belt in the passenger seat of Will's roomy old car.

'I don't think he is.' Will sighed and started the engine. 'I've tried to talk to him but he seems to have shut everyone out—including his mother. Bella worried about him at the beginning of her illness—she was diagnosed with cancer a week after Brad's fourteenth birthday—but she doesn't talk about him now. I think it upsets her that she can't give him the support she wishes she could. She told me a while back she'd run out of emotional energy.'

A painful mix of sadness and helplessness churned in Sophie's gut. The combination of poverty, illness and social isolation had delivered a cruel blow to this family. It wasn't fair.

'Isn't there anything more that can be done for Bella?'

'What do you mean?' Will frowned.

'She needs twenty-four-hour care… It's not fair on her son. There must be somewhere like a hospice… In Sydney—'

Will's grimace deepened.

'We're not in Sydney.'

Her boss seemed to want to wind up the conversation, but Sophie was determined to have her say.

'Isn't there residential care for the terminally ill here?'

Will began to back out into the street but braked at the kerb as a car sped past, the young driver going way too fast. He put the gearstick in neutral, wrenched the handbrake on and took a deep sighing breath.

'I wish there was…for patients like Bella.' Will's voice was thick with emotion. 'Do you think I don't know that Bella, and hundreds of people like her, deserve pampering and dignity in their last days? Or at least to have the choice of where and how they die. Particularly those who have little in the way of family support.' He paused. 'But who pays?'

Sophie looked away and began fiddling with her watch band.

'The government?' she suggested quietly.

Point made. Sophie felt foolish, naive and totally put in her place.

The hospice she was familiar with was a private facility attached to one of the major private hospitals, paid for by wealthy patients and their health insurance funds.

Will put the car in gear, released the handbrake and looked in the rear-view mirror but he didn't start reversing. He hadn't finished.

'The only government-funded hospice in this city is always full and is basically a converted wing of an old, now-defunct psychiatric hospital. And palliative care seems to be way down the list of priorities for Heath Department funding. I honestly think Bella is better off staying at home. At least for now.'

Will eased the car onto the road.

'She has access to twenty-four-hour advice, home visits through the palliative care service, and both she and Brad have chosen the home-care option.'

Will accelerated.

Sophie understood his frustration. She had a lot to learn—not only about working in Prevely Springs but about how much of himself he gave to his patients. She glanced at her companion. He had dark rings under his weary eyes and his tense grip on the steering-wheel indicated he wasn't as relaxed as his tone suggested.

What drove him to work so hard? As an experienced GP, surely he could choose a less demanding job. No one was indispensable.

But looking at Will… He seemed attached to his work and his patients by steadfastly unyielding Superglue.

Maybe she could be the one to ease his burden, to help him

discover that there was a life away from work, to bring on that gorgeous smile she'd seen light up his face at least once that afternoon.

Purely as a friend, of course.

As if sensing Sophie was watching him, Will glanced at her as he slowed, approaching a corner.

'What's up?' he said, crinkling his brow in a frown.

Nothing that your amazing smile won't fix.

'I'm concerned about Brad.' Which she had been before she'd become distracted by the enigmatic man sitting next to her. She continued. 'What sort of life does he lead? What's in store for him in the future?' She paused to take a breath, aware she had Will's full attention. 'How can a fourteen-year-old shoulder the responsibility of being the primary carer for his mother? It should be the other way around.'

Will accelerated around the corner and Sophie recognised the street where the clinic was located. 'All valid concerns.' He sighed as if the weight of the whole world's problems rested on his shoulders. 'He seems to have shut the real world out and replaced it with a virtual one, I'm afraid. I'm at a loss as to how to help him.'

'Would it be okay with you if I tried to talk to Brad?' Sophie knew it was an impulsive offer, and any support she gave would be a drop in the ocean compared to the Farrises' hardship, but the boy seemed so isolated and withdrawn. She wanted to do something positive for Brad and Bella.

'You'd have nothing to lose because I've got little to offer him at the moment.' Will looked almost as weary as Bella. 'Maybe twelve or eighteen months down the track…'

His voice trailed off, as if he'd started a conversation he didn't want to finish, but Sophie was interested.

'What do you mean?'

'It's a long story.'

'I'm not in a hurry.'

He rewarded her with another of those charismatic smiles, apparently surprised she was interested.

'I'm in the process of trying to get a youth-focused community centre up and running.' Will parked on the road, a block away from the clinic. 'See, over there?'

Sophie looked in the direction he was pointing. On the far side of a sports field a building of about the same vintage as the clinic stood neglected at the end of a weedy driveway. Several windows were broken and the parts of a low front wall that weren't hidden by metre-high weeds were covered in graffiti. It had a chain-link fence around it, displaying a 'DANGER KEEP OUT' sign.

'Looks like it's ready for demolition.'

Will's scowl suggested he didn't agree.

'That's exactly what the council wants, but they haven't got the resources to replace it. Since they closed the place down about a year ago they took away the one place local kids, like Brad and his mates, could hang out without getting bored and up to mischief. But if it's up to bureaucracy, it's unlikely to happen.'

Will tapped his fingers on the steering-wheel and for the briefest moment he looked desolate. Why was finding the fate of a rundown old building so painful?

'So what's going to happen to it?'

'I'm trying to save it.'

'How?' Will was a man who seemed to have an insatiable need to take on projects that most people would discard into the too-hard basket. Surely he had enough to do, looking after the health needs of Prevely Springs, without taking on their social problems.

Will revved the engine and pulled out onto the road.

'The cost of renovating and refurbishing is much less than a new build, especially if the skills of local people could be utilised. I've submitted a plan to the council and...' His sigh suggested he wasn't overjoyed with their response. He focused his attention on traffic as he indicated to turn into the clinic.

'And…?'

He parked and turned off the engine.

'To cut a long story short, they wanted detailed plans and costing to present to the building committee and if they approve it goes to a general meeting. But—'

'Go on.'

'The wheels of local government turn slowly. It's unbelievably frustrating. Three months down the track, I'm still waiting for approval. But what's turning out to be a bigger problem is that the planning department tells me I'm going to have to show the community can raise funds for half the cost of renovating a very old building that the council think is only fit for demolition.'

'Before they give approval?'

'That's right.' The smile was gone and Will looked despondent.

'So it's not going to be a help for Brad and kids like him any time soon.'

'No.'

Will reached into the back to get Sophie's bag, a signal that the conversation was over. But Sophie wasn't about to be put off.

'How much?'

Will could no longer disguise his disillusionment.

'An impossible amount.'

'Nothing's impossible.' Sophie knew about fundraising for the sort of amounts that *would* be impossible if you depended on cake stalls and bring-and-buy sales. For some of her mother's friends, raising large amounts of money for charity was a very acceptable occupation.

'How much?'

'Two hundred thousand dollars.'

'Oh.'

'An awful lot of money.'

'Yes, I can understand the problem.'

But not impossible.

Sophie didn't want to labour the point when she had nothing tangible to offer. In Sydney in the same situation all she'd have to do would be to ask her parents to help. Her father would pull strings and know all the right people to ask for financial backing. And her mother revelled in organising high-profile events for charity. It helped that it was fashionable to donate to philanthropic worthy causes in certain circles.

But Prevely Springs was nothing like the eastern suburbs of Sydney. She doubted the community would even be considered *worthy*, let alone high profile enough to get the desired publicity that usually went with large donations.

Someone she hoped she could help, though, was Brad.

'Can I go with you on your next visit to Bella Farris and I'll try to break the ice with her son.' At least she could attempt to break down some barriers with the withdrawn teenager.

'Sounds great,' he said, and the expression on his face changed to one of appreciation. Sophie felt a real buzz in response to her boss's approval. 'No harm in trying, but don't expect too much. You might end up disappointed.'

Then Will promptly changed the subject, ending their conversation about Bella and her son and the future of the derelict building on the next block.

'You must be keen to see the flat.'

At the thought of a comfortable bed, Sophie felt sudden overwhelming tiredness.

'I guess I am.'

'It's only a short drive to Sabiston. You can follow me.'

'Okay.'

Sophie glanced across at Will, who was concentrating on changing stations on his car radio. His face was blank. What was going on in his head? What impression had her unconventional intrusion into his life made? Their lives were so different.

He appeared to be a very private person, not bound to convention or what people expected of him.

She could live with that.

Then she thought of Bella and her introverted son and realised how small her problems were in the grand scheme of things. She felt humbled and even more determined to make a go of it.

CHAPTER THREE

SOPHIE followed in her own car as Will headed west towards the coast. The scenery transformed as soon as they crossed the railway line. Grey-slabbed roadside pavements and graffiti'd walls of grubby corner shops made way for expansive, grassed road verges, quiet streets lined with jacaranda trees and suburbs dotted with slick shopping malls.

Sophie hit the brake pedal as Will indicated to turn into the narrow driveway of a two-storey block of about a dozen art deco flats clustered around a neatly kept garden and a small brick-paved car park. The neighbourhood reeked of old money and good taste.

The surrounding residences were large and palatial without being ostentatious. The neighbouring property was a prime example—a rambling old house with an immaculately kept grassed tennis court and a garage nearly as big as Sophie's old flat back home. It reminded her of her parents' house in Manly.

She eased the car into the last remaining resident's space as Will climbed out of his car and walked across to open her door.

'I just need to collect the keys.' He gestured in the general direction of the neighbouring house. 'Do you want to meet your landlord?'

'Okay.'

'He's a colleague of mine and we went through medical

school together. Andrew Fletcher. He's one of the top cardiologists around town.'

'He must be doing well for himself,' she said.

'Yeah, I guess so.'

Sophie deduced they weren't great friends. She couldn't be sure but she thought there was a hint of bitterness in Will's voice, though he didn't seem the type to be jealous of those better off than him. They walked silently up the long drive to the front door. Sophie noticed the camera above them as Will rang the bell. A gravelly voice grated through the intercom. There was the sound of several other people talking and laughing in the background.

'Will, I was expecting you earlier. We're round the back by the pool. Let yourself in the side gate and come and join the party.' The camera swivelled like a giant reptilian eye. 'And great to see you've brought such a gorgeous-looking friend.'

'Party?' Sophie was confused.

'I knew nothing about it. I just told him I'd call in to get the keys some time this afternoon.'

Will opened one side of a pair of heavy wooden gates and then he politely followed her through to the party where they were greeted by a man Sophie assumed to be Andrew Fletcher.

'So you must be my new neighbour? How delightful to meet you.' The bare-chested man still dripping from the pool briefly glanced at Will before holding out his hand to Sophie. His grip was a little too firm and he held her hand a little too long. 'I'm Andrew Fletcher. Sorry—I didn't catch your name.'

He had the lean, muscular build, dazzling blue eyes and classically honed features of a Hollywood movie star. Looks designed to catch any woman's eye—and he knew it.

He was eerily like Jeremy in both looks and manner, and the similarities made Sophie feel uncomfortable. She glanced across at Will, hoping for some indication from him as to whether to take this larger-than-life show pony seriously. Will's expression suggested he disapproved of the man's blatant flirting as much as she did.

'Sophie. Sophie Carmichael.' She desperately tried to stop her voice trembling but didn't quite succeed. To her surprise, Will responded to her uneasiness by moving close, grasping her hand and giving it a reassuring squeeze.

'Great to meet you. I hope…' his fleeting look in Will's direction barely acknowledged his presence '…you *both* will come and at least have a drink with me and my friends.'

Andrew's manner tripped a switch for Sophie and she felt nauseous. She couldn't control the sudden churning in her gut as his roving eyes played havoc with her emotions. She wanted to tell him to back off, but she didn't want to offend Will or his friend.

'The party's only just starting to warm up,' he said with a grin.

She liked the man less with each word he uttered.

This stranger was a double of Jeremy, and she had a sudden compulsion to leave before the nagging nausea in her gut got any worse.

It was then he must have noticed Will's protective gesture. Obviously not used to being rebuffed, Andrew leaned close, his breath smelling of seafood and alcohol.

Without thinking what she was doing, Sophie shrank away from Andrew and snuggled a little closer to Will. His body felt warm, strong, secure…and sexy. He made her feel safe, cared for, protected…in a way Jeremy never had.

Whoa… What on earth had come over her? He was her boss. They'd known each other barely a couple of hours and were merely acting out a charade of being more than colleagues.

She pulled away and stole a quick look at Will's face and saw a twinkle of amusement in his eyes.

'Sophie and I have other plans, haven't we?'

He was rescuing her. It was as if he had read her mind and had decided to play the knight in shining armour.

'I…er…'

'Well, you *are* a dark horse, aren't you, mate?' Andrew winked and slapped Will on the back in a misguided gesture of friendship. He'd added his own interpretation to their show of intimacy.

Will also recoiled from the man, and his grip tightened on her hand in a subtle indication of new-found solidarity. Andrew prattled on, completely unaware of the undercurrents between the two of them.

'I had no idea.' Andrew's attention firmly focused on Will, the look on his face bemused but curious. 'How long have you two—?'

'We met years back.' Sophie interrupted, trying to think quickly and say something that wouldn't exaggerate the untruths. 'And Will has kindly offered me a job for a couple of months at a time when I need to get away from Sydney.' She attempted a look, implying that was all the information she was prepared to give.

'Ah. I see. Will's playing the good Samaritan.'

Will's free arm found its way onto Sophie's shoulder and his facial expression turned into one of exaggerated concern. She was relieved when he finally spoke.

'We appreciate the offer. Perhaps another time.' He hesitated, sending Sophie a look. 'So if we could just get the keys…?'

'Okay, I'll be five minutes,' Andrew said as he loped off towards the house.

'What was that all about? For a minute there I thought you were going to faint.'

Will dropped Sophie's hand and stepped back from her, folding his arms across his chest. He looked as confused as she was. His tanned cheeks were flushed and the understanding in his eyes a moment ago had turned to bewilderment. She could already tell he was a man who liked his world to stay in a predictable orbit, but Sophie was as surprised as Will at her reaction to Andrew Fletcher.

'It's difficult to explain,' she finally said.

'I'd like you to try.'

'It's just…'

'What?'

How could Sophie explain her reaction? Why she'd needed such a dramatic out from Andrew's advances? He reminded her so much of Jeremy—charming, handsome, generous, rich, but not capable of fidelity—it was scary. In the end, Jeremy's unfaithfulness had been their undoing.

When had he fallen out of love with her? The fact that he might never have loved her had left Sophie feeling totally gutted. She'd been used—put on display like an expensive accessory and then discarded when he'd become bored with her and traded in for a new model.

Andrew was cast in the same mould.

But all men weren't animals… Not if her instinctive reaction to Will's kindness was anything to go by. It made it even more difficult for her to explain her impulsive behaviour. She figured she had nothing to lose, though, by telling the truth.

'He reminded me of my ex.' She couldn't help the grimace.

'Oh.' Will seemed uncomfortable with the direction the conversation was headed. Too much information? Too personal?

As Will dropped his arms to his sides Andrew walked through the French doors.

Grabbing Will's hand again, Sophie said in a pleading voice, 'Do you mind? He's coming back.'

Will smiled, apparently with renewed understanding and what Sophie thought was a hint of empathy. 'Just this once, but after we leave here—'

'I know. I'm sorry. I owe you for this.'

Andrew returned at that moment, handed over the keys to Will and grinned.

'I'll let you two go off and get reacquainted, then.'

He waved them off, then added as his eyes did another quick

but obvious head-to-toe appraisal of Sophie, 'Remember I'm next door if you need anything.'

'I'm sure she won't,' Will said brusquely as he put the keys in his pocket.

What on earth was it about Sophie Carmichael that had made him behave in a totally irrational manner? wondered Will.

They walked down the driveway of Andrew Fletcher's house, Sophie's hand still enfolded in Will's protective grip. She offered no resistance and he was reluctant to release her cool, tense fingers. He knew he should. Sophie was probably thinking he was taking advantage of her vulnerability.

But it felt so natural, comfortable…and so sensual.

Oh, God.

What had happened to his well-ordered life?

Will had totally lost his bearings. His day had started out simply enough. Not surprisingly, he'd been tired. It had been a busy week and 'tired' seemed to be his default setting these days. The usual Saturday morning at the clinic, demanding work, but nothing he couldn't handle, had been predictable.

It had been after morning surgery, when Sophie Carmichael had crunched, strode and then nudged herself into his life that his world had tilted on its axis.

In the space of a few short hours she'd roused the full spectrum of his emotions. He'd tumbled through frustration, amusement, impatience, confusion and…desire.

Desire? He'd almost forgotten it existed.

'That went well,' Sophie said as they reached the end of Andrew's drive.

'You think so?'

Will reluctantly released her hand and dragged his mind back from what was turning into a totally unachievable fantasy. Thank heaven she had no idea what he was thinking.

Sophie smiled. The comment was probably her way of saying how uncomfortable the encounter with Will's colleague had been for both of them. Will already had an idea what made this fascinating woman tick. She was naturally intuitive, dangerously unpredictable, and seemed to act at times solely on impulse.

And he liked it, he grudgingly admitted.

She'd also shown good judgement in her reaction to his successful, good-looking colleague. Andrew normally had any pretty woman he set his charismatic sights on under his spell in less than five minutes.

But not Sophie.

'You've obviously known Andrew for a long time but…and I might have got the vibes wrong…you don't seem to be best mates.'

She was dead right. But what could he say? He could hardly burden her with the traumas of his past.

'You're pretty close to the mark. But I didn't mean to—'

'No need to apologise. If he's anything like my ex-fiancé…'

The words stuck in her throat and her cheerfulness drained away as rapidly as the healthy colour in her cheeks.

Will felt totally at sea. Talking about problems on a personal level, especially with a woman, wasn't something he did. At least, not outside his consulting room. What was the point? It wouldn't make what had happened all those years ago go away.

But Sophie looked so dejected, as if she carried deep sadness inside. He couldn't just jump into his car and drive away without showing he cared. And, much to his surprise, he *did* care. A lot.

'Andrew and I haven't got much in common now. Our career paths diverged years ago and I guess we're both busy with all our commitments.' He cleared his throat. 'Er…what was it about Andrew that reminded you of your boyfriend?'

They were approaching Sophie's flat and Will rummaged in

his pocket for the keys. He stopped on the doorstep and waited for Sophie's reply.

'Um…it's difficult to explain.' Her eyes lost focus for a moment but then she continued. 'I thought he loved me but it turned out…' She swung her gaze back. The pain was there in her eyes, hot and cruel. 'It turned out he was a first-class bastard.'

It only took a moment for a rampant blush to flood her face and she began to stutter. 'N-not that…um… It's not that I think your friend…'

There was no way Will would use the word 'friendship' in the same sentence as Andrew Fletcher after what he'd done. But Sophie didn't need to know that. She had her own demons to deal with.

'I mean, Andrew might be a nice guy… It was just a gut feeling… I'm sorry.'

Will felt awkward, not quite sure what to say. He wanted desperately to comfort her, offer reassurance, but he'd been out of the social scene for so long… Giving her a hug was probably totally inappropriate, and he certainly didn't want her to think he was cast in the same mould as Andrew. He respected his women friends and had decided long ago if he ever embarked on a serious relationship again it would be for life. And that certainly wasn't going to happen any time soon. The baggage he carried was too heavy to share.

To disguise his discomfort he unlocked the door, and the heaviness of Sophie's mood lifted.

'There you go,' he said, stepping aside. 'Furniture's basic, but you should have everything you need. I've left some supplies that I hope will keep you going until you have a chance to go shopping. There's a deli—you probably saw it as we turned in from the main road…'

He still stood on the threshold, but Sophie had waltzed in and in two short minutes claimed the place as her own. She'd opened the kitchen blind and exclaimed at the quaintness of the small private garden on her back doorstep. She'd sat on the couch and plumped the cushions before smelling the small spray of freesias he'd put in a sauce bottle on the tiny gate-leg table in the corner.

'Did you do this?' she exclaimed as she opened the cupboards and then the fridge.

Youth and happiness, untarnished by life's encumbrances, glowed on her face. The mood was contagious and Will wanted the moment to go on for ever.

'I guessed what you might need. Don't worry about throwing things away. Just give the non-perishables back to me if they're unwanted.'

'No. Everything's perfect. I love it.'

She was back in the doorway, reaching out for his hand again, but this time like an excited child. 'What are you standing outside for? Come in. The least I can do is make coffee.'

Damn, he had a meeting with a builder.

'No. I have to go. I—'

Her expression changed. Was it disappointment?

'Oh, of course. You're a busy man and you must have commitments on the weekends.' Her eyes were questioning. He was sorry how quickly Sophie's mood had changed. 'I'm sorry to have taken up so much of your precious leisure time. I'm sure your family…'

What leisure time? What family?

Lately nearly all Will's time away from the clinic had been consumed by his efforts to get his pet project off the ground. Any sort of social life was out of the question and he had no family demanding his attention. Will's heart clenched shut at the memory of the family he'd once had.

The family he'd lost, the family he'd failed…the family he'd destroyed.

And now… The residents of the Springs had infiltrated his life to become his kin. He'd long been aware that the older generation who had known his grandparents kept a watchful eye on him. And the young—the children of his adopted extended family—were the driving force behind his desire to do everything he could to give them the opportunity to achieve their full potential.

Could he ever repay his family?

He'd long ago realised the neighbourhood he'd been brought up in was the only place he felt truly at home. He'd be asking too much to expect Sophie to understand, her background being so different from his.

'No need to worry about family commitments. I'm unattached—no rug rats keeping me awake at night.' He feigned cheerfulness to disguise his loneliness.

The already rosy colour in Sophie's cheeks darkened and Will wondered what had made her blush. Did his single status make a difference? Maybe she would feel *safer* if he was married, considering what she'd just revealed about her ex-fiancé. Or did she consider him dating material?

Surely not.

His brow involuntarily crinkled in a frown as he dismissed the thought as fantasy. He rearranged his face into a smile. 'I've enjoyed your company, and any other time I'd love to share a coffee…' He glanced at his watch and then cleared his throat, wishing he could stay a little longer with Sophie. 'But I have a meeting with a builder for quotes on the renovations of the hall at the community centre.'

Sophie was silent for a moment.

'Right,' she said. 'Maybe another time.'

'Maybe.' He hesitated. 'I'll see you nine o'clock Monday morning, then.'

'I'll be there.'

As he walked to his car, Will was struck by the discomforting revelation that he was looking forward to it—looking forward to Monday morning, the beginning of another long working week…and the opportunity to see Sophie Carmichael again.

In fact, he could hardly wait.

CHAPTER FOUR

MONDAY, Sophie's third day in this strange new city, and she still felt jet-lagged. She forced herself to start her day early, and while munching her way through a couple of slices of toast reflected on the events of the weekend.

Despite the shaky start, Sophie's luck had turned—for the better.

Saturday afternoon she'd made it to the shops just before closing and bought toiletries, a change of underwear, an oversized T-shirt for sleeping in and a simple and conservative shirt-dress that would suffice for work if she was still without her suitcases.

It was with a sense of relief that she wasn't locked into the image of well-groomed sophistication that was expected in Sydney. She'd made the right choice in leaving most of her designer suits and dresses at home because she doubted the newest trendy styles or the fashion label you wore had any credibility in this town, where most families had barely enough money to buy food and keep roofs over their heads. She'd already realised your credibility was more about the kind of doctor you were and how you related to those people, like Bella Farris, who deserved to be treated with respect.

Which got her thinking about her boss.

The brooding, deliciously mysterious Dr William Brent...

Already he'd proved to be a caring, insightful and forgiving employer. The fact that he seemed to have a mission in life to improve the lives of the struggling people of Prevely Springs had got her thinking…about fundraising. She'd had a few ideas floating around in her head, and when she'd written them down it was quite a list. At the first opportunity she planned to present her thoughts to Will, with the offer to take on board the organising. She felt excited at the prospect.

She'd received some good news on Sunday afternoon as well. Her luggage had finally been located and was on its way to Perth via Brisbane and would be available to pick up in the morning.

Guiltily she'd imposed again on her boss's good will and asked for some time off to collect it.

'Take the whole day,' he'd said, almost nonchalantly. 'I've waited so long for some help, another day won't make any difference.'

She'd thanked him but hoped she wouldn't be tied up all day.

She'd also had time to clarify what she wanted from her short stay in Western Australia and define some simple rules to try and ensure the next few weeks went as smoothly as they possibly could.

She was in the ideal place, working with people who didn't know her, to cast off the shackles of her past. She would shed labels like 'ditzy', 'selfish' and 'impulsive' and replace them with 'sensible', 'hard-working' and 'well organised'.

Firstly, she'd embrace the work at Will's practice with professionalism and enthusiasm. She'd concentrate on the positives and endeavour to learn as much as possible. Realistically, her stay would only be six weeks—time enough for the storm at home to have passed and for people to forget and move on to the next scandal.

Secondly, she'd have as little impact as she could on her employer's generous good nature and prove to him she could be independent, self-sufficient and an asset rather than a liability.

And, thirdly, she'd steer clear of any personal relationships.

She'd made the journey west to recover from one disaster and she wasn't about to launch into another.

That was the plan. With minimal variables and few distractions. Easy.

Feeling confident and empowered, busy and productive, she picked up her luggage from the airport and even had time to do a little shopping.

When she finished her morning business it was lunchtime, so she headed back to the flat with a week's supply of groceries, a slab of fresh-baked *focaccia* bread, a bag of fruit muffins and a packet of her favourite coffee. The plan was to have lunch, change her clothes and head out to Prevely Springs to spend a couple of hours meeting the staff and familiarising herself with the clinic layout, computer system, the protocols and procedures. Of course, if she saw Will she would treat him with the friendly respect he deserved.

After eating and flipping through Will's information booklet, she went to the bedroom and spread the contents of her suitcases on the bed. She shed her casual clothes and chose tailored charcoal-grey trousers and a smart, snug-fitting, soft pink and muted grey striped shirt. She glanced in the mirror on the back of the bedroom door, happy with what she saw—conservative, practical and just right for her first day at the office.

She fastened her shoulder-length russet-coloured hair with a beaded clasp at the nape of her neck, smeared clear gloss on her lips and then sighed.

'Let's get on with it,' she muttered.

Mondays were always busy. The clinic, theoretically, had an appointment system. Patients who just rolled up knew, unless it was an emergency, the minority who booked took precedence. What purists might have seen as unmanageable chaos worked reasonably well for the clientele of Prevely Springs Medical Clinic. The patients understood they would usually have to wait but they also knew Will Brent was a hard-working, caring doctor who would never turn a genuine patient away.

Will was sitting in his consulting room at three in the afternoon, trying to snatch a bite to eat between patients, knowing the waiting room was overflowing. He'd also promised to call in and see a baby who'd just been discharged from hospital after treatment for bronchiolitis. After that he'd check on Bella Farris. His working day wouldn't be finished until well into the evening. He frowned as he sipped tepid tea and his frown deepened as the phone rang.

'It's Sandie.' Will wished he felt as cheerful as his receptionist sounded.

'Yes.'

'Thought you might like a fresh cup of tea.'

He sighed with relief. If that was all she wanted…

'Great. Thanks.'

'And there's someone to see you.'

Will suppressed his impatience. Pharmaceutical representatives always seemed to call unannounced when he was busiest. He lowered his voice.

'Sandie, I really haven't got time to—'

'Trust me. This is someone you'll be happy to see.'

She hung up the phone and a few minutes later stood in his doorway with two steaming cups and a plate of delicious-looking muffins on a tray. Behind her…

Sophie Carmichael grinned. Will didn't know whether to laugh or cry. He'd organised to meet her early the following morning to show her the ropes and settle her in. He just didn't have time today. Though he couldn't deny the pleasure he felt at seeing her again, looking like she'd just stepped out of the fashion section of a career-woman's magazine, he wondered why she'd turned up a day early. Another mini-catastrophe? She seemed to attract them like iron filings to a magnet.

'Hello, Will.'

She sat opposite while Sandie cleared a space for the tray.

'I'll leave you to it, then,' the receptionist said. She threw a conspiratorial glance at Sophie.

'Sophie.' He forced a smile as he leaned across his desk and extended his hand. At any other time he'd have been pleased to see her, but now… It must have shown on his face.

'Don't look so worried, Will. Drink your tea while it's hot. I'm here to help.'

'To help?' He gulped a mouthful of his drink.

She handed him a muffin.

'Sorry. I'm really busy. I'd love to chat and show you around but I haven't the time. Tomorrow morning—'

'It's okay. Your very efficient and competent nurse Lisa's already shown me most of what I need to know. And Sandie's asked around the waiting room and at least half of your patients are happy to see me. I should have time to do the home visit as well and be back before you set off to see Bella Farris.'

She broke off a piece of cake, popped it into her delightful mouth and wiped a crumb from her blouse. For once he was speechless. He needed time to absorb what she'd said.

'I want to talk to Brad, remember?' Sophie paused, waiting. 'If that's okay with you, of course.'

He finally spoke. 'You want to work, see patients now?'

The long and mundane afternoon that had stretched ahead was suddenly filled with light. Sophie was the first ray of sunshine to break through dark clouds after a storm.

'That's right. And Sandie's kindly told your next one you'll be at least ten minutes.'

'Oh.'

'So you may as well make the most of your break and eat.' She smiled. 'The muffins are scrumptious.' She seemed happy to cheerfully carry on the conversation alone. 'And that sandwich looks disgusting.'

He obediently took a bite of the cake and she was right. Delicious, just like her smile. He felt the tension in his body begin to melt away.

'I found this wonderful hot-bread shop on the way back from sorting out my luggage. Pity it's not close by…' She paused in mid-sentence and studied his face for a moment. 'Are you all right?'

'Yes. I'm fine.'

If you discount the peculiar lightness in my head and the urge I have to take you in my arms, kiss you thoroughly and swear my undying gratitude.

'You've made my day.'

'Good. If it's okay with you, I'll start helping to clear the waiting room.' She took a sip of her drink and then stood as if to leave, but waited—apparently for his permission.

'Yes, of course. If you're happy to—'

'I am.' She looked at her watch. 'You officially have six more minutes left of your break so I suggest you make the most of it.' She turned in the doorway. 'And if I'm not back by the time you finish, give me a ring. If you haven't got my mobile number, Sandie has it. I can meet you at Bella's.'

And with a delightful swish of her hips she was gone.

Working in Will's practice was like stepping into another world for Sophie. Although her afternoon went smoothly—the patients who had elected to see her had fairly straightforward problems—she'd noticed the majority of people she'd seen were…*so different* from what she was used to. They'd learned not to bother the doctor unless they were genuinely, seriously ill. Wasting her or Will's precious time meant someone who legitimately needed attention was put further back in the queue. And even though most couldn't afford the sort of fees her father's patients paid, there'd been a sense of heartfelt gratitude from several people she'd seen that could never be measured in dollars. It was almost as if the people of the Springs were used to being rebuffed by authorities purely because of their social status. They considered time spent with a doctor who was prepared to listen and take their problems seriously a privilege rather than a right.

For the first time in a long time Sophie felt the beginning of a return in the confidence and drive she'd had as a new graduate when she'd been ready to take on the world. In hindsight, her self-esteem had probably been eroded over the past two years without her even realising—by Jeremy. He'd never taken her career seriously, and had considered her work to be only a convenient and lucrative means to keep her happy and occupied until they married and started a family.

And her father was just as controlling. When he had realised she was determined to have a career in medicine he'd decided, without even consulting with her, that his practice, under his watchful eye, was where she should stay. She'd been shocked to overhear him talking to Jeremy about maternity leave and reducing her hours when the grandchildren started coming along—as if she had no say in the matter.

The fact that Jeremy's new girlfriend was pregnant had been the final straw for Sophie. She'd tried so hard to please her fiancé, forsaking her needs for his, and he'd not shown a morsel of remorse at trading her in for a flashy new model who was going to present him with a baby long before he was ready. When *she'd* broached the subject of children, he'd seemed put out that she'd even consider taking on the responsibility of a family before he finished his specialist training in the well-paying field of ophthalmology.

It made her wonder if the little chat he'd had with her father about job flexibility and maternity leave was a complete sham. Maybe it had just been a ploy by her father to make sure she stayed in the family practice to take over when he retired. The fuss he'd made when she'd told him she'd applied for and been accepted for a job in Western Australia had been over the top. Even after she'd explained she'd most likely be back in a month or two.

Will wasn't like that.

The thought entered her mind without warning as she real-ised how intimately her new employer was part of what she was feeling.

She'd had her first taste of how the other half lived…and worked and suffered. It validated her reasons for coming to WA, and she was beginning to experience the type of satisfaction in her work she'd longed for.

By five o'clock the waiting room was nearly empty. Only two patients remained and they both insisted on seeing Will.

Sophie headed for the reception area. Home visits were something she'd have to get used to as they were an integral part of the holistic style of medicine Will practised, rarely encountered in city practices these days.

She breezed into the reception area with renewed energy.

'From what you told me, I shouldn't be long,' she said to Sandie.

Sophie gathered the printed notes listing the details of the infant she was going to visit, as well as the hospital discharge summary. She had her own medical bag, but Lisa had kindly put together a bundle of the clinic stationery, which, she noticed with a smile, had been freshly printed to include her name and new provider number.

'Are you coming back?' the receptionist asked.

'If Dr Brent is still here. We're going to see Mrs Farris. I met her on Saturday.' Sophie could tell by the look on Sandie's face she knew Bella and the nature of her illness. 'I can meet him there if he finishes before I come back.'

Sandie smiled. 'Will rarely finishes before seven, sometimes as late as eight on a Monday. And that's without home visits.'

'It doesn't surprise me. He's the only doctor for… How many patients did you say were on the books?'

'Way too many. He works too damned hard.'

'Mmm.' Sophie knew it too, and she'd only known him a few days. If he kept going as he was, he'd burn himself out.

Her respect for him was growing by the minute. 'I'd better get going.' She gathered her gear and turned to go.

'Sophie?' Sandie's voice was quiet, kind.

'Yes. Have I forgotten something?'

'No. I just wanted to tell you what a difference you've made this afternoon. Thanks.'

'Just doing what I'm paid to do.' But Sophie knew that was never the case in medicine. To be a doctor, and especially in a practice like Will's, you had to be prepared to give that very substantial bit extra.

Sophie drove into the clinic car park half an hour later as Will walked out the back door, punching a number into his mobile phone. He stopped when he saw her.

'Perfect timing. I was just about to ring you,' he said as she stopped beside him and lowered the window. He looked a little less weary, and the hint of a smile as well as a barely perceptible spark in his almost black eyes was all Sophie needed to tell her she had been a help to him that afternoon.

'Are you going to see Bella Farris now?'

'That's right. Shall we go together?'

'Sounds good to me. Climb in.' She pointed to her passenger seat but Will looked reluctant. 'The more I drive, the more I get to know my way around the neighbourhood.'

He seemed to accept her logic, put his bag and a pile of medical journals on the back seat and settled himself next to her. 'Thanks,' he said, fastening his seat belt.

'No problem.'

'I don't just mean for the lift. You did really well this afternoon. Sandie told me a couple of patients were singing your praises.'

Sophie had enjoyed the afternoon of what was sometimes called bread-and-butter medicine. Simple problems with relatively simple solutions. So different from the wealthy patients of Sydney's eastern suburbs where she'd worked in her father's practice.

'Don't worry. I'm not about to poach your patients. Every single customer who consulted me this afternoon let me know they were loyal to you and only saw me because they knew you were so busy.'

Will laughed. 'Poach as many patients as you like. Just remember when you get your own following they'll…'

Sophie knew what he was going to say and understood why his voice trailed off.

'They'll give me a really hard time when they find out I'm leaving?'

'Mmm. Something like that.' It was a conversation-killer; neither of them was contemplating the future beyond the following day at this stage of their professional relationship.

'Is it left here?' Sophie asked when she thought she recognised the street.

'Yes. To the T-junction and left again.'

Sophie turned into the quiet suburban street. A group of grinning teenagers bounced their basketball precariously close to the car and then went running off in the opposite direction.

'Tell me about Bella. How long has she been ill?'

'Her cancer was diagnosed about three months ago. She'd had stomach pains and what she described as indigestion for only a couple of weeks before the scan.'

'Pancreatic cancer is often untreatable at the time of diagnosis, isn't it?'

'Incurable is probably a better word. We can still treat the symptoms as part of palliative care. Best quality of life is the general aim. And then a peaceful death.'

Sophie looked across at Will but he was staring out of the side window, a distant look on his face.

'Is Brad an only child?' Sophie understood why withdrawal into the realm of computer games was attractive to the teenager. In his fantasy world he probably had control and, from what

Sophie had seen, he played at a level of skill that assured he was a winner most of the time.

'No. He has an older married sister. She lives in Karratha, which is roughly fifteen hundred kilometres north of here, and has a young family of her own. She'll come down for Bella's last days and will take Brad back to live with her and her husband.'

Sophie recognised the group of townhouses as they turned the corner and she eased her car into the ragged driveway of the Farrises' house.

'Brad's father?'

'A drunk and a bully, so Bella told me, and long gone. She doesn't know where he is and doesn't want to. He'd left before I started seeing Bella.'

'She cares about Brad, though.'

'Yes, she does. His future is her biggest concern at the moment.' He paused and looked at her with narrowed eyes. 'Perceptive of you to see that.'

'I guessed, that's all.'

'Yeah, well, you guessed right.' Will got out of the car and then leaned into the back seat to get his bag. 'Come on. Let's go.'

Will knocked and then opened the door, calling out as he did so, 'It's Dr Brent and Dr Carmichael. Can we come in?'

He didn't appear to expect a reply, and when they entered the house the TV was on but Brad was in the kitchen, stirring the contents of a saucepan on the stove.

'Hi, Brad.' Will nodded towards the boy.

'Hi.'

'Smells okay, but you didn't have to go to all that trouble.'

Brad smiled, then went back to stirring.

'Mum said she feels like some tomato soup.'

'Good. She must be a bit better. Has Shelley been?'

'Yeah.'

'And? Did she say anything?'

'Nothin' much.'

Will slouched against the brick pillar supporting the wall dividing the living area from the kitchen. He gave the impression of having all the time in the world.

'Don't give me that. Shelley'd talk the nuts off a prize stud bull.'

Brad's smile turned into a grin for a moment.

'She said Mum's a bit better.'

'Good.'

'And that I'll end up as fat as her if I don't stop eating rubbish.'

'Ha.' Will's eyes twinkled. 'Now, that's a scary prospect.' He went over to inspect the soup and crinkled his nose. 'You won't get fat on this. We'd better go up and see your mum,' he added.

Brad put the lid on the pan, turned off the hotplate, and hovered as if waiting for them to make a move.

'Come on, Dr Carmichael.'

When they went upstairs and into the back bedroom Sophie could see the improvement in Bella—her smile was less forced, her colour better and her face not so lined with pain. A half-drunk glass of milky liquid stood on the bedside table.

Will picked up her chart and spent a few moments looking through the nurse's notes. 'Nausea's settled?'

'Yes, and the pain. That little pump works like magic.' Bella pulled aside her pyjama top to reveal the butterfly needle inserted under the skin of her chest and the battery-operated pump that slowly and steadily moved the plunger of the syringe to administer a constant supply of pain-relieving medication.

'Are you keeping any food down now?'

'A little. I've opened my bowels too.'

Will looked over at Sophie and explained, 'Hopefully the dexamethasone has begun to act to reduce gut inflammation and swelling.'

'Whatever. It's working,' Bella said.

'Good. Can I examine you?'

Bella dutifully lifted her top.

'Do you mind if I go downstairs and have a chat to Brad, Mrs Farris, while Will checks you over?'

'Call me Bella. I don't mind. But he doesn't talk much. Seems to spend most of the time when he's not at school playing electronic games.' A look of sadness crossed her face. 'His friends don't come over any more. I wish…'

'He seems a good kid. He was making soup when we arrived.'

It was the only way Sophie could think to reassure the woman whose mood had taken a dive when they'd started talking about her son.

'He is.' She hesitated. 'I wish things were different.'

Sophie glanced at Will, wondering if her decision to try and find out how the boy was coping was a wrong one. He nodded his approval.

'I guess we can only do our best with what we've got.' The comment seemed totally inadequate in the circumstances.

'Yes, you go and talk to Brad.' Bella's smile returned. 'And good luck.'

Will heard the laughter as he came downstairs, and then a whoop from Brad followed by Sophie's less animated groan. They were both sitting on the couch. Sophie's eyes were glued to the TV screen and her thumbs were on a game console control pad as if it was an extension of her hands.

'Ooh.' Sophie's voice was a little louder this time, easily heard against the background noise of racetrack engines revving and squealing brakes. 'Gotcha!' She threw her head back and laughed for a second, then her eyes shot back to the action on the screen.

'Watch out. Ha!' Brad exclaimed, and by the look on his face he was obviously winning the computer racing driver game.

Will stopped to take in the sight of Sophie. With her

privileged upbringing, she was an attractive, sophisticated
career-woman, and yet she was currently playing with young
Brad with the enthusiasm and lack of inhibition of a child. Will
hadn't seen Brad laugh like that since his mother had been diagnosed with incurable cancer. Even before Bella's illness he'd
seemed an introverted, though intelligent kid, content with his
own company.

Though he wasn't sure where Sophie was going with Brad,
the boy was enjoying himself, which was an enormous positive
step. As long as she didn't let him get too close to her.

'What's the game?' Will stood behind them at the bottom
of the stairs. Neither had been aware of his presence.

Brad's head shot round.

'Mario Kart, out of the archives.' It was Sophie who
answered.

'Am I supposed to know what that is?'

'Nup.' Brad was still engrossed in the action on the
screen.

'Is she any good?'

Brad glanced briefly at Sophie before he answered. 'Not bad
for a girl. But she's played before.'

Sophie put down her control pad and let her driver succumb
to the inevitable humiliation of coming last in the race.

'I remember when computer games had only just been in-
vented. The Mario Brothers games were my favourite. I've got
a kid brother,' she said, as if that explained everything.

Will had never been a fan of computer games, and Sophie's
comment reminded him of his age. He was nearly a decade
older than she was.

Sophie got up to leave. She tapped Brad on the shoulder.

'I might come sometimes when Dr Brent visits your mother.
Is that okay, Brad?'

'Okay.'

'And don't forget your mum's soup,' Will added.

'I won't,' he said as he turned the machine off.

Will and Sophie let themselves out and walked to the car.

'That went well,' Will said.

'It did, didn't it?' Her eyes glistened in the fading light. 'I think I might have made it to first base with him, but his biggest challenges are yet to come.'

Will knew exactly what she meant, but he suspected Sophie might be the one to make his journey a little less painful.

'I don't know how you did it, but you managed to put a smile on Brad's face,' Will said as he climbed into the passenger seat of Sophie's car.

'I played a computer game with him, that's all.' Sophie positioned herself in the driver's seat. 'And maybe my inner child's a bigger part of my psyche than in the average grown-up.'

Will laughed. 'If that's what it takes to get Brad out of his shell, I'm all for it.'

Sophie reversed out of the driveway. The street was quiet, no cars or people. The only sign of life after dark in this eerie place was the occasional flicker of a television screen seen through a curtainless front window and the sound of a distant barking dog. So different from Sydney, where even the suburbs seemed alive with folk going out to restaurants, walking dogs, visiting friends. It was as if by some mutual agreement the residents of Prevely Springs observed a curfew. If Brad felt isolated, Sophie could understand why.

'It's only the first step with him and I have no idea what the next one will be.'

'But you've made a start. That's more than I've managed.'

'Mmm.'

They drove in silence to the end of the road. Sophie didn't need directions this time. The maze of streets was beginning to look familiar.

'How much time do you think Bella has left?'

'Not long. Maybe a month—two at the outside.'

'She knows that?'

'Yes. We've talked about it. She's already put her affairs in order, made plans for Brad, that sort of thing.'

'Does Brad know?'

'He knows his mother's dying. We had a family conference a few weeks ago. Her daughter Gemma travelled down from Karratha. I didn't think it was fair to talk in terms of *how many weeks*.'

'No, I guess not.'

They drove past the park, part of the community centre complex. A restless group of youths had gathered under a streetlight, pushing and shoving each other. One lunged towards the car, pulling a face and making an unsavoury gesture until he saw Will. Then he smiled sheepishly.

'You know him?' Sophie asked.

'I know most of them. Always in trouble, mainly because they've no direction. Nothing else to do. In a different situation…' Will seemed to focus on some place in the distance.

'At least Brad isn't roaming the streets.'

'Yes. That's one positive, I suppose.' He sighed.

Sophie sensed Will had a bond with the people of Prevely Springs that went deeper than the doctor-patient relationship. There was only so much one person could do, though.

She stopped the car outside the clinic.

'Do you want to share some take-away?' she said on impulse. Will looked so despondent.

'No, thanks. I have a couple of things to finish off.'

'Work?'

'If I don't do it now—'

'Never leave until tomorrow…'

'That's right.' He opened the rear door to retrieve his gear, a look of determined acceptance on his face. 'You know how to get back to the flat?'

'I'll be fine. See you in the morning.'

Will smiled. 'Yes. I will, won't I? It's great to have you on board, Dr Carmichael.'

'My pleasure,' she muttered, easing her car away from the kerb.

Those two words weren't a clichéd reply. It was the absolute truth.

CHAPTER FIVE

'WILL works too hard,' Sophie said to the two women in the tea room. It was Friday lunchtime, after a busy morning consulting, and Sophie's observation was partly due to the fact her boss was working through his lunch-break…again.

'Tell me something we don't know,' Lisa replied as she removed the cling wrap from her sandwich.

'And he's taken on much more than he can possibly handle with the youth centre. Has he mentioned it to you?' Sandie addressed her question to Sophie.

'Mmm, on my first day, when we went and saw the Farrises.' Sophie took a sip of coffee. 'We were talking about Brad, and Will was lamenting the lack of facilities for young people in the neighbourhood.'

'He's right about that, but one man can't move mountains. Apparently the council have told him he has to show he can raise a six-figure sum before they'll even consider his proposal, let alone approve it. And it's not as if the residents have any spare cash to give away.'

'Has he said how he plans to do it?' Sophie had been mulling over her own ideas all week but hadn't had a chance to discuss them with Will.

'Apparently he has some well-to-do colleagues he was going to ask to sponsor the project, but he didn't seem too overjoyed at the prospect,' Sandie volunteered as she went across to the kettle to refill her cup. 'When it comes to the Springs, he seems to want to shoulder the entire load himself.'

'Mmm—he's not someone who's comfortable with the cap-in-hand role.' Lisa chuckled. 'We were all amazed he finally decided to take on an extra set of hands.'

The women carried on eating and drinking in silence until Sophie decided to share her thoughts, find out what Sandie and Lisa thought about her wanting to help.

'I have a few ideas.'

Her companions looked at her with surprise.

'To raise a couple of hundred thousand dollars?' The look on Lisa's face turned to incredulity.

'Like to share them?' Sandie pulled her chair a little closer and put down her cup.

'I wouldn't mind sounding you out on local knowledge but I'd rather run them by Will before I...' Sophie grinned '...go public.'

Sophie had a feeling that if she told Lisa and Sandie the details of her plans they'd be common knowledge before the day or at least the weekend was out. She wasn't ready for that yet, and she doubted the residents of Prevely Springs knew her well enough to trust her. The proposals had to come from Will.

'Are the youngsters around here into sport?'

'Playing or watching?' Lisa asked.

'Both.' Sophie could see she had the women's full attention. 'Any particular sport?'

Sandie and Lisa exchanged curious glances before Sandie answered.

'Aussie rules footy, I guess.' She looked at her friend for confirmation and Lisa nodded. 'You probably know there are two national teams in the West, and I'd say the majority of the football supporters around here go for the port team.'

'The underdogs.' Sophie had enough knowledge of the sport to know of the rivalry between the two West Australian teams and that the Fremantle team, though not usually as successful as their opponents, had an incredibly loyal following. 'Are there local amateurs? Do the kids play?'

'Pete, my husband, plays for the local team and coaches both boys and girls in the under-twelves.' Lisa paused. 'Where are all these questions leading?'

'I'm not sure yet, but you've been a great help.' Sophie grinned. 'Just one more question. What's the spectator capacity of the Springs sports ground?'

Lisa answered. 'I'll ask Pete. The local team never plays to a big crowd but at full capacity it would be around a couple of thousand at the most.'

Sophie looked at her watch.

'Thanks, ladies. I'd better be getting back to work.'

The information Sophie now had gave her more to think about, and by the looks on Sandie's and Lisa's faces she'd given them food for thought as well.

Sophie packed her things at the end of the Friday afternoon session. Her first week had been busy and she was looking forward to a relaxing evening—a long, hot shower, a supersized serving of her favourite take-away, and then watching back-to-back crime shows on TV.

She was just about to leave when the phone rang.

'Hello?' she said a little impatiently, hoping the call wouldn't lead to a delay in the start to her weekend.

'Thank goodness you're still here. I thought you might have left already.' There was no mistaking the urgency in Sandie's voice.

'What's the problem?'

'I wondered if you could see one last patient.'

'An emergency?' Sophie's heartbeat quickened and the muscles of her neck and shoulders tensed.

'Not exactly.' Sandie hesitated.

'Go on.'

'It's a woman who normally sees Will, but he's still got four patients in the waiting room. I buzzed him and he didn't want her turned away. He okayed you seeing her as long as you let him know if you have any problems.'

'Right. I just need a few minutes to log back into the computer. What's her name?' Sophie resigned herself to missing at least the first half of *City Crime*, but hoped the rest of the evening would go to plan.

'Beverley Sanders. And…er…she's got her daughter Brianna with her. Dr Brent said to tell you to check Brianna's notes as well.'

'Okay. Tell them I won't be long.'

'Thanks. You're a lifesaver.'

Sophie replaced her bag in the file drawer at the side of her desk, locked it and put the key in her pocket. She sat in front of the computer screen and waited the few seconds for it to reboot, then logged in with her password and entered the medical records.

Beverley Sanders…

Age thirty-one—the same age as Sophie. In fact, their birthdays were within a few weeks of each other. Marital status—de facto. Three children aged four, seven and fifteen. History of depression and a coded reference to her having been a victim of domestic violence.

Her life hadn't been a bed of roses.

The woman had seen Will a fortnight ago, and the brief notes alluded to a long consultation about problems she was having with her oldest daughter. He had requested she bring Brianna along when she saw him in a week's time.

The visit obviously hadn't happened and Sophie had a good idea why. Fifteen-year-old girls with difficult behaviour rarely admitted to having problems at all, let alone came willingly to attend the doctor for help.

Sophie did a quick calculation—Beverley had been sixteen when she'd had Brianna.

She did a check of the teenager's notes. The entries were sparse—a note documenting her refusal to have the rubella or the cervical cancer vaccine; three stitches in her forehead a year ago after a fall—Will had underlined that—and an entry a fortnight ago referring to her mother's visit: *'Problems at home with Brianna—?drugs'*.

Will had mentioned to Sophie that drug use and abuse was a big problem in the neighbourhood, and increasingly among high-school kids. He'd drilled her in what to look out for and how to question teenagers without being threatening or intrusive. He'd revealed that helping these youngsters was a special interest for him.

Sophie took a deep breath. Clenching her hands into fists to stop a slight tremor, she headed for the waiting room.

'Beverley Sanders?' she said. She glanced at the waiting patients but they were all male. Had Beverley and her daughter decided not to stay?

'Sandie?'

The receptionist was on the phone. She grimaced, then pointed to the front entry, before miming the action of drawing on a cigarette.

The message was clear. Her patient had gone outside for a smoke. The prospect of Chinese food and a quiet, relaxing evening was gradually fading as Sophie realised these last two patients would almost certainly take time. A lot of time.

Sophie walked across and opened the front door.

'Beverley Sanders?' she repeated, this time louder.

A woman emerged from behind the open driver's side door of an old car, stubbing out a cigarette as she slammed the door shut. She was overweight and dressed in the most unflattering cropped stretch pants, topped with a sleeveless, scoop-necked T-shirt at least a size too small. The outfit accentuated her obesity. Her straw-coloured hair straggled over her shoulders and her neck was swarthy and lined from too much exposure to the sun.

She hammered on the windscreen.

'Come on, Brianna, the doctor's waiting,' she shouted, and then shrugged an apology to Sophie. 'Sorry—you've no idea what it took to get her this far.'

The woman looked desperate…and weary, as if, with every choice she made in her life, she ended up with the short straw.

There was something about the look in her eyes, though, that indicated she was a survivor and wasn't about to give up. She deserved all the help she could get, Sophie decided.

Beverley hit the windscreen again and a thin girl Sophie surmised was Brianna emerged with a sour expression on her face. Sophie suspected the challenge she'd been wishing for had just arrived on her doorstep and was about to shuffle into the clinic scowling and under protest.

Sophie smiled her warmest welcoming smile.

'I'm Dr Carmichael. You must be Mrs Sanders?'

The woman nodded.

'And Brianna?' The girl looked away and said nothing, but ambled behind her mother in the direction of the clinic doors.

'Challenging' was an understated description of the fifty-minute consultation that followed.

'What brings you here today, Beverley?' Sophie's usual opening line sounded totally inappropriate and even a little snobbish. She felt the woman withdraw a fraction before she glanced at her daughter, as if to make sure the girl hadn't absconded.

'I've had it with Bri.'

'I told you not to call me that,' the teenager snapped. 'My name's *Brianna*.'

'See what I mean? She's like that all the time. But a lot worse. Arguing, shouting, swearing like a loser about the tiniest thing. And then she'll sink into a dark mood and won't talk to me or her stepdad for days. She went into a flaming rage a couple of weeks ago and slapped her little brother for changing the TV channel. That was the last straw.' Beverley was bravely holding back tears. 'The bruising on Joel's face lasted a week.' She paused and then added quietly, 'She used to be such a beautiful, well-behaved little girl.'

Sophie looked over at Brianna, who was still scowling and restlessly tapping one heel on the floor.

'Go on.'

'She sneaks out at night, falls asleep in class or doesn't show up at school at all. She's been suspended twice for smoking dope…and if it happens again she'll be expelled.'

'Okay.' Sophie needed a minute to organise her thoughts. She was determined to at least try and help.

'Brianna?' She'd surprised the girl. Brianna looked as if she didn't expect to be included in the conversation. 'Are things at home difficult for you too?'

The girl's facial expression relaxed for a moment, but then went straight back into rebellious teenager mode.

'What difference does it make?' she muttered.

'I'm not sure, but I think it would be worth trying to find out.' Sophie made sure she kept her tone neutral. It would be a big mistake to take sides. She fixed her gaze firmly on Brianna, but her question was directed at her mother as well. 'Would it be all right if I had a chat to each of you on your own? Maybe starting with you, Brianna?'

Beverley stayed silent, so the decision was up to the fifteen-year-old, but the girl was obviously reluctant to agree with a suggestion made by an adult on principle.

'What's the point?' she finally said. At least she'd acknowledged the question.

'We won't know until we give it a try.' Sophie glanced over at Beverley, who nodded her approval, looking relieved.

'Well?'

'Yeah, okay.' It was almost a whisper.

'Good.'

Her mother was standing already.

'If you sit in the waiting room, I'll call you when we've finished.'

Beverley walked wearily to the door and closed it softly behind her.

Challenge number two was about to begin.

The six-thirty call from Sandie, telling Will that Beverley Sanders had finally fronted up with her daughter in tow, had been unexpected. That the girl had come at all surprised him, and he could only imagine the effort her mother had made to persuade her. He had to see them. There was a good chance he might not get another opportunity. He often worked well into the evening when he was theoretically supposed to finish at six.

'Sophie's seeing her last patient and you've got another four waiting. Would you like me to ask her if she can see Beverley Sanders and her daughter?'

The receptionist had cleared her throat. Sandie had worked with Will since he'd first set up the clinic, over ten years ago, and had a good knowledge of the backgrounds of their regular patients. He assumed she already had an opinion of what their new assistant could cope with. In fact, a young, fresh, female doctor might be what Brianna needed to open up. His suspicions, from what her mother had told him, were that the teenager was experimenting with harder drugs—he knew all the tell-tale signs first hand—but he was interested in Sophie's assessment.

'As long as Beverley is agreeable.'

'And I'll tell Sophie you're in the next room if she needs any help.'

Sandie had amazing insight.

'That's exactly what I was about to say.'

'Good. I'll buzz you if they refuse to see Sophie.'

That had been nearly an hour ago. Will had finished

consulting, but Sophie's door was closed, which meant she was still working. He wasn't sure whether to be worried or impressed, and was keen to know the outcome of the visit.

He'd wait.

And he didn't have to wait long.

As he began to go back to his office Sophie's door opened and Beverley and Brianna emerged.

'Hello, Dr Brent.' Although she wasn't smiling, there was a sense of relief in Beverley's body language. Her daughter, shoulders hunched and head down, looked at the floor. She seemed calm, though, not agitated or angry, as he'd expected. 'I hope you don't mind us seeing the new doctor.'

The apology was unnecessary and he smiled.

'Of course not. We work as a team.'

'Good. Dr Carmichael wants us to come back next week.'

'Make sure you make an appointment before you leave.' Will smiled. He wanted to reinforce the fact he had no objections.

Brianna started heading towards the waiting room but Beverley looked as if she had something more to say. Sophie's door was still open, but from where Will stood, a little past her office, he couldn't see her. She could probably hear their conversation, though, which was the most likely reason Beverley leaned close to whisper, 'That woman's a gem. Brianna actually talked to her. Make sure you do everything to persuade her to stay.'

'I'll do my best.'

The woman had a rare smile on her face as she turned to follow her daughter, and Will did an about-turn to find out how Sophie had managed to perform a miracle.

Sophie hunched over her desk with one hand supporting her head and her gaze directed at the computer screen.

Will knocked quietly.

'Sophie?'

She sat up and swung round abruptly on her swivel chair,

looking surprised. Perhaps she *hadn't* been aware of the conversation taking place in the corridor. She ran her fingers through her hair. She had beautiful, shining hair, a rich reddish brown with glints of coppery gold when the light caught it in a certain way. She'd left it loose, and he liked it better that way than tied or clipped back, her usual style for work. He imagined it would be soft to touch and sweet smelling.

Her hand went back to her head, flicking stray strands behind her ear.

'Is there something wrong with my hair?' She was blushing and he reprimanded himself for blatantly staring. He hadn't realised…

'No.'

Everything was right with it.

'Sorry. I…er… It's been a long day,' he added—a lame attempt at justifying his behaviour.

'I know you've had a long day, Will, and I won't keep you—I'm sure you've got plans for the evening—but I wanted to have a quick word about Brianna Sanders before the weekend…to make sure I've done the right thing.'

Plans for the evening? Right. Buying a take-away on the way home and falling asleep watching TV after an aborted attempt at making an impression on the pile of journals in the corner of his study.

Of course he had plans.

'As a matter of fact I haven't any plans for tonight.' He moved one of the patient chairs back so he could sit facing her without his knees tangling with hers. He'd just had an outlandish thought. 'Have you?'

She grinned. 'Take-away and an early night. I think I'm too tired for anything else.'

'Do you like Chinese?'

'It's my favourite.'

'How about we share a Chinese take-away and go back to my place…?' He hesitated, but Sophie showed no sign of protesting.

'Or yours, if you prefer. And we can discuss your first week, as well as Brianna Sanders, on a full stomach.'

'That sounds good to me. I've got a couple of things I want to talk to you about.' She did her best to suppress a yawn. 'I can't guarantee I'll stay awake, though.'

'Not a problem. My house has two spare bedrooms.'

Whoops. He hoped Sophie didn't put the wrong interpretation on his invitation for a sleep-over. But she seemed oblivious to any inappropriate implications.

'Your place, then. I'll follow you in my car, but you'd better give me the address just in case I get lost,' she said as she unlocked the drawer to retrieve her bag.

Suddenly Will was no longer looking at the prospect of another dull evening at home on his own. He felt energised, with a feeling of lightness replacing the heaviness that usually encompassed his entire body towards the end of his working week.

Maybe it was time to at least consider there might be a life for him outside his job. He somehow put to the back of his mind that Sophie Carmichael was out of bounds.

Sophie couldn't deny she was curious to see where Will lived. She felt comfortable with him. He was so conservative she doubted he had an ulterior motive; her problem, though, was that she kind of wished he had. She felt certain that somewhere beneath his sombre, sober, serious exterior he hid a sense of humour. She'd had glimpses of it but he usually kept it well hidden.

The weird thing was she wanted to be the one to crack his shell. The idea had come on her slowly through the week and left her surprised and confused. She'd fantasised about showing him the therapeutic value of letting his hair down and having a good time.

He was the sort of man who probably didn't understand the meaning of the word flirting. It most likely hadn't occurred to

him that if he smiled a little more often, if he wore more flatter-
ing clothes, if he even thought about asking a woman out, he'd
be inundated with attractive ladies eager for his company.

There was something holding him back, though. Maybe
something in his past he wasn't able to let go of. Perhaps he'd
suffered the female equivalent of Jeremy. Someone who had
hurt him badly. Whatever, whoever it was it had a firm hold on
him.

But at the moment he was probably just as weary as she, and
needing an uncomplicated end to a hectic day. She put thoughts
of trying to analyse the man out of her mind.

Sophie followed Will to a busy Chinese restaurant and he
insisted on her helping to choose their meal.

'My place isn't far from here,' he said as he loaded several
containers of delicious-smelling take-away into his car. Sophie
followed him along the main road and then into a narrow brick-
paved street softly illuminated by old-fashioned lamps. The
street was still in or at least on the edge of Prevely Springs, but
had a character all its own.

The row of Federation houses, though built to the same plan,
were each different. One had a bright blue front door with lace
curtains and white miniature roses falling from a muddle of ter-
racotta pots in the front yard. Another was all trendy grey paint
and shiny black security screens. Sophie pulled up behind Will
as he parked in the driveway of the last house in the row.

Will's house.

It surprised her, but it suited him somehow.

The small garden of straggling native plants had found their
own special state of disorder. They softened the façade of the
old stone building, which stood aging but proud and defiant. It
quietly declared its protest against modernisation.

Will was out of his car and leaning towards her window.

'This is it,' he said, almost apologetically.

'I like it. It's so—'

'Don't you dare say quaint.'

'No.' She smiled. 'I was going to say it's so *you*.'

He grinned. 'I won't ask if that's meant to be a compliment or an insult.'

Will went back to his car, collected the food and then led her through a faded picket gate with a predictably squeaky hinge, up the low stone steps onto a dusty veranda. She could just make out intricately patterned tiles in the muted colours of earth and sky. It was like walking back in time.

'How long have you lived here?'

Will unlocked the door, flicked on the hall light and then turned to face her. 'Nearly my entire life, I guess. It was my grandparents' house. I spent a couple of years travelling...' He hesitated, as if deciding whether to continue.

'And?'

'The first two years of my life I lived with my mother. But I don't really remember...'

His voice trailed off and he gave her a look that told her he didn't want to talk about his past.

'Come through to the back and we'll eat.'

Sophie assumed he'd been brought up by his grandparents but didn't delve further. She followed him down the central passageway. The dark, closed-in front of the house opened up to a paradoxically light and airy, open-plan kitchen and informal living area.

'I'm responsible for the extension,' Will said, as if he needed to explain. 'I love the old house but it was time for change.'

Despite the contemporary features—a full wall of timber-framed glass doors, pale, polished wood floors, modern kitchen appliances—it all somehow blended with the history of the place. The furniture was a mix of old and new: a modern sofa; two antique high-back chairs; an ageless rocking chair.

'Sit down.' Will indicated the sofa. 'I'll bring plates and you can serve yourself. Okay?'

'That's fine.'

'Would you like some wine?' He opened the fridge, check-ing the contents. 'Or beer?'

'No, thanks, but don't let me stop you.' She'd be asleep before she finished her meal if she had even one drink.

'I'll just have water, I think,' Will said as he selected a bottle of spring water from the fridge. 'Okay?'

'Perfect.'

The meal was tasty and satisfying, and Will sustained an easy conversation, explaining the operation of his medical practice, discussing staff and a few of his more challenging patients.

He cleared the plates and returned with two cereal bowls heaped high with ice cream. A bite-sized chocolate bar was jammed into each serving.

'I won't be able to move if I eat any more.'

'Just eat what you can. I won't be offended.'

'I'll do my best.'

They ate dessert in silence, until Sophie could eat no more. She put her bowl on the table and pushed away.

Will leaned over for her dish. 'I'll make coffee.'

Sophie snatched it away. 'No. You've done enough. I'll make coffee while you finish your ice cream.' She smiled. 'And then we can talk about Bev and Brianna.'

Sophie stood in the kitchen—his kitchen—with her back to him, washing dishes and making coffee.

She looked so at home.

Had it been such a long time since he'd entertained a woman that he'd forgotten what it was like?

But Sophie wasn't just any woman. He hadn't spent the last week working with her with his eyes closed. But there never seemed to be a spare moment in the day at the clinic where he could speak to her for more than a few minutes, let alone relax and enjoy her company.

His gaze fixed on that glorious mass of wavy hair that caught the light in a magical way, so that he wanted to touch it to see if it was real. The proportions of her compact body were just right—sculpted shoulders, lean, lightly muscled limbs, gently curved spine and a perfectly rounded bottom that moved tantalisingly as she turned to put each clean dish on the drying rack.

Whoa… Where had that come from?

An abrupt awareness of his long-suppressed libido had Will's thoughts darting in all directions and totally confusing him. He wanted to run his fingers through Sophie's hair and inhale the perfume of it…of her. He imagined slowly exploring the nape of her neck with his lips and then spinning her round and grasping that adorable rear so he could pull her close. Close enough to let her know how his body was reacting.

And—oh, Lord—his body was certainly reacting. If he didn't put a stop to this totally inappropriate train of thought, he was likely to seriously embarrass himself.

He rearranged his legs, put his hands deep in his pockets and sank a little further into the soft cushions of the couch, trying desperately to think of something so boring it would take his mind off Sophie…and sex…*sex with Sophie.* Not an easy task, but it worked.

Just in time.

She'd finished making coffee and presented him with a tray laden with a steaming plunger, two mugs and a small glass jug he'd forgotten he owned filled with milk.

'You found everything?'

The front view was even more…sexy. It was the only word Will could think of to describe the glimpse of the creamy white skin of her breasts, soft and rounded, edged with peach-coloured lace that Sophie had unknowingly exposed as she'd leaned over to put the tray on the coffee table.

Sophie sat down.

'Except the sugar.'

'I spoon my sugar straight from the packet.'

'Which I'm afraid I couldn't find.'

'Oh. I think I ran out yesterday.'

The mundane conversation about his failings as a house-keeper clinched it. He could stop worrying. Uncrossing his legs, taking his hands out of his pockets, he poured the coffee. Mercifully, his only thoughts were of when he would have time to do some shopping on the weekend. And how much he needed that mug of coffee.

Sophie slipped off her sandals and settled in the corner of the sofa, tucking one foot up on the seat and arranging herself in the collection of cushions so she was looking directly into his eyes. She was so relaxed. Her life was uncomplicated, her privileged upbringing enviable, her view of the world unsoiled by the reality of the kind of life he led. She yawned.

'I'm sorry.' She giggled, as if she was tipsy with tiredness. 'I think I'm going to need this coffee or I won't last the distance. We planned to discuss Brianna Sanders.'

Her eyes closed a moment, but then opened as he put her drink on the coffee table in front of her.

'Thanks.' She reached forward and then took a sip.' Shall we get down to business?'

'Of course. Brianna Sanders.'

CHAPTER SIX

MANY of Will's patients were living reminders of his past, and he suspected he was about to add Brianna Sanders to the list. If she *was* using drugs, for whatever reason, she had little hope, without help, of fighting her way out the hole she and her so-called friends were digging for themselves,.

When Will had taken over the suburb's ailing medical practice the statistics for physical, psychological and social dysfunction as well as actual deaths related to drug and alcohol abuse in Prevely Springs had been appalling. There had been some improvement over the years Will had been working there, but he knew there was so much more that could be done—and one busy GP just couldn't do it. Not on his own.

He'd tried his best, though.

Before Sophie Carmichael had breezed into town Will had been close to giving up.

But her fresh and optimistic outlook had revived him.

Yes, she was young, naive, and a little bit flighty at times, but she was eager to work. She certainly wasn't shy of a challenge either, if the time she'd spent with her last patients was any indication.

He was keen to know how she'd coped.

'So, how did things go with the Sanderses this evening?'

'That's the problem, Will. I'm not really sure. Beverley would have jumped through flaming hoops if she'd thought it would bring back the "well-behaved little girl" she said

Brianna used to be. She was receptive to every suggestion I made. But Brianna… Trying to talk to her was like trying to milk a bull.'

Will noticed a tiny muscle twitching in one of Sophie's eyelids.

He knew exactly how she felt. Tired and frustrated.

He sighed.

'That bad, huh?' he said. 'Bev told me Brianna's behaviour and personality changed soon after she started school last summer, after the Christmas vacation. She was fine before then. Does that ring any alarm bells with you?'

'I saw your note in Brianna's records about possible drug use, so I was tuned in to it being a potential reason for her behaviour. At first she said her main problem was she couldn't sleep and she wanted sleeping pills. I refused and said we had to find a cause for the insomnia before treating it, then asked her directly about drug use. She went so far as admitting she binge-drinks with mates but not that often. Maybe once a fortnight. She smokes dope when she can get it as well. The insomnia sounds more like a symptom of using uppers, but she denied taking speed or any of the similar drugs.'

Was it Will's imagination, or had Sophie's attitude subtly changed when she'd mentioned the drinking? He sensed a slight increase in her muscle tension. She clenched one of her hands into a fist and her eyes lost focus—just for a moment or two. He was used to reading body language, and he trusted his instincts. If Sophie had some sort of baggage related to alcohol it was probably best he know about it—particularly in view of his own past problems.

But she was now totally focused and back on track, and he wanted to hear more about her encounter with Brianna.

'Sounds like you're making progress with the girl.'

'I hope so. But I reached a dead end as far as her revealing anything more about drug use.'

'Do you think you're gaining her trust?'

'I'm trying, but we're not there yet. For the rest of the consultation I decided not to pressure her and went along a different track. I asked if she had any plans for when she left school.'

'And?'

'She surprised me. Said she'd always liked cooking and wanted to be a chef. She'd never mentioned it to her mother, though. And it's all bound up in low self-esteem. Her stepfather keeps telling her she's a useless piece of work and he can't wait to be rid of her. He certainly doesn't want to spend any money on her education and his attitude seems to be eroding any progress Bev makes. Bev's reached the point where she's run out of energy to stand up for Brianna.' Sophie paused and took a sighing breath. 'So Brianna resorts to bad behaviour, including drug use. It's a no-win situation.'

'You think she's using amphetamines?'

'Probably. The signs are there. If she is, I can't see her stopping unless we tackle the underlying causes.'

Sophie's emotional involvement with Brianna and Bev Sanders, even after one visit, was written all over her face. The sadness in her eyes, the frustration in the frown furrowing her forehead, the bewilderment and uncertainty in her expression all touched Will's heart. His dilemma was whether to let her go with her feelings—and risk being let down—or to warn her against the hard reality that change had to come from the patient herself. All a doctor could do was try and teach the skills to make positive decisions that could turn lives around. Will had been in that dark and self-destructive place and been lucky enough to see sense. Many others didn't have the strength of mind.

He had to caution her.

He wanted to comfort her.

'Sophie?'

She stopped fiddling with a loose thread on one of the cushions and looked up.

'Yes.'

'You've done good work with Bev and Brianna, and it sounds like you've got what it takes to tackle their problems.'

'Thanks,' she said. An appreciative smile lit up her face. 'This is new territory, and it's great to have your reassurance I'm on the right track.'

This is a woman with many layers, Will thought, and Sophie was beginning to reveal that what lay below the glitzy surface was a dedicated, caring doctor and a woman who was taking his breath away simply by being in the same room—there was no other way he could think to describe what he was feeling.

He had to get his mind back on the reason she was there. To discuss a challenging patient.

'But don't get too close to the issues and problems in what sounds like a pretty dysfunctional family.'

'I'm not sure what you mean. When you're trying to help someone, it's pretty difficult not to.'

'Maintain a degree of detachment…as protection against disappointment.'

Despite her outward sophistication Sophie had a soft centre, and Will felt the need to protect her from the kind of mistakes he'd made too often himself.

'You've made a good start with her. The fact she admitted to abusing marijuana and alcohol is a pretty big step on a first visit.'

That momentary look was there again—a mix of sadness and suppressed distress that Sophie was unable to hide. Will felt a compulsion to find out what had triggered it.

'I hope you don't mind me asking…and you can tell me to butt right out…but do *you* have any kind of personal issue with alcohol, or other drugs?'

He knew what he was saying was confrontational but he had to clear the air. If Sophie had any unresolved issues…

She blushed fiery red and then looked down at her inter-locked fingers in her lap. He hadn't expected that kind of reaction. Will regretted being so frank.

'I'm sorry. I was out of—'

'No, that's okay. It's not something I talk about.' She paused and her eyes reconnected with his. 'And I probably should— even though it happened a long time ago.'

'A long time ago? What happened?'

'When I was sixteen, my best friend—I'd known Jessica nearly all my life—was killed in a car accident that shouldn't have happened. Her so-called boyfriend was driving, showing off and speeding. He was breathalysed at four times the legal limit. You know the scenario. It's in the papers every day. He walked away with barely a scratch and little in the way of remorse.'

Sophie's hands trembled and her eyes shone bright with unshed tears. But she hadn't finished.

'Since then I always get edgy when I'm with anybody who drinks to the point of getting drunk.' She managed a smile. 'And I've been known to fly right off the handle at anyone who drinks more than one or two and says they're going to drive.'

Sophie's life hadn't been as charmed as he'd thought. Money certainly offered no protection against the tragedy she had experienced. Neither could it erase the memories.

Will felt compelled to comfort her.

He moved a little closer and put his hand on hers.

'I'm sorry,' he said quietly.

A single tear escaped from her brimming eyes and she wiped it away with her sleeve. Then she grasped Will's hand, pressing it to the dampness on her face. He needed no other invitation. He leaned across, put his arms around her and kissed her forehead.

Sophie was no doubt feeling vulnerable, her emotions fragile, but she was so beautiful…soft…and warm. She didn't protest or pull away but snuggled close to his neck. With the slightest tremor in her hands, she intertwined her fingers behind his head.

Will held her closer and nuzzled into her beautiful, silky,

sweet-smelling hair. His lips found the corner of her eye and touched her lids gently, one after the other, until the dampness was gone.

A tiny guttural sound issued from her throat and he could feel her heart beating even faster than his own. Will wanted to consume her, but it was Sophie who opened her eyes, tilted her head a little and then pressed her lips against his open mouth.

What was supposed to be a comfort-giving hug had inexplicably turned into something much, much more.

Their kiss was exhilarating for Will; an awakening. At first it was merely gentle pressure of sensitive skin against skin, then a hesitant probing of the nectar-sweet recesses of Sophie's mouth as she opened up to his intimate caress. The hungry exploration that followed left Will breathless. As the kiss deepened Sophie's hands traced a tortuous pattern down his back until she reached the belt of his trousers and pulled at his shirt until it was free. The touch of her palms as they skimmed the skin of his lower back sent a stab of molten heat to his groin.

This shouldn't be happening!

For at least a dozen compelling reasons.

Will opened his eyes and eased himself away from Sophie, who seemed to sense his passion had ebbed. He hoped she understood.

'I didn't mean to take advantage of the situation,' Will finally said, after what felt like an interminable silence.

Sophie ran her fingers through her hair and straightened her rumpled shirt. She was still close enough for him to feel the warmth of her breath and see the gradual rise of colour from the pale skin between her breasts to her neck and then her cheeks.

The physical intimacy they'd shared had taken him totally by surprise. It was out of character, inappropriate, and wouldn't happen again.

Sophie moved away and picked up her sandals from the floor.

'I'm sorry if...' Will had no explanation as to why, but he needed to apologise.

She looked up and gave him a half-smile.

'Don't be. I was as much to blame as you.' Her smile broadened. 'I guess we're both tired, got caught up with the moment, forgot that doctors should always listen to the left side of their brains. Impulsive decisions are not our forte. No harm done.'

'It won't happen again.'

'No,' she said quietly, slipping on her sandals. She glanced at her watch, her composure having fully returned. 'It's getting late. I'd better go.'

'The offer of the spare room still stands,' Will added, knowing she wouldn't accept and not blaming her.

'Thanks, but, no, thanks. I've been too much of an imposition on you already... And I sleep better in my own bed.'

Will wasn't about to labour the point to tell her she definitely was not an *imposition*.

'I'll see you tomorrow, then.'

Sophie didn't sleep particularly well in her own bed. She kept reliving how it had felt to be enfolded in Will's gentle arms, how a comforting kiss could turn into a deeply arousing revelation of passion and how, if Will hadn't pulled away, she could have easily been persuaded to take the kiss to the next stage.

No! She'd vowed to stay away from men...from *relationships*...from setting herself up for the same mistakes she'd made with Jeremy. It was too soon; she was too vulnerable. She had to fight the feelings she was beginning to have for Will Brent with all her might.

Where had it come from—the embrace, the kiss, the wanting more? She searched her mind for a logical explanation.

Maybe from a place in her heart that had been locked for too many years.

She'd not confided in Jeremy about her friend's death. He'd never been good with *personal,* or *emotional*, or anything involving a woman shedding tears. He was a typical macho, self-absorbed male who believed life's tragedies should be dealt with promptly before moving on.

But Will was different. She'd never met a man like him. He was totally selfless in so many things he did. He was kind, caring, understanding and also…very sexy.

Had she used him purely to fill the emptiness left by Jeremy? The thought horrified her.

After making herself a mug of warm milk, trying to read a magazine and then listening to a relaxation CD, she finally fell asleep at close to three in the morning. She then slept soundly and wasn't woken by her alarm. Her mobile phone began ringing at just after seven o'clock. She fumbled amongst the debris left from the previous night's sleeplessness and finally found it.

'Hello?' She half hoped it was Will, telling her how much he'd enjoyed last night and asking when they could do it again. But the voice on the line was gruff—annoyed, even.

'Sophie?'

'Yes, Dad. Is anything wrong?' Her father had rung her twice already during the week, supposedly to check how the job was going and how his 'favourite daughter' was settling in 'all on her own'. His previous calls had been at a more civilised time, though. Sophie suspected his agenda was to check up on how Will was treating her. He didn't seem to understand how she could *choose* to work in his practice, treating people from a social demographic he mistrusted and tried his best to avoid.

'Well…er…not wrong exactly, but there's something I thought you should know.' There was no loving greeting or even a stilted enquiry as to how she was. He obviously had something important on his mind.

She sighed, resigning herself to the fact that the extra hour of sleep she'd been hoping for, due to her later start at work on Saturday morning, wasn't going to happen. She was wide awake.

'And what's that, Dad?'

'I bumped into a dermatologist at a lunchtime meeting yesterday—someone who went to university in WA at the same time as your Will Brent. I tried to ring you last night but couldn't raise you.'

'I went out, Dad, and came home late. I left my phone in the car.' The last part was true, but she wasn't about to give him any more detail. If he asked for extra information, she'd say it was a night out to do with work. But he seemed more preoccupied with imparting his own important information. 'What did you want to tell me?'

'Well…er…' Her father cleared his throat. 'Apparently Dr Brent had problems in med school.' He paused, but Sophie stayed silent and let him continue. 'He nearly got booted out in the early years of his training—failed some exams—but was given a second chance.'

'Dad!' She was annoyed at her father's muck-raking interference and felt she had to defend her boss. 'You know nothing about what Will Brent's like, or his background. He's a good, caring doctor. He's not well off, like us, and I imagine he had a battle supporting himself while he was studying. I admire him for what he's achieved and I like working with him. It makes no difference to me whether he failed a couple of subjects.'

'I haven't finished, Sophie.' Her father's voice was now hard as steel, and she knew he had more dirt to turn. 'He was a drunk.'

'What?' Sophie couldn't believe what her father was saying. 'What do you mean?'

'He apparently had a problem with alcohol.'

She laughed. 'But what med student *doesn't* go over the top with drinking?'

He obviously didn't see the humour.

'You don't understand. He had a big problem. He was abusing

the stuff—an alcoholic. The only reason he was allowed to continue studying was because he vowed to give up drinking completely.'

Sophie felt tears brimming. Why was her father telling her this? Through some misguided sense of protection?

'Okay, you've said what you wanted to say. I have to go now, Dad. I need to get ready for work. I'll keep in touch,' she added out of politeness, and then pressed the 'end call' button. If her father thought she was being rude, that was his problem.

Sophie had agreed to work alternate Saturday mornings. Having an extra doctor, even for only a couple of hours, was a godsend for Will. He told himself so a dozen times as he tried desperately to put Sophie Carmichael and that exquisitely sensual kiss out of his mind.

'Oh, God, what have I done?' he muttered.

He had no room in his life for a woman...and definitely not Sophie. He had nothing to offer her. And he had no right to lead her on, even in the name of a brief affair. He didn't do affairs. He'd tried it a couple of times and the result had been anger and tears.

Should he talk to her? Or just pretend it hadn't happened?

As he drove into the clinic he still hadn't made up his mind.

Half expecting her to be tight-lipped about what had happened the previous evening, he wasn't surprised that after a polite 'Good morning, Will,' she hurried off to her room.

He saw little of her after that, and it was small consolation that her coolness, at least for the time being, solved his dilemma of whether to confront her.

But he wanted to clear the air. The fact that what he'd offered as purely a hug of reassurance had turned into something much more was regrettable.

Though at the time he'd certainly felt no regret. He'd been so caught up in the bombardment of physical sensations and long-

forgotten emotions he'd just wanted to hold Sophie—beautiful,
tempting, sexy Sophie—in his arms for ever.

The thought of revealing how he felt frightened him.

He'd dreamed about her last night. She'd floated into his
bedroom wearing a pure white, gossamer, full-length nightgown. She'd sat on his bed and offered him her hand, saying,
'Take me now. You might never have the chance again.' But
when he'd reached for her hand she'd disappeared—like all
the beautiful things in his life, all the people he'd really cared
about, she had been snatched away.

He couldn't face that happening again—he had to talk to
Sophie before she left.

Amazingly, they'd run to schedule—it was only just past
midday, and the waiting room was empty, so he assumed Sophie
had finished as well.

As he went to find her Will's mind whirled with twenty different ways of explaining and apologising for taking advantage
of her vulnerability the previous night.

She was in the treatment room, tidying up after a procedure.
He knocked softly, and when she turned she forced a smile.

'What can I do for you?' she said casually.

'I need to explain about last night.'

She resumed her task of clearing the trolley. 'There's no
need, Will. Forget it ever happened. It was the result of a set
of unexpected circumstances. Nobody's fault. Let's just leave
it at that.'

She'd summed it up perfectly. The kiss had meant nothing.
He meant nothing to her. He tried to hide his disappointment
but she was right.

'As long as you understand…and as long as it won't affect
our professional relationship.'

'Of course not. See you next week,' she muttered.

She pushed past him, the brief touch sending a pulse of
bright heat through his veins. Will wondered how he would
cope with the next few weeks—not because of overwork, or

tiredness, or the constant demands of his patients, but because of working side by side with Sophie… Unfathomable, untouchable Sophie.

He sighed. Why was life so complicated?

CHAPTER SEVEN

WILL was in a good mood. Sophie was proving to be a real asset to the practice. She'd been seeing more of Will's regular patients, which had definitely eased his workload. The clinic income was picking up as well—partly due to news of a female doctor in the neighbourhood spreading to the women in the area, particularly the older ones, who were reluctant to see *him* for any problem that might involve 'intimate women's complaints'.

He began wondering how to persuade her to stay. Purely for the benefit of the practice, of course.

He was trying his best to ignore the fact his relationship with Sophie had subtly changed since that unexpected kiss a week ago—without much success. He'd begun viewing Sophie more as an attractive, very feminine woman rather than simply as a colleague.

Despite his determination to keep their relationship on a professional level, it had become increasingly difficult to treat her purely as a very able assistant as she settled into the routine of working in his practice. He found himself at times behaving quite irrationally. He ironed his shirts; he'd resurrected a bottle of aftershave he hadn't used for years; he'd even tried to restore some order to the chaos that was his desk. And he'd been sure his face had turned cherry red when Sophie had caught him staring at his reflection in the tea room window, attempting to rearrange his unruly hair.

'If you're trying for the rugged, tousled look, you've definitely succeeded,' she'd said with a laugh.

He'd been unable to come up with a witty reply so he'd simply said, 'I just realised I'm overdue for a haircut.'

Sophie had grinned and sashayed out of the room, leaving him confused.

So when Andrew Fletcher's secretary rang one evening, to invite him and Sophie to one of Andrew's famous dinner parties, he'd had mixed feelings about whether to accept. Sophie would benefit from meeting some of the local specialists, but he knew how uncomfortable she'd been in the company of Andrew during their brief encounter when they'd collected the keys to her flat.

There was also a compelling reason for Will to attend. It presented the ideal opportunity to talk to some of Andrew's wealthy friends about raising money for his project. A possible complication of them going together, though, was that it would perpetuate the pretence that he and Sophie were a couple. Will wasn't good at acting, and dreaded having to explain to Andrew. He'd also have to make it clear to Sophie it wasn't a date.

The first thing he needed to do was check with Sophie before accepting and now, Friday lunchtime, was the ideal opportunity.

'Sophie!'

The sole occupant of the tea room, she had her head bowed over a journal with a steaming mug at her side. She glanced up with a look of mild surprise on her face. Will rarely had time for breaks, and he realised, guiltily, that he hadn't managed to have lunch with the staff since Sophie had started working with him.

'Mind if I join you?'

'No, of course not.' She closed the journal and took a sip of what smelled like real, fresh-brewed coffee. 'Can I make you one?' She stood before he had a chance to stop her. 'I bring my own and brew it in a plunger.'

'I'd love one. I'm not that keen on instant either, but—'

'I know. You need spare time to make it and, more importantly, to enjoy it.'

She was dead right, Will thought as he watched her swish the grounds, depress the plunger and pour him a mug full of the drink he thrived on.

Sophie had her back to him, and when she reached up to get the sugar from an overhead cupboard he was treated to a delightful glimpse of thigh and an accentuation of the curve of her bottom under her snug-fitting skirt. He sighed.

'Busy morning?'

Fortunately she'd totally misinterpreted his admiring response. She brought his cup to the table and sat down.

'Steady, I guess. I certainly haven't been rushed off my feet.' He hadn't yet told Sophie how much difference her working with him had made. 'I can't remember the last time I had a proper lunch-break. It's thanks to you I'm beginning to enjoy the luxury of having some spare time.'

'That's great to hear.' She seemed to accept the compliment graciously, but moved on quickly. 'Have some.' She pushed a plate of what remained of some lightly toasted rolls and savoury pastries towards him.

'I saw Brianna Sanders yesterday, and I was hoping to see you today for your opinion,' Sophie said.

'Well done. You must have struck a chord with her. Bev didn't hold out much hope that she'd co-operate. Any progress?'

'I think so, but it's hard to tell. I don't want to send her running by accusing her of using, let alone abusing illegal drugs. I'm still trying to gain her trust.'

'Sensible move.'

'I spent thirty minutes with her just talking about the problems of being a teenager. You know—bossy, controlling parents, annoying younger sibs, school, boys, sex. She really started to open up—until I asked her if there was a drug problem at her school.'

'And?' Will was impressed with her approach. For someone with her social background Sophie had remarkable insight into how Brianna's mind worked.

'She reverted to one-syllable answers so I wound the consult up and asked her to come back next week.'

'From what you've told me, you're on track with her. In my experience with kids like Brianna, the most important thing is getting their trust. After that, it takes time and lots of patience. They eventually start listening and accepting that the advice you give isn't all rubbish just because they perceive you as being too old to understand.' Will took a second bite of a mini cheese and spinach quiche. 'This is really good.'

'I know. I ate way too much.' Sophie looked at her watch and stood up, pushing her chair under the table. 'And I'd better get going. I think I'm fully booked this afternoon.'

'One last thing, Sophie.' Will hadn't touched on the main reason he wanted to see her.

'Yes?'

'I had a call yesterday from Andrew Fletcher's secretary.'

The tiniest flicker of a frown creased her forehead.

'He's having a dinner party next Saturday night. Apparently a gathering of colleagues. He wondered if you and I would like to come. His secretary said Andrew thought it might be helpful for you to meet some of the local specialists—put faces to names, that sort of thing. I think they call it networking these days.'

Sophie took a few seconds to process the information, but her reaction was difficult to read.

'Tomorrow night? It's a bit short notice.' she said.

'No, the following Saturday.'

'Oh.' She hesitated. 'Are you going?'

'I honestly haven't decided.' He paused, carefully considering what he would say next. 'Obviously it's not a date…but if you want to go, and you don't want to arrive on your own, I'd be happy to accompany you. I'll probably know most of the people there.'

'And you'd be a buffer between Andrew and me.' She smiled.

'If you like.' He smiled wryly in return.

'What time?'

'Between seven-thirty and eight.'

'Okay.' Her eyes suddenly lit up. 'It could be a perfect way to plug our…er…I mean your cause.'

She was thinking along the same lines as him, but her enthusiasm for a task he wasn't looking forward to surprised him. The last thing he'd expected from his new recruit was willing involvement in his obsession with rescuing the derelict building down the road in the name of trying to aid a group of young people many would regard as beyond help.

'I'll come round to the flat and we can walk across together.' Will grinned. An otherwise long and boring evening in the company of Andrew and his cronies might turn out to be pleasurable…with Sophie as his companion.

'Okay. It's a date.'

Will was frowning. She'd said the wrong thing, mentioning the word *date*, which made her even more nervous at the prospect of telling Will about her ideas for fundraising. She had no valid reason to be anxious, though. After all, Sandie had wheedled information from her a week ago and had done a lot of the groundwork—information-gathering, the compilation of lists of potential participants and donors. Her local knowledge had been invaluable. And now Sophie was eager to share their secret with Will. They already had a solid, workable plan. But not much time.

She summoned up the courage to say, 'Have you got a minute to spare? There's something else I want to talk to you about.'

Sandie breezed in as Will looked at his watch.

'You won't believe this. Your first patient's cancelled and

there's no one waiting.' She paused, and looked from Sophie to Will and back again, then grinned.

'Am I interrupting something?'

Will looked suddenly awkward.

'Of course not.' Sophie had the feeling she was rescuing her boss. 'I was just going to discuss our…er…research over the past week.'

Sandie's face lit up with a smile of anticipation.

'I wondered when you'd finally summon up the courage,' she said with a wink. 'I have a couple of minutes. Mind if I stay?'

Will looked more and more bewildered as their conversation continued. But he remained silent. Sophie sat down again.

'That would be great.'

'What's all this about?' Will finally said, after noisily clearing his throat.

'The community centre.'

Sophie held her breath, wondering what her boss's reaction would be to what some might consider meddling.

'I have some ideas for raising the money you told me you need.'

Will smiled indulgently. Sophie could tell he wasn't taking her seriously—probably thinking she was about to propose selling raffle tickets or chocolates at the front desk.

'Go on,' he said, with eyebrows raised questioningly.

Sandie sent her an encouraging glance.

'It's just an idea, but I thought of a football match.'

'A football match?' Will seemed to be trying his best to suppress a laugh. 'Remember we need to raise nearly a quarter of a million dollars.'

'Listen to her, Will. She's done this kind of thing before. You'll be surprised,' Sandie said with a knowing look.

Sophie took a deep breath. 'The idea is to reach outside the district—attract people who have money to spend and offer value for their hard-earned cash.'

Will listened attentively so Sophie continued.

'The national league season doesn't start for another six weeks, and there's interest from both teams in playing a practice match—like a pre-season derby—before the competition kicks off.'

'How do you know?' Will's interest was increasing.

'I contacted both teams' publicity departments and actually spoke to one of the coaches,' Sandie contributed with a grin. 'Of course, the media has got so much mileage out of…er…. the transgressions of one of their high-profile players they seem keen for a diversion that will show the clubs in a good light.'

'And where would this match be held?'

'The local ground is way too small, but I have three dates we could have East Park's oval free of charge. Two of those days, Sunday the twelfth or Saturday the eighteenth, are possibilities for both teams.'

'Free?'

'It's all in the marketing. If you can convince them it's free advertising—'

'You *have* done this before,' Will interrupted.

'Once or twice.' Sophie grinned and then went on. 'The capacity of the ground is ten thousand, give or take a couple of hundred. At ten dollars a ticket, plus some celebrity packages, the sale of food and drink, as well as a fashion parade and an auction, that would be at least half the money you need. The rest, I hope, will come from corporate and individual donations.'

'Fashion parade?' The expression on Will's face was one of disbelief.

'At half-time. That is where I really shine. You have to believe me—I know about fashion.'

'Sophie's already got tentative involvement from— What's the latest tally?' Sandie was as excited as Sophie.

'Sixteen.'

'Sixteen boutiques around the city and inner suburbs.

They'd donate clothes. We plan to get local teenagers to model them, and then auction them. And Sophie's confident we can obtain just about everything we need, including insurance, as donations.'

Both women stopped talking and looked expectantly at Will, who seemed overwhelmed.

After an interminable pause Will spoke.

'You think you can organise an event of that scale in...' he seemed to be doing a quick calculation in his head '...four or five weeks?'

'Of course. Having a deadline's part of the buzz.'

Will frowned and Sophie suddenly felt all their hard work in the last week had been wasted. She should have realised her conservative boss was unlikely to take on an event of such magnitude.

But then his face broke into a grin.

'What the heck? Go for it, girls.'

Sophie now had official approval to get things moving and it needed to happen fast.

'Where's the boss?' Sophie asked Sandie on her way out of the clinic at the end of the afternoon session. The waiting room was empty so she assumed Will had finished for the day.

'House call and then he's going home,' Sandie said as she picked up the phone, which never stopped ringing.

Sophie waited for her to finish her conversation before continuing. The receptionist turned on the answering-machine.

'I want to organise a meeting.'

'When?' Sandie was sorting patient records ready for filing the following morning.

'As soon as possible. I was hoping for tomorrow afternoon—say, about two o'clock? I've already checked with Lisa, and she and Pete can come as long as we don't mind her youngest tagging along.'

'Suits me. I have nothing else planned.' She grabbed her

handbag from under the desk and extracted a bunch of keys. 'Doug said he could help with the building side of the project and has some ideas. Would it be all right if he came too?'

Sophie smiled. She could feel the momentum building already. 'The more the merrier,' she said. 'I'll contact Will tonight and only let you know if it's not a goer.'

The women left the building together.

'See you tomorrow afternoon,' Sandie said with a wave.

When the phone had rung the previous night, just as Will had been taking the first large bite of pizza, his initial reaction had been one of dismay. Although he employed a locum service to cover emergencies after hours, he'd made it quite clear he wanted to be contacted if there were any problems with his patients. In effect, that meant he was available seven days a week.

But hearing Sophie's voice had instantly lightened his mood. Her enthusiasm was contagious and even if he'd wanted to, he hadn't been able to refuse her invitation to what she called 'a planning meeting', which would be held on Saturday afternoon.

When he opened the door to the tea room at twenty minutes to two the following afternoon he was greeted by Sophie's vibrant, twinkling eyes and disarming smile. She was alone and leafing through a large folder. Looking at her, all flushed cheeks and cheerfulness, infused him with a wonderful feeling he couldn't quite define. In the mix there was definitely hope—something he'd almost forgotten existed—with a good dollop of anticipation and a large pinch of…pleasure. Yes, there was no doubt he was pleased to see her and wished he could claim her company all to himself.

'The others should be here any minute,' Sophie said as she gestured towards the chair next to her.

'Who else is coming?'

'Sandie and Doug, Lisa and Pete, as well as a good friend of Doug's called Charlie Mundy and his daughter Colleen.'

Will swallowed hard and then cleared his throat. Charlie had been one of his grandfather's best mates. Will had gone to school with Colleen and she was now a teacher at the local high school. Since the death of Will's grandparents Charlie had always been there for him—if ever he needed a confidant, a shoulder to cry on or just someone to talk to who understood.

'Why Charlie?' The question had to be asked.

'I hope you don't mind, but from what Sandie told me he'd be a great bridge to the people we're trying to help. He apparently has widespread contacts in Prevely Springs so he's volunteered to be our community liaison person.'

Before Will could reply, Caitlyn appeared in the doorway.

'Okay if I go now? All the filing's done and I've switched the phone over, so hopefully you won't be disturbed.' She paused at the sound of chattering people approaching the back door. 'Looks like the team has arrived.'

'Off you go, then, and enjoy the rest of your weekend,' Will said.

A few moments later the room was filled with a noisy mob carrying plates of sandwiches, steaming meat pies and an enormous chocolate cake. Lisa busied herself with boiling the kettle and Sandie introduced Sophie to Charlie and Colleen, who were both beaming, then Colleen approached Will and gave him a hug.

For a few seconds Will was overcome with emotion.

He was no longer alone.

Surrounded by true friends, he was suddenly aware they were as passionate about the future of the Springs as he was. By his side sat the woman who had made it happen—the woman who was, as each day passed, quietly permeating nearly every aspect of his life; the woman he could very easily fall in love with...

The realisation struck him like a blow to his chest. He felt winded, unable to breathe, as his heart thudded in his chest.

No! He mustn't let it happen. Love led to one place only—a dark, hurtful torment of disillusionment. His grandparents had loved him—and he'd been their ultimate disappointment; he'd loved Tanya with all his being—and she had been snatched away; he'd dreamed of another kind of love, a mother's love, but he knew his dream would never come true.

'Is something the matter, Will? You've turned deathly pale,' Colleen said as she stepped back from him.

All eyes turned to him as he found his breath.

'I'm fine.'

Sandie chipped in. 'You're working too hard…and I bet you missed breakfast this morning.' She piled a plate with food and pushed it towards him. 'Am I right?'

'About breakfast, yes,' he said as he selected a sandwich. 'The food looks fabulous.'

Content with his answer, Sandie summoned the attention of the group and they all got on with the business of how to turn the fortunes of Prevely Springs around.

The meeting went better than Sophie expected.

They formed what could loosely be called a committee, with Sophie and Will sharing the helm, Sandie taking the jobs of treasurer and fashion parade co-ordinator, Doug volunteering to round up volunteers to help on the day, and Lisa and her husband taking on organising the football match. Colleen, as well as liaising with the neighbourhood schools, was put in charge of publicity, while her father was to be the voice of the committee in the community.

A good deal of the initial groundwork had been done, and Sophie had no doubts in her mind that their close-knit team would turn Will's dream into reality.

She sighed as the excited group collected the debris of a

very busy and productive afternoon and left Will and herself to tidy up a couple of loose ends.

Will looked totally exhausted.

'Do you want another coffee?' she said as she put a bundle of papers in her bag.

'No, thanks,' Will replied.

He slumped back into the seat he had recently vacated to say goodbye to the rest of the crew. He looked…in need of a hug. Sophie resisted the temptation.

'I won't keep you long. It's just the issue of…er…petty cash. There'll be expenses along the way that we can't expect the committee to take care of,' she said.

'Of course.'

After Will offered Sophie a paid afternoon off a week in the lead-up to the event, and a generous cash amount to start the ball rolling, he got up as if to leave and then hesitated.

'Sophie,' he said, and the weariness in his eyes was replaced by what she thought was a spark of appreciation.

'Yes?'

'I just want to thank you. You have no idea—'

'There's no need. I've enjoyed every minute…and what else would I do in my spare time?'

She smiled and Will took a step towards her, looking dangerously, enticingly attractive. He stood motionless for a moment and then lifted his hand to touch her cheek before grazing his fingers along a burning line to the angle of her jaw.

She wanted so much for his lips to soothe, his fingers to caress, his body to meld intimately with hers. But he dropped his hand and stepped away, leaving Sophie bewildered. How could such a simple touch leave her so…aroused? Had he any idea…?

'Sorry… I didn't mean to...'

Of course he knew, and was feeling just as vulnerable and out of control as she was.

But yielding to her gut feelings, to her body's reaction, was out of the question.

She stuttered a reply. 'N-no…no, of c-course you didn't. You must be tired. You must be… *I'm* sorry…' By now she was burning hot all over and her heart had gone into overdrive. She leaned down to pick up her bag in an attempt to hide her embarrassment, but only succeeded in dropping it and scattering the contents over the floor.

Will grasped her shoulders and spun her around so her face was mere centimetres away from his. She closed her eyes, not sure if it was in anticipation of a kiss or to block out the smouldering desire in Will's eyes.

Oh, Lord, I want this so much.

CHAPTER EIGHT

IT HAD taken all the self-control Will could muster to stop himself enfolding Sophie in his arms, pressing his impatient body against hers and kissing her thoroughly.

The situation had been awkward to say the least and could have easily turned into a monumental blunder…if his mobile phone hadn't rung.

Saved by the bell.

His conversation with the locum doctor had brought them both back to reality, and Sophie had taken the opportunity to make a hasty exit while Will was still on the phone.

Neither of them mentioned the incident through the week, though Will had half expected Sophie to bow out of their dinner engagement with Andrew Fletcher. On Friday, he reminded her of the dinner party and she said she was keen to meet Andrew's friends and hoped they were generous as well as wealthy.

She continued to tackle the fundraising project with gusto. He sometimes wondered why she was prepared to offer so much at the same time as giving him the impression she was having a ball doing it. After a great deal of thought he'd finally decided to not question her motives and let her, and Sandie, and half the population of Prevely Springs get on with the task of bringing Sophie's ambitious plans to fruition.

So when Will arrived home after work on the afternoon of the dinner party his mood was buoyant. For the first time in years he felt…happy, optimistic, and confident of a positive future for himself and the people of the Springs. He was on a high that had nothing to do with mind-altering drugs, but an awful lot to do with Sophie Carmichael.

He hummed softly as he showered. Then he pulled on a T-shirt, a pair of faded knee-length denim shorts and cast his gaze downwards to take stock of himself—something he rarely had the time or inclination to do. In fact, his house didn't even boast a full-length mirror.

He frowned. The casual crumpled look was definitely no longer fashionable.

The shorts, trendy in their day, were at least ten years old. The T-shirt, black with the graphic of a 1980s rock band emblazoned on the back, could probably only redeem itself as a collector's item.

But what did it matter? He wasn't trying to impress anyone, was he?

An image of Sophie popped into his mind. She seemed to be having an impact on him in many unexpected ways. He reluctantly admitted *she* was the reason he was thinking about clothes. And for some scary reason he didn't understand, it mattered what she thought of him.

He was a few months short of his fortieth birthday.

'You're as old as you feel,' he muttered as he did an about-turn and went into the bathroom. 'And I refuse to feel old.'

Will opened a new packet of disposable razors and squirted shaving foam onto his palm. After he washed his whisker-less face he patted his cheeks with the expensive cologne he'd bought on impulse the previous week, and dragged a comb though his still-damp hair. The reflection staring back at him from the mirror made him grimace. The hair was too much. It made him look like a pomaded Mafia boss. He rearranged his dark mane into its usual state of untidiness with his fingers.

'That's better,' he muttered, but he knew some subtle shift in his thought processes had occurred and he wasn't sure whether to be alarmed or pleased. The adrenaline he usually channelled into his work had taken a different direction and he found these strange thoughts he was having and his peculiar behaviour oddly exhilarating.

He made a snap decision to visit the city shops—something he hadn't done for years.

His expedition took up most of the afternoon. That evening, as he pulled on his trousers, buttoned his shirt and fiddled with his strange new hairstyle, he thought of Sophie's reaction—but it was too late to be having regrets.

She was the reason for it all.

What was done was done and was probably long overdue. He couldn't turn back the clock.

Half an hour later he drove into the car park of the flats where Sophie lived, feeling way out of his comfort zone, but he reminded himself she had only been the catalyst. He had to admit he felt younger, less tired and for the first time in years he experienced a spark of… What? A zest for living? New-found energy? The desire to look good to impress a woman?

And there was no doubt in his muddled mind who that woman was.

Sophie had no excuse for taking so long deciding what to wear. She only had two choices—her deep burgundy equivalent of the *little black dress* or a more conservative outfit of black flared silk trousers paired with a floaty, swirly, off-the-shoulder top she'd bought that morning.

She stood in front of the mirror for a final inspection, grimacing. She missed her three-times-a-week workouts at the gym and had put on a kilo or two. Prodding the skin of her thigh, she wondered, with alarm, if the slight bulge was the beginning of cellulite. Turning to the side and pulling in her stomach before inspecting her backside, she scowled.

'Too clingy. Too revealing,' she muttered as she smoothed the body-hugging fabric from her midriff to the mid-thigh hemline. 'I'll change into the trousers.'

At that moment there was a knock on the door and Sophie looked at her watch. Surely it wasn't Will already? But it was half past seven—he was right on time. Slipping on her high-heeled sandals, she went to open the door.

She was gob-smacked.

All thoughts of her own appearance evaporated.

It was hard to believe the slickly dressed, tall, dark and handsome hunk was the same man she'd worked alongside for the last three weeks.

He looked gorgeous!

She tried to keep a straight face, but by the look on his face she hadn't been as successful as she'd hoped.

The transformation was hard to believe. He was a picture of casual but sophisticated elegance. He wore sleek black tailored trousers sitting snugly on lean, relaxed hips. His long-sleeved deep blue-green shirt revealed just enough of his perfectly proportioned torso to make any red-blooded woman want to see more, and accentuated his naturally olive skin. He was clean shaven with the hint of a sexy five-o'clock shadow.

And his hair... It had been cut fashionably short and professionally styled to look ruffled. The deep brown, almost black colour was natural, but caught the light in a way that glinted with an almost silver sheen.

He surprised her by grinning and doing a self-conscious twirl. The look on his face was apologetic—embarrassed, even.

'Like it?'

What did he expect her to say? That he could come and decorate her living room any day he liked?

'Not bad. A definite improvement.' She chuckled.

He laughed as well, but gave the impression he wasn't completely comfortable with his new look.

'I'll take that as a compliment,' he said with a lingering, hesitant smile. 'And don't *you* look stunning?'

She felt his gaze drift from her hair all the way to her toes and suddenly remembered her dress—the deep V of the neck-line that exposed way too much cleavage, the too-short skirt and the clinging fabric revealing bulges she hadn't realised she had.

He was staring at her.

She definitely had to change.

'Can I come in?' he said.

'Yes, sorry—of course.'

'Just sit down while I get changed. I won't be a minute.'

'Get changed? Why? You look fabulous.'

'Are you sure? The dress isn't too…er…?'

'It's perfect, Sophie.' He grinned. 'As long as you can cope with the admiration of all the men present.'

He was almost flirting, but not quite. And she liked it. If Will approved, she'd stay with the dress. It was stretch fabric and would probably…stretch.

'Let's go, then,' she said as she grabbed her purse and linked her arm in his.

Will knew that every pair of eyes at the party, including the women's, would be on Sophie. She was dressed to kill.

He felt protective of her, though, despite the fact he couldn't lay claim to being anything more than her employer and friend providing the courtesy of accompanying her to a party where all the guests would be strangers.

What if she were his date?

He dismissed the thought, realising it was futile to even imagine the possibility of crash-landing in paradise.

They walked the short distance to Andrew's house, weaving their way through the cars belonging to guests who had already arrived—a BMW convertible, a late-model Range Rover and a vintage Porsche. It was like cruising the showroom at Perth's major dealer in luxury cars.

'Specialists must earn good money here,' Sophie said as they reached the elaborate covered entry to Andrew's house.

'The ones Andrew fraternises with do.' He tried to keep the sarcasm out of his voice. These days Will was rarely invited to functions like this and he had a good idea why.

'The Porsche belongs to Sam Baxter, an extremely popular and successful plastic surgeon who specialises in cosmetic surgery,' he added. 'His wife runs a skin clinic that does dermabrasion, Botox, laser treatment and the like. Exceptionally lucrative and dependent on full-paying private patients. I'm not sure who owns the other cars.'

Sophie didn't reply and appeared to be absorbing the information. She'd feel quite at home with Andrew's guests, he was certain. He pressed the buzzer and a few seconds later the door was opened by a middle-aged man in a dark suit. He promptly took the drinks and seemed to know who they were without introduction.

'Dr Brent, Dr Carmichael, please follow me,' he said formally.

Will glanced at Sophie as they both followed the man into a large, tastefully furnished living room. Andrew broke away from an earnest conversation with Lance Braithwell, a fellow cardiologist. Their host extended his hand to Will and kissed Sophie lightly on the cheek.

'Fabulous you both could come.' His gaze fixed on Sophie, swinging from her dress and its delectable contents back to her face. 'You look absolutely gorgeous, Sophie. Come and meet the other guests.' His hand, the one not holding a bright blue cocktail, found its way to the small of her back as he guided her towards the Baxters. 'What would you like to drink?'

Will took the opportunity to slip away, find the kitchen, and organise his own drink. He felt sure Sophie and her admirers wouldn't miss him.

The kitchen was a hive of activity, and Will was barely noticed as he scanned the contents of a huge fridge dedicated purely to liquid refreshment. He finally found what he was looking for—a particular brand of dry ginger ale which, in the right glass, could pass as light ale. He'd devised various strategies over the years to avoid drawing attention to the fact he was a teetotaller, or the reason why. He always kept a small amount of wine and beer at home for visitors but had never been tempted to imbibe.

He totally understood Sophie's distrust of drinkers and their sometimes irresponsible behaviour. He had no intention of re-visiting a time in his life that had nearly been his undoing by revealing a part of his past he'd rather forget. It was best Sophie didn't know.

Ignoring the questioning look from the teenager washing dishes, he selected a heavy-based beer glass from a crate near the sink and filled it close to the brim. Task accomplished, he made his way back to the party and was content, at least initially, to stand quietly in the background observing, before embracing the task of fundraising.

Not surprisingly, Sophie was sitting on a couch, talking animatedly to an admiring audience of three men, including Andrew, and she gave the impression she was quite capable of looking after herself.

'You must be Will Brent.' A young woman with a tangle of blonde hair, wearing a sleeveless denim mini-dress in the unlikely colour of purple, metallic black ankle boots and a jumble of silver jewellery, sidled up to him. She looked as if she'd be more at home at a rock concert. She'd startled him out of his reverie and he came close to spilling his drink.

'That's right. I don't think I've met you before. You are…?'

'Angie Baxter.' She smiled mischievously. 'Doctor, daughter of Sam and Olivia, recently appointed registrar to Andrew.'

It was difficult for Will to hold back his surprise and she must have picked up on it.

'Surprised? That such conservative parents could pro-duce—?'

His laughter cut her sentence short.

'A little. You don't exactly fit the mould of Andrew's usual guests.'

'Neither do you, or so I've heard.'

'And do you believe what you've heard?'

'Now I've met you…definitely not. In fact, you scrub up nicely for someone who's supposed to hang out on the wrong side of the tracks and work so hard he's forgotten how to have fun.'

Just then Sophie appeared, and for a reason totally unknown to him Will suppressed the sudden urge to explain or apologise or both, as if she were his date.

'Who's forgotten how to have fun?' Sophie said innocently.

'Excuse me.' Angie seemed to lose interest in Will. 'There's something I need to see Andrew about, now he's free. Hope you don't mind?'

'No, of course not,' Will assured her, with a little more enthusiasm than he'd planned.

Sophie stared at him with a quizzical twinkle in her eye.

'I hope I didn't interrupt something important.'

Will shrugged. Sophie was teasing and he liked it. It implied familiarity and being comfortable in the other person's company. He dropped his voice and leaned close.

'I actually found her a bit scary. Would you believe she's Andrew's registrar and…her mother and father are here!'

Sophie laughed. 'No, it wouldn't surprise me at all. Are the Baxters her parents?'

'That's right. How did you guess?'

'They're slightly…how can I put it?…bizarre as well. Olivia's just offered me a cushy job in cosmetic medicine. No interview, no CV or references required. Sam said I qualified for the job on the basis of my looks alone—as an advertisement for their treatments. I wouldn't trust him as far as… Well, I just wouldn't trust him.'

The lightness of Will's mood suddenly took a dive as he began to understand his colleague's motives in wining and dining Sophie Carmichael. She was probably seen as a desirable and youthful addition to the social set Andrew and his cronies moved in. Not only was she decorative and charismatic, but also clever, and the type of graduate who would jump at the chance of a well-paid, relatively undemanding job at such an early stage of her career—particularly if she wanted to marry and have children. That type of long-term job in Western Australia would also solve her problem of getting away from her ex.

'What did you tell him?' Will guessed Sophie had refused the offer, but also hoped she hadn't offended the couple. He'd planned to ask them for either a hefty donation or ongoing sponsorship for the community centre upgrade and he wanted them onside.

'I just thanked them politely and told them I couldn't make any commitments at the moment because I didn't know how long I would be staying in Perth.'

Will smiled, surprised at the intensity of relief he felt. 'Full points for diplomacy,' he said, hiding his emotion, something he was expert at.

'Oh, and of course I mentioned our fundraising, gave the cause a bit of a plug, and they seemed interested. Said they'd be keen to hear what you had planned.'

'That's fabulous.'

He felt like scooping her into his arms and thanking her properly…thoroughly…with a heartfelt kiss, but…

A young man Will hadn't met, who'd recently joined Andrew's private practice as a partner, introduced himself and spirited Sophie away to meet his wife. Will took the opportunity to put on his most charismatic face to work the room, and before he had a chance to catch up with Sophie again the butler appeared, ringing a tiny bell, and announced that dinner was served.

By the end of the main course Sophie had had enough. Her permanent smile made her face ache, she was fed up with the never-ending stream of doctor and lawyer jokes, and she could no longer keep up the façade that she was enjoying herself.

Everyone drank more as the evening progressed.

Except Will. He seemed to make the same glass of beer last all night and contributed very little.

The other guests were letting their hair down, getting louder and cruder, and when the conversation degenerated into cruel criticism of those who weren't there to defend themselves she decided she would make her excuses to leave at the first opportunity.

Also, the tone of the evening as it progressed made her feel edgy—particularly as it looked as if they were all going to drive home.

She wanted to leave. With Will.

Somehow she had been persuaded to sit between Lance Braithwell, recently divorced, and Andrew, perennial playboy. She didn't know how to escape. Will was at the other end of the table, tolerating what appeared to be an endless, one-sided conversation with Angie Baxter. He looked as if he'd reached his limits as well, but she had no idea how to join forces with him and tactfully make an exit.

Finally she had her chance when it was announced that dessert, coffee and liqueurs were being served by the pool and the party moved outside. She approached Will.

'Enjoying yourself?' she asked with what she hoped was tact.

Will shrugged. 'Are you?'

'Not really.' She leaned close and whispered, 'They're boring, Will. They've had too much to drink. I think if I left at this stage of the evening they wouldn't even notice.'

Will responded to her frank assessment with a hoot of laughter.

'Well said. You're absolutely right.' He grasped her hand, moved back from the pool into the shadows and began to walk purposefully towards the side gate. 'I'm game if you are,' he added, with a mischievous grin on his face.

They were both breathless as Will furtively closed the gate. Then Sophie began to giggle. Her mood was contagious as Will tried to muffle his laughter.

'Shush,' Sophie whispered. 'They might send a search party.'

Will grasped her hand and they jogged down Andrew Fletcher's driveway as fast as Sophie's high heels would allow. A few minutes later they stumbled up the single low step to Sophie's flat and stopped a moment to catch their breath. Will released his grip on Sophie's hand and stood hesitantly.

'Well…' he finally said. 'I guess I'd better get going.'

Sophie could barely see Will's expression in the dim light but his body language suggested disappointment. It was only ten-thirty—hours before Sophie's usual Saturday-night bedtime—and she wasn't ready for her first night out in Perth to finish so soon. She didn't want the evening to end, and deep down she knew it was because she wanted to spend more time Will.

She assumed, from his inability to let go and have a good time, the dinner party had been an ordeal for him. He definitely wasn't comfortable with Andrew's crowd, and she suspected the evening had been purely a means to an end—a way to take his dream a step closer to reality.

Her eyes became accustomed to the gloom and she noticed Will was hovering, as reluctant to part as she was.

She had nothing to lose.

'It's too early, don't you think?'

Sophie was aware of Will tensing and she wondered why. Had she misread his body language? She paused, waiting for his reaction, but he stood motionless in the half-dark.

'I'm not sure what you mean,' he finally said.

'It seems a shame to waste the new clothes, the whole new look by having an early night.' She smiled and reclaimed his hand. 'And I feel I need an antidote to the after-effects of spending several boring hours in the company of Sir Andrew and his friends.'

He laughed. Her attempt at humour worked.

'Great.' His eyes seemed to twinkle in anticipation. 'I'm a bit out of touch with the late-night scene, though.'

'All the more exciting. We'll both be venturing into the unknown.'

'Okay, let's find ourselves somewhere to party.'

As they walked hand in hand to Will's car, Sophie felt a sense of freedom, as if the shackles that bound her to the past had been broken.

The reason was the man beside her.

But she didn't dare think of the future.

CHAPTER NINE

SOPHIE's suggestion took Will totally by surprise. He wondered if she'd homed in on his reluctance to say goodnight.

But where could he take her? It had been longer then he'd like to admit since he'd set foot in a late-night bar or club, but he didn't want to appear completely out of touch.

'Where would you like to go? Somewhere quiet? I remember a piano bar in one of the old pubs in the city.' He paused to take a breath. He could hardly believe what he was about to say. 'Or perhaps you'd prefer some real excitement. A nightclub, maybe?'

He held his breath and prepared himself for Sophie's laughter but her answer was deadly serious.

'After Andrew, clubbing sounds good to me.'

'Oh.' He felt a tingle of combined exhilaration and trepidation travel from the base of his skull all the way down his spine. Late-night revelling was probably second nature to Sophie and her sophisticated Sydney set. He didn't want to disappoint her.

Did he know any decent nightclubs?

The only one that came to mind was The Quarterdeck. Andrew had invited him to celebrate one of his divorces there a few years back, but Will had politely declined. He remembered, though, that his colleague had said it catered to an older and more sophisticated clientele than the usual night spots.

Sophie was still standing on her doorstep, looking at him expectantly and waiting for a reply.

'You're serious, then?'

'Absolutely.' She was challenging him, probably thinking *fun* was a word that had disappeared from his vocabulary. And she was right.

But he *so* wanted to spend more time with her. And if risking making a total fool of himself was the only way to do it...

'I've heard there's a place in Fremantle that's okay.'

'In the port city?'

'That's right. It's called The Quarterdeck.'

'Sounds good to me. Are you okay to drive?'

Will understood Sophie's concern, but wasn't going to explain he'd been drinking a soft drink.

'I'll be fine. I've only had one all evening,' he said.

She seemed satisfied with that and smiled.

'Shall we go, then?'

There was an undercurrent of tension buzzing in the air as Will drove the ten kilometres to central Fremantle. Was he nervous about spending the rest of the evening with her? Had she put their professional relationship at risk? Comfort-zone boundaries were being stretched again, Sophie thought as Will expertly eased his car into a narrow space about a block away from the nightclub.

'Ready to party?' Will said with a smile that looked a little forced, and Sophie wondered if he was having second thoughts.

'That's what we're here for.'

He made his way around to the passenger side of the car and opened the door for her while she quickly checked her make-up and dragged a comb through her tussled hair.

'You look gorgeous,' Will said, appearing slightly embarrassed.

He locked his car and then took her hand. She could easily

get used to cradling this man's warm strong fingers in hers. It felt right, somehow.

'It's this way,' he added.

They walked the length of the narrow side street in silence and then turned into the main road, which bustled with activity. Crowded bars spilled their patrons onto open-air drinking areas. Late-night diners filled the many restaurants and a queue of about twenty people snaked its way towards the entrance of The Quarterdeck. Sophie sighed with relief when she saw that most of the patrons were in their late twenties and thirties—a mixture of couples, groups and singles.

'Do you think the queue means we have to wait for people to come out before we can go in?' Will asked as they took their place at its tail.

'I doubt it. It's still early and unlikely that the place is full.'

Will laughed. 'You call eleven o'clock early? I'm usually tucked up in bed by now.'

Sophie sent him a sideways glance.

'Lucky you.' Her tone was light, the words easily taking on a double meaning, but she didn't have a chance to gauge Will's reaction. The line moved forward as a large group at the front gained entry and it wasn't long before the entrance fee was paid in exchange for the mark of a small rubber stamp on the backs of their hands and admission to a loud, hot, pulsating den of night-life.

Sophie felt energised.

Will looked bewildered.

'Come on!' she shouted. 'Over there—near the bar. There's a table free. You'd like a drink before we dance, wouldn't you?'

Will nodded mutely and didn't complain as she led him across a dance floor crammed with a seething mass of people.

'Let me buy you a drink.'

'No, I—'

'Just the first one, to thank you for bringing me out to rage. It's the least I—'

But her voice was drowned out by the music and he seemed so overwhelmed he was beyond protest.

She'd have to get something special, she thought, and decided at that moment she would be skipper for the night. If he wanted a drink or two on what she presumed was his first Saturday night out for…well…probably longer than she could even guess, he wouldn't have to worry about driving.

Shouldering her way through to the bar, she scrutinised the cocktail list and found the one she wanted—the one she'd been introduced to by her best friend Anna on the night of her last final-year exam.

'What's in your All Night Long?' she requested when she finally caught the attention of one of the bar staff.

The barman listed the familiar ingredients.

'And pineapple juice?'

'That's the one, darling. With a dash of lemon and lime.' The brawny bartender winked. 'You want one?'

'Yes, and a pineapple juice in the same type of glass, thanks.'

After he'd carefully measured and mixed the drink, Sophie couldn't help taking a sip of the delectable cocktail she'd bought for Will, hoping he'd accept it in good spirits. It was just as she remembered—the perfect combination of smoothness and bite, designed to be sipped slowly, every drop savoured.

She glanced across to where Will sat and smiled. He was vigorously shaking his head at three young women who were vying for his attention and the seat he seemed to be guarding jealously—presumably for her. Always the gentleman.

He looked relieved when she arrived back at the table and the women left them in peace.

'That looks fancy.' Will grinned as she placed the drinks on the table.

'My favourite special-occasion drink.'

'Special occasion?' The music began again after a short break and Will leaned close to her so he could be heard. His breath was warm on her cheek and she could tell he was becoming swept up in the heady, effervescent mood of the place. His cheeks were slightly flushed and one leg began to move with the throbbing rhythm of the music. Sophie anticipated little persuasion would be needed to get him up to dance.

'My first night out in a new city.' She'd almost said *first date*, but checked herself just in time. It was ludicrous to even contemplate them being a couple.

'And *my* first night out for longer than I can remember.' Will stirred his drink with the bright plastic swizzle stick, its top shaped like an anchor, and took a sip. To her dismay, he frowned. 'What's in it?'

'That's a secret between me and the barman. Don't you like it?'

'It's not that.' He hesitated. 'I don't drink…when I'm driving.'

'I'll drive,' she said with a smile, and pointed to her drink. 'Just pineapple juice.'

'We can swap, then.'

He moved the glasses with a determination that showed he wasn't going to argue, and Sophie suddenly remembered what her father had told her—what she'd dismissed as manipulative and misguided gossip.

Maybe Will didn't touch alcohol at all. Other than at Andrew's, where his one drink had seemed to last for ever, she'd never seen him have an alcoholic drink. In fact, she hadn't seen him pour his drink at the dinner party and couldn't be absolutely sure what it was. Perhaps she'd have the courage to ask him later.

By that time the volume of the music made conversation near impossible and they were both content to watch the rabble of clubbers, Will in apparent wide-eyed wonder. She was enjoying herself more than she had in a long time. It felt so good to be out having uncomplicated fun with a man she liked and knew she could trust. It was easy just being with Will.

Swept up in the moment she stood and grasped his hand.

'Come on, let's dance.'

Will grinned and downed the last two mouthfuls of his drink.

'You don't know what you're letting yourself in for,' he shouted.

'Let me be the judge of that.' Sophie doubted he heard her reply.

They managed to blend in with the roiling mob, but despite the crowd around her Sophie's awareness suddenly focused. Her partner, gradually shedding his inhibitions, grabbed one of her hands and swung her in an intimate arc until their bodies collided with reckless anticipation. It was as if she and Will had the dance floor to themselves. He pulled her towards him, his pelvis pressed hard into her belly and his hips swaying to the primal pulse of the music.

His lips grazed her forehead and left her skin smarting and her body confused. He inclined his head and said in a rasping whisper, 'I'll stop if—'

'No, don't stop.'

It was probably no more than ten minutes that Sophie and Will spent locked in an abandoned embrace, oblivious to anything other than the music and themselves, but for Sophie it felt like a lifetime.

She didn't want it to end.

Her awareness of every muscle of Will's body, the firm pressure of one hand in the small of her back and the other sliding seductively from just below her shoulder blade to her backside and back and his warm, uneven breath touching her forehead had every nerve ending painfully primed for pleasure.

She wanted him.

If it was purely lust, she didn't care.

If this extraordinarily sexy man was willing, what was the

harm? If they both had a physical need, an infuriating itch that desperately needed scratching, then why not?

Rules were made to be broken.

When the music stopped she had no doubt he was just as aroused as she was, and when he said, 'Shall we go?' Sophie knew he wasn't asking because he was bored or disenchanted with the club. He wanted to be alone with her.

He wanted *her*.

She answered, 'Yes,' without hesitation, and didn't know how long she could wait.

They were both breathless as they walked towards the corner of the street where Will's car was parked, but there was no doubt in his mind—Will knew what he was doing. Although the music, the dancing and the mesmerising feeling of being part of a like-minded crowd had loosened him up, his head was clear. He'd even given himself time to think through what had happened on the dance floor.

It was a wonderful, magical but purely physical desire he felt for Sophie. The unfamiliar set of circumstances—the atmosphere, the noise, the combined raw energy of the patrons in the club—had triggered a bubbling to the surface of something he'd kept inside too long.

His sexuality.

He'd just had no need for it, and he'd viewed it as a hindrance to the things he considered important in his life.

But now…having kissed Sophie on an impulse a fortnight ago, having been so close to making love to her on the dance floor…he knew the urge was more powerful than mere reasoned restraint.

And Sophie was hot—there was no other word for it.

The experience was invigorating, all-consuming and tantalisingly acute. He didn't need to waste words on asking Sophie how she felt or what she wanted either.

He knew.

They rounded the corner, and now they were away from prying eyes he needed at least to kiss her.

He pinned her against the rough brick wall and she groaned.

'I hold you responsible,' she said, with the barest hint of a smile.

'Full responsibility accepted.'

The words were barely out of his mouth before his lips found hers. Her mouth was delicious. She tasted of fruit, a hint of coffee, and something he could only describe as sexy and very feminine.

Her hands were on the back of his head, steadying, possessing and ensuring the captured kiss lasted as long as *she* wanted.

And it lasted. Long and lingering.

She pressed her mouth hard against his and then bit his lower lip before opening up to him. Their mutual exploration left him gasping as he realised his whole body was responding.

And Sophie knew it.

Her lips still caressed as she pressed one teasing thigh between his legs while her other leg somehow tangled around his knee, almost straddling him, exciting him beyond endurance.

She pulled away and opened her eyes, a startled look on her face.

'Not here,' she whispered.

'No.' He caught his breath, slightly embarrassed that he'd become so immersed in the moment he'd lost sight of where they were.

'Come back to my place,' Sophie said, her voice laced with the same urgency *he* was feeling. 'It's closer,' she added with a cheeky smile that drizzled into his being like melted chocolate. He had no objections.

'Okay.'

The word was barely out of his mouth when a skinny, scantily clad girl of about sixteen or seventeen emerged from a lane-way twenty metres or so from where they stood. She looked stoned and desperate, and Will found himself alert—primed for danger. He'd be surprised if she was on her own, and a number of scenarios went through his head.

He had no problem if she turned out to be simply a passer-by or genuinely needed help but, with his experience of how some of the teenagers in Prevely Springs managed to survive, he had to be sure.

Sophie was busy adjusting her dress and hadn't noticed. She looked up as the girl began to stumble towards them, crying. Then Sophie moved so fast Will didn't have a chance to stop her.

Sophie wondered why Will hesitated when the girl was obviously distressed and needed help. It was instinct to go to her and find out what was wrong.

'What's the matter?'

The teenager's tears turned to sobs. 'I… My friend…'

Sophie grasped the girl's shoulders. She made no sense.

'What's your name?'

She stopped sobbing and took a ragged intake of breath.

'Emma.'

Sophie felt a firm hand on her own shoulder and turned to see Will with a look of disapproval on his face.

'What's she told you?' he asked.

'Nothing yet. Just her name.'

Emma was shaking now, her skin mottled despite the mildness of the night.

Sophie ignored Will and moved towards the teenager, putting her arm around her shoulders and confirming she was cold.

'We can't help you if you don't tell us what's wrong, Emma.'

'Be careful, Sophie.'

She glanced briefly at Will but continued. 'Your friend? Is there something wrong with your friend?'

'We took some stuff. The guy said it was like speed but better because it'd make us feel good without the aggro. We'd chill out and relax.'

Sophie began walking towards the lane-way, aware of Will at her heel.

'What happened then?'

'Everything was cool, but then my friend Lexie, she was sick, and had some kind of fit. The guy, he just ran, left us, and I can't get Lex to wake up.' She began sobbing again. 'You've got to help us. She mustn't die.'

'Okay, where is Lexie? Can you show us?'

It was the first sign from Will that he was prepared to help. He leaned towards Sophie and spoke quietly, as if he didn't want Emma to hear.

'Let me go first. You stay back—just until we make sure it's safe.'

'What?' Sophie didn't understand why he wouldn't believe the girl. Anyone could tell she was scared witless.

'Just trust me on this one. I've been in the same place as Emma. I know how her world works and it's not always kind.'

Sophie dropped back as they followed Emma into the lane. They were only a few metres in when they saw the other teenager slumped against a skip bin.

Will started to run.

'She doesn't look good,' he called as he reached the girl, who appeared to be unconscious.

Sophie wasn't far behind.

Will checked she was breathing then laid her on her side. He inspected her pupils—not easy in the dim light—and barked an instruction to Sophie.

'Ring for an ambulance. Tell them we've got an unconscious teenager with a probable drug overdose and it looks like she has some respiratory depression. Do you know the name of the street?'

Emma's frightened form emerged from the shadows. 'Genevieve Lane, off Alcott Street.'

'Good girl.' Will's tone was reassuring and Emma managed a smile.

Sophie reached the emergency services on her mobile phone and was connected to the ambulance base communications officer. She relayed what she knew, and added that although there were two doctors in attendance they had no equipment and could only administer at-the-scene first aid. She made it quite clear it was a life-or-death emergency.

Lexie was lucky. There was a large tertiary hospital nearby, and an ambulance was promised in five to ten minutes. Her chances of survival and recovery were good, even if she stopped breathing and needed CPR before the paramedics arrived.

'Five minutes.' Sophie relayed the information to Will, whose fingers were on Lexie's neck, feeling for her pulse.

'Good. The sooner, the better.' Will directed his gaze at Emma. 'You did the right thing. I think she'll be okay.'

Sophie saw some of Emma's anxiety dissipate and was glad Will's sensitivity had returned.

'Can you wait for the ambulance at the entrance to the lane to show them where we are?' he added.

Emma shuffled back to the street.

'You really think she'll be okay?' Sophie asked, sensing there was nothing more that Will could do other than maintain the girl's airway and monitor the vital signs he was able to measure without equipment.

He took his eyes off his patient and looked at Sophie long enough for her to see that his expression was one of unfathomable pain. She knew now was not the time to ask why.

'I think so. It's possible she's a street kid, but I don't think she's on hard drugs. More likely a one-off dose of a party drug. They're often contaminated. Her history—the short time between euphoria and then vomiting and convulsions before she passed out—suggests it might be GHB.'

'No reversal drug?'

'No, the opiate antidote has no effect but we always give it. You have little to lose in a comatose patient, but if they've been using narcotics it can mean the difference between life and death. A good proportion of heroin ODs are resuscitated at the scene and don't even need hospitalisation.'

'I've heard they often refuse to go to hospital when they wake up.'

'Right, and you rarely get any thanks.'

Sophie felt the bitterness in Will's words but had no time for reflection on her colleague's attitude to drug-users.

They heard the ambulance siren gradually getting closer, and Emma waved frantically from the pavement at the end of the lane.

'They're here,' she shouted, as the bright green and white vehicle pulled up. The driver stopped briefly to talk to Emma and then slowly reversed down the lane.

A briskly efficient woman jumped from the passenger seat, gathering her resuscitation kit. Her colleague followed with a stretcher, an oxygen cylinder and another large bag.

'I'm Liz. What have we got here?' She leaned over the girl, looking and feeling for respiration, slipping an airway into Lexie's mouth, feeling her pulse, checking her pupils.

'Took an unknown oral drug. Her friend said she started vomiting, then fitted and finally lost consciousness.'

She glanced at Sophie. 'And you're both doctors?'

'Mmm.'

'Looks like it was this kid's lucky night, then. What do you think she took?' She was addressing Will now.

'I'm not positive, but my first guess from the history and the fact she's unusually cold, has a bradycardia, respiratory depression and is out of it—'

'GHB?'

'Right.'

'Second callout tonight.' Liz's partner spoke as he was preparing to insert an IV line.

'That's Geoff.'

He nodded while positioning the cannula into one of the fragile veins in Lexie's forearm.

'He was about the same age but in much worse shape. Had to be intubated.' He taped in the tube, connected the bag of fluid and then drew medication from an ampoule, which his partner checked.

'We'll give naloxone here, though, and if there's no response she'll need to go to the ED. Do you think she's likely to arrest?' Liz asked.

'She's been unconscious but stable since we've been here—about ten minutes—with no deterioration in her resps.'

Will threw a glance in Sophie's direction. She felt redundant.

'Do you want me to go in the ambulance?' He'd directed the question to the paramedics.

'No, there's no need. They're expecting us and it's only five minutes to the hospital. Any response?' Liz asked Geoff, who was carefully giving increments of the antidote drug at one-minute intervals. The effect to reverse opiate toxicity was usually rapid—within minutes. Lexie's lack of response suggested she hadn't OD'd on heroin or related drugs.

'Nah, and that's the max—two milligrams. I think it's time to move her out.'

'Can I go with her?' a small voice interrupted.

Sophie suddenly felt guilty about neglecting Emma.

'Of course. The doctors will need your help.' Liz smiled at the girl. 'And when Lexie wakes up, I bet she'll want a hand to hold.'

The two paramedics with all their paraphernalia wheeled Lexie the short distance to the ambulance.

'Thanks for your help,' Geoff called.

As Liz passed Sophie, she said quietly with a wink, 'Enjoy the rest of the evening. Lucky you. He's gorgeous.'

CHAPTER TEN

THE magic of that breathless, heady encounter, when Will had pressed Sophie's willing body up against the wall and kissed her, had dissolved as soon as Emma had staggered from the lane-way. By the look on Will's face it was unlikely to be re-captured—that night, at least.

'She should be okay,' Will said, as if he was talking to a colleague after a successful resuscitation.

'What will they do at the hospital?'

'If she shows no signs of deterioration she'll most likely be admitted for monitoring and observation. Although she didn't improve before the ambulance arrived, the kid stayed stable, so I doubt she'll get worse.'

'That's good.'

'And they'll do toxicology, of course.'

'Mmm.' Sophie had seen enough kids with drug habits to know resuscitation from an OD was only the tip of the iceberg. 'Will she be followed up?'

Will turned and looked at her with sadness in his eyes.

'Appointments are made, but you're lucky to get fifty per cent to show up. The biggest problem is trying to break the cycle.'

Sophie knew what he meant. Treating the effects of drugs didn't address the cause—the set of circumstances that had led to young person's substance abuse in the first place.

'The youth centre should make a big difference.'

Will slowed his walking pace a little and looked directly into Sophie's eyes. His weekday weariness had returned.

'Before you came on board I was beginning to wonder if it would ever get off the ground.' He sighed. 'I thought the process would be easy but I still feel I'm fighting an uphill battle.'

Will still gave the impression he was shouldering the whole load and Sophie wanted to let him know he was no longer alone.

'But we're trying to get the people of the Springs involved. The folk who will benefit. The centre will have more meaning if they've actually helped to make it happen.'

'That's not been the major problem.' A hint of a smile brightened his gloomy expression. 'Grass-roots support doesn't make any difference to how slowly the bureaucratic wheels turn.'

Sophie couldn't think of anything reassuring to say, so she stayed silent and her thoughts returned to the two teenagers they'd helped. Emma had seemed a caring kid, at least, and Sophie had the feeling the girls weren't addicts—she hoped they had just been experimenting and had the sense to learn from the night's experience. The type of centre Will was working so hard to set up would be ideal to follow up kids like Emma and Lexie—to try and keep them on track, to break the cycle of cause and effect.

Will and Sophie had been walking and talking and were now only a few metres from Will's car. Sophie was disappointed that Will was so distant. He hadn't even offered to hold her hand. Perhaps what had buzzed between them a short time ago had been illusory—purely a result of the near frenzied atmosphere of the club and their mutual loneliness.

Not reason enough to jump into bed together.

Will opened the car door for her.

'Thanks.' Sophie smiled but Will's face was impassive.

'I'll drop you home.' It was a statement from Will, not a question.

They travelled the entire journey to Sabiston in silence, and when they arrived at Sophie's flat she was wide awake. She knew it would take time for her to relax enough to sleep. She craved company, Will's company.

'Do you want to come in—?'

'No, I—'

From the look on his face he'd misunderstood.

Sophie smiled. 'Just for a coffee. I'm a bit wound up after what happened and could do with the company…just to talk.'

He grinned sheepishly.

'Yes, I'd like that.' He paused and took longer than he needed to turn the engine off and extract the key from the ignition. He glanced briefly in her direction but seemed embarrassed. 'What happened between us...'

He wanted out.

'Impulsive—in the heat of the moment.'

'A mistake.'

Not in Sophie's view, but they both needed time to reassess the consequences of a short affair with no possibility of a future. From what she'd gleaned of Will's personality in the short time they'd known each other, he wouldn't embark on anything without giving one hundred per cent.

'Right,' she lied, but knew it was for the best.

They got out of the car and made their way to the flat in the light of the dim car-park lamps. The soft yellowish glow cast shadows and a light breeze stirred leaf litter from the single plane tree behind the flats—the only sound, other than their footsteps, to disturb the clear, moonlit night. The atmosphere created was eerily sensual and Will looked particularly handsome with his shadowed jaw, ruffled clothes and uncertain expression.

Sophie wondered if she'd made a mistake by inviting Will in when she had the sudden urge to reassure him by putting her arms around his beautiful body and just holding him. He seemed so vulnerable and alone.

She turned on the light.

'Come in, Will. Make yourself at home,' she managed as she regained her composure.

Sophie looked around the small living-dining room and wished the furnishings were less sparse. The single sofa and the modest two-place dining setting provided the only seating, and she needed to maintain some distance from Will.

'Sit down.' Sophie made a sweeping gesture, leaving Will to make the decision of where to sit, suddenly wondering why it mattered so much. 'I'll make coffee. Okay?'

'Great.' He pulled out one of the chairs from the table and sat where he could watch her prepare the drinks. 'Need any help?'

'No, thanks.'

It was polite small talk. Sophie relaxed as she added water to the kettle and coffee to the plunger.

'You've settled in, then?'

'Yes. The flat's great. There's a park a block away, a supermarket nearby. I've even had a cup of tea with my elderly next-door neighbours.'

Sophie brought a tray with mugs, coffee-maker, milk and sugar to the table. She poured Will's drink the way she remembered he liked it—black and strong—then nudged the sugar in his direction as she sat opposite him.

'Okay?'

'Fine.' He stirred a generous spoonful of sugar into his cup and then absently added another. He looked up at her. 'Have you managed to get any spare time since you've been here…to enjoy yourself?' He chuckled but it sounded unnatural, contrived even. 'Done any sightseeing?'

'No sightseeing. I've done some shopping, and I swam a few laps in the pool at the local gym this morning.'

'Good.' He looked as if his mind was somewhere else and they both sipped their drinks in silence for a very long minute or two before it began to feel uncomfortable. As Will adjusted the cuff of one sleeve and began fiddling with the button on the other cuff Sophie recalled something Will had said when he'd attended to Lexie. It had played on her mind at the time.

'Do you mind if I ask you something personal?'

He looked at her, initially with slight irritation, before he rearranged his face and laughed.

'My personal life is as boring as mud. Fire away.'

Sophie boldly continued, despite his dismissal.

'You said you'd been in the same place as Lexie.' The smile froze on his face. 'What did you mean?'

He looked away, as if gazing through the window at something in the distance, but the only view was the early-morning dark. Sophie assumed he was thinking, deciding if he trusted her enough to give her an honest answer.

'It's a long story.' He focused back on Sophie and locked her eyes in a frighteningly intense look. 'How much time have you got?'

She was wide awake and had all night. Neither of them had to work the following day.

'As long as it takes.'

Was he about to close off from her? Or had he decided to reveal a secret he guarded as if it was a curse?

Their coffee was going cold. Sophie felt like something stronger.

'I've got a bottle of Chardonnay in the fridge. Would you share it with me?'

He didn't hesitate.

'No, thanks. I don't drink—'

'And drive.' She finished the sentence, remembering what he'd told her in the club and still dismissing her father's revelations about Will's past.

'Do you mind if I have one?'

'Of course not.'

Will stood, scraping the chair awkwardly on the hard floor but not seeming to mind. He collected the half-empty cups and put them on the tray.

'I think I overdid the sugar,' he said with a grimace. 'I'll get the wine. You go and sit on the couch and make yourself comfortable.'

'You sure? I can—'

'Don't worry. I think I know where everything is.' He'd already opened the fridge and found the bottle. He held it up for her to see. 'Wine—fridge; glass—glasses cupboard; cork-screw—knick-knacks drawer,' he said, with just enough cheeky sarcasm to make her laugh.

'Okay, I believe you. You're capable of finding your way around my kitchen.'

She crossed the short distance to the sofa and sat in one corner of the large and comfortable couch, slipped off her sandals and tucked her feet under her bottom. She no longer felt nervous about being physically close to Will and decided she'd go with the flow and let the rest of the evening take its own course.

As Will found the corkscrew and uncorked the wine he tried to decide how much of his past he was prepared to reveal to Sophie. He had no family left who would remember and he'd never told anyone else—not even Tanya. He'd never wanted to. Though his mother's death and his own brief experience with drugs had had a profound influence on the choices he'd made in his life, he didn't like to dwell on the past. He hoped he'd moved on.

There was something about Sophie's gentle probing, though, that demanded an explanation of his behaviour with the teenagers earlier in the evening. He'd reveal whatever he was comfortable with, he decided.

He found a diet cola in the fridge, brought the wine bottle and glasses to the coffee table and poured Sophie's drink. He sat down, angling himself in the corner between the arm and the back of the seat. The couch was roomy enough so they weren't touching. He wasn't quite sure why but it seemed important that there was at least a small physical distance between them.

'So, tell me about yourself.' Her smile was tentative.

'You know a little already.'

'The important stuff?' Sophie sipped her wine.

'Some. You've seen my house. You know it belonged to my grandparents and that they brought me up.'

Sophie didn't prompt him to continue but he could tell she wanted to hear more.

'I can't deny I had a happy childhood. They did the best they could, but June and Albie were getting on in years. June was in her early forties when she had my mum—the miracle baby from God who arrived after so much waiting.'

'And your mother's dead?'

'She abandoned me when I was two and died of an overdose of alcohol and benzodiazepines three years later, when my grandparents thought she'd come off the hard drugs. They were devastated, but I was too young to comprehend.'

It was easier than he'd thought, exposing the naked truth of himself that he'd kept buried in a dark place too long. Sophie put down her drink and reached for his hand. Her steady warmth comforted him.

'My grandparents were completely honest about everything. As soon as I was old enough to understand they told me how my mother had died and that there was no way of knowing who my father was… But they loved me and would do anything for me. That was something they didn't have to tell me, I knew. They seemed to invest everything in me. I was the son they never had. They didn't want to make the same mistakes they'd made with my mother. I was their golden-haired boy. And I let them down.'

'How?' Sophie's voice was a soft whisper and her eyes were moist with the tears *he'd* never been able to shed.

'Can't you guess?'

He knew it was an unfair question, but he needed a moment

before he could go on. The telling was a kind of pain that had to happen before he could be set free. How had he not known it before?

Sophie shrugged.

'Drugs? That would explain…'

'Yeah, I guess it explains a lot, but it doesn't make it right.'

He took a gulp of his drink, then another.

'I did the predictable teenage thing. Got in with the wrong crowd. Started wasting my life and my grandparents' money on drugs. I spent a year deadening my brain with alcohol and dope before I started on speed.'

'Heroin?'

'No, fortunately I didn't get that far, but on my seventeenth birthday I ended up in hospital, out of my brain on a cocktail of uppers and some prescription antidepressants that one of my so-called mates stole from his mum.'

He took a deep breath. The memories came flooding back as fresh in his mind as if it were yesterday.

'I was lucky I didn't kill myself.' He couldn't help smiling.

'What's funny?' Tears trickled down Sophie's face and his own eyes were moist.

'The irony of it.'

'Irony?'

'I had a deep loathing for the police and it was probably them who saved me.'

Sophie moved closer to Will so her head rested on his shoulder. Her arm entwined in his and she held his hand tight, as if she was afraid of losing him.

'What happened?'

'They were called to the party. I was remorselessly abusive, though I gather not physically aggressive. They took me in via the hospital, because I emptied the contents of my stomach in their van and promptly passed out.

'The doctors in Emergency punished me with two lots of

gastric lavage, and I reckon they found the most junior intern and inexperienced nurse to treat me. And I don't blame them. I deserved to have my stomach pumped.'

'Even if you didn't need it?' Sophie was smiling too.

'For sure. A bastard of a tube stuck down my gullet, the biggest funnel I'd ever seen, and unlimited quantities of fluid being pumped in and out… I tell you, that was a defining moment for me.'

He'd never been able to see any humour in the downward spiral his life had taken in his teen years. It was a liberating experience to laugh at some of the events of so long ago.

'So what happened? You must have finished school to get into medicine and get your degrees.'

It was so easy to tear his heart open for Sophie.

'Albie died. It was only a month after I got into trouble. I blamed myself totally. I believed I'd killed him even though he was eighty-one, had diabetes and ischemic heart disease and was probably a heart attack waiting to happen.'

'And you survived all that?'

'My grandfather was in hospital a week before he died. I stopped taking drugs the day of his heart attack and went in with June every day to visit, sometimes staying so late the night staff booted me out when they started their shift about ten.' He laughed. 'They all thought I was an angel—the perfect grandson.' The slow sigh came from deep within. 'I had lots of time to think—to re-evaluate the reason for my existence and to decide how best I could help my grandparents. June was so proud her grandson was training to become a doctor…' The words stuck in his throat. 'But she didn't live to see me graduate.' Will held back tears. 'She died of a stroke five years after Albie passed away.'

He looked down at Sophie, grasped her chin and tilted her head so he could see her face.

'You must have been highly motivated to study medicine,' Sophie said.

'I had a good brain, so my teachers always said on my school reports, just a bad attitude. So I decided to use my brain, took university entrance subjects at college, gained entry to medicine as a mature student and...' He kissed Sophie's forehead. 'Here I am.'

'Looking after people like your grandparents. Battlers. And kids like the one you used to be.'

'You've got it.'

Sophie brought his hand up to her lips and kissed it lightly. She took a few moments to absorb what he'd said.

'And you've...er...never married?'

Her question stabbed directly into his heart.

'No.' He felt drained and wanted to close the subject, but Sophie persisted. Her intuition had kicked in again.

'Why not?' She rubbed her thumb across the back of his hand and the repetitive action was surprisingly soothing. What did he have to lose?

'I came close. Her name was Tanya. We were both too young. I was in the second year of my medical degree, June had just suffered her first stroke, and I was still weighed down with guilt.' He cleared his throat and swallowed, but it didn't stop the husky emotion in his voice. 'Andrew came along and swept Tanya off her feet.'

Sophie attempted a smile. 'You're a survivor, that's for sure.'

He wasn't about to tell her that had been the second time in his life he nearly *hadn't* survived. He'd used alcohol, not drugs, after Andrew and Tanya had cruelly betrayed him, to numb the pain. A time in his life he'd rather forget.

He hoped Sophie understood now who he was, why he continued to work in a rough neighbourhood notorious for its high level of poverty and crime. If he pulled even one kid out of the gutter and set him on the road to a better life, he felt he'd begin to repay the debt he owed his grandparents.

'So, having my practice in Preverly Springs is my way of paying back my grandparents, Sophie Carmichael.'

'I can see that,' she said softly, and then they both gave up on suppressing enormous yawns.

Will looked at his watch. 'Lord, it's two o'clock. I'd better go.'

Sophie stretched. 'You're overtired and I'd guess emotionally drained.' She patted his hand as they stood. 'Would you like to stay here tonight?'

Of course he would.

But he knew he couldn't. There was too much at stake. Sophie was…like no other woman he'd ever met. Underneath her bubbly, carefree and pampered exterior was a heart so big and kind and loving he could easily fall head over heels for her.

In fact, he was beginning to feel it happening already.

And love… Well, it meant commitment.

The night of lust-driven sex that could easily have happened if they hadn't been interrupted earlier in the evening didn't sit right in his conscience. She deserved better—and he wasn't in the position to provide anything more.

The attraction was there, he had no doubt, but the circumstances were all wrong. It could never work.

He smiled and then kissed her lightly on the cheek, trying his best to give the impression he'd read nothing more into her offer than the provision of spare blankets so he could sleep on the couch.

'Thanks, but, no, thanks.'

Sophie seemed to understand.

'Okay.' She hesitated a moment before wrapping her arms around him and hugging him. Then she stepped back and looked directly into his eyes before continuing.

'I can imagine how hard it must have been…'

He shrugged. The conversation was becoming too intimate. He'd opened his heart to this young woman and shared part of himself that he'd offered to no one else. Now he needed time alone, to try and make some sense out of what to do next.

'I'm fine.' He gathered his keys and they both walked to the door. 'I'll see you Monday.'

The previous evening had been a powerful experience for Will. He'd gone to sleep thinking of Sophie and she was still in his mind when he woke the next morning. Not only had she shown him how to relax and have fun again but she'd rekindled emotions he'd kept buried for half a lifetime.

She'd also awakened sexual feelings he'd kept in check for so long he'd been surprised and a little awed by their ferocity. But the physical awareness hadn't happened overnight. Thinking back, his attraction to Sophie had probably begun the day he'd met her and had been simmering in the background, waiting for the right moment to reach boiling point.

He'd come close after they'd left the club last night. It would have been so easy to succumb…

But now the previous night seemed like a dream. Sophie was easy to be with, easy to work with…easy to love. But she was from a different world. He could tell she missed her young, upwardly mobile friends and the hectic social life she'd left behind. Her suggestion to go out after they'd left Andrew's had most likely been a result of sheer boredom rather than any desire to spend more time with him. He was crazy to think she had feelings for him. Any sort of future together was out of the question.

She had her whole life ahead of her, and was just starting out in her career. She could pick and choose the work she wanted; in fact, she had what some might consider an ideal job waiting for her back in Sydney.

He wondered if *she* realised the full implications of embarking on a personal relationship with him. The medical practice he'd literally saved from the gutter, his patients, the work he did with people mainstream society often rejected was his life. He couldn't move away. Not in the foreseeable future.

If the unlikely happened and she decided to stay on, it had to be for the right reasons. Not staying out of guilt, or pity, or purely because she needed an escape from a difficult period in her life. She was on the rebound and he happened to be the first eligible male she'd bumped into…

He needed his partner in the practice to be as committed as he was.

She seemed to be getting over the break-up with her fiancé, and she'd have no problem finding new suitors. He didn't know how to live in her world and she would probably tire of him before too long.

They'd had a fun night out together…but that was all. They were totally incompatible for anything more than a one-night stand. He didn't do one-nighters. It was total commitment or nothing for him—in his relationships as well as his work. Maybe he was a perfectionist, setting high goals for himself, but he'd seen the mess his mother had made of her life and there was no way he was going to repeat any of her mistakes. He knew commitment to a life with him wouldn't be easy and she would have to be a very special woman…his Ms Right.

He pulled on faded jeans and shrugged into a crumpled shirt, wondering what he'd done to deserve a life full of so many complications.

He'd just have to stop thinking of his Ms Right…especially in terms of Dr Sophie Carmichael.

CHAPTER ELEVEN

SOPHIE spent most of Sunday trying to clear her mind of thoughts of Will. She cleaned the flat until it gleamed, spent an hour at the pool, caught up with her e-mails and replied to them all—but the thoughts wouldn't go away.

When her phone rang just as she was about to order take-away, she half hoped it was Will.

'Hello?' Sophie recognised her parents' Sydney number and wondered why her father was ringing again. She'd only spoken to him the previous day.

'Darling, how are you?'

She sighed. It wasn't like him to ring her for a friendly chat. She hoped he wasn't about to lecture her yet again on the morals, verified or not, of her boss and the merits of packing her bags and going home.

'I'm fine, Dad.' She cleared her throat, knowing there was a reason for his call, wondering how long it would take for him to travel the circuitous route before he actually told her. 'How are you?'

'Missing you, Sophie, but otherwise excellent.'

'Great.'

Her father coughed, and she imagined him formulating in his mind some request he was going to make or some important news he was going to impart.

'It's wonderful to hear from you, Dad. A pleasant surprise, and I really appreciate your call. Was there anything...?'

'I wondered how you were coping with the work over there. You've been away a while now and I thought you'd have an idea when you were coming home.'

She wouldn't be surprised if he'd been making more enquiries about Will's practice. He'd informed her on his last call that he'd tracked down another couple of doctors who'd worked in the West. He'd already tried to find out about Prevely Springs and appeared to enjoy collecting ammunition to use against her employer. He'd never be happy with the simple truth, though.

'I'm enjoying it, Dad. The practice is very different from home. Most of the patients are low income or on benefits, so their problems can be challenging. But that's what I'm here for—a change and to broaden my experience.'

'What's he like, this Dr William Brent?'

He said each word of Will's name as if he'd been forced to say something particularly unpleasant. Sophie's skin tingled at the thought of telling her father the truth of how she felt about Will. For a start, he didn't hail from Sydney, hadn't been to a private school, and definitely came from the wrong side of the tracks. The cards were stacked against him. She had no doubt her father practised his own kind of snobbery—particularly when it came to the company his oldest daughter kept. And he'd liked Jeremy. Sophie's father hadn't even tried to hide his disappointment when they'd broken up, choosing to ignore the fact her fiancé had been two-timing her.

Will was playing in a totally different field but she didn't expect her father to understand.

'He's dedicated, experienced, hard-working.'

'Has he contacts over there? Are you meeting the right people? Have you managed to catch up with David and Felicity Barr?'

At least he wasn't harping on about Will's alleged drinking problem. Perhaps he'd decided to woo her back home by other means.

'Not yet, Dad. I haven't really had time.'

The last thing she felt like talking about was Andrew Fletcher's dinner party, knowing her father would approve of his guest list.

'No, of course not.' He paused. Maybe he was finally going to disclose what he'd really phoned about.

'So you'll stick out the next few weeks, you think?'

'Yes.'

'And then you'll be back?'

'Look, Dad, all I can say at the moment is that I plan to stay for the time I've committed to, and then who knows? If things work out I might stay on—'

'For another few weeks?'

'Maybe. I'm not sure yet.'

'Oh, it's just that Janet Willis has dropped a bombshell.'

Janet was a GP about her father's age and had been working at his practice for as long as Sophie could remember. Sophie got on well with her—the only other woman in a male-dominated practice.

'Why? What do you mean?'

Janet was as steady as a rock, dependably calm in a crisis, and took her fair share of the typically demanding, well-heeled female patients who often just needed a sounding board. Sophie's first concern was that she was unwell.

'Is she sick?'

'No, nothing like that. She's leaving us.'

Now Sophie understood. For her father, that would have as much of a negative impact as if Janet had been seriously ill. She let him explain.

'Her daughter Pippa and her husband look like they're staying in the UK. Pippa's pregnant and is having a difficult time of it. Janet's going over to help.'

'So she's coming back?'

Sophie couldn't really understand her father's concern. Janet had taken several months' leave to help her daughter with her first baby, and that had been before Sophie had started working with the practice.

'That's the thing, darling. She isn't. She has registration in England and a job. Richard has some contacts, and of course they'll have no problems with visas.'

'Are they going soon?'

Ross Carmichael ignored her question. Something he often did when he wasn't happy with the direction of the conversation.

'So you must see, Sophie, I need you back home as soon as possible. This little *jaunt* of yours… If you're worried about what people think about that fiasco with Jeremy—'

'No, Dad. I'm over that. I just want to get on with my life.'

'Of course you do. I understand. So as soon as we can get you home… I can talk to this Dr Brent if you want me to. I'm sure we can work something out.'

At that moment Sophie realised how much control her father had had over her life, for longer than she wanted to admit. Well, she'd tasted freedom now. If she wanted to stay in Western Australia, if she wanted to continue working with Will for a week, a month or a year, it was going to be *her* decision. She needed time to think. She might well decide to return to Sydney when the eight weeks was up, but she wasn't going to be bullied by her father. She was determined to make up her own mind.

'No, Dad, I'm staying.'

'What did you say, Sophie? I must have misheard.'

'I'm staying. I've agreed to at least until the end of the month, and I'll let you know my plans from then on.' Her father was strangely silent. She took a deep breath. 'So I suggest you advertise for a replacement for Janet as soon as you can.'

'But, Sophie, you can't—'

'Yes, I can.'

And then Sophie did something she'd never done before. She

hung up…before her father had finished what he'd wanted to say. She'd actually had the last word.

It felt good.

The next day, when Sophie arrived at work, she could hear animated chatter followed by muffled laughter coming from the tea room and was curious to know what was going on.

'What's the joke?'

Lisa and Sandie fell silent and exchanged looks, suggesting they might not want to share the reason for their amusement.

Sophie smiled. 'Should my ears be burning?'

Sandie stirred milk into the drink she'd made and cleared her throat. 'No need to worry. We're not talking about you, and you'll find out soon enough, so we might as well tell you.' Again she looked at Lisa and the nurse nodded.

'Go on,' Lisa said.

'It's the boss.'

'The boss?' Sophie was intrigued.

'We think he's had some kind of life-changing experience on the weekend. It took a double-take to recognise him when he breezed into Reception this morning.'

Sophie suddenly realised what they were talking about. She prayed that the increase in her heart rate and the sudden rush of whole-body warmth wouldn't give her away. Lisa didn't seem to notice as she continued where the receptionist had left off.

'He's bought some new clothes that are actually *trendy*—not mass-produced department-store stuff.'

'And had a haircut,' Sandie added with a grin. 'He looks absolutely gorgeous. If I wasn't a happily married woman…'

Both women fixed their gaze on Sophie. It took all she had to maintain her composure. Did they know?

'We thought he'd either won the Lotto or… We wondered if *you* might have had something to do with it,' Lisa said slowly.

'Me?' Sophie laughed and raised both hands to her shoulders, palms outwards. 'Why would what Dr Brent wears have any-thing to do with me?'

Sophie didn't want to hear the answer, and thankfully the conversation was interrupted by Caitlyn.

'It's getting busy at the front desk.' The girl was addressing Sandie. 'And the phone's going non-stop. I could do with a hand.'

The women's attention shifted.

'Sorry, Caitlyn. I'll be right there.'

'Thanks. And you've got three patients waiting already, Dr Carmichael,' Caitlyn added, before she did an about-turn and hurried back towards Reception, with Lisa and Sandie not far behind.

Sophie took a deep breath, trying to pretend Saturday night hadn't happened. The logical part of her brain told her that if Will took the relatively small step of reclaiming some of his time for a social life he would find the perfect woman. He already had his female staff drooling and they were only the tip of the iceberg. It was just a matter of time.

The trouble was, her heart was sending her a completely different message. She wanted him for herself.

Sophie's day sped by with no time to stop and talk to Will, let alone admire his revamped appearance. Every time their paths crossed he was civil but economical with words. It was diffi-cult to know what he was thinking. She was over the halfway mark in her stay and had begun to seriously think about the possibility of staying on.

The hints from Will about how he felt hadn't happened, so she was still undecided.

From her first day she'd found the work and the people she treated in Prevely Springs a challenge. The rewards weren't measured in terms of money and prestige, though, but they were certainly there for the taking if you were prepared to give that little bit extra. Job satisfaction was in a different league from the humdrum routine of treating the wealthy, who were often unnecessarily preoccupied with their own health, back home.

Home?

Did she really want Sydney to be home…for the rest of her life? She was beginning to have serious doubts now she'd experienced a way of life so different, so unpredictable, so interesting…and so full of possibilities.

After her father's phone call the previous day she'd felt angry and annoyed. He'd automatically assumed she'd do as he wanted and run back to Sydney because he *needed* her. He took absolutely no account of *her* needs and, in retrospect, he probably never had. All the important decisions directing the course of her life had been his. Medicine, general practice, Jeremy…

Maybe it was time to start taking control. Extending her stay with Will Brent could be the first step, but she still had a few weeks to make up her mind.

She tidied her desk, gathered her things and walked the short length of corridor to Will's room. His door was open and he sat at his desk, tapping away at his computer keyboard. He looked up when she knocked.

'Finished consulting for the day?' she asked.

'Just about.'

'Are you calling in to see Bella Farris tonight?'

'I am. I wasn't sure whether you wanted to come or not.'

'Do you mind if I do?'

'Of course not. I'll be ready to go in ten minutes.'

A short time later they set off in Will's car.

'Shelley phoned this morning and warned me that Bella's deteriorated. She suggested we contact her daughter.'

Will glanced across at Sophie, probably to gauge whether she understood the full implications. Although Sophie had only seen the Farris family twice, she felt she'd made an impression on Bella's withdrawn son. His mother's death would be an enormous stress for him but her training hadn't prepared Sophie for the reality of dealing with a fourteen-year-old's grief.

Her instincts told her she might add to his distress by deserting him. Brad and Bella Farris were two more reasons for her to stay on.

'She's in the last stages?' Sophie asked, choking back emotion she'd thought she'd be able to control.

'That's right.'

They made the rest of the short trip to Bella's house without speaking. When they arrived Brad was outside, manoeuvring a battered skateboard down the slope of the drive. He smashed into the letterbox and then repeated exactly the same sequence, the second time flattening the post. He seemed oblivious to their presence and the damage he was doing.

'He's angry,' Will said quietly.

'At his mother?'

'That's right, and probably at himself for what he sees as his helplessness; at me for not being able to provide a cure; at life in general for dealing him such a cruel hand. We'll have to tread softly with Brad over the next week or two.'

'You think that's all the time Bella has left?'

'I can't say until I see her, but from what Shelley said—'

Will's sentence was cut short by the thumping sound of Brad skidding past the car and apparently stopping by turning sharply into the back of the wagon.

'He's an accident waiting to happen. Let's get him inside.'

Sophie climbed out of the car while Will gathered his bag.

'You've been practising. I reckon that gives you an unfair advantage,' she said to Brad as he scooted past.

The last time Sophie had seen Brad he'd told her he planned to borrow a skateboarding game from a mate—an oldie but a goodie, he'd said, and had seemed keen to share it with her. She figured relating to the introverted teenager on any level was better than nothing.

Brad picked up his board and walked towards the house. Despite his distant expression, Sophie noticed the slightest smile. He left the front door open and when Sophie and Will stepped inside he was already setting up the games console. Will nodded in the direction of the boy.

'You don't have to come with me to see Bella.' He winked and whispered, 'I think you might have more important work to do with Brad.'

Sophie responded to his cue, walked across and sat beside Brad.

'I hope you've got the skateboarding game?' she said cautiously, trying to gauge the boy's mood.

'Yeah.'

He turned on the TV and loaded the game. The screen lit up with graphics and colours reminiscent of the 1980s.

'How old is this game?'

'Vintage.'

'Love the intro music.'

Some of the catchy digital sequences sounded vaguely familiar to Sophie, and dated the game as ancient, but Brad didn't seem to mind. The relatively simple game was no doubt for Sophie's benefit.

'You're seriously weird,' Brad said.

She'd obviously caught his attention by mentioning the music. He looked at her and grinned, and she took his comment as a compliment.

'I'll show you the moves,' Brad generously offered. 'There's a load of different courses. Do you wanna start with a race or ramp event?'

'A race, of course.'

Brad laughed as he selected 'Downhill Chase' and wasted no time in setting up the beginning of a two-dimensional urban obstacle course.

'I'll do a demo and then you can have a go on your own.'

The conversation they were having involved the longest strings of words Brad had uttered in the time Sophie had known him. It was a positive step.

'And then we race and see who's the better man,' Sophie said.

The next ten minutes Sophie spent crashing into fire hydrants, falling off ledges and causing traffic accidents—many times over and in no particular order. Brad, of course, reached four-figure scores and was merciless in making no allowances for Sophie's inexperience and lack of skill.

'I think I've had enough,' she finally said when her skateboarding alter ego ended up in an underground sewer. 'But you carry on.'

As Brad finished the course with his highest score yet, Sophie wondered how his enthusiasm and skill in electronic gaming could be transformed into more productive pursuits. He needed something in his life that would allow him to move forward after his mother died. He'd already alluded to not hitting it off with his sister's husband, but there was no alternative to him moving to Karratha when the time came.

What was he good at?

'You're way too good for me,' she said as Brad went to replace the cartridge with a single-player game.

'Nah, you're all right.'

Another compliment. Sophie was getting the hang of the understated language only teenagers understood. She laughed.

'No, I'm not. I'm hopeless.'

The noise of the new game began.

'You any good with computers?' She wasn't sure where her tentative question would lead.

'Okay, I s'pose,' he said, without looking away from the screen. It was as if he needed the buffer of the game to lessen the stress of a face-to-face conversation.

'Do you do computer studies at school?'

'Used to.'

'Why did you stop?'

'No point.'

'What do you mean?'

He stopped the game momentarily and looked at Sophie as if the question was out of line.

'I haven't got a computer at home. Most of the other kids in the class have.'

He concentrated his attention back on the game, signalling the conversation was over, and Sophie knew it would achieve little to try and pursue the subject of computers further.

'I might go up and say hello to your mum, then.'

Sophie had gone as far as she could with Brad that afternoon. She also knew the time she had to help the boy was limited.

The change in Bella was dramatic. When Will had called in a few days ago she'd been holding on and he'd estimated her life expectancy to be in months. But now…

Her morphine dose had increased steadily. From the nurse's daily notes Will gleaned she was eating very little and was becoming weaker as each day passed. It was an effort for her to keep her eyes open.

'I'll organise oxygen for you, Bella, and see you as often as I can. Every day, if possible. Are you in pain?'

She opened her eyes. 'Nothing I can't handle.' Her husky voice was barely a whisper.

'I think we should contact Gemma.'

'Yes, Gemma needs to be here. It's not fair on Brad.'

Will saw a different type of pain in Bella's eyes. It was a kind of grieving pain. For the loss of time she wanted to spend with her son.

'Do you want me to ring her?'

'Yes. Thank you.'

'Okay.' He grasped the woman's cool hand. 'Shelley or one of the other palliative care nurses will continue coming twice a day and I'll see you tomorrow evening. By that time we should know when Gemma can come to help out.'

She nodded, exhausted by the effort of being examined and having to carry on a conversation.

Will gathered his things and turned to leave. He was surprised to see Sophie standing in the doorway.

'Have you been here long?' he said quietly.

They moved into the passage.

'Long enough.'

He thought he could see moisture in her eyes. She definitely wore her heart on her sleeve.

'Are you all right?' Will asked.

'Yes, I'm fine.'

He paused, but didn't want to press the matter.

'And Brad?'

'It's hard to tell. We didn't talk much but I think he's slowly coming out of his shell.'

'Good. Maybe we can talk about it in the car.'

They made their way down the stairs and said goodbye to Brad. Will hoped Sophie was making some progress with him because his own attempts had been unsuccessful.

When they reached the car he opened the door for his companion and the thought entered his mind that had been plaguing him all day.

What could he possibly do to make her stay?

Sophie could tell by the brief discussion they'd had in the car on the way back to the clinic that Will had developed the kind of emotional attachment to Bella that the training manuals suggested should be avoided. Sadness for a dying patient on a certain level was acceptable, but Will's involvement went deeper. If he responded to all his patients going through similar ordeals with the same intensity, he was headed for emotional burn-out. The usual debriefing process in this type of situation involved talking things through with a trusted colleague. To her knowledge, Will had no one to fulfil that role. Sophie wished she could help but didn't know how, without appearing too pushy.

When he asked if she would mind working on her own on

Wednesday afternoon while he took a couple of hours off, she was happy to co-operate. He definitely needed down-time from work, and what had come to be known as the Springs Footy Derby was occupying most of his valuable spare time. Sandie soon set her straight, though. She should have known Will needed more than a couple of hours to turn off from the job.

When she returned from a lunchtime home visit the receptionist confided that leaving her in charge of the clinic was an unprecedented occurrence.

'Dr Brent has very important business to attend to,' Sandie said mysteriously.

'Oh,' Sophie answered, not wanting to pry. Sandie would tell her if she thought it worthy of a few minutes' gossip time. Sophie had learned in the time she'd been working at the practice that you told Sandie nothing you didn't want to become common neighbourhood knowledge by the end of the day.

'Aren't you interested in what it is?'

An answer wasn't necessary as the receptionist decided to tell Sophie anyway.

'He's meeting with the IT company that produces our medical software. He's been saying it's needed an upgrade for ages. You've probably noticed it's always crashing and there's two new versions come out since the 3.5.' She finally took a breath. 'But apparently our hardware is too old to cope, so Dr Brent's getting prices to replace the lot.'

'What? He's thinking of getting new computers, monitors…?'

'Even printers.'

Sophie's interest was mildly aroused by Sandie's revelations and it set her thinking. When she visited Bella and Brad Farris the following day she had the germ of an idea, and after returning to the clinic she made a couple of phone calls. The responses were positive. Although she had no clue whether her plans would work, she felt it was worth a try and wanted to discuss the matter with Will.

She hadn't had the opportunity to broach the subject with him but decided she'd make the time.

Today. Thursday evening.

She'd been out on a late home visit, and was pleased to see Will's car still in the carport but the patient parking area empty when she got back. Hopefully he'd finished for the day and would be free to talk to her. She nearly collided with him as she opened the back door to the clinic.

'Hello, Sophie. I thought you'd gone home.'

'Hi, Will. I've just been out to see Jim Cooper.'

'Anything I should know about?'

'Dizzy spells. He's only a couple of days home from hospital after a heart attack and I think the starting dose of ACE inhibitor is too high. His systolic blood pressure's fallen to a hundred and he has symptoms typical of postural hypotension.'

'Did you reduce the dose of the new medication?'

'Yes, he agreed to come in and have Lisa check his BP every day over the next few days.'

'Good.'

Will looked as if he was in a hurry to leave, but Sophie wasn't going to be put off. The time she had to organise things was limited.

'Can I have a word about another matter?'

He looked at his watch. 'I was on my way to see Bella. Can it wait until tomorrow?'

Sophie smiled. 'I called in to see her and Brad at lunchtime. That's what I wanted to talk to you about. Her condition has picked up since Monday and we had a good chat. I asked if she felt she needed to see you as well… She said to tell you she's feeling better.'

Will looked relieved. 'Okay, but let's not stand in the doorway. How about a coffee?'

Will made the drinks and they both settled in the tea room.

'Fire away,' Will said after he'd taken a long sip of his coffee and visibly relaxed. 'What did you want to talk about?' he added, looking genuinely interested.

'Well, you know how I've been seeing Brad Farris?'

'And getting through to him, from what Bella and Shelley tell me. Amazing after only a couple of visits.' He paused as Sophie took a moment to absorb his praise. 'Sorry, I'm interrupting.'

'That's okay. It's good to know others are noticing his… change in attitude.'

She ran her finger around the rim of her cup, wondering if Will would think her suggestion forward—arrogant, even. She was probably basing her opinion on her father, who had always been resistant to any changes in his medical practice that hadn't been his idea. Will had nothing in common with Ross Carmichael other than a medical degree. Will waited attentively for her to continue.

'I wondered what you had planned for the old computers.'

'The old computers? Sandie's dealing with all that. I gather they're so outdated they're worth next to nothing. I think Sandie said something about donating them to a senior citizens' group.' He sipped coffee and ran his fingers through his hair. 'But I don't really understand what that has to do with Brad.'

'Well, I was talking to Bella about how Brad was performing at school and she said he was going really well until the full impact of her illness struck home.'

'I'm not surprised his work suffered.'

'He was good at maths, topped his class in computer studies and kept up with his other subjects. One of the brightest kids in his year.'

'And now?'

'He's barely scraping through, and not doing homework or handing in assignments. He's dropped out of computing, which was an elective for the kids in his year who needed more of a challenge.'

'What are you getting at?'

'He says there's no point. He hasn't even got a computer at home and he'll be moving north when…'

'Bella dies.'

'Yeah, there's no softer way to put it. He feels he'll be a second-class citizen, living with his sister and her young kids. He doesn't get on with his brother-in-law, who's made it quite clear he'll tolerate Brad only until he's old enough to go out to work. I gather as soon as that happens he'll be out on the streets. So…I was wondering…'

'Y-e-s?' Will said the word slowly.

'If there was any chance of giving Brad one of the old computers?'

Will looked surprised but was smiling.

'I think that's a great idea,' he said. 'We'd need to clean the hard drive—'

'Which you'd have to do anyway, even if it was going to the tip. I talked with Howard.'

'Howard Lin?'

'Mmm, when he was checking out the rooms for the new cabling this morning. He said he'd be happy to clear the hard drives, as well as set up a recycled computer—no charge. And he could organise the loading of basic software for Brad as early as the middle of next week if they start the installation here tomorrow and work all weekend.'

'You told him about Brad?'

'Sort of. In general terms. I also told him we didn't have much time.'

Will leaned back in his chair and whistled. 'Well, well. You've been a busy lady, haven't you? And you think this will turn a corner for Brad?'

'I do—even though the sceptics might call it a long shot. I hope it will give him a sense of identity and put those skills he uses in his hours of gaming to some use. Bella says she's left provision for an allowance for him in her will.'

'You've talked wills with Bella?'

'She brought it up. It means he'd have enough spare cash to at least get an internet connection if his sister isn't already connected, but I'd have to see how Brad responds. I don't want him to abuse our goodwill.'

'So you haven't mentioned it to him?'

'Of course not. I needed to discuss it with you first.' *And I might not be here for much longer.* She didn't dare voice her thoughts.

Sophie caught her breath, seeing the subtle change in Will's expression, as if he'd read her mind. She'd put off the inevitable discussion of what she'd do at the end of her eight weeks' trial. The truth was she still wasn't a hundred per cent certain.

'That's fine by me.'

'What?'

For a moment Sophie thought he was talking about her leaving Prevely Springs.

'Go ahead. Set things up with Brad and the computer. After all, you may not have much time.'

CHAPTER TWELVE

THE next two weeks flew by at whirlwind speed, and Sophie could hardly believe the derby was actually happening...the following day. The committee had gathered for its final planning meeting and the atmosphere in the small room at the rear of Prevely Springs Medical Clinic was electric.

'I don't believe you've put Brianna Sanders in charge of one of the food stalls,' Will said as they worked their way through the checklist. They'd reached item five—catering.

'She wants to be a chef. She's truly passionate about cooking and I'm confident she can do it. She's a bright, responsible kid—'

'Who fell by the wayside and needed someone like you, Sophie, to bring her back from the brink,' Colleen said with a grin.

'Exactly,' Sophie replied. 'And of course her mum's going to be helping her for most of the day.' Sophie attempted a persuasive smile before continuing. 'Anyone have any problems with that?'

The group was silent.

'Next item—public address system,' Will said with authority.

It took a couple of hours to work their way through the complete list and at the end they all sat back with satisfied expressions on their weary faces. Apart from a health and safety issue with the construction of the catwalk for the fashion parade, and a last-minute change of supplier for the drinks stalls, the preparations had gone extremely well.

'There's just one last thing I need to mention that isn't on the list,' Sophie said.

'And what's that?'

'Bella Farris.'

Everyone knew and in some small way had touched the life of the gravely ill woman. A mood of sadness descended.

'You all know she's determined to come tomorrow?' Several people nodded and waited for Sophie to continue. 'We've put everything in place we can think of to make it as easy as is humanly possible. Will's arranged transport by ambulance, and Shelley will escort her into one of the executive boxes on a gurney, hooked up to oxygen.' Sophie paused and took a deep breath. 'She wants to come for the last quarter of the match and I wondered…'

'Yes, go on.' Will's voice was husky with emotion.

'It was a last-minute idea and I ran it by both football clubs only this afternoon.' Sophie cleared her throat, giving herself a moment to hold back threatening tears. 'I wondered if you'd all agree to dedicate the match to Bella.'

There was a moment or two of feet shuffling and fumbling in bags for tissues before Sandie spoke.

'That's a wonderful…touching…generous suggestion, and I'm pretty sure I speak for everyone when I say, go for it Sophie.'

There were sounds of agreement, and Lisa got up from her seat to give Sophie a hug, followed by Colleen, and then Charlie reached across the table and vigorously shook her hand. Sophie had touched a nerve in the work-weary group who were teetering on the brink of the previous month's hard slog coming to fruition. It wasn't long before they were all standing, smiling, crying, hugging, congratulating and back-slapping.

Only Will stood back. Quiet and serious. Until the last member of the committee took their leave.

Then he finally spoke.

'I… I…'

Will wanted to say so much, but the words stuck fast in his throat. He felt the sting of unshed tears and the remorseless thumping of his heart.

He wanted to say so much…

'What's the matter?'

Sophie looked bewildered.

'Is it something I've said…something I've done?'

'It's everything about you, Sophie Carmichael.' A hundred clichés rolled through Will's mind, but it stuck on those three words that were always so hard to say. 'I… I…'

She had embraced with enthusiasm this rag-bag of a neighbourhood he called home; she'd breathed new life into a community that had seemed programmed to self-destruct; she'd touched so many hearts…including his; she'd unlocked a window in his tormented soul and let in the sunshine.

She'd turned his life around.

He loved her! Why was it so painful to tell her?

'I…just wanted to say thank you.'

'It was teamwork. You worked as hard as me,' she said without hesitation.

'But—'

Sophie took a step forward and spread her arms wide, ready to hug him. He needed no further encouragement. He wrapped his arms around her and felt the warmth of her body pressed against his chest. Her breathing synchronised with his as he gently stroked her shoulder, moving his fingertips to the bare skin at the base of her beautiful neck. She tensed, but as he continued the caress he felt her muscles relax.

'I don't know how I can ever thank you, Sophie,' he whispered, before placing his hungry lips on her forehead. She tilted her head to look in his eyes and invited him into the depths of her own.

'Just don't ever change, Will.' She tightened her grip around his waist and drew him even closer. 'You're one in a million.' Sophie pulled away and reached around behind her back to release his grip.

They both stood, embarrassed and emotional, until Sophie finally spoke, putting an end to their intimacy.

'Big day tomorrow. We really should be going.'

'Yes, you're right. We should be going.'

Sophie sighed with relief as the final siren sounded and the capacity crowd erupted into a roar of cheering, whistling and raucous singing. The game had been close, with only two goals the difference, but in the end it didn't matter to Sophie which team won. The big winners of the day were the people of Prevely Springs.

The event had been a resounding success in more ways than one. The people, the lifeblood of the community they were trying to rescue, had turned out in force. Will had revealed to her he'd never, in the more than thirty years he'd lived and worked in the Springs, seen the community work together with such energy, motivation and optimism for the future—not only for themselves but for the next generation.

Sophie felt a hand on her shoulder and looked around to see a beaming Will standing behind her. They'd been too busy to spend much time together throughout the day, but during the little contact she had had with her boss she'd noticed a change in him.

He'd lost some of the intensity that had kept him on a narrow, joyless path of endless work and personal sacrifice. The frown he'd once worn like an identity badge had been, at least for the day, replaced by the generous, heart-melting smile he'd previously saved for rare special occasions. And the way he had treated her...

'We need to go down for the presentations,' he said quietly.

'Yes, of course.'

For the final fifteen minutes of the game Sophie had joined Bella, Brad, Gemma and Shelley in the glass-enclosed viewing box overlooking the ground. Bella had somehow summoned up the energy to cheer and clap when her beloved team hit the front in the last few minutes. She now looked exhausted, was battling to keep her eyes open, and welcomed the oxygen she'd initially rejected.

'I'll just say goodbye to Bella. It's been a huge thrill for her to be able to come today.'

Sophie touched Bella's arm and she opened her eyes.

'Hey, you two. Shouldn't you be somewhere else…sorting out the awards…making speeches?' She paused for breath and her angular face broke into a grin. 'I can't thank you enough.'

Will leaned forward and grasped her hand.

'There's no need. Think of how much giving you've done over the years. It's about time you got something back.'

The woman sighed, then glanced at Shelley, Brad and Gemma, who'd kept a watchful eye on her during the afternoon.

'Off you go,' she said. 'I'm in good hands.'

Bella pulled her hand from Will's grip and waved him and Sophie away.

'We'll call in and see you on Monday.'

As they left the happy foursome Will reached for Sophie's hand and intertwined his fingers in hers as he strode towards the exit. His grip was strong, assertive, and seemed somehow to exemplify the subtle change Sophie had noticed in him through the day. He seemed to be chipping away at the barriers that had unyieldingly prevented him from venturing into any sort of personal relationship.

The biggest change, though, was the transformation that had happened gradually over the past few weeks. He had begun to share the burden that had weighed him down for most of his life. A small chink had appeared in the armour he wore when anyone tried to get close to him. He was learning to trust, to confide and to share.

What a mysterious and complicated man he was.

And the more he revealed, the more Sophie loved him.

She loved him. There was no doubt in her mind.

But Sophie had no time to dwell on her thoughts as Will guided her up the steps to the catwalk—which had now been transformed into a dais—ready to take his place at the head of the queue of speechmakers.

Will was handed a microphone and he cleared his throat. The crowd stilled to near silence as he began to speak.

'Firstly I'd like to thank…'

He methodically worked his way through the long list of sponsors, donors and helpers. When he reached the end he took a deep breath and again stilled the crowd with his steady voice.

'And I also have an important announcement…' He swallowed and cleared his throat again before continuing in a strong, sure voice. 'You all know the match was dedicated to Bella Farris, one of the brave, quiet achievers of our community.' The silence continued. 'I have pleasure in announcing that this morning I received approval from the council to name the Prevely Springs soon-to-be-revamped sports ground—an integral part of the project we hope will breathe new life into the area…' He paused and smiled. Sophie held her breath in anticipation. 'The Bella Farris Recreation Reserve.'

Sophie glanced up and saw the look of surprise and pleasure on Bella's face.

That moment made all the blood, sweat and tears worthwhile.

The applause rolled in like a mighty wave and then subsided. Will hadn't finished.

'And I also want to acknowledge the driving force, the

creative energy and the…' He looked at Sophie, his eyes full of tender gratitude. She was close to tears. 'The inspiration for us all to at least have a decent go at achieving what I thought was an impossible goal.'

He grinned.

'Dr Sophie Carmichael.'

Sophie sat in dappled shade in a corner of her small courtyard garden, reflecting on the events of the previous day. It was like a vivid, poignant dream. The takings from ticket sales, the fashion auction, food and drink had come to the amazing sum of one hundred and twenty-five thousand dollars. The final count on personal and business donations was expected to reach a cool hundred thousand at least. Even after costs, they'd reached their goal with money to spare.

Now she had to think of the future. In the frenzied build-up to the derby she'd hardly given the matter a second thought, but Will wanted her final decision…tomorrow.

She still hadn't made up her mind.

Her biggest problem was an agonising battle being played out between her head and her heart.

Her rational, objective mind told her to go home to Sydney. She'd had the break she needed to get over Jeremy. He was history. And although the experience of working in Prevely Springs had been positive, the only reason to stay on was if she was prepared to stay long term.

It wouldn't be fair on Will. He wanted a committed, long-term partner, and Sophie didn't fit the job description.

But her crazy, irrational, subjective heart was sending her completely different messages.

She'd fallen in love with Will Brent.

It was a scary realisation.

She couldn't ignore the strengthening feelings she had for her boss. She'd become accustomed to Will's daily presence in her life and she'd miss him if she left. More than she was willing to acknowledge.

She was undoubtedly attracted to him physically. But it was more than that. She yearned for him to enfold her in his arms; she craved to spend every moment of her days and nights with him; she was willing to share with him her deepest secrets. But even more alarming were her recurring fantasies of becoming his wife and soul-mate, having his babies and growing old with him…in Prevely Springs.

She was beginning to feel at home.

But their different upbringings and life experiences put them worlds apart. She was willing to work on those issues if Will was prepared to as well, but it wouldn't happen if she went back to Sydney.

She went inside, sat at the tiny kitchen table and opened her laptop. When she'd finished the letter she'd written to Will to formalise her intention to continue working at the Prevely Springs Medical Clinic she placed it in her bag, ready to give to him first thing Monday morning.

CHAPTER THIRTEEN

THE call came from Shelley just before lunchtime. Fortunately Will was between patients and only had a couple waiting that he hoped could be rebooked.

'Bella's asking for you,' she said simply to Will, and then lowered her voice. 'She wants to say goodbye.'

Will swallowed hard.

'I'll be there in fifteen minutes,' he promised.

He quickly logged off the computer, collected his medical bag and hurried towards Reception.

'I'm off to see Bella and I need you to somehow rearrange my bookings. I want the whole afternoon free. If you could ask Sophie—'

'Don't worry. I'll sort it all out.' She paused. 'And if you're a bit late tomorrow—'

He knew where she was coming from. She'd worked with him long enough to know that with some of his patients it was difficult to maintain professional distance. Bella was one of them. But whatever happened, he saw no reason why it wouldn't be business as usual the following day.

'It should be fine. Just leave things as they are for now,' he said.

When he arrived at the Farris house Shelley opened the door. 'Gemma's upstairs with Bella, but Brad's shut himself in his room. I'm not sure what to do to help,' she said from the doorway.

Will walked into the house with the nurse.

'How's Bella?' he said, knowing the news wasn't good.

'She's lapsing in and out of consciousness but quite lucid when she's awake.'

'Has she asked to see Brad?'

'No. She just asked for you.'

'Okay, I'll go up and see Bella and then I'll try and talk to Brad.'

When Will entered Bella's room it took him a few moments to focus in the gloom. The curtains had been drawn but he saw Gemma, close to tears, sitting next to her mother, holding her hand. On the bedside table sat a large vase of brightly coloured gerberas—Bella's favourite flowers.

'Hello,' he whispered. 'Is your mother awake?'

Bella's eyes slowly opened and she smiled.

'Thanks for coming.' She sighed and then took a deep breath. 'I have something…important to say…to you.' She closed her eyes briefly and then opened them again.

'It must be important,' he said.

She ignored his comment and gathered her energy. He waited.

'Dr Carmichael…'

'Yes? You want to tell me something about Sophie?'

'Shh.' Bella put her finger to her lips and continued. 'She's sweet…on you.'

Will couldn't help a smile and was rewarded by the brief twinkle in Bella's eyes.

'She told you that?'

'No, not exactly…but you don't have to…be a mind-reader…'

'You're wrong.'

'You're telling a dying woman…she's wrong? Humour me… Dr Brent…and don't let her slip out…of your grasp.'

She closed her eyes again and this time didn't open them.

Will glanced at Gemma, whose previously suppressed tears now trickled down her cheeks.

'She's a matchmaker from way back and I've never known her to get it wrong.' The young woman blew her nose and then sighed. 'Is there anything else we can do for Mum?'

'Just be there for her,' he said quietly, and then added in his thoughts as a fuzzy image of *his* mother flashed into his mind. *And love her.*

'Thank you, Dr Brent,' Gemma whispered as she stood to give him a hug. 'Mum's had nothing but praise for the way you and Shelley and the other nurses have cared for her.' A smile emerged from the tears. 'And the derby was one of the high points of her life. She hasn't made a big deal about it, but the match, the dedication, naming the sports complex... She was really chuffed.'

Will stood in silence for a few moments, not knowing what to say. 'You should be thanking Sophie,' he finally said. 'She did most of the work.'

Gemma gave his hand a squeeze before she sat down again. 'Can you let her know how grateful we are?'

'Yes, of course.'

Gemma wiped her eyes and sniffed.

'Shelley said she'd stay, but there's no need—'

'I can't do anything more for your mother but I'd like to stay. Not only for Bella but for you...and Brad.'

Gemma's tears began to flow again and she nodded.

'I realise she's not got long, and Mum would like that, I'm sure. To have the people she cares about by her side.' Her voice trailed off. 'If only we could get through to Brad.'

'Let me try,' Will offered.

'Thanks.'

Gemma's attention returned to her mother, whose pattern of breathing had changed. Bella's hands began to twitch. Will slipped quietly out of the room and made his way along the short passage to Brad's room. The door was closed. Will knocked softly.

'It's Dr Brent.' Will waited a minute before adding, 'Can I come in?'

There was no reply, but when he tried the handle the door opened without resistance. Brad huddled in the corner of his room where the computer was set up on a small table next to his desk. Will sat on the bed.

'How's it going, Brad?' Will intentionally left the question open, so Brad could choose the direction of the conversation.

The boy closed down the screen. Brad turned to face him.

'Okay, I guess.'

'The computer?'

'Cool.'

'Did Howard set it up with some decent software?'

'Yeah. It's not the latest version but it's all I need. He set up an e-mail account. And it's got word processing and stuff so I can use it for school. He said we could look at an internet connection when I move.'

'To Karratha?'

Brad's expression changed. He sighed.

'Yeah.'

'Not looking forward to it?'

Brad's silence said it all.

'You'll miss your mum.'

Brad turned away. He was crying, so Will waited a minute before he moved across and put his arm around the boy's shoulders.

'She loves you very much, you know, and if she had any power to change things she would. She's done the best she can.'

'I know,' he whispered as he sniffed and wiped tears away with his sleeve.

'Maybe you could go in and see her?'

'Maybe,' he said as he turned back to the computer and loaded a game.

It was Brad's way of telling him he wanted to be on his own, and Will certainly didn't want to force him out of his comfort zone. He had the feeling Brad would see his mother before the afternoon was out.

'I'll be downstairs with Shelley if you need me,' Will said as he softly closed the door.

Bella passed away peacefully two and a half hours later. Both Brad and Gemma were with her, and it was as if, content that she had tied up the loose ends in her life, she was free to leave.

Will stayed on to make sure Gemma and Brad were okay, as well as performing the medical tasks that had to be done. It was late afternoon before he finally left. He phoned Sandie to let her know his patient had died and that he was going straight home.

'If you need me for anything, don't hesitate to phone,' he said with a calmness he didn't feel.

'We won't need you!' Sandie stated with her usual assertiveness. 'Sophie's managing perfectly well with the few extra patients we couldn't reschedule. Go home. Forget about work for the rest of the day and relax. You deserve it.'

But taking her advice was easier said than done.

When he got home he felt physically and emotionally exhausted but he couldn't relax.

He kept thinking of Brad. Orphaned and bundled off to live with his sister and her family at a time when his loss would be causing him most pain. Will had no doubt that Gemma loved her brother. She would probably manage to provide for his physical needs but she could never replace Bella.

Will knew that first hand.

Although Will's grandparents had assured him his mother, in her own way, had loved him, he'd never fully forgiven her for abandoning him and then dying before he'd had a chance to find out for himself.

Brad would need the strength of Superman to survive the future—*the great unknown future*. He hoped with all his heart that the boy would find the staying power to make his way in the world without succumbing to the kind of mistakes he himself had made in his youth.

To add to his worries, Will also had recurring troubling thoughts of Sophie.

Bella had been at least half-right with her home-grown wisdom. Although he doubted Sophie was 'sweet on him', as Bella had put it, he wished—perhaps naively—there was some way of ensuring she stayed in WA so he could at least find out whether his deepening feelings for her were reciprocated. Today she was supposed to let him know if her intention was to continue working at Prevely Springs or to leave.

Not knowing added to his restlessness.

Will turned on the TV to try and take his mind off ruminations that were making him more uptight, but early-evening television wasn't the solution. He selected a CD from the 1980s that, if he played it loudly and immersed himself in the dark lyrics, could help him forget today's problems.

After cranking the volume up to a level just short of annoying the neighbours, he went into the kitchen to see what he had to make a snack.

Standing in front of the open fridge, he stared at the bottle of wine and six-pack of beer he kept for the visitors he rarely had; thankfully he'd never been tempted to have a drink. His resistance to temptation was a sign of his strength of character. After his disastrous experience with alcohol abuse when he'd been a student, he'd pledged to never drink it again.

But tonight he felt edgy.

He felt dangerously close to breaking his pledge.

And he knew what he had to do.

* * *

Although Sophie finished late, and was feeling the strain of a long day, she wanted to see Will.

Sandie had told her of Bella's death that afternoon and she guessed Will would take it pretty hard. If he didn't want to talk about it then that was okay—at least she would have offered. She also wanted to know how Brad was doing.

She'd also not had the opportunity to let him know she'd decided to stay on, and she particularly wanted to give him the news personally. If he was feeling down, maybe her decision might cheer him up.

As she drove into his street she remembered the first time she'd visited his home. She recalled his gentlemanly hospitality, the way he'd shrugged off her enquiries about his upbringing and his comforting hug when she'd revealed a painful secret from her past. The hug turning into a wonderfully sensual kiss should have alerted her to the possibility she might fall in love with the man.

And she had…tumbled head over heels in love with Dr Will Brent. She realised it hadn't happened overnight. It had crept up on her like the subtle arrival of warm, life-giving sunshine after a cold, desolate winter and now she couldn't imagine the loneliness of life without him.

She pulled up in front of his house and saw lights on. As she walked up the front path she heard muffled sounds of an old rock band, and when she knocked on the front door she wasn't surprised there was no answer as the music originating from somewhere in the depths of the building was loud. Using music to numb emotions was something she could relate to, but she felt oddly apprehensive.

Should she tell Will how she felt about him, and risk a knock-back? Could she cope with another humiliating rejection? Jeremy's heartless behaviour still stung.

Nothing ventured, nothing gained…

As she headed along the narrow side pathway to the back of the house the volume of the music increased and she quickened her step. Taking a deep breath, she rounded the corner. Bright lights shone through the curtainless expanse of glass dividing the kitchen-living area from the patio. She knocked loudly on the central door.

'Will, it's me,' she shouted, and waited a minute or two before peering through. It took a while before she located Will. He was sprawled on the sofa, his head on the armrest and his mouth slightly open. She could see the slow, steady movement of his chest as he took each breath. The remains of a sandwich sat on a plate on the coffee table and Will clutched an empty tumbler.

He looked peaceful and was sound asleep. Sophie smiled, deciding it wasn't fair to wake him. It was probably better to let him sleep off the stresses and strains of his day undisturbed.

Sophie wasn't sure what prompted her to scan the rest of the room before she turned to leave, and what she saw took the bottom out of her world. Her father's words echoed in her mind as the heaviness of disappointment descended from her heart to the pit of her stomach.

He was a drunk...had a problem with alcohol...an alcoholic...

At first she'd dismissed the spiteful words as being unsubstantiated malicious gossip. Then, when Will had opened his heart to her and told her about his drug abuse, she'd believed his addiction problems were in the past.

But now...

The evidence was there, before her eyes. A jumble of beer bottles stood empty on the kitchen bench and a wine bottle lay on its side on the draining board of the sink.

Even if he wasn't an alcoholic, he obviously still had a problem with binge-drinking in times of stress. A lethal combination.

Regardless of how strong her feelings were for Will, she couldn't even contemplate a relationship with a man who drank to excess, no matter what the reason. Alcohol and irresponsible driving had killed her best friend. It was a time in her life she would never forget…never forgive.

Her eyes brimmed with tears as she marched out of Will's yard to her car. Her idyllic plans for the future disappeared down a deep, gloomy hole.

How had she managed to be blindfolded *again* to what stood blatantly before her eyes?

She fumbled with the remote and finally unlocked the car door, hunched behind the wheel and slammed the door shut. But she didn't start the engine. Her hands were shaking, her body felt drained of energy and her mind was a tumultuous riot of conflicting emotions. She needed time to pull herself together and reconcile what she'd seen with what she knew. She took several deep, tremulous breaths until she calmed down, until her mind was clear enough to look at the situation objectively. She couldn't have got it all so completely wrong.

Had her immediate, emotion-fuelled response been simply a spur-of-the-moment gut reaction?

Will wasn't a quitter.

Neither was he a drunk.

His strength, at times, seemed limitless, and it didn't make sense that he would find solace in alcohol. He'd been close to Bella but Sophie felt sure he could cope with her inevitable death. It was part of his daily work.

What her father had told her was based purely on hearsay. It didn't feel right and she had no reason to believe his gossip-mongering—especially when his motivation was surely to encourage her to go back to Sydney.

There must be another explanation.

Sophie gazed into the darkness, collecting her thoughts. *She loved Will…*and she was fast becoming hooked on a lifestyle and neighbourhood that, for the first time in her working life, was providing her with a gratifying sense of fulfilment. It was a good feeling. One she didn't want to relinquish.

And why should she?

The confusion in her mind suddenly cleared and she knew she had to talk to Will.

To find out the truth.

Tonight.

The noise tore into Will's sleep-addled brain like an angle grinder cutting through sheet metal. He opened his eyes and tried to concentrate. The high-pitched, intermittent sound was close but it wasn't music.

It was coming from outside.

A car horn blared…almost continuously…urgently.

What on earth was going on?

He strode barefoot to the front door, and when he opened it his reaction to what he saw was reflexive, almost primitive.

'Hey, what the hell do you think you're doing?' he shouted as he ran down the front steps and saw Sophie's car parked in the driveway.

Sophie's car?

Why was she parked in front of his house?

The two shadowy figures banging on the windscreen and shouting obscenities were suddenly silent, and then ran. Will thought he saw the glint of a knife in one of troublemaker's hands but he had no time to investigate—he had to see if Sophie was safe.

He thanked God her door was locked as he leaned over to peer through the window. Even in the gloom he could see her shrink back and that she was sobbing. She was terrified.

'It's me—Will,' he said calmly, with his face close to the glass.

'Will?' She fumbled for the controls and the window slid down. He heard the click of the central locking.

'They've gone and I doubt they'll come back.' He opened the door and her gasping sobs wrenched at his heart. 'Come inside,' he whispered. He had an overwhelming need to protect this fragile, frightened woman huddled in the dark.

She accepted his offered hand, and then suddenly she was in his arms, clinging to his shirt as if her life depended on it. He embraced her and hugged her close until all her tears were spent.

'Come inside,' Will repeated as he steadied her stumbling gait and guided her towards the house.

He led her to the sofa and sat next to her. She began to shake again like a frightened animal. He enfolded her in his arms and held her close.

'What happened?' Will said gently. 'What are you doing here?'

Sophie turned, and her eyes—reddened from crying, pupils still wide and dark with fear—met his. She sniffed, cleared her throat and leaned slightly away from him. It seemed an eternity before she finally spoke.

'Bella...'

The worried expression on her face was edged with pain. He waited for her to continue.

'Sandie told me she passed away this afternoon and I just wondered...' She looked away. He wanted to soothe her, keep hold of her and never let her go.

'You wondered?'

'I thought you might want someone to talk to.'

Will's heart did an uncomfortable somersault. *She* was worried about *him*. In the guise of comforter she'd apparently landed herself in the midst of a terrifying altercation...on his front doorstep. Guilt burned in his gut. It had been a long time since anyone had cared about him that much...

They sat in silence for a few moments. Will felt Sophie's breathing steady and her heart rate slow. He reached for her hand.

'I'll call the police.'

The force with which she withdrew startled Will.

'No!' she said. 'They didn't hurt me or damage any property, and they were only kids—probably fourteen or fifteen. I panicked. I overreacted. There must be better ways to keep them off the streets.'

Now she was *defending* her attackers. It was difficult to comprehend how she could so easily forgive—after what they'd done.

'But they were—'

'No.' She reached for a handful of tissues and blew her nose. 'Forget about the louts.' Her gaze was now steady and her eyes dry. 'There's something else I want to talk to you about.'

It hadn't taken Sophie long, once she'd recovered from her distressing experience with the teenage hooligans, to realise Will wasn't drunk. His eyes were bright and brimming with concern, his movements steady and purposeful, and his breath smelled of herbs, piquant cheese and coffee.

She had no doubt in her mind that her tall, dark and handsome rescuer's head was clear.

She'd accepted his offer to make her a mug of tea and he was busy in the kitchen. It gave her a chance to collect her thoughts and work out what she was going to say. A few moments later he was back by her side and putting two steaming cups on the coffee table.

He smiled.

'What was it you wanted to talk to me about?'

Sophie paused to take a breath and wondered if she was doing the right thing, but she decided she needed to know.

'There's no easy way to say this. It's about…er…'

'Go on, I'm listening.' Will was frowning now.

'I know you don't drink, and I think I know why. My father—'

'Let me guess,' he interrupted. 'Your father has done some research and found a skeleton or two in your boss's closet.'

Sophie felt ashamed of her father's behaviour as much

as reluctance to bring the problem out into the open with the man Ross Carmichael had accused of crimes he'd had no evidence for.

No secrets, she reminded herself. Honesty. She'd start right now.

'Something like that. He rang me a couple of times…' Sophie paused to take a deep breath. 'He told me he'd heard you'd had an alcohol problem when you were a med student.'

Will surprised her with laughter.

'And I bet he told you once an alcoholic, always an alcoholic, and to run a mile.' He brought the back of her hand up to his lips and kissed it tenderly. It somehow seemed the natural thing for him to do. 'That's in the past. I haven't touched a drink for nearly twenty years. And I don't intend to in the future either.'

'But…' The mess of empty bottles still littered his kitchen.

'But what?' Will said looking bewildered.

She clenched her hands in her lap. What she was about to tell him wasn't going to be easy.

'I was about to go home when those boys came out of nowhere.'

'Go home? I don't understand. Had you changed your mind?'

Sophie took a slow sip of her tea. She could feel the intensity of Will's gaze. He looked bewildered.

'I knocked at the front door. There was music but you didn't answer, so I went around the back.'

He smiled. 'I got carried away—sorry. Loud vintage music has the effect of numbing my brain when I get stressed—rarely fails to work.' His expression changed and she wondered if he'd suddenly realised what she'd seen. 'I've had one of those days.'

'But the bottles?'

'What bottles?'

'Over there on the sink. Wine and beer…empty…' Sophie's heart began to thud. She wondered if she'd just ended their embryonic relationship before it had had a chance to breathe fresh air. But Will was smiling again. He certainly didn't look like a guilty man.

'Ah, the bottles. It's confession time. They were empty because I tipped them down the sink.' He grasped her hand again, with a grip that indicated he wasn't about to let go. 'I keep a small amount of alcohol in the house for visitors.' He chuckled. 'Not that I have many. I pride myself in having the willpower not to touch it, and I haven't in twenty years. A couple of times I've come pretty close, and today was one of those occasions. So I tipped temptation away and I must have been sound asleep when you knocked.' He paused. 'Do you believe me?'

Sophie nodded. How could she not believe this open-faced, eager, gorgeous man?

'So your father was right. But it's definitely past history.'

Sophie smiled.

'I'm glad,' she said, and wondered how she could have not trusted him. There was nothing in this wonderful, giving man not to love.

'I love you, Will Brent.' The words came straight from her heart and spilled from her mouth before she had a chance to stop them.

Impulsively, she leaned across and kissed him on the mouth, and then sat back, startled at her own bravado. Will was silent. Stunned. Had she blown it?

'And I want to stay in Prevely Springs…if you'll have me.' It was a last-ditch attempt to get a reaction.

It worked.

He broke into a broad grin.

'Of course I'll have you, Dr Sophie.' His warm, soft lips found hers and he kissed her long and hard, with a passion that took Sophie's breath away. When he finally released her he sighed and whispered with a mischievous twinkle in his eye, 'But will you have me?'

She leaned across and rested both hands on his shoulders.

'Is that a business proposal?'

He laughed and encircled her delicate wrists with his firm, gentle hands. He kissed one palm and then the other.

'No, it's a marriage proposal.'

Sophie replied without hesitation.

'I will.'

EPILOGUE

A year later

SOPHIE stood in the newly refurbished kitchen of Brent's Place. The building's official name was The Albert and June Brent Community Centre, but long ago, when the rebuilding had only just begun, the name had been abbreviated—and had tenaciously stuck. It hadn't detracted from the elderly couple the centre was dedicated to, though. Will had made sure of that. Over the past twelve months, singing the praises of his grandparents had almost become a mantra, and had been instrumental in bringing the disparate community together to achieve their goal.

'Dr Brent, do you want these in the oven yet?'

Sophie still wasn't used to the title she shared with her husband of seven months, and it took a couple of moments before she registered that Brianna Sanders was addressing *her* and not Will. She was usually called simply 'Dr Sophie' by the adults of the community, to save confusion.

She smiled at the sixteen-going-on-twenty-five-year-old who was transforming into a confident and beautiful young woman. Brianna no longer needed drugs to give her a high. She was part way towards her goal of becoming a chef, and judging by the wonderful food she'd helped prepare for the opening of the centre Sophie had no doubt she would succeed.

'Stack the trays in the oven and we'll fire them up in about half an hour.'

'Okay.'

After she'd loaded one half of the commercial-size double oven with a variety of savoury pastries, the tall, slim teenager peeped through the hatch, which provided a view of the gymnasium. For tonight's celebration it had been decorated with brightly painted posters provided by the year-eleven art class of the local high school and converted to a hall with seating for about a hundred.

'There are hardly any seats left,' Brianna said with a broad grin.

'I think nearly the whole of Prevely Springs is here.' Sophie beamed as well.

Will had cleverly involved a substantial number of the residents in the building and renovating process, which had not only provided a focus for many of the bored and unemployed young people but had also brought the generations together, with the older folk all too willing to share their knowledge and skills. And they'd come out in force for the official opening of the new facility.

Sophie scanned the room and saw many familiar faces.

'Is that Brad over there?' Brianna seemed to be doing a double-take.

'I think it is.' The boy had grown taller in the last year, lost some weight and had shed the veil of gloom he'd worn like a shield before his mother had died. Sophie and Will had seen him only a couple of months ago, when he'd first moved back to Perth. The boy had kept in touch, via regular e-mails, and had been over the moon when he'd been one of only two students from his school in remote Karratha who had won a maths and computer studies scholarship to one of the academically focused colleges in Perth. He'd been billeted by an elderly couple who lived near his college and seemed to exude new-found confidence, settling well into his new life.

'He's sure changed,' Brianna said, as her gaze lingered on Brad.

'Interested?'

Brianna laughed and gave Sophie a friendly punch in the arm.

'He's only just turned fifteen. I'm not that desperate.'

'No, I guess not. You can take your pick.'

At that moment she saw Will heading from the back of the hall towards the small stage where the Lord Mayor, several councillors and half a dozen of their benefactors, including Andrew Fletcher, were already seated. Will seemed to be looking for someone, and when he glanced in her direction he waved and beckoned her to join him.

'Looks like we're nearly ready to start and my services are required elsewhere.' She smiled at Brianna. 'Sure you can manage in here?'

'Of course I can,' she said, with a maturity beyond her years, and Sophie had full confidence in her abilities.

As Sophie joined her husband and they walked hand in hand down the central aisle to the stage, the audience began to clap and then burst into clamorous cheering. From the heat in Sophie's cheeks she could only imagine the colour of her face, but Will was beaming and apparently revelling in the noisy show of approval.

He gave her hand a squeeze and leaned close to her. If she wasn't mistaken, Will was close to tears.

'I wish Albie and June were here to see this.'

Sophie fixed her gaze on his and marvelled at how lucky she was to have found her soul-mate and life partner—in the most unlikely of places. She loved him so much.

'I think they're here in spirit, Will.'

He smiled. 'I think so too.' He paused at the steps on the edge of the stage and took a deep breath. 'And I have the feeling I can finally let go.'

Sophie knew at that moment that Will had fulfilled a self-imposed obligation that had been weighing him down for too long. He'd reached a turning point and she hoped he could finally move on.

As they climbed onto the stage together the audience stood as one and continued cheering, and Sophie felt a heady mixture of elation and pride.

She was home. In Prevely Springs. With the man she loved. Her free hand moved to the barely perceptible bump in her belly, instinctively protecting their tiny unborn child.

She smiled. They were a family.

What more could she possibly want?

Medical Romance™

THE TORTURED REBEL
by Alison Roberts

Beautiful helicopter pilot Becca Harding has spent long years trying to forget SAS medic and emergency specialist Jet Munroe, but she's never been able to forgive him. Now, thrown together again, it's time to stop running from their past, and the scorching attraction still lingering between them.

DATING DR DELICIOUS
by Laura Iding

It's Hannah Stewart's first day as a surgical intern at Chicago's busiest hospital and she couldn't be more excited—then she meets Dr Jake Holt, her new boss…the man she had a completely out-of-character, one-night stand with! Jake has a strict "no relationships at work" rule, but his new intern is proving to be a distraction impossible to ignore…!

On sale from 5th August 2011
Don't miss out!

Available at WHSmith, Tesco, ASDA, Eason and all good bookshops
www.millsandboon.co.uk

2 FREE BOOKS
AND A SURPRISE GIFT

We would like to take this opportunity to thank you for reading this
Mills & Boon® book by offering you the chance to take TWO more
specially selected books from the Medical™ series absolutely FREE!
We're also making this offer to introduce you to the benefits of the
Mills & Boon® Book Club™—

- **FREE home delivery**
- **FREE gifts and competitions**
- **FREE monthly Newsletter**
- **Exclusive Mills & Boon Book Club offers**
- **Books available before they're in the shops**

Accepting these FREE books and gift places you under no obligation to buy, you may cancel at any time, even after receiving your free
books. Simply complete your details below and return the entire page
to the address below. You don't even need a stamp!

YES Please send me 2 free Medical books and a surprise gift. I
understand that unless you hear from me, I will receive 5 superb new
stories every month including two 2-in-1 books priced at £5.30
each and a single book priced at £3.30, postage and packing free. I
am under no obligation to purchase any books and may cancel my
subscription at any time. The free books and gift will be mine to keep
in any case.

Ms/Mrs/Miss/Mr ——————— Initials ———————

Surname ————————————————————
Address ————————————————————

——————————————— Postcode ——————
E-mail ————————————————————

Send this whole page to: Mills & Boon Book Club, Free Book Offer,
FREEPOST NAT 10298, Richmond, TW9 1BR